IT'S TIME FOR A SAVIOR...

In a land that has long been occupied and oppressed by foreign dictators, the time for heroes is ripe, it is time for legends to arise and free their country from tyranny. Two adolescent teenagers accustomed to the laid back life of their small and peaceful village of Pavanti where little excitement happens, is about to change. An ensuing attack by an expeditionary force from the main Rakirian army turns their tranquil village into a smoldering ruin and throws the boys into opposite ends of their world, which is suffering under the yoke of oppression. Meanwhile, an evil is approaching that threatens to destroy their world, to face it they must have the courage, to fight it they must have brawn, and to defeat it they must have wisdom. Aided by a beautiful foreign princess and a wise peasant girl, the youths from Pavanti must rise and incite revolt.

I0628963

Stephen and Jason this one is for you guys.

Acknowledgments

The biggest thanks goes to my sister Oksana, thank-you so much for your help on the proofing you did. I will always be grateful.

D. Michael Whelan, I am blessed to have had you help me with this project. Your editing skills, and attention to detail have helped to advance this novel. Thank you. You have a gift for positive criticism, and the feedback I received from you certainly helped me grow as a writer.

Matthew Sweeney, finding an artist/illustrator with your talents was truly a blessing. Thank-you for all of your patience and willingness to revise and truly create a fantastic cover.

Special thanks to my dear wife Julia, your patience and encouragement have meant so much to me and were vital for the publication of this book. My two daughters were a source of inspiration as well as a meaningful distraction from my writing. I would also like to extend my gratitude to the rest of my family. You guys are all awesome, and your encouragement, excitement and support meant a lot to me during this process.

TABLE OF CONTENTS

LEGENDS OF ROSMIR
BOOK 1: REVOLT

VICTOR L. PAVLOV

PROLOGUE

The Rakirian Viceroy, Ragin, struggled to keep walking through the blizzard of objects pelting him to avoid being dragged every time he slowed because he was blinded by the concuss of being struck. He felt the bite of the rope around his wrists and the pull of the ox dragging him onwards.

The stench was horrible, but the taste in his mouth was much worse. Even as he tried to block the rank odor, and spit the bile contents from his mouth, more of the warm brown matter washed over him, the brown mixture of human feces and urine being emptied from the latrines above cut off the little air he already had. His stomach lurched again and again, to the point where he couldn't walk. Suddenly he was on the ground; his body dragging on the rough stone of the street scraping and tearing at his skin. He struggled onto his feet, but his feet failed him as the ox continued to drag him. The fecal matter burned his eyes, but even with his blurred vision he could see the angry mob around him. A half-crazed woman ran at him, all the while cursing, and then he felt the strike of club slamming into his shoulder before the woman was dragged away from him by a rebel. The pain where the club hit seemed irrelevant even as pebbles, stones and rotten vegetables continued to prick him with every step he took.

Ragin could see the crowd around him in a haze, but their shouts, just like the pain from the objects that they threw at him were very real. The rebels were going to hang him then cut his head off and send it to Rakon, the capital of the Rakirian Empire while the flesh from his body would be plucked by crows. But first they had to get him to the gallows alive. The way this crazed crowd was behaving he would be lucky to arrive at the gallows in one piece much less alive.

The past two weeks were worse than hell. The pain from the torment and the humiliation that he had suffered were beyond his imagination. The thought that humans could inflict so much pain on others was disturbing to him; yet he wasn't naïve to think that it rarely happened. Many of his officers would torture to extract information or even to set an example on the subjects that he had been in charge of governing. He had never stopped it, and hardly thought much of it, that is until he had experienced it firsthand. His tormenters would remind him that he was only getting what he had done to others. He had never tortured anyone he had tried to plead, but to no avail. They only laughed at him in return.

Ragin was a Rakirian Viceroy in charge of this northernmost province of Rosmir. There was nothing further north except the mountains of Celesta, mountains so tall that no man had ever scaled them, much less seen their peaks. It was to be his first time here, and he had been excited to see the legendary mountains that marked the northern boundary of their planet. Though the mountains were fabled to reach paradise itself; it was hell that oftentimes rained down from above. Sometimes molten rock, still red hot, would fall to earth and start wildfires. Other times instead of rain bringing forth water, it would bring forth ash, or ash mixed with water. This ash rain was fabled to be the fountain of youth; it was said that it prolonged a person's life by a score of years.

It was because of this ash that he had even requested this post from the emperor. He had thought to prolong his and his wife's life as well as make a lucrative business selling this ash across the empire. He had thought that he would be the richest man in the empire within ten years. Almost a year had passed, and he hadn't made a single trip. He was simple too busy strengthening his castle and dealing with a distrustful and rebellious population. The taxes had to be taken from the people by force, and he had collected them from all except for the people of Celesta. It was a delicate situation, and he had decided to head the expedition personally to ensure that no treachery was committed towards the populous. He wanted to win them over; so that his future business could thrive with local support.

It has been two weeks since he and his men had set out to come here, to Celesta. The going had been slow; since the horses that they rode and the oxen that were pulling the supplies tired quickly from going up a constant hill. Even though he and his men were on horseback, they noticed that their energy was diminishing as the air became thinner. When they looked back down the road they had come on, they saw it winding through beautiful green pastures with not a tree taller than ten feet in sight; and the road below seemed to vanish into the clouds. It was strange to be walking above the clouds he had mused. It had felt like paradise indeed. Everything here seemed more vivid. The color of the grass was a deeper green, and the sky seemed bluer still. They had set their course for the rising mountain walls; which always seemed a half day's walk away. But five days later, they hardly seemed to get any closer to the mountain walls. Each day, they realized that the mountain walls were much farther away than they first anticipated.

At the end of the fifth day, exhaustion had set in. The animals were completely worn out, and they themselves were beyond weary. Even breathing seemed like a chore. Thus, they had built a makeshift camp and had fallen asleep, including the guards on duty. The rebels attacked them and took them by surprise. It was still light outside, but the skirmish hardly lasted fifteen minutes before Ragin and his men were crushed. Their weapons had seemed lighter in the thin air, but with little oxygen they were soon winded, panting so hard that their lungs burned while the rebels hardly broke a sweat. He didn't see a single rebel out of breath.

They bound him in chains and threw him across his own horse. At the time, he wasn't the least bit worried. He was the Viceroy of Rakiria. Influence, wealth, and power were at his behest. He would forgive them their taxes and even offer them gold in return. He would tell them of his plan to make them all rich together. It had seemed so reasonable and simple, but that's only because he was naïve. The rebels didn't want his money; their only thirst was for vengeance that could only be satisfied with Ragin's blood. By the end of his first night he was fully aware of his circumstance, he was pretty much a dead man. Yet even as he was being tortured, he only prayed to the gods that his wife and children would be safe in the castle below.

During his first week of captivity, he would often wonder how long it would be before anyone from his hometown noticed that he had gone missing. Today he had received that answer when the rebel leader had him that they intended to ship his head back to Rakiria as a message to stay away. He had attempted to reason with the rebel that such an act would bring all of the Rakirian armies north, and then he and all his people would be butchered like pigs. The man had laughed at him.

Suddenly the ox stopped, and the crowd seemed to be at a further distance from him than before. His vision was still blurred, and he couldn't see anything clearly more than a few feet away. His breath was suddenly cut short, and he felt himself drowning before realizing that a bucket had been dumped on him. He shut his eyes and mouth instinctively and held his breath. When he first felt the liquid, he expected more fecal matter, yet what he felt was just water. When his lungs threatened to explode he sucked in the air through his open mouth and tasted the clean water on his lips. Another bucket of water crashed over his head, and someone came up and wiped the water from his eyes with a clean towel. His vision cleared, and his breath left him at the sight before him. On the gallows stood his wife and his five children— two of his older sons and three younger daughters. The youngest was only five. The rebels even built a platform to accommodate her height and to ensure that she couldn't step off the bucket on her own.

He sensed something of an animal rising from within him, and suddenly he was like a hound unleashed. He sprang at the nearest rebel, but the rope around his wrists only pulled him back. He screamed and yelled and finally he was on his knees begging, but all he got in return was more laughter of the people around him. His children were looking at him. His younger girls were crying and calling for him, but the two older boys, ages sixteen and fourteen, didn't even allow a tear on their face. Even his daughter at just the age of ten stood astutely observing the scene. He had taught them well to maintain their poise and to keep their dignity. Aside from the clothes and luxuries, it was dignity and poise that separated a noble from a peasant. Yet here he faced them, their teacher in noble dignity, and not a trace of dignity left in him. When he looked up at his wife, her face was turned away from him, facing towards the valley below. He wondered if it was the crocodile tears rolling down his face that shamed her to the point where she wouldn't look at him. This was how they would see him and remember him, as an animal, before their souls left the earth.

The rebel leader, a man almost seven feet tall with blond hair and piercing blue eyes was a stereotypical Northern man. All the people here were tall; Ragin had noted. Even the women were abnormally tall, slender, and very beautiful. He had reasoned that it was all due to the ash water. The ash water that they drank and that same ash water that watered their crops gave them good health, strength, and their physique. Initially, when he had set out to acquire this ash, he dreamed that his sons would be the tallest and the most handsome men in the entire Kingdom and his daughters by far the most beautiful if only they drank of the ashen waters of Celesta. Now none of it mattered as they stood there near the gallows.

Two rebels grabbed him from both sides and forced him to his knees as another two men came up and with their dirty fingers, forced his eyelids open. The horror suddenly struck him as he realized that the Rebel leader had stopped talking, and everyone's eyes were on the gallows. The executioner stepped up and kicked the wooden platform away from his youngest daughter, and just like that she was swinging from a rope. The barbarism of it all shocked him as his mind seemed to go numb. His life was over, and so was his family's. He tried to look away, but the men holding him were much bigger and stronger than him, and his forced eyes took it all in as another daughter dangled from a rope. Then one after another, from the youngest until the oldest, his children were executed before his eyes. Even as his eldest son, his heir, was executed, there was not a single tear on his son's face. His son had learned to accept fate well—much

5

better than he did. He looked at his son whose wide eyes seemed to stare into the world with the same dignity as when he were yet alive, while his body swayed in the breeze. With every child that was sent hanging by their necks, the crowd yelled and only grew in ecstasy. His wife who had refused to meet his eyes the entire time now stared at him, and her stare was condemning as if this was entirely his fault. His fault for dragging them from the comforts of Rakon, the Rakirian Capital, into this northern land filled with savages. He was helpless. How could he have known? Now all he wanted was his wife's forgiveness.

"Please," he croaked, "let me speak to my wife."

The rebel looked at him, his eyes steely blue and without a trace of pity before turning to face the gallows and signaling the executioner. With dread, Ragin watched as the executioner stepped up and sent his wife swinging, he watched as her body dropped before being jerked to a sudden halt by the rope. Her body swayed in the breeze, but her condemning eyes stayed fixated on him. His fault, they reminded him.

Big hands grabbed him by the arms and dragged him up onto the platform where his family hung, and all the while he could hear the derision of the crowd as they hooted with joy. His head was forced onto a wooden block, and a rope was pulled across the back of his neck to keep it in place. He watched as men, women, boys and girls, ranging from the elderly to the infants, stood watching his execution, and thought, *may your gods protect you from the wrath of Rakiria that is to come upon you*.

They say that a person's entire life flashes before him when he is about to die. That was true for Ragin. In a split second he seemed to envision his whole life up to this very moment. Time had seemed to stop. His senses were heightened, especially his hearing. He seemed to pick up on every sound that he had always taken for granted, but some sounds were even more distinct than others, like the creaking of the boards as the executioner moved into place at his side, the stillness and serene quiet of the crowd, broken only by the wailing of babes and their mothers trying to hush them... The grunt of exertion from the executioner as he hoisted the axe, and it was the last sound he heard forever.

The Rakirian Emperor Duragino was just wrapping up a meeting with his war councilor when his cup-bearer came in carrying a small wooden crate. The cup-bearer was a youth in his early twenties, but he was already held in high esteem by all in the royal court. Not only was he the emperor's personal server and taster of food and wine, but he was also his confidant. The cup-bearer bowed before the emperor.

"Rise," the emperor commanded.

The youth rose and offered the crate to the emperor, "Your Eminence, this just arrived from Celesta, a northern province of Rosmir."

Emperor Duragino read the letter attached to the crate; which was addressed to him from Viceroy Ragin. "Open it." He commanded the general beside him.

General Tibernum was a man in his sixties but still as nimble and fit as a man in his thirties. He drew his sword and pried the wooden lid of the crate. The wooden crate was lined with waxed leather, and a wax seal went around the lid to waterproof it. As soon as the lid came off, the pungent smell of rotting flesh filled the air.

"Aaaugh! What is that smell?" The emperor asked. The cup-bearer quickly offered the emperor a clean handkerchief. The emperor took the hanky and covered his nose with it. "Well, what is it?"

The general reached in and pulled out a leather bag out of the box. It was soaked and was dripping fluid, yet the general's face showed no signs of squeamishness. He sat the bag on the table, and his hand went inside the bag. His eyebrows furrowed in puzzlement, and he brought the object out of the bag.

Groans, followed by fits of coughing resounded throughout the room as everyone's hand went up to cover their noses. Their eyes, however, stayed focused on the thing before them. The misshapen ball of rotting flesh and hair made the object quite obvious.

"Whose head is that?" Emperor Duragino asked, his voice low and brimming with anger.

The general pulled out another article from the bag: a hand with a ring still affixed to the finger. The general's mask evaporated into a sour look as he pried the ring off the finger. The cup-bearer was ready with a clean towel, and the general wiped the blood and gore off the ring and then his hands. A clean bowl of water was ready for him as well, and he washed his hands and the ring before offering it to the emperor.

Emperor Duragino took the ring and looked at the emblem engraved on it. "Ragin." He whispered. His furious eyes fixed on the old general. "General Tibernum, I want this dealt with right away. I will make an example of this for the entire Empire to see how I repay treachery and rebellion. Send in an army and have it carve a path of blood and destruction all the way to Celesta itself."

Tibernum took a deep breath. "Our forces are stretched very thin, My Lord. Our wars in the south have really depleted our resources and manpower significantly, but I could muster together a force of around 10,000 fresh recruits."

Duragino scowled angrily. This wasn't what he wanted to hear; nevertheless, it shouldn't be such a problem. Rosmir was conquered roughly 50 years ago, and currently it was part of the Rakirian Empire. Only a small peninsula is all that was left unconquered. That enclave shouldn't pose a threat since the Rosmirians on the Peninsula of Caminia are only concerned with defending themselves, and they rarely leave the safety of the peninsula.

Duragino looked intently into Tibernum's eyes before he spoke. "I want you to raise this army and find them a suitable commander."

"Yes My Lord." General Tibernum hesitated before finally turning to go.

"General, what is it?" Emperor Duragino asked.

"Can I offer a humble suggestion?" Tibernum requested; for the burden of sending out an order to spare no one was too great for him to bear.

"Make your suggestion."

"My Lord, the empire is in great need of fresh labor; I ask that the young be spared. They can still be of so much value to the empire."

"It is the young that always stir up the trouble."

"If we take the young as prisoners, the young men can be recruited for our armies and the women can serve as maids and nurses on the battlefield." Even the children can be placed into schools and be indoctrinated in our culture. We will force them to assimilate and become one with our empire."

Emperor Duragino frowned at the suggestion, and the muscles in his jaw flexed as he contemplated this request. "General, I fear you may be going soft in your old age, opting to show mercy, when vengeful slaughter is what is required." Duragino sighed. "Yet, there is wisdom in your words. See to it that it is done."

CHAPTER 1: BOLSHOI FALLS

Pavanti, Rosmir

A crowd of rowdy boys and girls had gathered on the banks of Bestri River to witness the village's two daredevils attempt to make a river crossing on the most dangerous, fast flowing rapids filled with sharp rocks and only a mile away from Bolshoi Falls. When one of the boys in the village had said that that part of the river couldn't be crossed, Achledis, the younger of the two boys was quick to argue that it could be and had sworn that he would prove it. Now they were about to embark on this suicide mission.

Now he stood at the water's edge next to the little boat that would take him on his adventure with his gaze fixed on the waves crashing against the rocks that jutted out dangerously all throughout the river. His long blonde hair flew in the wind; tall and broad shouldered he was deaf to the shouts and taunts of the crowd as he meditated on the task at hand. Most people in the crowd were taking it as a sign that he had second thoughts and wouldn't go through with the dare. His friend Vitaeus, however, who was slightly taller, with short dark hair and a lean build, knew better than that. Though he was only a year older, he was the one always following Achledis' lead no matter how foolish it was.

Though, in this current adventure, he had been trying to talk some sense into his friend, but to no avail. Taking the canoe down the rapids where a 30 foot waterfall was only a mile away was madness; any person would agree. Achledis didn't see it that way. He saw it as a feat that had to be conquered.

Even now, looking at his friend, Vitaeus saw no fear in his eyes, only a certain confidence. Vitaeus knew that it would be impossible to talk him out of this; Achledis' mind was made up. Even if Vitaeus had refused to go, then he would simply go on his own.

Some girls standing nearby were shouting for the boys not to go. Vitaeus looked at them, then back to Achledis. "Listen to them, they all want you to live; I want you to live."

"Oh come on, let's go already!" A big boy with fiery red hair shouted. Vitaeus knew that Red, as he was called, was an instigator who was always pleased when someone else got hurt.

Achledis, who was standing there staring at the fast flowing rapids, smiling the whole time, looked up suddenly. His eyes met Vitaeus's. "Let's go." He said as he grabbed the little skiff and started to pull it towards the water.

Closing his eyes briefly, Vitaeus said a little prayer, and his shoulders slunk defeated. He wasn't sure why he agreed to do these suicide missions with his friend, but deep inside he knew that he just didn't want to see his friend die alone.

The boys put the front of the skiff in the water and climbed in; with Achledis taking the front as he planned on guiding it through the rocks. Vitaeus was forced to push off. Vitaeus nudged the bank with his oar half-heartedly; hoping that it would still be stuck and delay this stupidity. The boat shot into the water and was instantly racing away.

Vitaeus shouted from sheer terror. The roaring water swallowed out the roar of the fans on the bank and the cries of the terrified girls.

"Woooooh, Yeaaaa!" Achledis shouted in turn; he was smiling as he fought the rocks and steered them further away from the bank. Right behind him, Vitaeus was pale and barely breathing. His heart was pounding loudly in his chest, and for a moment it was all that Vitaeus could hear. He couldn't understand his friend, how he could get such a kick out of this and have absolutely no fear. For Achledis, this was being alive, living as close to the edge as he could get. Vitaeus had diagnosed him long ago as being an adrenaline junky.

Suddenly terror struck Vitaeus further as the roar of waterfalls became acutely distinct. The skiff had only made it halfway across the river. Now they were nowhere near shore; with no chance of making land before going down the waterfall.

"Waterfalls, row to shore!" Vitaeus shouted as he rowed frantically.

Achledis suddenly got serious and started rowing towards shore in more earnest, but nowhere fast enough, as the roaring water got louder up ahead. The mist could be seen just ahead and closing in fast. Vitaeus was rowing in a panic and was shocked when Achledis stopped rowing and turning towards him shook his head calmly. "Hold tight!" He shouted and lay flat down in the boat holding onto to both sides of the little skiff.

We're dead, Vitaeus thought as the boat jarred violently against boulders that were protruding from the water gashing holes in the boat that neither boy noticed, before plummeting over the edge. Vitaeus felt his stomach lurch into his chest as he felt the weightlessness as if airborne, but it was only for a split second...

Achledis awoke, being shaken roughly, and he started to cough violently.Vitaeus was sitting just a few feet away, completely dazed and confused about what just happened, and how exactly he had ended up on the beach. He looked at his friend Achledis and blinked a couple of times.

"Grandpa, this one's alive too," said a feminine voice.

Achledis started laughing, "Well we made it! We are alive, haha!"

The old man who was now stooping over him frowned angrily, "You two are remarkably stupid. You are lucky the falls didn't kill you. If I wasn't around, both of you surely would have drowned."

"Thank you, sir, thank you for saving our lives. I don't know how we got in the river. I can't remember a thing, but it's clear that you saved our lives, and I am truly grateful," Vitaeus said.

"Yea, thank you," Achledis repeated. "You too ma'am," he nodded towards the girl who was hauling the fish out of the boat. She was slender and beautiful he thought, and his heart skipped a beat when she looked back at him with a scowl on her face. Her wet blonde hair, hung down to her shoulders, her green eyes blazing with anger.

"Don't thank me! If it were up to me, I would have let you two fools drown. This wasn't an accident. The girls in town told me about how two boys with something to prove were going to attempt this stupidity."

"Going over the falls was definitely not part of the plan!" Vitaeus was quick to correct as his memory came flooding back.

"Well, all I know is that I was fishing with my granddaughter when I saw your boat shoot out of them falls there, and shortly afterwards, I spotted your bodies on that wreckage of a boat. Luckily, you managed to stay on it; being unconscious and all. I think it's a miracle. I'm just puzzled why any local would take a boat into the waters up north knowing full well that a waterfall isn't much further away." The old fisherman, known as Perat said with anger in his voice.

CHAPTER 2: THE HIDDEN CAVERN

Achledis was exhausted. The sun was directly overhead, and the pile of wood that needed to be chopped up didn't seem to be getting any smaller. Besides, his head throbbed and his body ached from the beating he received at the falls. Maybe his father would come out soon to tell him that he could run to the lake with Vitaeus, Achledis thought. In the meantime, however, he better continue working. After splitting another log, his father appeared leading their two horses as they dragged two more large logs to be chopped up into pieces. A feeling of dread passed over Achledis, thinking this was never going to end.

Wood being the primary source of fuel for heating and cooking meant that chopping wood and stocking up was a way of life.

"Achledis," Achledis's father Kalim called. "You have done well for the day, but your mother wants to prepare some fish for dinner. You better go get it, but before you go, come in and get a bite to eat."

"Yes Sir," Achledis replied.

Achledis was overjoyed. That was his father being himself; always giving you a compliment and a break while making it sound like it was just another chore. Kalim had been harder on Achledis this past year as he trained him for his upcoming manhood. Achledis was now eighteen years old and has been the one doing most of the wood chopping, which helped to create his broad shoulders and rippling muscles.

Kalim also encouraged Achledis to do pull-ups, sit-ups and pushups. Swimming across Pavanti Lake and back every morning was something that Kalim stressed to Achledis will help him attain an excellent physique and endurance.

Achledis was just finishing up his meal when Vitaeus knocked on the door. Achledis's mother Svetani invited him in.

"Hello," Vitaeus said and politely declined the invitation for dinner.

"Vitaeus you need to start eating more. My goodness, you are starting to look extremely skinny." Svetani teased her son's friend.

"Oh thank you ma'am, I just had my dinner. It must have been an entire cow; I swear. I don't know why I can't gain more weight," Vitaeus replied, his wolfish grin displayed as always.

"He is a lean mean wolf." Kalim replied as he came in through the door after taking care of his horses.

"Ok, I'm done! Let's go Vitaeus; we got a lot to do." With a quick kiss to his mom and a quick compliment, "the meal was great mom," Achledis tried to scurry out.

"Hey wait a minute! What's the rush Achledis? Vitaeus just got here, and I haven't seen my second son in almost a week." Svetani called out.

"Oh come Svetani, the boys really better get going. With their skill at fishing, we will be lucky to have any fish tonight." Kalim joked.

With their fishing rods in hand, the boys hurried to the lake. At the lake, the boys got into their little fishing boat and started to row out to Rostrif Island. On the way, they both caught a couple of fish, which they placed into a little cage that was tied to the boat and dragging, in the water, to keep the fish alive and fresh. Both boys agreed that they needed another adventure, and they were going to try and find it on Rostrif Island.

As the boys approached the Island, Achledis jumped to shore while Vitaeus parked the skiff under a bush hanging over the water.

"Achledis!" Vitaeus called out, his voice sounded overly excited.

"What is it?"

"You have to take a look at this; it looks like an entrance to a cave or something."

Achledis excitedly got back in the water and underneath the thick bush; which concealed Vitaeus and the boat completely.

Straight ahead was a small opening, but large enough for a man to crawl through on his hands and knees.

"Wow! This is awesome!" Achledis exclaimed quietly. Both boys were motionless for a while as if still stunned.

"What are you waiting for?" Achledis said as he scrambled towards the opening.

"Achledis wait," Vitaeus called, but his words seemed to bounce of the entrance as Achledis proceeded in a hurry.

"Achledis I mean it! It could be dangerous."

Achledis paused, "Dangerous? How dangerous are we talking here Vitaeus? I know you better than you think, and you just want to be the first one in."

"It could be booby trapped." Vitaeus warned.

Once through the entrance, the tunnel thinned out to a point where Achledis had to crawl on his belly going up hill the whole way. Achledis' hand nudged a rock out of place, and suddenly he was airborne as his entire body catapulted through the space towards his right. He hit a rock wall and crumpled.

"Achledis? Are you ok? I thought I heard you starting a rockslide in there, and if you did, don't expect me to dig you out."

Vitaeus' voice sounded so distant, Achledis thought as he tried to shake the grogginess so he could call back for help.

"Vitaeus, be careful. You were right, it is booby trapped. I need you to get a torch in here. I need to see where I'm at."

"Are you safe?" Vitaeus called.

"All I know is that I'm on a slim ledge, but be careful. Watch out for the trap."

"All right stay there; it might take a while for me to make a fire for the torch. Sit tight, and pretty please don't get yourself killed."

Vitaeus took a flint from his pocket and gathered some dry kindling. Five minutes later he had a nice fire going. He found a Fente branch and peeled the bark off the tip. The sap from the Fente was oily and burned long and bright. It had always been a natural source of energy in Rosmir.

Vitaeus made his way through the little tunnel on his stomach, keeping the torch in front of him the whole time. That way he was able to see what was between him and the torch. He noticed a mechanism made of wood, and it was more like a gate. When the water level in the lake rose, the water in the slot would fill up and cause the board to float up and seal the entrance to the cave so that the cave wouldn't get flooded. Further up, he noticed an opening to his right *so that must be close to where Achledis flew out*, he thought and decided to proceed ahead with more caution.

"Achledis, your still there?" Vitaeus called out.

"Yea, I can see your light. Vitaeus be careful, you're getting closer to the trap."

"Well, about that you need not worry," Vitaeus retorted. "Thank the Creator He gave me more sense than to you."

"Oh shut-up. Just get me out of here."

Vitaeus looked over to his right and saw Achledis on a narrow ledge; the two boys looked down and gulped. They didn't say anything instead the silence said it all. The chasm that separated the two was so deep that the light from the torch couldn't reach the bottom below. At the end of the ledge, next to the rocky wall, there was a sock chute that seemed to lead to the bottom. Vitaeus saw Achledis looking at it, and knew what his friend was thinking of doing next.

"Achledis, don't even think of doing it because there is no way that I'm going to go down there to save your hide. If you die down there it's your own doing, and I am not responsible."

"Vitaeus come now, we wanted an adventure, and we got one. I for one am not done yet. I'm not ready to go home, but I am ready to go down."

"We don't know how old that sock chute is; it could be rotted out at the bottom."

When Achledis didn't respond Vitaeus continued. "So you will go down the sock chute and explore the chasm, but what if you can't come back up? What if there isn't a way out?"

"Ok, so I'll tie the bottom of that sock chute around my waist and climb down, using the chute as a rope. You will have to give me that torch; so that I could get a better look around."

Vitaeus got a look of exasperation as he cursed under his breath. "Achledis, the people who designed all the mechanisms in this cave aren't stupid. I am looking at this trap that catapulted you across, and it's almost invisible. This rock that you bumped is weighing down the pin on this mechanism that's keeping this door down. If the rock is moved, it releases the pin, and the trap door will launch you across a space of an eight foot wide chasm. That's a lot of force that this mechanism can generate." Vitaeus had a grave look on his face. He got that look a lot whenever he was pondering over a puzzle or a riddle. "But then I don't get how the door automatically re-attaches itself." He spoke to himself as he pondered thoughtfully.

"Vitaeus, while you're thinking over some stupid mechanism, I am still waiting for that torch over here." Achledis yelled.

Vitaeus glanced over at Achledis annoyed and turned back to his puzzle. This spot offered enough height for him to be on his hands and knees once again. He crawled carefully to the other side of the door. He moved the rock and again the door shot out and what looked like a rubber rope slammed it back shut instantly, reloading itself for the next victim. Up above him was some kind of lever that Vitaeus didn't notice previously, and he bumped it down, but it didn't seem to do anything.

Meanwhile, Achledis was pulling the last of the sock up and was about to start tying it around himself when Vitaeus stopped him. "Hey throw the sock over here so that I can pull you onto this side. I want to open this door, I think that there might be something below."

Achledis paused to think it over. He wanted to go explore the chasm, but he was also intrigued of what could be under that trap door. He pulled up the sock chute until there was enough slack, and threw it to Vitaeus. Vitaeus started to wrap the chute around a rock that jutted out from the wall until it was tight; he misplaced his foot and accidentally bumped the booby trap. After a few seconds, he realized that the mechanism didn't launch him across and that he was still standing unperturbed. Achledis started to make his way over; unaware of what almost happened to Vitaeus.

"Whoa," Vitaeus yelled out in relief. "I just bumped this booby trap rock and nothing happened."

Achledis just finished crossing the chasm and gave Vitaeus a puzzled look, *"What do you mean by nothing happened?"* Achledis was on the opposite side of the door from where Vitaeus crouched.   He pulled the rock again, and again, nothing happened.   Something dawned on Vitaeus as his wolfish grin appeared.

"Of course that's what the lever is for, uh that makes a lot of sense" Vitaeus mused.

"What lever?" A confused Achledis asked.

"This one right here," Vitaeus pointed above them. "Now let's try to open this door."

The two boys gripped the edge of the door and opened it rather effortlessly, and as they opened it their eyes opened wide with surprise. The lever w make the spring that caused the door to shut with such force to go down into a slot relieving the pressure, and the band that re-shut the door automatically was unwound by the lever.

"Wow," Achledis gasped.

A simple rope ladder descended into the cavern below, and the two boys scurried down. They found themselves in a large room with wooden crates lining up along its walls and lots of weapons. Swords, battle axes and bows of different sizes hung on the walls.There were crossbows and even exotic looking knives. There were certainly enough weapons to equip a small militia, and the boys excitedly were inspecting every weapon in the room.

"Vitaeus, you have to see this!It's a giant map." Achledis called out excitedly.

In the middle of the room was a large circular stone slab; that was used as a table. On the table lay a map and a letter. The map was of the peninsula of Caminia, located in the Northwestern border of Rosmir, and the proposed plan to defend the Peninsula from the Rakirian invaders.

As Achledis stood there studying the map of Caminia, Vitaeus took the letter and opened it gingerly. The ancient paper was dry and threatened to break in its brittle form.

"What's in the letter?" Achledis asked.

"It's some kind of order from the Rosmirian Colonel Kurandin to hide an ancient book titled Wisdom of War in the cave. This cave here I assume. From the sound of it, the colonel was preparing to surrender Seredine, and he wanted to make sure that this book didn't get into enemy hands."

"I don't need a book to tell me how to wage a war. I would charge in and make sure my men fought with heart; there is nothing more you can ask." Achledis said.

"And the rest of us prefer to use our heads for what they were designed for, to think with, not as battering rams."

Why was the book not taken to Caminia? Vitaeus wondered. As history goes, following Rosmir's defeat at Seredine, at the hands of the Rakirian army, the remaining part of the crumbled Rosmirian army that wasn't routed at Seredine, rushed to stage a last defense at Caminia. At the beginning, three makeshift forts were built to keep the Rakirian army at bay; while a large castle was being built behind the forts for a long term resistance.

The peninsula had excellent natural defenses such as a steep hill leading up to the forts and an isthmus that was only a quarter mile wide at its narrowest point. The shores of the peninsula were high walls of rock; making it almost impossible to mount an invasion from the sea. The Rosmirian defense quickly dotted its shores with forts to ensure that an invasion from the sea, no matter how impossible, didn't happen. The weakest point was a beach in south Caminia that was a couple miles wide, but the Rosmirians have built a fort just as wide to ensure that no enemy was landing on that beach. Since then the fort has evolved into more of a formidable fortress and took the name of Nitami Fortress, after Nitami Beach where it was located.

Vitaeus set out to look for the book, Wisdom of War. Even though Achledis grumbled about how the chasm might be more interesting, he too joined in the search.

CHAPTER 3: EXPLORING THE CHASM

It was late into the night before the boys gave up looking for the book and started to head back home. Before they did, however, the boys swore a pledge to one another that they would keep the cave a secret. A light could be seen coming from the unshuttered windows of Achledis's house as the two boys separated. The house was still and quiet when Achledis entered. His mother was sitting at the table in an uncomfortable slumber. Quietly he placed the fish on the table and tiptoed up the stairs to his loft.

He woke up in the early morning being roughly shaken by his father, who had a stern look on his face. Kalim who usually didn't like to show emotion was furious inside, and Achledis sensed it instantly.

"Get up!" Kalim growled. "Do you have any idea what your mother and I went through last night? I was looking for you two up and down the lake late into the night. I was just about to go and get the whole town riled up for a manhunt; thinking that you boys drowned. Now I find you sleeping comfortably in bed?"

"Pa, I'm sorry, I didn't realize that you were looking for me, and I had no idea that you and Ma were so worried. After finally catching a few fish we simply fell asleep on the beach." Achledis explained.

"Good, your rest will be critical for you now as you will have so many chores to do, because while you were sleeping, I was awake looking for you!" Kalim put an emphasis on the last word as he walked away.

"Oh and by the way, you're grounded for the next week as you will have too much work to go anywhere. I will hunt and fish; you can tend to the livestock and bring in the wood.

For the next couple of days Achledis did his work from sunrise to sunset, and all the while he kept thinking about the secret cave. There was a secret book somewhere in there, and the fact that it was snuck out of Seredine during the siege and hidden in the cave made it that much more mysterious. They found a chest of books, but no book on 'Ancient Wisdom of War'. He knew that Vitaeus was obsessed with finding it, and he had to admit his curiosity was now fully aroused as well. Yet he still wanted to explore the chasm in the cave first. There was a sock chute that lead down there; so there must be something to go down to, he reasoned.

It was his secret with Vitaeus. It was their place that no one else knew about, and that made it unique. They were two adults acting like kids when it came to the cave; Achledis knew that. But it was times like this that he didn't want to grow up; because growing up and becoming mature, adhering to rules of proper etiquette seemed boring. He knew that day when he would be expected to act in such a way, however, wasn't far off.

Considering that Vitaeus wasn't showing up, Achledis could only assume that he too got grounded by his father.

We need to sneak out tonight and go to the cave again. Achledis thought. Aside from the secret room, the boys still had to explore the rest of the cave and take a ride down the chute to the bottom of the chasm. What lay at the bottom was beyond anything that Achledis could imagine, and his curiosity was driving him crazy. *Tonight will be the night that we find out what's at the bottom of that chasm,* Achledis decided.

That night after Achledis was sure that his parents have fallen asleep, he slipped out of bed and jumped out his window from the second story loft. As he approached Vitaeus's cottage, he heard a soft thud and footsteps racing towards him; so he ducked in some nearby bushes. Vitaeus came into view jogging, and as he ran by Achledis's hiding place, Achledis jumped out and tackled Vitaeus. The boys wrestled into a stalemate before Vitaeus realized that he had been wrestling his best friend.

"Achledis, what are you doing here?"

"I wanted to ask you the same, but I think that I have gotten it figured out." Achledis chuckled.

"I have been thinking about that cave all week, and against my better judgment I decided that I had to sneak out and risk getting my hide skinned." Vitaeus replied.

Finding the entrance by moonlight turned out to be easier than expected. After lighting the torch, the two boys crawled through the tunnel until they got to the chasm. Achledis dropped a rock and waited as seconds ticked by before hearing a thud. The boys quickly disabled the trap door before it tossed them across the chasm. Then Achledis, who was more than willing to be the one to go down first, swung himself on a rope across the chasm to the ledge on the other side. Vitaeus dropped one of the lit torches down into the chasm so that Achledis could have some lighting. It took his breath away to see the lit torch as a mere speck of light down below. Achledis stood by the chute as if having second thoughts.

"Not going to back out, are you Achledis?"

"No way!" Achledis said firmly and looked at Vitaeus with a side glance that seemed to ask, "Why would you even ask something like that." With that, Achledis jumped inside the cloth chute and zipped down. He slowed to almost a standstill down towards the end as the sock chute became so narrow that it almost constricted him from passing through. Achledis wiggled his body in the tight chute and felt that he was starting to slip through. As the tight, but elastic cloth slowly gave way, Achledis popped out through the bottom end and dropped another seven feet onto a rocky floor.

"Ok I made it!" Achledis shouted

"What do you see?"

"It's a small rocky chamber which has another small drop, which is filled with water and, and..."Achledis hesitated. He was sure that these was small deadly poisonous snakes that he could see swimming around in the water. "Snakes!" Achledis yelled. "There is also what looks like a hole that's filled with slimy looking mud."

"What else is down there?" Vitaeus yelled.

"Aside from some skeletons and bones in the water, there isn't much." The disappointment in Achledis's voice was clearly audible, but at least his curiosity on the chasm was finally satisfied, Vitaeus thought.

Achledis had just finished climbing the rope that Vitaeus had tossed down to him. As he clambered back on the ledge beside Vitaeus, he said thoughtfully, "That hole with slimy mud has to have a purpose, but what could it be? There is a reason that there is a chute leading into this chasm; it must be there for something."

"Achledis when you think, I get nervous. So stop thinking. When the trap door throws the intruder, the lucky ones do not fall into the chasm, to their death, but land on the narrow ledge. They are encouraged to go ahead and go into the pit safely, with the aid of the chute. Once they are at the bottom of the chasm, they stumble into a pit of hungry snakes." Achledis shrugged in acceptance to Vitaeus's explanation, but deep down something bothered him about it. There has to be more to it than that, he decided.

CHAPTER 4: THE ATTACK

Dawn was just breaking when the boys exited the cave. Their only fear was that they wouldn't get home in time before their parents woke up and realized their absence. In the cave they simply lost track of time, and now they were horrified to see the pre-dawn light peering over the horizon. To add to their delay, a heavy fog was set across the lake, and the two boys tried their best to maintain a straight course as they rowed blindly. After some time the boat finally hit land, and as assumed, the boat was way off course. The boys tied it off under some heavy brush next to the weeping willow tree and raced to their homes before their absence was discovered.

Achledis tried to slip through the door quietly, and as soon as he did, he came face to face with a stern faced Kalim.

"Where have you been?" Kalim's voice was harsh and accusing. "Did you forget that you were grounded, or is that why you're sneaking around at night?"

"I uh, went and tried to do some fishing. I decided to add fishing to my chores," Achledis stammered. His excuse was lame, and he regretted opening his mouth at all.

Kalim suppressed a smile and tried to be angry with his son, but affection and pride got in the way. Knowing his son, he was surprised it took this long for him to sneak out; he wasn't the type to stay confined to the property for too long. Speaking softer, Kalim continued, "Forgot your fishing pole didn't you, or were you trying to spear the fish in the dark?" As an afterthought, he nodded at Achledis's empty hands. "I guess that explains the absence of fish."

Svetani came around the corner and saved Achledis from further embarrassment. "Well now what are you two boys doing up so early?"

"Achledis and I are going to go and do some fishing, my love," Kalim said as he stooped to kiss his wife.

"Well you better not sneak out without getting some breakfast."

Just as Svetani was serving breakfast, they heard yelling and the thundering of horses' hooves. Kalim ran to the door to see what was going on and came back quickly going straight for his sword and ordered Achledis to grab his bow.

He stood and looked grimly at his son. "Son, protect your mother! I know you can; I have seen your skill with that bow." His eyes drifted toward Svetani, and he locked eyes with his wife. His eyes were calm and showed no signs of panic, but Svetani knew her husband was being strong, for her sake. "Now go! Both of you, go to the woods, I will catch up with you shortly." Stooping down, he kissed Svetani, allowing his lips to linger for a moment; then he turned and hurried towards the door.

"Kalim, what is it? What's going on?" Svetani asked. Achledis looked at his mom, and though she tried to look brave, the quiver of her voice was very distinct, and betrayed her courage.

"It's the Rakirians. I see plumes of smoke rising from the direction of Pavanti. Now a small party of them is at the top of the knoll, heading in this direction. You two have to go somewhere deep in the forest and hide. I will come for you when this is all over."

Svetani wrapped herself tightly around Kalim's waist and didn't want to let go. "No! You must come with us," she begged, tears flowing freely down her face.

"Go my love, go. I will come for you. I trust Achledis will be able to take you to a safe place." Kalim looked at Achledis, and as their eyes met, he knew that his boy was going to do just fine.

"Dad, you and mom should go. I will distract them. You taught me well, and you said yourself that I can fight!"

"No Achledis! Do as you are told, and take your mother to the woods and don't you dare look for trouble, or a fight. Your mother's safety depends on it." Kalim kissed Svetani and held her for a moment as she sobbed, and then gently, but firmly, he pulled back and whispered. "I love you darling, don't forget that." Kalim struggled to finish the statement as he suddenly pulled back, hiding his own tears. Shoulders squared, he turned and walked to the door, casting a single glance at his beloved wife before slipping outside.

Achledis grabbed his hunting knife and bow and ran out the door, with his mother close behind. Roughly fifteen paces from the door Kalim was quickly losing ground in an overmatched battle against three Rakirians. Survival didn't seem to be an option; Kalim's only hope was to last long enough for his wife and son to make their escape.

Seeing his father in peril, Achledis abandoned all thoughts of flight.Whipping out his bow, he zipped an arrow through the throat of the first attacker. Kalim glanced back quickly, and Achledis saw the surprise and relief on his father's face. Achledis knocked another arrow into his bow string, and it zipped at the second attacker.At that moment Kalim stepped into the path of the arrow and tried to jab the Rakirian with his sword. His arm was knocked off course as the arrow sliced into his forearm, and the sword fell to the ground.

The two remaining attackers hesitated for a split second; the foe that had been able to hold them off was now a sitting duck, unable to grasp a sword. As they prepared to execute Kalim, they committed an error that would cost them their lives; they dropped their guard against Achledis. The third arrow shot out from Achledis's bow, flying straight and true, right through the eye of the second Rakirian.

The last Rakirian was rattled to see another compatriot shot down by the boy's accurate shooting. Suddenly the boy tossed his bow aside to the ground and charged him; taking out a large hunting knife as he did. It all happened too fast for the Rakirian. *Is this boy crazy, I have a sword*, he thought. Then the boy was upon him.

Achledis's senses became more vivid.He saw the Rakirian's braced sword as he charged him and at the last moment, slid under the drawn sword, plunging the knife right into the man's gut. The Rakirian collapsed onto Achledis and Achledis pushed him off drawing his knife back in one fluid motion.

As Achledis looked down at the wide eyed corpse lying at his feet, pride swelled up in his chest. He looked at his parents as they stood speechless, looking at him in admiration.

"Dad, I'm sorry about your arm; you jumped right into it."

"Oh, forget the arm son; it will heal.Bsides you more than made up for it." Kalim proudly put an arm on Achledis's shoulder.

"Um, Kalim," Svetani stood frozen as she stared somewhere behind Kalim, "Here come the rest of them." Turning around, Achledis and Kalim saw as twenty Rakirians charged down the hill yelling.

"Mom, Dad, go to Rostrif Island, and I will find you there. There should be a boat tied under the bush, next to the big willow. Take it Rostrif Island."

"No, Son! You have to come with us; we have to run now," Svetani pleaded.

"Achledis come! You can't fight them; there are at least twenty of them descending the hill." Kalim yelled as he grabbed Achledis and started to pull him along.

Achledis pulled back sharply from his father's grip, "No, I'm going to stay and stall them; I will get away, once you're both out of sight."

"Then you and your mother go while I distract them." Kalim pleaded.

Achledis motioned with a toss of his head at his dad's useless right arm. "You can't fight with that; besides dad, mom is your girl. It's your responsibility to get her away from here safely."

Kalim locked eyes with Achledis for a moment, and the two had an understanding. Kalim's eyes simmered, and he fought back a tear as he knew that Achledis's mind was made up. His son had grown into a man, and he just realized it now.

The Rakirians were considerably closer now, and they suddenly broke into a run with swords drawn.

Achledis looked at his parents and shouted impatiently, "Go, go, just go!" Then he whipped out his bow and started shooting one arrow after another. After five Rakirians had fallen in their tracks, the others stopped running. A large burly Rakirian took out his spear, and after winding up, he let the spear go. The shaft sprang out of the big man's hand and whizzed by Achledis; the force of the air was felt on his face. As Achledis watched the shafts flying by, he heard his father yelling, "No!" As he dived in front of Svetani taking a single spear through the back, the shaft came out the other end, piercing Svetani through the chest too.

A rage swept through Achledis as he watched his parents get murdered right in front of his eyes. Grabbing his father's sword and a Rakirian shield, Achledis charged into battle.Though the shield was heavy, Achledis barely noticed as adrenaline carried its weight. As he was nearing the Rakirian soldiers, he received a round of spears into his shield. In a smooth motion he flung his shield forward at the sword drawn in front of him as the Rakirian staggered from the impact. Achledis lunged at him, stabbing the man through the belly. As the man sagged, Achledis launched himself on him, jabbing his sword right through the chainmail and into the chest of another Rakirian. Suddenly a loud crack resounded as a Rakirian slammed his shield across Achledis's head. A black veil covered his eyes, and he drifted off into the darkness.

As Vitaeus got closer to his house he thought he smelled smoke. Vitaeus paused and quickly looked around; he thought he could hear screaming in the distance. There it was again! Breaking into a run, Vitaeus tried to force out the nightmares that his mind was racing through. As he got closer, he could hear men laughing and taunting a woman mercilessly.

Vitaeus slipped through the trees quietly and peered at his parents' house. It was engulfed in flames. His father lay in front of the door in a pool of blood, and his mother was being shoved toward a group of men.

A blind rage consumed Vitaeus. With strength he never knew he possessed, he charged and tackled the man who shoved his mother. Springing up, he grabbed the sword that fell to the ground, but the man had kicked his feet out before he got a chance to use it. A volley of kicks slammed into Vitaeus, and they continued to fall until he was too weak to attempt getting up. With blood oozing from his nose and mouth, darkness settled over him. The sound of his mother screaming for them to stop kicking him grew fainter and fainter, and he barely felt the pain from the impact of the kicks. Then there was nothing.

CHAPTER 5: CAGED LION

The midday sun was scorching overhead when Achledis came to. Achledis let out a groan as the wooden wheels rolled over a rut in the road, causing the wagon to jolt violently and sending bolts of pain coursing through his head. Apart from the pain, thirst was the next thing that Achledis noticed. The heat of the day seemed to evaporate every drop from his body, leaving his mouth dry, and his tongue feeling like rubber.

In his delirious state, Achledis wasn't sure where he was, but he could smell the stench of nasty body odor before he saw or felt the mass of bodies piled all around him. He gagged as he got a strong whiff of sweat and urine. Achledis sat up to get fresh air, grunting from the effort. That was when he noticed that his hands and feet were bound. Then the memories of the day's events came flooding upon him, and Achledis set his jaw firm at the memory of his parents' murders at the hands of the Rakirian marauders.

"Murdered, my parents were murdered," he mumbled to himself in disbelief. This couldn't be real.He didn't believe that any of this could have happened; it was like a nightmare, *a terribly real nightmare. I need to wake up,* he thought. The searing pain in his head, however, and the discomfort of dehydration were real, and he knew that this was no nightmare. This was now his life.

The feeling of utter helplessness and sudden loneliness drained Achledis as he realized that he would never see his parents again, never hear their voices, feel the gentle touch of his mother, or the guiding hand of his father. His thoughts turned from pity to vengeance as he slumbered off into a troubled sleep. His last thought was that his parents' deaths were impossible to avenge. Even if he killed the entire Rakirian army and put every single one of their cities ablaze, he knew his vengeance would never be satisfied. The lives of his parents were priceless; there was nothing more valuable in the world that he could destroy to avenge them. He wondered about his best friend Vitaeus, and whether he had survived the attack. Perhaps he had been taken prisoner too? Achledis didn't even dare think of the other possibility for fear of making it true.

In his uneasy sleep, Achledis dreamed about a mighty lion, a beast like no other. It was big, powerful, and fierce. Its roar was dreadful and chilling, and Achledis could see the fear of the keepers that tried to contain the lion. They would bind the lion with chains, but the lion would break them and kill all the keepers around him. The keepers were persistent and would put bigger and stronger chains on the lion, but the result was the same. In its rage, the lion broke the chains and killed the keepers. The keepers then attempted to lock the lion in a cage, but in its fury, the beast would break through the door as if it wasn't there. Achledis realized that nothing could hold this ferocious lion down, neither chains nor cages, and he saw himself as the lion bringing death and destruction upon his tormentors.

As the dream started to fade, he could see the calm, but stern look of his father emerge. He looked at Achledis with those unwavering eyes, eyes full of confidence. His mother's face appeared for a moment; he could see her laughing eyes and smile. As he tried to reach out to touch her face, the image was suddenly gone.

A sharp elbow slammed in Achledis's face jarring him awake. It was a girl that lay next to him; she was trying to shift into a more comfortable position. He observed her out of the corner of his eye as she shifted around in discomfort. Her tan skin and white blonde hair, streaked even blonder from being in the sun, seemed to bring out her beautiful swan green eyes, but even with such beauty, there was something more that seemed to draw Achledis in. It was her restlessness he realized.

"Can't get comfortable?" Achledis asked.

The girl glanced at him as if annoyed with the stupid question.

Achledis shrugged his shoulders and rolled his eyes to the side as if indifferent with her response.

"Well we are packed like fish being taken to the market. There's no room to move around, and I can't feel my hands and feet anymore." She said.

Achledis readily agreed and offered his hand, "I'm Achledis."

"Hi, I'm Desiani. I saw you rolling your eyes at me; hope I wasn't too rude."

"Calling it rude would be a polite way of putting it," Achledis joked. Desiani scowled at him, and Achledis's grin quickly faded. There was something familiar about her he realized, but he couldn't remember where he might have seen her before.

"So where are you from?" He asked.

"Same place as you."

"Pavanti?"

"Yes."

Achledis studied the girl with more interest; her green eyes seemed to be laughing at him. She bit her lower lip, and by doing so revealed the dimples in her high cheekbones. She could see his discomfort, and she enjoyed exploiting it.

"Why, you don't remember me?" Her eyes squinted accusingly. He remembered her all right; it didn't take long for him to remember where it was that he had seen that beautiful face. She was the girl that was with the old fisherman who had pulled him and Vitaeus out of the water after they went over the falls. He wasn't about to admit it; so he shook his head slowly.

Desiani, in turn, put on a hurt look as her eyes dropped in a pout. "I'm hurt. I saved your life, and you can't even remember the face of your savior."

Achledis let his eyes open up wide really slowly, as if recognition had just dawned on him. "Hmm, yes, I guess it is you since you were pretty rude back then too."

"Thanks, you're not so nice yourself if you haven't noticed."

"Would you two stop talking already? I'm trying to get some rest here; my head is killing me." Complained a male voice from somewhere inside the mass of bodies.

"Red, is that you? Shut up you lard! I'm trying to talk to a beautiful girl, and I don't appreciate you getting in the way." Red was the bully in the town of Pavanti, and Achledis didn't like him at all. He had put the kid in his place many times when he would pick on other kids weaker than him. He remembered him standing on the bank yelling and prodding for them to go when Vitaeus and he were attempting to cross Bestri River. He was a kid that enjoyed other people's pain, and Achledis cared very little for any pain that he might feel now.

"See, I rest my case,. You are a true gentleman." She said, trying to hide a flattered smile. She had blushed when he had referred to her as a beautiful girl.

"Actually I am, but Red isn't. Let's not pay any attention to him. Now more importantly, why have I not seen you around town before?"

"I moved to Pavanti last fall. I've been in town a lot, but I never ran into you."

"Yea, I've been kind of busy lately."

"Oh yeah, doing what? Attempting suicidal stunts and getting rescued by old men and young girls?" She tried to suppress a giggle.

"Something like that." Achledis smiled back casually.

"So, who were you trying to impress?"

"Impress?" Achledis asked, clearly not following.

"You took a boat over a cliff. I assume you had some kind of reason; besides being stupid, like maybe you were trying to impress someone?"

"No one, it was something I believed that could be achieved, and I set out to prove it. I turned out to be slightly wrong.That part of the river is a lot faster than I had anticipated."

"Right," Desiani said doubtfully.

"Oh, okay so tell me why are you so rude? You think your beauty gives you the right to talk down to men?"

Desiani was stumped by the accusation before finding her feet and responding quite hotly. "No, I'm actually rather sweet most of the time. I just don't like guys who have more brawn than brain. Guys kind of like you, stuck up, because they have silly girls

34

who gush at them when they pass by." Desiani stopped suddenly, unnerved by Achledis's sudden smile. Achledis couldn't stop the smile; even if he had tried to suppress it. Desiani's fiery passion amused him, and he liked it in her.

"Why are you smiling like that?" Desiani said suddenly feeling bashful.

"I was just watching your eyes. Such passion burning in them when you rant, and those dimples when you smile like now, wow!" Achledis laughed aloud, "How do you do that? It's so different, but I like it."

"Stop," she said, but the tone in her voice told him that she wanted him to continue heaping her with praise.

After riding in silence for a bit, both in their own thoughts, Achledis's mind wandered back to the events of the day. He remembered how his parents got murdered and felt the rage well up within his chest once more.

"Why would Rakiria attack us? They have already occupied our land, and lord over us. What was the need for them to come and murder so many innocent people, to pillage our land, and take so many of us from our homes? Why?" He almost shouted. His teeth were clenched tightly now to prevent himself from shouting yet again. Desiani looked at him, surprised by the outburst. His fists were clenched tightly together, and he seethed angrily.

Personally, she hadn't lost anyone close to her. Her grandfather had gone fishing that morning and chances were that he was okay. She remembered how she was lying in her bunk in the loft when she heard the door come crashing down and the Rakirian soldiers running in. She remembered how one of them had grabbed her roughly, a wicked grin on his face, when another soldier stepped in and punched him in the face, pulling Desiani away from him. The kind Rakirian had personally escorted Desiani to the wagon, and as he tied her ropes he apologized for the other Rakirian.

Now as she looked at Achledis who was still seething, she put her hand on top of his to comfort him. "Do they need a reason?" She asked. "They do what they want, when they want.

35

Perhaps they needed to replenish their slaves; the men will be forced to join their armies. Rakiria is always in need of more manpower with all the wars that they are fighting women will make excellent slaves for households. Look around, do you see any old people? All the prisoners are under thirty."

"I'll be damned if I fight for those accursed beasts. I would sooner kill them before I kill for them." Then lowering his voice, he whispered to her, "One day I will destroy them Desiani. I will make their empire fall to its knees."

"Everything will be all right. Together we will figure out how to get you back to your family and friends. Be thankful that you were only snatched away and not murdered." Desiani said reassuringly.

"You think I was merely snatched away from family and friends?" Achledis's face grew red with rage. "Really? That's what you think this is? Well my parents were murdered. They committed no crime, but they were murdered anyway. These dogs are without honor, and I would love to kill every one of them."

"I'm sorry; I didn't know," Desiani said as she gently put her hand on his shoulder comfortingly. She felt the muscles in Achledis's shoulder ease under her touch.

The call to stop for camp was finally made, and the two were more than happy to get some needed rest from the bumpy wagon ride. Their bodies were aching from being crunched with other bodies that were all equally exhausted and restless at the same time.

Two lines were formed: Male and female. Guards escorted them in opposite directions, beyond the clearing and into the trees. Those with fuller bladders urged others to go as fast as the ropes on their feet allowed them to go. Though the bonds on their hands had been undone to give them freedom to do their business, their feet were still tied; allowing them only to put one foot in front of the other foot. Guards walked alongside the line with crossbows trained at the prisoners, daring anyone to attempt an escape. Every now and then, a guard would prod someone back into line, shouting for the prisoners to keep the line straight. The guard that was leading the procession raised his hand in the air as he shouted for the prisoners to stop and do their business quickly. Everyone was anxious to finally relieve themselves. Some had already gone at least once in their pants but eagerly tried to go again; while the opportunity presented itself.

Once back at camp, Achledis saw Desiani further up in line getting her food; which consisted of a delicious smelling broth. Achledis salivated as he smelled the soup. He wasn't sure if he was just that hungry, or if the Rakirians knew how to prepare a delicious stew for themselves and their prisoners alike.

He noticed a Rakirian soldier, who was standing to the side supervising the line, kept glancing at Desiani. He approached Desiani slowly from behind and nudged himself against her back as he took a slice of bread away from her. Smirking, he pointed that she was only allowed one. Desiani recognized the guard as being the same one that had grabbed her from her bunk earlier that morning when she was first captured. The move he made was so provocative that Desiani pretended to stumble and threw the contents of her hot soup into the soldier's face. Quickly recovering, Desiani apologized innocently. The soldier looked at her with anger burning in his eyes; his face was red from being scalded by the hot broth.

"You did that on purpose!" He shouted as he slapped her violently across the face.

Desiani winced in pain and tears flowed instantly. There was a shocked silence in line as everyone noticed the scene unfold. The soldier grabbed Desiani by the hair cruelly and pulled her roughly out of line.

Achledis reacted instantly as he half ran, half stumbled towards the soldier, slamming a knee to his groin.Then grabbing the soldier's head he twisted it until it snapped. As the corpse of the dead soldier crumpled to the ground, Achledis snatched his sword and cut the ropes that bound his ankles. Turning around he braced himself as two Rakirians attacked him.

Like the lion that had been teased and taunted while being caged, Achledis was now free to have his vengeance. Instead of waiting for the two to attack him, he sprang at one soldier, and his sword was so quick that the other soldier had to give ground. Achledis deflected the second swordsman's sword with ease; even as he stepped up his offensive. He feigned a lunge on the foe to his left and at the last second pulled back and with an over the shoulder arc as he sliced off the head of the soldier on his right.

The Rakirians where lining up with crossbows ready to fire. Right before they were given the order to fire, Achledis lunged and stabbed the other swordsman through the chest as he brought him abreast so that their eyes were only inches away. The soldier's eyes bulged with surprise and instantly glazed over as he realized that he was seconds from death. Achledis grabbed the soldier and pulled him close as twenty some darts raced towards him but struck the Rakirian soldier that he had used as a shield. He felt a burning sensation across his left cheek and right ear where the darts grazed by, but there was no pain, just a trickle of blood. Without losing another moment, Achledis scrambled under one of the wagons before running into the trees.

CHAPTER 6: SILVER WOLF

A pounding, dull and heavy, yet steady like that of drums to a certain cadencewas the headache that made Vitaeus grimaced. He was trying to bear the pain in his head in silence, but a flash of pain shot through his brain and he let out a groan. Where he was? He didn't know, and it was too dark to tell. He reached for his head and felt a damp cloth on his forehead. He struggled to sit up, but ended up rolling instead as sudden and excruciating pain forced him to grab his head in his palms and suffer through the agony.

"Creator have mercy." He whispered as he clutched his head. He was on his knees and elbows on the ground; his palms holding his head steady. There was nothing steady about any of it. Where am I? He wondered.

"Dear, is that you?" A weak and tender feminine voice called. "Are you awake? Oh praise the good Creator."

Vitaeus heard a rustling as if someone was groping their way in the dark and then the soft padding of feet. Sudden light appeared almost blinding his eyes before he noticed a woman standing at the doorway holding an oil lamp.

The woman stood at the doorway, her quivering hand swept up to her mouth, and her eyes were pools of water that were overflowing. Vitaeus stared into her eyes and puzzled at them; they were kind and so familiar.

"My dear boy, thank the good Creator you are alive." She said as she rushed to him, stooping to kiss him tenderly. She held him affectionately as her tears rolled down the back of his neck and down his spine.

"My head hurts." He said.

"I know my son; you took quite a blow to the head. I will go get you some herbs that will help numb the pain." His mother replied.

"Where am I?" He asked.

"We are staying at Perat's house. Do you remember anything?" She asked.

"You mean the attack?"

"Yes," She replied, her voice full of relief.

"Though the effort does nothing to improve the pain in my head, I remember it."

"Let me get you something for your pain."

His mother Riani disappeared for the herbs, and Vitaeus looked around him. He had been lying on a straw mat on the floor in a small room that was fairly bare. The wooden floor was polished of any splinters; he saw that much. The walls were rough wooden logs, with a kind of muck in between to seal up any holes. A small window was to the left, sealed tight, and the opening covered with tanned leather. His thoughts wandered to the attack. He couldn't remember much; just the image of his slain father and his mother struggling against Rakirian soldiers. The thought was more than he could take. Just then his mother reappeared.

"Here, take this. This should help ease your pain, and this will help you sleep."

"I slept long enough; I think." He replied.

"You got hit on the head, and you need to rest."

A jolt of pain coursed through his skull just then, and he figured she was right. He needed to be put out of his misery. "Mom, thank the good Creator that you're alive. I, I..." Tears welled up in his eyes and a sudden lump in his throat cut of any more words that he might have had.

His mother looked strong at that moment. Though her eyes were red around the rims; they were dry.

He lay down with a goose feather stuffed pillow under his head, and the pain seemed to subside instantly. He wasn't sure what cured the pain, if it was the medicine or the soft pillow which wrapped snugly around his head. "What happened?"

"After I saw you get knocked out, I was beside myself," his mother began in that soft voice of hers. "I struggled and fought them, but there were too many of them. They held me down." Her face twisted slightly at the thought. "They acted like wild beasts..." Her voice cut off again. "I felt so helpless, but then the Rakirians started to drop with long arrows sticking out of them, the rest scattered quickly, leaving me."

"They didn't hurt you did they? They didn't get the chance?" Vitaeus asked his voice hopeful.

"No, not in that way they didn't. Perat got there in time with his bow."

"I hid you in a thicket by the river until the battle had moved on and the last of the Rakirians were gone. With Perat's help, we brought you here."

"What about Achledis and his family? Did you check on them?"

"Yes," She wiped more tears as they sprang up and shook her head sadly at her son.

"No, he can't be dead, not Achledis. I saw him defy death so many times that he couldn't just die by a Rakirian sword." Vitaeus said, his voice growing in despair.

"Kalim and Svetani Serdonis are both dead, and Achledis is missing. Their house was burned to the ground."

"I must bury them." Vitaeus said. But the herbs he took had already made him drowsy, and his voice was heavy with sleep.

"Rest now my dear. We will talk more in the morning." His mother put a fresh damp cloth on his forehead, but Vitaeus was already sleeping. Dreaming of a silver wolf who was reasserting its role as the head of a pack and more importantly as head of the animal kingdom.

CHAPTER 7: EVADING CAPTURE

Achledis ran aimlessly, armed with only the short sword that he acquired during the skirmish with the guards while escaping the Rakirian prison camp. He ran as fast as his legs would carry him, slowing down to a jog only after he felt like he put enough distance between himself and his pursuers. He crossed a frigid creek several times, getting out of the water on rocky soil, careful to leave his wet prints only on rock.

Feeling more relaxed now that he felt he lost his pursuers, Achledis slowed to a walk. The guards, weighed down with heavy armor and weapons, probably stopped the pursuit a long time ago. His adrenaline had carried him for much of the way, but he knew that if it wasn't for his father's rigorous training, his energy and strength would have given out a long time ago. Now that he felt safe, fatigue suddenly overcame him.

With darkness starting to settle, Achledis started thinking about where he would spend his night. All around was wilderness; no town or civilization that he could turn to for a nice dinner and a clean and comfortable bed. He would do just about anything for the two things that he had always taken for granted. Slowly he realized that he would be lucky if he found a roof over his head on this night. Though the skies were clear, and there was no danger of rain, he knew that a cloudless night also meant a frigid night, and he didn't have so much as a blanket.

He sat against a tree in a small clearing in front of the creek and thought about starting a fire but discarded that idea. Exhausted he lay down. His mind wandered to all that had occurred to him that day. He tried to shake the image of his parent's death from his mind, but he found it hard to do. The spear slamming through his father's back and impaling his mother was too much to take. He remembered his friend Vitaeus and sadly realized that he never did see him with the prisoners. When he was going to the bathroom, he looked through all the wagons that he passed, and even while standing in the food line he kept searching for his friend. He had spotted a lot of people from Pavanti, but Vitaeus was nowhere to be seen. *Had Vitaeus even got home before the attack? Perhaps he got away. What of Vitaeus's parents?* The Konis's were like his second parents, and their whereabouts was another thing that he didn't want to dwell on.

As he began to doze off, Desiani was on his mind, and he found himself planning on how he was going to rescue her. *Crazy,* he thought that on a day that he lost his parents, possibly his best friend, and had been taken captive, he could still distract himself so easily with a girl he met in a cramped prisoner wagon. He smiled to himself as he thought of how passionately she described her contempt for cocky men such as him, and the way her beautiful green eyes had burned with passion. The way she walked when she headed towards the female line, so graceful, like a swan on a placid lake. An amazing creature she is, he thought to himself.

With that, he probably would have fallen asleep except that he heard footsteps as they broke on dry twigs and branches and the whispering of voices. Instantly, Achledis sat more alert. He was very excited. This might solve his problem for food and shelter. As he opened his mouth to call out, he had a gut feeling not too. Instead he listened intently. As the voices grew closer and the snapping twigs got louder, he heard the men conversing in Rakirian. The hair on his spine stood on end as he braced himself behind the tree, a short sword in hand. The way the guards were whispering and attempting to walk quietly, there was no doubt that they were pursuing him.

With the settling darkness, many objects seemed to be more abstract, and with that knowledge, Achledis allowed himself to peer from behind the tree and make a visual of his pursuers. He noted that they only had leather vests for protection and none of the heavy armor that was standard for a Rakirian guard. They must be scouts, he decided. It would explain why these two haven't lost his trail and were dressed so lightly. They carried loaded crossbows and had their fingers on the trigger as they entered the clearing and made their way to where he hid behind the tree. He ducked his head back behind the tree; armed with a short sword against two crossbowmen, he didn't stand a chance at this range. His only chance was to ambush them as they walked past the tree.

He noticed that their conversation had suddenly ceased, and everything was still. The incessant sound of crickets chirping was the only sound to break the foreboding silence, and Achledis realized that he was holding his breath. *Could this really be the end?* He thought. *Is this how his life would end; being shot down with a crossbow from a distance, where he wouldn't have a chance to fight back. No!* He decided. *He would not die; he would kill them and live.* Calmly he closed his eyes and sucked in all the air he could manage into his lungs; then he breathed out slowly. He focused on one sense that would help him the most right now, his hearing. With his ears, he strained to hear sounds, indicating the direction of their approach. He heard twigs snapping almost simultaneously from the right and left of the tree. They had split, Achledis realized dreadfully, and were trying to come up on both sides of the tree. Somehow they knew that he was here. Perhaps the trail he left was too obvious, or they were just being cautious. His mind raced as he tried to find a way out of this predicament. The scout on the right could arc out nice and far if he wanted to. The scout to his left was limited by the creek, however, and the furthest he could get was ten paces from the tree. Thus, Achledis concentrated on listening to the approach from that direction; while allowing his eyes to scan the darkness to his right, which was now illuminated by the soft glow of the moon. Any sudden movement from the right and he would have no choice but to react swiftly to his left, where the guard would be considerably closer.

The sound of a pebble skidding across a rock alerted Achledis that his pursuer was extremely close, and the muscles in his legs tensed, ready to pounce like a cat on its prey. His heart was beating wildly, but he barely noticed. His focus was solely on the target that should emerge at any time. He had to make the decision. Should he attack the guard to his left before he came into view? It might have that element of surprise; which would give him an advantage. What if he was further than fifteen paces? What if the Rakirian intentionally tossed the pebble to get him to show his face; so he could shoot him from a distance? There were too many ifs and buts, too many unknowns. It was too late to climb the tree; he would make too much noise and allow his antagonists to shoot freely at him. He had no choice. He had to attack he decided, and before he could change his mind he charged out from cover, screaming and howling.

The Rakirian was maybe twelve paces from the tree, at the water's edge, trying to maintain distance between himself and the tree when Achledis came charging out. Unnerved by the sudden appearance of the enemy, he raised the crossbow and took aim; he was an excellent shot and there was no reason for him to panic. His finger tightened on the trigger, and the quarrel shot out towards its target. At that moment, however, Achledis stumbled over a root but recovered quickly. As he moved in at an incredible speed with the short sword held out in front, the quarrel harmlessly flew by. Hurriedly the scout fumbled to draw his own hunting knife. Before he could draw it, Achledis's sword had severed his neck, and the scout crumpled to the ground dead.

A second bolt flew by Achledis's head, and Achledis turned quickly to locate his second adversary. He saw him a good fifty paces away scrambling to reload the crossbow. Achledis grabbed the dead scout's crossbow and bolts and scrambled into the bushes.

The second Rakirian with the crossbow loaded and ready once again looked to where Achledis had been but couldn't see him anymore. He had failed to note where he went, and with this present darkness, he knew that it might be impossible to locate him. He had to withdraw for the night and try again in the morning. He had found new respect for this Rosmirian youth and decided not to risk following him in the dark where an ambush could be set for him at every bush and tree. Besides, it would be impossible to track him this late at night. As he turned to go back, he suddenly felt the sharp bite and impact of an object as it struck his right arm. Instinctively he dropped the crossbow and looked in shock at a bolt protruding from his dominant arm. As he looked up he could see a shadow racing towards him, the outline of a short sword held high overhead. Screaming, he turned to run, but his foot tripped over a root sticking out of the ground.

The Rakirian felt the cold blade at his throat; even as a heavy foot stepped on his chest. He could see the outline of a man standing over him; an angry scowl was the only feature that he could make out in the darkness. A chill ran through the Rakirian's body as he sensed fear swell up within. He raised two fingers pressed together into the air, a universal symbol of defeat and surrender.

Angry, Achledis didn't want to let this man off so easily. He wanted to kill him and every one of his kind. There was a hatred for this people that had come into his land. As he pressed the sword slowly into the Scout's throat, however, he saw the man's eyes bulging with fear so that the whites of the eyes illuminated in the moonlight. Achledis realized that he couldn't murder someone so helpless, but he couldn't bear allowing this man to go back into the service of Rakiria.

"Please, I want to live," the Scout croaked.

"And what will you do if I let you live? Where will you go?" Achledis asked suspiciously.

The scout seemed stupefied by the question and stopped to think as something told him that his life depended on his answer. "Where would you like me to go?" He finally asked.

"Go home to your wife! If we ever meet again, I swear to you that I'll do things to you that will make you regret ever being born." The Scout nodded enthusiastically. "Now strip down and go."

As the scout ran off into the darkness naked, Achledis gathered the scout's belongings: the large knife, the quarrels for his crossbow, some biscuits, jerky, canteen of water, and a thin woolen blanket; everything else he tossed into the creek. Achledis had an uneasy knot in the pit of his stomach. He wasn't sure if he did the right thing; for mercy could be a weakness that could kill him some day. There was no way for him to judge if the Scout wouldn't simply rejoin the Rakirian army and carry on as before.

CHAPTER 8: THE FUNERAL

The sun was already shining in the eastern horizon, displaying colors ranging from yellow, orange, pink, and blue as Vitaeus walked on briskly. He chose the path through the forest to get to his burned house, rather than use the main road; just in case any more Rakirian scouts were around. The pine needles blanketed the forest floor like a soft carpet against his bare feet, an occasional needle would prick, but he hardly noticed. His mind was elsewhere; the dream he had was still on his mind. It was a common belief throughout Rosmir and perhaps other places as well that dreams held secret meanings or symbolized what may come or has already come. This dream contained animals, a powerful symbolism, but he didn't know what any of it meant. Animals fighting in an epic battle, but the foes and allies seemed so unlikely. Vitaeus had never had any reason to take much stock or ponder his dreams before, but this was different. This was a peculiar dream, and given the events of yesterday's attack, it somehow gave it more importance. He was no prophet, however, and it was beyond him to understand such things.

Vitaeus came out to the edge of the forest where the line of trees broke into a sprawling valley of grass below. Most days, Vitaeus would see all sorts of travel taking place on the roads below, but today there was nothing. The air was crisp and fresh, of an early summer morning. Vitaeus watched a hawk circling around in the air searching for prey. This was a place he came to often to reminisce, to think, to watch the sunrise in the horizon, but today he couldn't stand to be there a second longer as he continued on. He cut across to the nearest road, content that he hadn't seen any Rakirians. He needed a weapon, a sword at least, but all he carried was a small dirk that he borrowed from Perat's table. After getting on the dirt path, he followed it to the house that was home to him his whole life. Now it was a heap of charred and still smoking timber. As he came up to it, he froze at the sight before him.

Before the doorway lay charred bones and burned flesh of what had been his father. Nothing left for even the vultures to pluck on, he thought as he looked away, fighting back tears. The man that had been everything to him. He taught him all he needed to know; the person he looked up to his whole life. His father wasn't a typical country gentleman; he was more of a thinker, certainly well educated, articulate, and extremely good with the sword. His business had taken him away from his family often; at times, he would be gone for as long as a month, sometimes more, but mostly less. He owned a successful trading company with a fleet of his own ships, but he chose to raise his family here, a day and a half from the nearest port. This way he wasn't always stuck on business but had time to be home as well. At least that's what he always told Vitaeus, but Vitaeus suspected that there was a lot more to it. His father had been saying that this is the year that he would take him to show him his business. It was something that Vitaeus had anxiously looked forward to. His father had never taken him before and wouldn't even consider it prior to this year, but then he said that Vitaeus had finally grown into a man.It was time to show him and teach him the business of Losmir Arkonis.

Vitaeus had apparently lost track of time and had hardly noticed as two more people stood behind him sharing in his grief. He only turned to acknowledge his mother and Perat when he felt his mother's hand on his shoulder; he turned and met her embrace. Vitaeus had never seen tears in his mother's eyes before. She had always been such a strong woman, but right now Riani Arkonis, the wife of Losmir and mother of Vitaeus, wept. As Vitaeus held his mother, her weeping turned into deep sobs, and her tears ran freely and soaked into Vitaeus's chest.

Time passed, and no words were spoken. Perat stood to the side, his eyebrows furrowed together, and his eyes cast down in a deep reminisce. A shovel was stuck in the dirt next to him. He allowed mother and son to share in their private sorrow, but he was also there to mourn the extraordinary man he had known right along with them. Perat was known in the area as a fisherman, hunter and woods guide, but mainly as a fisherman.

Vitaeus hadn't known him too well; Perat wasn't one who enjoyed being part of society and usually stuck to himself. Vitaeus remembered being rescued by the old man, and his beautiful granddaughter. Vitaeus had just remembered about her, and realized that he hadn't seen her back at the cabin.

Vitaeus approached Perat slowly, and the older man met his gaze. "Thank-you for everything," Vitaeus said.

"Your father was a great man; perhaps the greatest of his generation, a lot like his own father."

"His father?" Vitaeus asked. "You knew my grandfather?"

"Yes, but that is a conversation for a later time." Perat replied. It was a phrase that Vitaeus had heard his whole life. He didn't know much of his family history; he grew up without any direct relatives or any knowledge of any. His family had a secret. He knew that his whole life. Only thing is that he didn't know what it was, and it was the same for Achledis and his family. Perhaps that was why their families had always been so close. Losmir and Kalim were as close as brothers, and Kalim would even go with his father on long business trips at times. Vitaeus had always believed that his father's business was somehow related to the secrecy of his family's past, but now he had to know the truth. It could not wait any longer.

"By later, I hope you mean right after I finish burying my father." There was a harsh edge to Vitaeus's tone. "Today I know the truth!"

Perat nodded, "As you wish; it is time you know."

Vitaeus snatched the shovel and headed back to where his mother stood before his father's corpse. Her eyes were swollen but dry, and she resumed her look of steadfast determination. Her light brown hair wasn't made elegantly but was tossed in a ponytail behind her. A breeze fluttered thin wisps of curls like banners across her face, but she took no notice. She grabbed the shovel from her son's hands.

"I must do this myself." She said, and her eyes glistened once more. "Such a pitiful funeral for such a great Lord."

Underneath the two willows Riani broke ground. Not far was a wooden bench and a small table where his father and

49

mother used to sip on white wine on hot summer days or drink their hot tea on brisk mornings. His father would write his letters there when the weather permitted. The memories of their lifetime together flooded over her and filled her with emotion as she shoveled the dirt hastily until her strength was spent. Vitaeus came up to her and gingerly took the shovel from her hands, which were red and blistered, and continued to dig. He shoveled steadily with less emotion and more purpose.

When the narrow grave was three feet deep, Vitaeus set the shovel in the dirt, and he and Perat picked up the charred body off the ground where it lay and placed it upon a purple blanket.

"A color worthy of a king." Perat had said when he had spread the blanket on the ground.

Riani gingerly wrapped the blanket around Losmir's corps, taking extra care to fold and tuck him in as if he were a child being swaddled in a blanket. No sooner had she finished when she cried out in anguish one more time and put the side of her face against where Losmir's face was covered. She held the corpse as she cried, her whole body quivering with each deep sob.

When she got up, Perat had a handkerchief ready for her; Riani whispered her thanks, her voice barely audible as she composed herself once more. Vitaeus moved first and stooped to pick up his father's upper body, and Perat got on the other end. Together they picked up Losmir's corpse and set it in the grave.

"Any last words for Losmir before we forever return his body to the earth where he came from and his spirit to eternal rest with the Creator who created him?" Perat asked.

Moments passed, and the only sounds were that of the breeze blowing the long thin branches and the wispy leaves of the willow before Riani stepped forward.

"Losmir, you were My Lord, husband and best friend. Together we set out to do a great thing and to change our world, but we didn't finish our task. Now I am alone and have to see it through without you."

Vitaeus waited till his mother finished speaking before he stepped forward and looked at the charred heap that was once his father. "Father, your life was one big secret to me, your past, your business and your future. I wanted to know so badly about what it is that you do, but you never trusted me enough to tell me. You always were a cautious man, making sure you covered every angle of everything you did, always striving for perfection. Your friend Kalim was the bold one, but you both had your secrets. Achledis and I never felt worthy enough to know them. Achledis always shrugged it off and pretended that it didn't matter, but it always mattered to me. It hurt that my father didn't trust his only son with his secrets. Now you can never tell me your secrets, and your promise to tell me one day remains unfulfilled. However, I intend to find it out and decide if your work is really worth carrying out, and most importantly, why it was always such a secret. You were a great man in many aspects, but who will know of your greatness? Who will mourn your passing except for the three of us that stand before your grave today? Will your business partners be in anguish? Rest in peace father. My only regret is that I didn't know you better."

Vitaeus picked up the spade with dirt and was about to throw it in the grave when Perat snatched the spade from his hand.

"I haven't said my farewell yet." He whispered through clenched teeth. Vitaeus nodded and took a step back.

Perat knelt by the grave and bowed his head in deep reverence, "Losmir, I served your father as I have served you faithfully. Yet I failed this one time. It was their scouting party that attacked and took your life. I didn't cover every angle like you would have had me do, and because of this, you lie in the ground with your work unfinished. Your son does have your and Riani's passion, however, and he will make a strong leader one day. He will finish the work that you set out to do. Rest in peace my liege and my friend. The memory of you will always be cherished." Perat took the spade and handed it to a perplexed Vitaeus. "Let's bury your father. Then we must bury Kalim and Svetani; for they also deserve proper recognition before their burial."

CHAPTER 9: FOLLOWING

Achledis woke up in the middle of the night to the sound of his own teeth chattering in the cold. Groaning, he pulled the thin woolen blanket over his head, hoping that by breathing inside the blanket, he could warm himself up. Shutting his eyes, he tried to fall asleep once again; for he was having a wonderful dream. But the cold seemingly got colder as it seeped into his skin; so that he started to shiver uncontrollably and his teeth started chattering worse than before. "Rocks and sticks, I knew I should have started a fire," he grumbled under his breath. Without further hesitation, he got up, gathered his belongings, and with the blanket wrapped tightly around his shoulders, he started his trek back towards camp.

As he walked, he chewed on the dry and tasteless biscuit, courtesy of the Rakirian scout, flushing it down with some cool water. The meager meal seemed to only rouse his hunger more, and he took out the jerky from his pouch and looked longingly at it. It was heavily salted and peppered, and he could almost smell the smoked meat. His mouth watered as he imagined the taste. Quickly he stowed it back into his pouch;knowing that he would need it later in the day. Not wanting to tempt himself further, he forced himself to focus on the predicament of rescuing Desiani.

Arriving at the camp in the predawn light, Achledis spotted a tall cedar tree on a slight crest that would give him the perfect vantage point. Its branches were at least fifteen feet off the ground and with a diameter of at least three feet; it was going to be a difficult tree to climb. Though Achledis had always been a good climber, this was going to be a challenge even for him. After hiding his belongings in a bush nearby, Achledis started to climb by hugging the tree with his body and slowly inched his way up by pulling himself with his arms and legs. The rough bark scraped right through his tunic against his arms and chest, and he stuck his hand into sticky sap a few times, but he pressed on. Finally a branch seemed to be right overhead but just slightly out of reach.

Weakened by hunger, Achledis was low on energy and being so close, but yet too far away to reach the branch frustrated him. He clung to the trunk of the tree and tried to focus his energy for one final push. He took a deep breath and pulled himself up the trunk. With one hand he reached out for the branch. The rest of his body swung out from the tree, and he was left hanging by one arm before reaching out with his other hand and pulling himself up onto the branch.

On the first branch now, Achledis rested and looked down the trunk that he had just climbed, smiling proudly at his conquest. His body was sticky.he smelled of tree sap, but he was safe on the branch. He cut his celebration short as he noticed the first rays of light peering out in the horizon. With renewed purpose, he climbed from branch to branch until he was up as high as the strength of the tree allowed him to go. His breath seemed to catch in his throat as he realized how high he actually was. He could see for miles around, and the camp was in perfect view.

He noted the layout of the camp and all the sentries on the perimeter of the camp as they stood or slouched, some even sat with their backs against the tree. Clearly they didn't expect any trouble and didn't take their sentry duty seriously. He noted a few guards that looked like they might even be dozing. Sneaking into camp didn't appear to be too difficult, but as he allowed his gaze to roam through the camp. He instantly noticed something strange. Aside from the rows of wagons with prisoners, parked in a neat square, with sentries lining the perimeter of the square in intervals, there was a wagon with a cage on top, parked aside from the other prisoner wagons. Four guards were posted on every corner of it, and it appeared that the cage was wrapped with what appeared to be a chain. He noticed the prisoner inside was slouched over asleep. The tiny prison did not even allow for the prisoner to stretch out in comfort. *Must be a high profile prisoner*, Achledis thought to himself as he tried to locate the wagon that he and Desiani rode in on, but it turned out to be an impossible task since they all looked identical. Achledis had no idea how he would locate Desiani, and thought perhaps when they were getting in line for food, he might locate her. But he would need to get closer in order for him to make out the faces. He spotted some bushes where he might hide close enough to the food line.

It was time to move out now, he decided, as he saw a couple of scouts dragging in a deer. Soon the camp would be up, and with soldiers milling around, it would be harder to sneak in and out of their camp.

Achledis was behind the last bush at the edge of the clearing, and the caged wagon was clearly in his view. The prisoner tossed and turned inside the small cell, trying to get comfortable, but it was all in vain. The frustrated prisoner sat up suddenly and slid to the corner with her back to the wall and her head resting on the side. The long golden blonde hair and stubborn chin could only mean Desiani. Pride for her swelled in his heart, followed by instant remorse at the realization of how difficult it would be for her to escape her prison.

He stared at the chain wrapped around the tiny cage, with the heavy lock that held it tightly in place and then at the four guards whose sole responsibility was to guard her. It was clear that breaking her out would be extremely difficult.

In the crisp morning air, while the camp still slept, Achledis pondered his move. He considered shooting the guards around the wagon with his crossbow, but they were all alert. If he shot the first one, the others would sound a warning. Then he would have a whole hive of wasps after him, and possibly Desiani, and he didn't want that. The heavy lock on the cage door made him think of yet another possibility; the guards may not even possess a key for it.

Achledis stood on a rock jutting out into the middle of the creek, the cold water spraying his feet and ankles as it rushed by. In his hands he held a spear, which he had crafted with the large hunting knife and now waited for some fish to swim within his reach. His stomach growled hungrily. The biscuit he had for breakfast had long since been digested and the jerky that he just finished didn't quell his hunger either.

He let his mind wander from the fish in the creek to Desiani's predicament and how he would go about rescuing her. Any way he put it in his mind, a stealthy operation was impossible: *With four guards right next to her caged wagon and a heavy lock to deal with, there was no way he could pull it off without arousing suspicion. That is unless he acted like he belonged there, but how?* He wondered. *Even if he disposed of the guards? Where would he get the key? He doubted that the guards would have it. But perhaps they did?* Either way, he couldn't count on it. A large trout swam right by his rock, bringing Achledis back to reality. Silently he cursed at himself for allowing such a nice one to get away. *The rescue plans would have to come later,* he decided. *First, I need to catch myself a meal.*

Half an hour later, he was roasting his two fishes over the fire. The fire was a risk since the smoke could be visible at the Rakirian camp, which was several miles away, but the risk was worth it as raw fish was something that he preferred not to try. Finishing his meal, he doused the fire with water and then covered the embers with dirt to prevent it from smoking.

Later that evening, Achledis climbed an oak tree where he could take a nap without much fear of being discovered in its dense foliage. He was careful to stay out of sight in case the smoke from his fire was seen. No sooner had Achledis settled in, when he heard several voices speaking in hushed tones. Achledis's body went rigid, afraid that even a small movement would give him away.

There were five soldiers; they walked by within ten feet of the oak tree where Achledis lay watching. Achledis heard them talking in Rakirian, about him.

"That naked scout who came in this morning testified to how he got bested," laughed a soldier. "He said the Rosmirian was as quick as a panther; the moment he turned away the Rosmirian struck at him."

"The fact that he allowed him to go shows that he is weak." Spoke up another with disdain in his voice.

One of the soldiers stumbled over a mound of dirt, unearthing smoldering embers. Instant silence fell upon the soldiers as they stared at the glowing embers. A soldier kicked the dirt aside with his foot revealing more glowing coals. They all began to look over their shoulders uneasily letting their eyes roam up and about. The air filled with tension.

Achledis weighed his options. He could continue lying here and hope that they wouldn't be able to track him to the tree, or he could start shooting them down with his crossbow right now. He watched as they found a few of his tracks and started to follow them in his direction.

CHAPTER 10: VULCANCRAT

Vitaeus sat back against the stone wall inside the chamber of books as he now called it, inside the secret cave and breathed in the dank air. It was almost eerie how quiet the world was when he was here. He felt alone in the world, and he loved it. It was his hideaway, his castle, a place of refuge. The walls were lined up with cases and chests, which included books and other ancient relics, such as ancient weapons, gadgets and maps. It fascinated him, and he needed to get his mind off of everything else that had been happening in his world.

The last time he was here, his best friend Achledis had been here with him, and now his whereabouts were unknown. Though the bodies of his parents had been recovered and given a proper burial, Achledis's body had not been found. After burying Kalim and Svetani, he and Perat had gone throughout the town collecting corpses after the vultures had finished feasting on them. They threw them on a giant funeral pier; which they had made out of the wreckage of the town. The hard work had taken all day. When they finished at night,they set the fire in the center of the town's square. During that time, not one person showed up to help, nor did they find any other living soul about. Everyone was either killed or taken captive; with only the houses and buildings remaining. Although most of them were also gone, and what remained of them was only wreckage of burned timber and collapsing stone. The town had become desolate and uncanny, and it was no wonder that his mother had insisted on moving away as soon as possible. She felt frightened, and if he was honest, it kind of scared him too. There was something unsettling about living in a ghost town where the inhabitants that you had known your whole life got slaughtered, and the town itself burned down and turned to ruin.

Vitaeus couldn't sleep. As tired as he was, the images of the day were engraved in his mind, and after a few hours of tossing and turning, he had escaped here to the cave. Yet the bloody images stayed with him; so he searched for a book to read. Anything to get his mind on something else.

Vitaeus walked up to a display. A map entitled Vulcancrat, and a journal with the same title lay beside it. A silver sword with a bluish tint to the metal lay inside a concave rock filled with water. Vitaeus let his fingers run over the pommel of the handle before he picked it up. The blue of the metal illuminated under the torch light as he held it up, but what amazed him at that moment was how light it was. The wet blade didn't have a hint of rust on it. *What kind of metal is it that it doesn't rust?* Vitaeus thought to himself. The blade had a perfect balance to it, and Vitaeus whirled it around and swung it side to side, He was amazed at how just right it felt; as if the blade was an extension of his arm itself.

This weapon must have cost a fortune! Who was the smith who forged it? He wondered. The metal itself was exotic. It was light and didn't rust, but was it strong? There was one way to find out, but he couldn't bring himself to do it. He didn't want to so much as scratch the blade.

A shield of the same metal leaned against a rock to the side. He had seen it earlier, but didn't give it any more thought than if it were just another weapon on display. Vitaeus crouched in front of it and saw his own reflection shimmering in its bluish silver surface. He ran his hands over the slightly abrasive surface of the cast metal. Picking it up, Vitaeus was once again amazed by how light such a large chunk of metal was. It didn't compare to anything that he was used to. He slung it on his back in hoplite fashion. The circular shield had a slight semicircle cut on either side of it; so that it wouldn't hamper a soldier's arm movement when slung over the back.

I wish Achledis would have seen this the last time we were here. How could we have missed this? Out of all the weapons in the room we didn't look closely in this corner. With the bad lighting, these weapons certainly hadn't stood out as being anything but ordinary at the time.

Vitaeus noticed something else gleaming in the dirt between the rocks at his feet, and stooping closer he noticed a handle. Naturally, he grabbed it and gave it a heave, but couldn't get it to budge. A trapdoor! Of course, how else would all this stuff get in here through that crawl space? There has to be another way inside. He thought. He grabbed the handle and focused his mind and energy on heaving the door open, and again he couldn't get it to budge. Feeling discouraged, Vitaeus sat back for a second and pondered the problem. For one, all he saw was a handle; he didn't actually see any door. He would have to uncover the handle fully and see what it was fastened too. With that in mind, he set to work laboring for several hours before he cleared away all the rock and dirt to reveal the outline of a trapdoor. The door had been buried under a foot of rock, and the handle that he had found was attached to a chain leading to the door. Drawing his breath, Vitaeus grabbed the handle and yanked with all his strength. The door opened with a lot more ease than he had anticipated, and Vitaeus staggered. Excitedly Vitaeus looked inside and pulled out a package wrapped in a blue blanket of a strange material. Inside the package, he found chainmail made of the same metal as the sword and shield. Next he pulled out a helmet, then a breastplate, grieves, and the rest of the armor that a knight wears. All of the same bluish, silver steel. But it was what was at the very bottom that made him lose his breath. The shiny stones glimmered and shimmered, and on top of them lay an ornate dagger. Its blade was thin with rivets running on either side of the bluish-silver blade. The handle was laden with rubies, diamonds, gems, and sapphires. Vitaeus held it above his eyes and watched as the light danced against the brilliant rocks. Vitaeus scooped up the stones in his hands and let them cascade back in. He picked out a diamond and studied it under the light; even in the light of a torch the diamond shimmered.

Who placed this treasure here? He wondered. He was no longer sure that he was awake. *This must be another one of my dreams,* he thought. *This can't be real.* But it felt real.

Vitaeus grabbed a handful of stones and placed them in his pocket. Even with what was in his pockets, he was already a very wealthy man. Next, he dressed himself in the armor and was amazed how well it fit him; it's as if it was tailored specifically to his build. The armor was super light, and again Vitaeus had to wonder how strong it actually was.

Vulcancrat, he read the title of the leather journal once more and picked it up. Flipping through the pages, Vitaeus skimmed through it quickly with half interest and was about to set the journal down when a title at the top of a page caught his eyes, _Vulcan Steel_, he read. Intrigued, Vitaeus started to read about this bluish-silver steel that was mined in the volcanoes of Vulcancrat, or Mountain Island, as it is known in our world. _The steel, though extremely light, is stronger than iron, and it doesn't rust. It is one of the few wonders I found on Vulcancrat._ The author wrote. Vitaeus's curiosity stirred like never before. He read on until his eyes got droopy, and he fell asleep dreaming of this fabled land where precious stones were as common as stones in the rest of the world.

CHAPTER 11: PLANNING A RESCUE

The Rakirians paused ten yards from the tree and conversed amongst themselves in hushed tones. Though Achledis could hear the sound of their voices, he couldn't pick up what was being said. Their eyes were anxiously skimming over all the tree tops and brush alike as if expecting Achledis to either come charging or swinging from a tree at any time to kill them.

Achledis lay still, trying to ignore the itch in his arm that kept wanting to go for the crossbow; a motion that would most assuredly give him away. Besides, the crossbow would take too long to reload, and after his first shot he could expect to start getting shot back in return. If he had a bow, he would have had the luxury of reloading quickly and possibly taking three soldiers out before they could get a chance to locate him. No, he decided his best chance was to lie still and pray that he didn't get spotted.

Their walk to the tree was slow and deliberate, constantly scanning the treetops and brush until finally they were standing right underneath the branch where he lay. A few soldiers seemed to be staring him in the face, but with his body covered in dirt and hidden where the foliage of the leaves was thickest, Achledis was hidden from their view.   Yet Achledis felt exposed. *My camouflage isn't good enough. Anytime now they will see through it and start shooting at me,* he kept thinking. Without the element of surprise, the odds were heavily against him. For every bolt he fired he would get between four or five back, depending if he managed to kill with his first shot. One of the Rakirian soldiers had been staring suspiciously into the foliage of leaves where Achledis lay hidden for a long time before shifting his gaze. Achledis let out a deep breath; which he held the whole time. He knew that even a twitch could be enough to give him away. Just then he felt something small fall on his back, startling him. He jerked.

In horror, he watched as the acorn fell to the ground right below where he lay. It hit the ground with a loud, hollow thump; instantly five pairs of eyes shot up to the spot where he lay hidden. *Here it goes,* thought Achledis. His luck just ran out. Just then he felt four sharp little claws on his back and a bushy tail sweeping side to side. The soldiers below saw a jerk of sudden movement, and five crossbows quickly went up as they aimed their weapons. The squirrel leaped out of the thick foliage unto another branch and scurried down before jumping onto the next tree.

"Just a squirrel," said one of the Rakirians, relieved.

"Could've been just the squirrel, but I need to make sure," said another as he fired his crossbow. The little dart flew to where Achledis lay hidden. Stunned, Achledis stared at the embedded quarrel inches away from his face. The soldier, who had fired his crossbow, studied the dense leaves overhead, searching for a motion that would prove he hit a live target. Finally satisfied that nothing moved, he motioned for his companions and once more they moved away from the tree glancing back occasionally.

Achledis waited for a couple of hours before coming down the tree. He knew he wouldn't fall asleep now; so he decided to make his way back to the Rakirian camp and was surprised to see that they had already moved out. Relief swept over him, seeing that there was no present danger lurking about. He walked to the spot where Desiani's prison once stood, and as he remembered her from earlier that morning, he was also reminded on how difficult the rescue would be. Fatigue swept over him, and he lay down in the soft grass, not caring what critters might crawl on him and fell asleep.

It was well into the afternoon before Achledis started in pursuit of the Rakirian war party and their Rosmirian prisoners. The trail was easy to follow, and by dusk Achledis had closed in on the group as they were setting up camp. Wasting no time, Achledis climbed a tall tree and studied the camp not far off. Like before, he watched the sentries take their posts around the camp and the wagons filled with prisoners taking turns to eat. It was the wagon in the center of camp, however, that stood out. It seemed as if the enemy was taunting him by placing it in there; making it easy for him to spot and to show him its impregnability. If he wanted to rescue the girl, he would need an army.

I will find a way to get her out, he reassured himself. There were just too many obstacles though. First, he would need to infiltrate the camp, pose as a prisoner getting in line for food to allow him to get close to Desiani's wagon, and then somehow avoid drawing suspicion from the guards when he got to the wagon. Of course, he would need to unlock a heavy lock with a key he didn't possess, unwrap a heavy chain that held the door shut tight, run fifteen meters to the nearest bush and make their getaway. Achledis cursed. It just couldn't be done, the mission was impossible.

No sooner had impossible crossed his mind before he remembered his father's constant reminder: "For every obstacle, there is a solution; it's just a matter of finding it. Be patient and keep an open mind."

"Thanks, Dad," he muttered under his breath. "You always make it sound so easy, but in reality it's quite difficult. How do I find a solution with so many obstacles? Clearly some things truly are just impossible." He closed his eyes and let out a deep sigh of defeat, suddenly remembering his best friend Vitaeus who thrived on problem solving. *Wish you could be here with me buddy; I could sure use that brain of yours right about now.*

Wistfully he recounted all the obstacles once more, and once again his dad's words came to him, reminding him that there was a solution to it all. It was out there, and it was up to him to find it. With vigilante guards posted on every corner of the wagon, he might as well abandon stealth. *Vigilant!* The word suddenly stood out in his mind. What if they weren't vigilant? What if they were distracted? *Yes, a distraction,* he thought, *a big distraction.* A plan started to form in his mind.

CHAPTER 12: REVELATION

The sound of rain pattering gently against the leaves and branches of the forest above and that of his own feet padding softly against the needles carpeting the floor was all Vitaeus heard. The cool air that the rains always brought with them felt fresh and therapeutic. During the rain, the whole world seemed to be frozen and in peace, he thought, but a rustling in the brush ahead seemed to contradict his thoughts. A fawn and its mother appeared, and they stood frozen watching him for a moment. The fawn looked with a great deal of curiosity as he jogged in their direction, but in her life, the mother had learned that man wasn't a friend to her kind. She nipped her young one, and they were off once more.

Seeing live game reminded Vitaeus of his hunger, and he wondered what there was to eat at Perat's. The livestock around Pavanti had either been freed or worse, slaughtered by the plundering Rakirians; so food would no longer be as readily available. The thought of food led to thoughts of his mother, and he increased his speed knowing that she was worried. When she saw him, her worry would quickly turn to anger.

Vitaeus had woken up to find himself in the cavern of books. He was dirty and hungry, and knew that he had better go home quickly before too many questions were raised by his lengthy departure. Besides, knowing his mother and given the recent events that had taken place, she would be exceedingly worried. He had jogged the whole time since he crossed the lake, and the hunger in his belly was only growing more intense.

He paused at the door to Perat's cabin, trying to prepare himself for the frenzy of questions and accusations that were to follow, but the door opened for him.

"Come in My Lord." Perat invited him inside; though his facial expression didn't appear so cordial. Ever since his father's burial, Perat had taken to calling him lord. Though Perat still hadn't explained why, Vitaeus was curious. He wasn't sure that he was ready to hear the answer. The bits and pieces that he had heard in the past couple days had his mind abuzz with questions, but he decided to keep them inside. At his father's funeral he had demanded to have answers that same day, but the whole day turned into one of nothing but funerals. At the end of the day, all he had wanted was sleep, but even sleep had evaded him.

His mother sat at the table finishing her meal of a potato and pigeon with berry sauce on top. His stomach rumbled loudly, but even then she didn't look up to acknowledge him. He took his boots off by the door; though wet, they weren't dirty as the carpet of pine in the forest had kept the mud off .

"Mother," Vitaeus called. "I'm sorry I'm late."

Riani turned slowly; the rim of her eyes were red, but resolute. "You're late? Is that what you call being gone from sunrise to sunset? Late! What do you expect me to make of that?" She asked.

Vitaeus cast his eyes downward, having nothing substantial to say in response. "I fell asleep."

"And left me worried," She finished. "You're a big boy Vitaeus, but you are still my son. All I ask is that you use your head. Not only am I grieving for the loss of my husband and friends, but I found myself wondering what ill could have befallen on my only son, my husband's greatest legacy."

"I..." Vitaeus began

But Riani waved him to silence. "Not now, I don't need to hear it. We have bigger and more serious things to talk about; so we must move on. Sit!" She commanded.

As Vitaeus sat down, his mother pushed the rest of her meal before him. "Eat."

Vitaeus didn't need to hear any more as he tore into the remainder of the pigeon, scooping berry sauce to go with it. The sweet tang of the sauce with the succulent taste of meat marinated in vinegar made his mouth salivate even more. Hungrily, he bit into the remainder of the potato that his mother hadn't finished, and before he knew it, his plate was empty. Yet he still felt hungry, but more food wasn't offered. Instead, Perat poured three cups of tea and sat down at the table with them.

Vitaeus remembered of Perat's granddaughter and wondered again where she was, but he wasn't sure how to ask the question or whether it was even appropriate given that the answer might be fairly obvious. But what the heck? The silence between the three of them was overbearing for Vitaeus. He couldn't take anymore,; so he looked at both of them and decided it was time for him to begin his interrogation.

"Who was father that you always called him lord? Since his death you started to refer to me in the same manner."

Perat nodded slowly as if he had expected that exact question, and his eyes wandered to Riani who gave a slight nod.

"To answer your question, I first need to tell you a bit of history that took place some 50 years ago. Back then, Rosmir was an independent country, with a strong army, and a great economy. Being on a peninsula, it had very defensible borders. Due south was the burgeoning empire of Rakiria, which stayed at peace with Rosmir; even though it was a tenuous peace at that. Rakiria had learned just how difficult it was to invade a peninsula 100 years prior; when it was brutally defeated by Rosmir in the Ten Year War. For a century, the Rakirians dreamed of conquering Rosmir, and 50 years ago their dream finally came true.

King Krepedes was a popular king, very much beloved by the people. The people's love and admiration for him perhaps contributed to his naïve nature, and he never suspected the enemies that were swarming around him or the plots against him.

Vitaeus waited patiently as Perat poured Riani and himself more tea. Long moments passed as Perat sipped his tea and listened to the pattering rain on his thatch roof above as he remembered the past. When Vitaeus's impatient fidgeting became a little more obvious, Perat finally continued.

"Like I said, 50 years ago the land of Rosmir was very different from what it is today. It was an independent nation with its own army. The land was filled with jovial people who celebrated life even during the harsh northern winters, and most importantly, the nation was at peace with the world. To the south was the powerful Rakirian Empire, but the isthmus between the two countries gave Rosmir a false sense of security. There was a castle on the border that was supposed to defend the rest of the peninsula from any invasion from the south. King Krepedes heard rumors of a Rakirian army massing on the border, but he didn't take a whole lot of stock in rumors. He too believed that the fortress on the isthmus would more than thwart any Rakirian plan of invasion; however, he succumbed to pressure and sent most of the army to the border. For over a year this went on, and there was even a diplomatic mission that came from Rakiria to improve trade between the two countries. Spies on the border continued to report that the size of the Rakirian army seemed to grow every month. Krepedes wasn't worried, but he did send more pitch and weapons to the fortress on the border. Another winter went by and come spring, the Rakirian army attacked the fortress. The battle went on for a month and the fortress held. But the Rakirians had just begun. They landed a large force of men behind the encamped Rosmirian troops and cut them off from the rest of Rosmir. In the next two months, Rakirian troops were landing on Rosmirian beaches daily, and just like that, seventy percent of the Rosmir army was effectively cut off and trapped on the isthmus. With supplies running low and facing the effects of Rakirian mining against its walls, the fortress surrendered and the entire Rosmir army on the isthmus with it. It was a defeat that shook all of Rosmir to the core; King Krepedes who was once beloved by his people was now an object of scorn.

As the Rakirian army approached the Rosmirian capital of Seredine, Krepedes and the royal family evacuated the palace and fled to the Duchy of Caminia. Caminia, being another peninsula jutting out of Rosmir's northwestern corner and surrounded by sheer cliffs facing out to sea, seemed like the best defensive position to take up. And it was; for Rakiria seized all of Rosmir under its control that same summer, with the exception of Caminia. Yet again, King Krepedes was lulled by a false sense of security, and again treachery followed." Perat paused, and his eyes seemed distant as he stared past Vitaeus and into a past world.

Vitaeus knew his history and wondered why Perat had to recite it for him; it was common knowledge that Krepedes was a naïve fool. History remembered him as Krepedes the Fool, but what did all of this have to do with his family history?

"This next part of the story I personally witnessed." Perat's voice was barely more than a whisper. "It was at the end of the first week of the king's arrival in Caminia, and Razim, the young Duke of all Caminia, still in his early twenties threw a ball in celebration of the king's arrival. The king and his family were by no means in a festive mood, as you can imagine, having fled their palace in Seredine; it was a traumatic event for them. Yet the ball was a necessary formality, and all the high nobles who escaped Seredine had all set out to enjoy it. There was a lot of feasting and drinking before the dancing began. The two eldest royal princes of eighteen and fifteen were dancing with all the young women of the court, but it was their twelve year old sister that truly stole the show that day. At only twelve, she was already a beautiful maiden, elegant and graceful on the dance floor. She curtsied like a little lady to perfection and stole the hearts of all men round about." Perat stood and started pacing before continuing with the story.

"Everyone in the royal family drank wine that night; except for the little princess, who was seven, and the little prince, who was five. All of those that drank the wine got sick. His majesty had to excuse himself and her majesty on the premise of feeling ill; the two youngest left with them. But the three elder royals stayed; even though, they too were visibly sick. Solyeta, the twelve year old princess, threw up while dancing with her courtier, and that pretty much brought the ball to a close. When morning rolled around, all but the youngest two of the royal family were already dead.

I was a squire to knight Valon, the king's right hand man, and I remember it all so vividly. Valon and I had slept outside the king's chambers that night, but by late morning, the king and queen still weren't stirring. Valon, under the orders of the king that they were not to be disturbed, hadn't allowed anyone inside. Yet he told me that in the next half hour if the king didn't make his presence known, he would be forced to check in on their health. Ten minutes hadn't passed when a high pitched scream resounded further down the hall, and a maid ran out, her face white as snow. Seeing Valon, she ran to him, stammering something about princess Solyeta being dead.

The news registered quickly, and Valon commanded me to secure the royal children even as he rushed into the king's and queen's chamber. I ran to the chambers of the crown prince, but he was already dead, with residue of dry vomit around his mouth. The fifteen year old prince who was second in line to the throne was also dead; they found his body doubled over as if he died in pain. The little princess Kapriona and the little prince were the only survivors.

The death of the royal family was hushed for a whole day. Duke Razim sealed the palace off with guards and made sure that no one left the building. Valon talked to the little prince and princess Kapriona about what had happened and explained to them that he needed them to be brave. Valon and the entire royal guard that was inside the palace, consisting of about 50 men, stood guard over the two young royals, not allowing anyone to get close to them. Duke Razim demanded that they be handed over to him, to be under his protection, but Valon refused, and on the third night it all came to a bloody confrontation. The Duke tried to take the royals by force employing pikemen and crossbowmen.

We had a rough escape plan hatched out beforehand, and so the operation went as smooth as could be expected under those circumstances. First, I lowered Valon onto the battlements below, followed by the princess, and then by our little prince. I went last. Princess Kapriona was only seven, but she was wiser and smarter than most girls her age. She knew her parents were murdered, along with her sister and brothers, and knew that her life was in danger too. As we stayed in the shadows of the city trying to find the most opportune time to escape, word came out about the murder of the Royal family and the kidnapping of the youngest royals. Valon was named the culprit of the whole plot, and the price Razim put on his head was substantial.

With the isthmus sealed off with the Duke's men, we had to travel to the only beach on the Duchy of Caminia, Nitami

Beach. There Valon found a man who agreed to take the Arkonis royals and Valon's family across the bay back to Rosmir for a hefty price. After dropping off the family on shore, Valon returned back to the ship for the remainder of their supplies, and that's where the captain of the ship murdered him so that he could collect his reward from Razim. Razim sent assassins in search of the two royals, and we had to keep moving further south, out of Razim's reach. Kapriona, who became even more mistrustful after Valon's death and constantly fearful for her life, disappeared one morning and has never been seen or heard of again. Though some of the royal guards believe that she was assassinated, I have always believed that she had simply run away thinking she would be safer alone. I brought Valon's wife and children and the little prince here to Pavanti, close to the Rakirian border, and far from the reaches of Razim. This is where they were raised. Soon after our arrival to Pavanti, we received news that Razim had changed Caminia from a duchy to a kingdom and had himself crowned king."

Vitaeus stared at Perat in a state of disbelief. "Are you saying that my father, my father was…"

"Yes, Valon was Kalim's father, and grandfather to Achledis, and your father was the little prince Losmir, the youngest son of King Krepedes, the King of Rosmir at the time of the Rakirian invasion. He was the lone survivor of the Arkonis family, who was the true heir to the throne of Rosmir, and with his passing those blood rights pass on to you."

CHAPTER 13: THE RESCUE

The gentle whisper of the wind on prairie grass was broken by the soft crunch of dry grass breaking underneath Achledis's feet as he crept to the camp under cover of darkness. He continued until he arrived at the spot where the herd of horses was directly between him and his destination.

A horse neighed up ahead as a slight breeze brought the scent of Achledis. Achledis smiled as he thought of the breeze; luck was on his side tonight. Stooping down, he tore the dry grass and made a neat pile of it. Then with his knife he struck at the flint until a large spark landed on a nice blade of grass and smoldered. Achledis gently blew air towards it, and a tiny flame sprang up. Instantly, the flame grew as it fed on the long dry grass around it. With the aid of the breeze, which suddenly grew stronger, the growing blaze started to make its way towards the horses and the camp further on.

As the fire approached, the horses stamped their hooves and neighed fearfully. A big gray horse reared up on its hind legs with its head tossing from side to side and its eyes wide with fear was throwing its head back angrily, He pawed his hooves in the air and took off in the direction away from the fire. The rest of the herd followed their leader as they galloped straight for camp and the startled soldiers.

The Rakirlan camp had quickly turned to chaos as some soldiers tried to contain the large battle horses; which pranced around wildly with fear. Other soldiers armed with buckets of water ran to meet the oncoming flame. A middle-aged colonel stood on the field bellowing orders; his loud and booming voice carried an aura of confidence that carried over to the soldiers.

This was Colonel Viserate's first campaign, and his chance at greatness. Morale had been high among his army as they marched through the Rakirian countryside burning down towns and villages, killing villagers, and taking prisoners. Whenever these Rosmir villagers stood up to challenge his army, he would crush them ruthlessly, and after every onslaught the feeling of power and invincibility made him feel even more immortal. He imagined his name, Viserate the Conqueror, lasting through the ages; along with the rest of the great Rakirian generals who helped build the Rakirian Empire.

The current crisis didn't make him panic or curse; quite the opposite. It was his opportunity to shine. He was like the eye of the storm. His men sensed his unwavering courage and calm head and responded by obeying his commands without hesitation or question.

Word of his army marching through must have spread ahead of him, and he was undoubtedly facing another pocket of resistance. Whoever started the fire didn't have the guts to meet him in open battle as his scouts had scoured the premises and found nothing. This was the first time his army encountered harassment, but nonetheless, he had been expecting it for some time. He anticipated that the rebels might have even prepared an ambush for him up ahead. He was itching for a battle if only for another chance to enforce his supremacy on this land. With pride, he watched as his men started to bring order to chaos. The fire that had seemed so large was now dying out as the continual flow of buckets full of water beat the flames down. The fearful horses were also brought under control. The disaster was averted, or so he thought.

A young soldier ran up to him, excited and out of breath. He was shouting something, but the colonel couldn't make out the words. He pointed towards the center of camp and shouted for the colonel to follow quickly. The excited soldier forget to salute the colonel before he started running back in the direction he came from.

He was Colonel Viserate and his men had to show the proper respect owed to him by his title. Forgetting to salute your commander was unforgivable; as it was a complete sign of disrespect. Nevertheless, the colonel followed the young soldier to see what new emergency had sprung up that required his immediate action. *I will have to discipline him,* he thought. *I can't let them forget how to address their superiors no matter how drastic the situation*. Coming up to where the soldier stood pointing, he looked in the direction of his finger, seeing nothing but grass at the side of a perfect wooden wheel.

The colonel's anger flared. This man was wasting his time with something that was more than likely a trivial matter.

"Well! What is it?" The colonel's angry roar instantly died away as he felt the blade of a knife at his throat.

"Release the girl!" The young soldier commanded. The authority of his voice sent a chill down the colonel's spine.

"It is you?" The colonel whispered. His face paled as he realized that this must be the one who escaped the other day. Already different tales were floating throughout the Rakirian camp about this Rosmir youth. The seriousness in the youth's commanding voice dispelled any notion of trying anything heroic on the colonel's part.

"Now do you have the keys or are you as worthless to me as the guard that I had to get rid of?" Achledis asked.

"Yes! I have it right here; just take her and go." The colonel said forcefully, keeping his voice steady and strong.

Achledis motioned for the colonel to undo the locks on the chains; which were tightly wrapped around the cage and the gate itself. The colonel was slow to comply as he noticed that a few of his men had noticed the situation and were slowly surrounding them. A few soldiers yelled out an alarm, and instantly the numbers of soldiers watching their colonel with a knife to his throat grew. Achledis's knife pressed a little deeper against the soft flesh of the colonel's throat, and that was all the urging the colonel needed.

"Tell your men to unwrap that heavy chain." Achledis commanded.

The colonel gave the command, but none of the soldiers made a move to comply.

"I guess they don't take one of us seriously, order them again! Make sure they know you mean it this time." Achledis commanded. With that, he stabbed the colonel through the shoulder where the coif and the espalier came together. The wound wasn't mortal, as the armor managed to deflect the thrust of the blade, but was deep enough to draw blood.

Viserate's breath caught in disbelief at being stabbed; fear of what could come next overwhelmed any plan he had. He was truly at the youth's mercy now; his title of colonel and all his men were powerless to save him.

Through clenched teeth, the colonel yelled at his men to comply; his once strong and steady voice now quivered with fear. The man was weak, Achledis realized. It is interesting how at the point of death you truly learn if a man is brave and strong or just another weak sapling, on the verge of breaking under the weight of fear. He had no pity towards this man in front of him; for he had come into his land, killing and raping the innocent. A thin contemptuous smile crept across Achledis's face as he watched the men jump to action, pulling the chain off and opening the door. He almost chuckled to himself to see the care they showed in helping Desiani off the wagon.

"Now get us two of your best horses, with dried venison, canteens full of water and two bows with two dozen arrows per bow. Tell them to hurry." Achledis commanded. Instantly, the men jumped into action before the colonel got a chance to repeat the command.

Achledis waited until Desiani was fully mounted on a big gray destrie, and flashed her a smile, "Ready darling?"

She nodded back with a smile playing on her face.

"Then you better go; I'm right behind you." Achledis told her.

As Desiani galloped off, Achledis grabbed the colonel, his fingers digging into the colonels cheeks and turned the colonel to face him. "Colonel, I mean no disrespect when I say that I don't trust you and your men. Here you shower me with going away presents, but yet I feel somehow unsettled by it all as if I might get stabbed or shot in the back by a couple dozen bolts as soon as I turn to go. To put me at ease, have your men lie on their stomachs with their feet in my direction."

The colonel bellowed the order, and his men instantly complied.

"Thank-you colonel, you have been gracious towards me and the lady this night. I hope that there aren't any hard feelings about that scratch on your shoulder." Achledis forced another smile as he tried to keep his anger under control; even though it threatened to explode at any time.

This was the man that was responsible for the death of his parents and for the hurt and anguish of his countrymen. He had an incredible urge to kill Colonel Viserate at that moment. Perhaps he would finally have vengeance for his parents' murders. To kill the colonel, however, would be dishonorable; since he had complied with all of his demands. His father always told him that without honor, a man is nothing. Achledis clenched his jaw as he forced himself to accept his decision; even as he acknowledged to himself that he would never get a better chance to have his revenge.

Achledis mounted his gray stallion, a beautiful and powerful beast. When Achledis commanded that they bring their best horses, it was clear that they had complied with his demand. Achledis double checked that the bag was full of venison and the canteen was filled with fresh water. Content that everything was satisfactory, he tapped his horse on the side with his heel and felt it respond instantly as it galloped off with powerful strides. Before Achledis made it to the tree line, two crossbow bolts whistled by, one grazing his shoulder.

CHAPTER 14: ABOARD THE WHITE SWAN

The cold water of the Rok Sea crashed against the stern of the carrack, spraying Vitaeus with its brackish water and tossing the boat in the waves. He barely paid it any mind; rather he inhaled the salty air as he allowed his mind wander back to the revelation of his family's past. Since Perat's revelation, a little over two weeks went by, and Vitaeus's only focus since was how to take the throne back. For it was his to take, and the Rakirian attack on the helpless village of Pavanti only proved to him once more that all the people of Rosmir deserved a king who would fight to defend them and not just the Caminian enclave. Yet he was partly aware that his true motive was vengeance; though he didn't dare voice it out loud.

Vitaeus could have never imagined that the answer to his most sought question since childhood would open a torrent of more questions. He didn't know where to begin, or even how to begin. What was he supposed to do? Rosmir was being pillaged, and its people raped and murdered. Yet he was a king without an army.

At his mother's insistence, Perat would guide her to the Rok Isles where his father had a wine business. It was the best place for her to go; even as Vitaeus set sail for Caminia where he would seek to find his way back into power. His father owned two ships, both of which were away on trade business; so his mother paid for her fare. Vitaeus was forced to seek out the ship's owner and purchase the boat with all the trade goods still on it from the Chain Islands for the sum of eight rubies and eight diamonds. The owner's eyes glinted with greed as Vitaeus purchased the boat. To retain the crew that manned the boat, he had to sell another two pieces of sapphires to get some cash.

He had a vague plan. It was unlike him to do something without planning it out to the smallest detail, yet there were too many unknowns. As Losmir used to tell him, sometimes in life one must wade in before he learns to swim, and this had to be one of those times. With him, he took his greatest treasures: the priceless Vulcan Journal, armor and weapons cast from Vulcan steel, and a pouch with precious stones. He traveled under the guise of being a trader from the Chain Islands on the other side of Rosmir.

"Your father had long been financing propaganda and ensuring that faithful friends circulate stories that the youngest son of Krepedes has emerged and is in hiding for fear of Razim's treachery. Though in Caminia, the story has been stifled, but in mainland Rosmir, the story has taken root. It's the hope of many people that their king will finally reemerge to liberate them." Perat had told him.

Vitaeus heard of those rumors, though never from his father. He had always thought of them as conspiracy tales and never gave them much credibility. Yet he was at the center of this conspiracy tale, and it had put everything in a different light.

"Your father was a meticulous planner, and I had often grown impatient with his apparent lack of action." His mother Riani had said. "Yet he always stressed that he had to forge a trail before he could build a road, and so he did. With the Rakirian army marauding through our lands, the people are desperate for someone who will protect them. They need a king, a real king, and not a usurper who sits in the safety of his peninsula with steep rock cliffs all around."

"To re-emerge without an army sounds like a good plan if I wanted to give Razim an opportunity to cut my head off and stick it on a pike." Vitaeus had mused. No, he had to proceed with caution, and his first plan was to see if he could purchase an island for a base. There, he could build a fortress, as well.

The ship lurched slightly as a large wave hit them. So far, the sailing had been smooth and the winds favorable, and they were expected to land at Nitami beach that night.

He nodded at a sailor cordially, but the sailor didn't even meet his eyes as he walked by briskly, the gold on his one tooth glinting. Vitaeus wondered how his mother was fairing through all this; as she sailed to the Rok Isles, a foreign country and no less an ally of King Razim in Caminia.

"Your father owns two ships and has a vineyard on the Rok Isles. The wine industry was his main trade, yet he wanted you to grow up here in Rosmir, in your own country." Perat had told him

Perat put an emphasis on your as if his royal bloodline actually meant something; it didn't. Fifty years was a long time, long enough for people to forget, long enough for people to be educated on the propaganda of whoever ruled the land. Even here in Pavanti, where the Caminian king had no real authority, his story or version of the tragedy that killed the Arkonis family was the accepted history.

The conversation that followed after Perat's revelation of Vitaeus's royal bloodline still rang in his head.

"But our family name isn't Arkonis,; it's simply Konis." Vitaeus had said.

"Konis was the alias your father used; he simply took out the Ar out of Arkonis."

Vitaeus stood suddenly and started to circle the small room, his mind still numb at the revelation that he had received.

"I always thought that you were just a fisherman." Vitaeus had said to Perat as he paced.

"I am a fisherman and a knight, knighted by your father. I swore my life to the service of protecting the Arkonis family, and you are the last of your bloodline. Therefore, the Rok Isles will be the safest place for you now. You will stay there until the time is more appropriate for you to make your move."

"The time will never be more appropriate! Fifty years is a long time." Vitaeus had replied sharply. In the end, he had decided against going to the Rok Isles and instead vouched for Caminia. It was on that peninsula that vengeance against his family had to be avenged and where the power of the nation rested.

"Land ahoy, land ahoy," a sailor shouted.

Sure enough, Vitaeus could see the first of the small islands that dotted Nitami Beach. In the distance, there was yet another island and the biggest of the archipelago; on it was a deserted keep, in much need of repairs. With the funds in Caminia in limited supply, Razim had to withdraw from the islands and focus more on the fortress on Nitami Beach to protect Caminia. Yet this was one of the places that Perat had suggested for him. Since it didn't have a lord, it shouldn't be too difficult for him to simply move in.

Vitaeus found the captain at the stern of the ship. With mistrustful black eyes he gazed at Vitaeus when Vitaeus approached him. His greasy black hair was woven into dreadlocks, and a thin braid from his beard hung a good six inches from his chin. Vitaeus was done trying to connect with the captain and the crew. They simply made no conversation with him and for the majority of the voyage spoke in the tongue of the Chain Islands; so that he couldn't understand them.

"Captain, I would like you to move the boat in closer to that island with the keep." The captain gave him a blank stare before turning around and starting to steer the boat in the island's direction. A sharp gust of wind seemed to catch the sail just right, and the ship slowed instantly, giving Vitaeus a chance to study the layout of the island. The perimeter of the island was at least ten miles around, with a large square keep on the south side facing out to sea, and a Motte-and-Bailey castle on the north side, which was no more than a square keep on a slight ridge and a wooden palisade around it. Vitaeus didn't see a soul on the island. The wild brush that had sprouted around the palisade made it obvious that it had been neglected for a long time.

The ship sailed by the Island, and the keep on the stony rise was soon out of sight. Another sailor came up and conversed with the captain. Vitaeus couldn't help noticing the suspicious glances he kept receiving from the sailor and the captain alike; it was enough to put Vitaeus on edge. He had heard lots of stories of mutinies at sea, and this crew seemed likely to turn on him. Based on what he saw between two sailors earlier, these sailors were no rookies to sword fights. Vitaeus kept his Vulcan sword at his hip. Though the sailors never saw the blade, they saw the ornate sheath it was kept in. This crew wasn't likely to ask him anything though, much less speak to him. The captain gave the sailor a sharp and curt response and the sailor walked away.

"Captain, give the wheel to your mate and follow me to my cabin. I need to talk to you right away." Vitaeus said.

The captain glowered at him, but yelled out for his mate, who instantly responded to the captain's command and took his position behind the wheel. Without waiting for Vitaeus to lead the way, the captain strode ahead for the cabin at the back of the ship, but before entering, the captain bellowed something in their language and instantly sailors started to move towards the cabin, fingering the hilts of their swords. The captain was a few inches taller than Vitaeus, and both had to crouch to get inside. The ceiling was also low, and they had to stoop to walk around. The captain took the only chair in the cabin and made himself comfortable, leaving Vitaeus to hunch at the small table across from the captain. Vitaeus knew that the captain quartered in this cabin on most voyages, but Vitaeus had claimed it. The captain had to resort to a smaller cabin; which mainly consisted of a small bunk inside. The captain glowered again, waiting for Vitaeus to begin.

"Captain, I want us to have a productive conversation and see if we can understand one another better. I am the new owner of this vessel, yet I feel like an intruder by you and the crew. I want to be a good owner and have a captain working for me that I can trust. My trust is lacking at the moment. Please tell me your grievances. Why are you and the crew so hostile towards me?"

"You new owner," the captain began pointing an accusing finger and speaking Rosmirian with a heavy accent. "But old owner owes us a lot of money, and we still haven't seen a kopeck. Very shrewd of owner to sell us off without paying us. The crew wants to sell this merchandise; in order to pay themselves what is owed. You haven't agreed on a price with me. You just told me to sail to Caminia, but the initial and most profitable course would have been to go to the Four Kingdom Island."

"Whoa, so this is about money?" Vitaeus asked.

The captain just continued his menacing scowl in response.

"How much are you and the crew owed?"

"Half of merchandise on this boat."

It was a very large sum, and Vitaeus suddenly remembered the gleeful look on the ship's owner's face when he purchased the boat from him. It all made sense now. He had indeed been extremely shrewd and had, in fact, duped Vitaeus. One of those diamonds alone was worth the wages of 100 men in a year. He had given away eight diamonds and eight rubies, yet Vitaeus remembered the sailors gathering outside the cabin as he and the captain had entered inside. The situation was exceedingly delicate, and Vitaeus had to play it just right. He kept his face emotionless as he nodded at the captain.

"You are right, the old owner was shrewd. He had told me that your wages were all paid through this year, and that had been part of the negotiations."

"He lied!" The captain slammed his fist on the small table as he stood up from the chair sending it sprawling.

"Yes he did, but I don't want you or the crew to be cheated. I will pay you as agreed."

"Need down payment now; before we land at Nitami Beach."

Vitaeus pulled out his sack of coins and poured them out on the table for the captain to see. "See, this is all I have. I will have to pay the rest when we sell the goods on the ship."

The captain picked up a golden dinar and bit it with his teeth, pocketed the coin and picked up a silver one; which he also examined closely before reaching out with his muscular arm and sweeping the coins toward himself. "Okay, the rest you pay later," he said as he pointed an accusing finger, but Vitaeus stopped him from taking all the coins.

"Let me." Vitaeus said, as he pointed at the captain's pocket and said, "You already have a gold and a silver. Here is one more gold for you; the rest I will pay to the crew myself."

The captain opened his mouth to protest, but instead just jerked his head and stood up leaving the coins on the table. The captain flung the door of the cabin open and stepped out, yelling something to the crew in his foreign tongue. The crew responded to his words instantly with jubilant shouts and a frenzy to get close to Vitaeus and the captain.

"What did you tell them?" Vitaeus asked.

"That you have promised to be fair and in a sign of goodwill will pay the crew some of what is owed from the previous owner right now."

"Great, now tell them to get in line, and I will pay them all silver." Vitaeus said, feeling relief wash over him.

The captain relayed the order. The crew hastily formed a line, but not before some more pushing and shoving occurred. Now instead of the scowls that Vitaeus had gotten used to seeing, he was seeing the yellow, crooked and sometimes toothless smiles of the crew members.

CHAPTER 15: MYSTERY

The gray stallion snorted in appreciation as Achledis slowed the horse to a walk. "Easy boy, easy now. You did well, and I'm proud to be your new owner." Achledis's smooth voice soothed the horse as he patted its neck to show affection.

Desiani laughed. "You think he understands you?"

"Of course, didn't you hear his response?" Achledis chuckled.

Initially the horses had been ridden in a gentle canter, in the darkness of the forest; so as not to risk the horses stumbling in the dark and going lame. As morning came, they exited the forest and rode out onto the plain, and the horses were pressed to create more distance between them and the enemy. Achledis and Desiani had set their course for Seredine, where Desiani still had family that resided there. It was the old Rosmirian capital; though now it was occupied by the Rakirians. They were still a week's journey away, and they knew better than to kill their horses on the first day of the journey. But the fear of being pursued kept them going faster than they intended. They slowed down only after rounding atop a crest and verifying there were no pursuers.

It was high noon, and the sun beat down without mercy, sapping every bit of energy on any mortal that happened to be on the plain at that hour. With the horses fatigued, Achledis knew that they had to find a suitable place to camp. He and Desiani dismounted and walked to conserve the horses' energy. Coming on top of another hill, a prairie bush stood out alone in a barren field; it was the relief that they needed from the scorching sun. The Creator up above was looking over them.

"Let's stop here." Desiani's voice croaked from dehydration. "That brush will offer some shade from the heat." Achledis looked at the withered bush void of any leaves and looked questioningly at Desiani. He noticed her face was a bright pink from the sun's rays, and her clothes covered in dust from the long ride. He realized that he too must be burned "We will place our blankets on top of the withered branches to block the sun's rays." She explained.

Achledis nodded in agreement. They would all benefit by taking shelter from the blistering sun; as traveling under this intense heat would only drain their energy more.

They camped on a hill that allowed them to have a clear view of the valley below. Huddled under their makeshift shelter, they were able to seek relief from the blazing sun. Achledis had given the horses a little water before joining Desiani. They were both too fatigued for conversation, and they ate their dried meat in silence. Their muscles and bones where sore from a long day in the saddle, and their scalded skin throbbed with heat. Achledis's left arm felt like dead weight. The wound on the left shoulder was still sore and too weak to support his arm. Being in the saddle all day and focusing solely on putting as much distance as possible between themselves and the Rakirian forces didn't give Desiani the opportunity to notice the wound until now.

"Achledis, you're hurt!" Desiani exclaimed.

"Oh it's just a scratch." Achledis retorted nonchalantly, but as Desiani took his arm gently to inspect the wound, Achledis gritted his teeth in pain. His grimace didn't escape Desiani as she noticed him tense up.

"It may be just a scratch, but if we don't address it, it will fester and become a real problem soon." She went in search of some herbal grass and returned shortly with a nice batch, ringing it to extract the juice. She made a salve out of it; with which she then applied the medicine to Achledis's wound and bound it with a strip that she tore off of her petticoat.

"You know, this wound was worth it. I would get one just like it a million times if it meant that I would get this kind of attention from you every time." Achledis joked.

"Why, you didn't know that I had a nice side to me?" Desiani retorted sarcastically. "Let's just say I'm trying to show my gratitude for your help."

"So this is about easing your conscience rather than the goodness of your heart?" Achledis teased back.

"Exactly." Desiani responded. "But I'll give you some credit; you were pretty fearsome back there. You left quite an impression on the Rakirians. Once Colonel Viserate found out that you killed his men in my defense, they became fearful that you would return for me too. That's why they locked me up and wrapped the door with a heavy chain to deter you from attempting any rescue. They put sentries around my wagon at all times. The sentries even compared you to the mythical Horcles, saying that you had to be immortal; for no mortal could move and kill the way you did."

Achledis chuckled heartily at the comparison with the myth of Horcles; a myth of a man in ancient times that was believed to be a god in a man's body. The legend told of how Horcles stood up for the weak and the poor against the oppressive tyrant of the time; until he banished all evil from the earth. With evil gone, and peace and goodness reining once again on earth, the gods recalled Horcles to the heavens. But before Horcles left, he promised that when a great evil rose up again, he would return.

"I thought it was a bit of a stretch myself. Rakirians can be superstitious, but who knows, perhaps they are right. Do you know who your father was?" Desiani asked in a teasing tone.

"If you're done humoring me," Achledis said, trying to end that topic and move the focus off him, "perhaps you could tell me how you were treated after I escaped. They didn't hurt you, did they?"

"No, they didn't hurt me, but tell me more about you. Like if your parents aren't the gods, then who are they?" Desiani noticed the pained look across his face before it disappeared.

"My dad was a woodcutter, and my mother was the best woman in the world."

"I'm sorry. I didn't even consider before asking..." Desiani's voice trailed off mid-sentence as if not sure how to finish it.

"You have nothing to be sorry about; I'm the one who should apologize for that curt response." His voice grew gentle as he thought back to his parents. "Kalim was my father. He was the woodcutter in Pavanti. My mother was Svetani." He stopped when he saw Desiani's eyes open wide in surprise.

"Kalim was your father?" She asked.

"Yes. Why? Did you know my father?"

"My grandfather introduced me to him and said that your father was one of the most honorable men he knew." Silence fell between them as Desiani strained to think back on something else. "It was early in the morning, before dawn even; grandfather was planning to go fishing at dawn when Kalim came. I was supposed to be sleeping upstairs in the loft, but I overheard them talking. I crept up closer to the ledge so that I could hear their conversation better. Kalim sounded a little alarmed, saying that he believed that his son and his son's friend discovered the secret on the island, and that perhaps it was time to let the boys in on the rest. My grandfather and your father argued for a while, but then they eventually agreed. Your father said that he would take you in the morning, along with your friend and his father, and they would finally reveal the secret to you about your families." Desiani told the story with excitement , barely pausing to breathe as she recalled the details. "It was weird, and I was curious about it. I even contemplated asking my grandpa about it when he got back from the fishing trip, but the attack occurred before he got a chance to get back."

"This conversation occurred on the morning of the attack?" Achledis asked in disbelief at the story he just heard from Desiani.

"Yea, not long after they both left, the village was attacked." Desiani said. Her eyes questioning him as if he might share the secret with her now.

Achledis's mind raced back to that morning. He remembered how his father met him at the door and recalled the knowing glint of a smile on his face as he caught him in his lie. He had told his mother that they would be going fishing. That's when he would have shared this secret with him. His mind started going crazy with what his father wanted to reveal to him, the secret on the island? Could it be the secret cave? He wondered and decided that it was very possible, but what about his family's history? Why was it such a secret? It was odd, but he recalled that his parents never spoke of his grandparents. When he asked his father to tell him about who his grandfather was, his father told him that he would be told when the time was right, and there was no more conversation on the matter.

"Did he share the secret with you?" She finally asked, giving up on him telling her without being prompted.

"Hmm?" Achledis sat up startled. "Um, no, we were supposed to go fishing that morning. I, I guess he never got the chance." His voice trailed off, and he turned away quickly to look the other way. Desiani took his hand and held it in hers. His hand seemed to swallow hers, but she tried to squeeze it regardless.

He smiled at her and nodded his thanks. "He wanted me to escape with my mother; while he fought off three Rakirians." Achledis began and recounted the story up until how his parents got killed and his helplessness as he watched it happen.

Desiani looked into Achledis's eyes as they stared with a firm determination into an abyss, his face pained and jaw clenched. She could sense a strength coming from him that was more than physical; he had a certain confidence about him. She had seen his courage firsthand, and his fighting and seeming invincibility had certainly left an impression on her. She put her arms around him and put her head on his shoulder to comfort him. The two sat there like that for some time, not saying a word, just enjoying one another's presence. Desiani wrapped her arm around Achledis's strong shoulders and felt him wince as she accidentally applied too much pressure on his hurt shoulder.

The sun was disappearing over a distant hill, leaving a glowing reddish-pink color on the horizon; while the valley was blanketed with an orange tint that radiated from the sunset. The beauty of the sunset, along with Desiani by his side, made Achledis believe that his life was almost perfect again, at least for tonight. Desiani too seemed dazzled by the beauty of the sunset.

When the stars filled the sky and the moon was high above filling the land with its light and leaving the sky a deep dark blue, Desiani went to sleep, nestled against Achledis's side; while he stayed up to take first watch. He caught himself glancing down at her a lot; as if he couldn't get enough of her beauty. He was acutely conscious of the warmth of her body nuzzled next to him.

It was early morning when Achledis found himself being shaken awake by Desiani. He opened his eyes and found himself looking into the most beautiful green eyes. So green, they almost radiated from her red and sun chapped skin. He allowed his eyes to wander and study her face; her prominent cheekbones were even more pronounced by her wide smile.

"Good morning my sleeping protector," Desiani giggled. "I thought you would wake me up when you were going to sleep. You gave me this speech on the importance of not falling asleep while on watch; something about a matter of life and death," she smiled at him teasingly.

Achledis groaned. "Well we're safe; are we not?" He grinned sheepishly.

As the two ate their dried venison, Achledis caught Desiani looking at him, and when Achledis looked in her direction, she pretended to be looking past him.

"What are you looking at?" Achledis fought the grin that threatened to spread across his face.

"Oh, ah nothing," Desiani stuttered. "Just wondering where our pursuers are; that's all."

"How disappointing, I thought you were checking me out."

She grinned flirtatiously at him. "I might have been doing a bit of that too." A goofy grin broke out on Achledis's face, and he winked at her in response. Well rested and full of energy, it was time for them to go once again. Seredine was still a week's ride away. Desiani tried to convince Achledis to stay there with her, by telling him of all the exciting things to do in a large city.

"How can I settle down while my country is being burned to the ground all around me? I must fight to help my people."

"Achledis, you are such an idealist; which isn't always bad. But you need to be realistic. You are young and hot headed, and I fear that you will do something rash and get yourself killed. Don't forget that Rakiria rarely is defeated in battle. They have more men and weapons at their disposal than we can only dream of."

Achledis looked at her from the corner of his eyes and realized that she just didn't get it. There could be no life of peace and leisure for him; especially after his parents were murdered. He could only guess what happened to Vitaeus.

"I can't comprehend the concept of peace as long as Rakiria is allowed to maraud our country at will, and to be frank, I don't want to understand it. I would rather die with honor and with no regrets for having fought on the side of freedom, rather than live and cower at the brutality of Rakiria. I can't settle and live peacefully when I'm always looking over my shoulder; wondering when Rakiria will come through looking for more slaves and young men for her armies."

"But how do you know that you will succeed? It's you against an empire." Desiani's voice was pleading; as if that would help her bring some sense to him. "You could try to fight. But if you die and your death won't bring any changes, then your death would have been in vain."

"Even if my life turns out to be a short one, it will be a life full of purpose, and there is nothing vain about that."

A long silence followed between Achledis and Desiani. Sensing the strong conviction from Achledis, she decided to let it go. His mind was made up. He was a man on a mission, and there would be no way of turning him from it. It left her sad but proud at the same time. She sensed greatness in him, an aura of immortality, and knew for certain that he was the hero that Rosmir needed and yearned for.

CHAPTER 16: NITAMI

Nitami Beach only had a couple miles of sand before the steep rock cliffs started up again. It was the only sandy beach that Caminia possessed, and otherwise, the peninsula was entirely surrounded by steep cliffs that met the waves of the ocean. The carrack had to sail through a narrow channel with thick, high walls on both sides to get to the main harbor. Soldiers walked on the battlements above, watching the ship sail by. Vitaeus could see large pots laden with tar above. Any unwelcome ship that did get as far as the channel would then be stopped by a chain stretched across the channel from wall to wall, trapping it from entering further. Then the ship would have hot tar poured on its deck from the walls above; the deck would then be lit on fire.

Caminia certainly was impregnable from the sea. Even on land, the narrow isthmus to Caminia with steep cliffs on both sides more than deterred any enemies from mounting an invasion. When Rakiria tried to invade 50 years ago, its armies got pummeled on the isthmus by trebuchets, and the invading army was decimated. Since then, Rakiria hadn't made anymore attempts to invade.Razim didn't provoke them further; being content with just being left alone.

When the ship docked, a ladder was pulled up to the side of the ship for the crew to start disembarking. Half the crew was given leave to go to shore; while the rest had to stay with the ship and guard the merchandise. Tomorrow would be a long day. The sailors would need to unload the merchandise and help take it to the market. Since the only port in Caminia was located in Nitami, the city didn't lack merchants; overland merchants that didn't possess ships would buy the goods in Nitami and take them overland to the other cities of Caminia to make a profit.

The massive gray walls of Nitami Fortress stretched in either direction of the beach with no end in sight. Circular towers spiraled skyward with trebuchets mounted on top, and a stone walkway was built from the fortress to the narrow channel walls that guarded the harbor. A cobble road led from the dock to the wall; the entrance was through a massive gatehouse, the size of a keep. Impossible as it may seem for enemy ships to get into the harbor, with the channel being so heavily guarded, those that managed to slip inside stood no chance of penetrating the massive walls.

No wonder Razim felt so secure; his kingdom was impregnable from the outside. Vitaeus thought to himself as he chose to take a walk alongside the wall, rather than go inside the city. He walked to the point where the sandy beaches came to an end. There, the sharp slope of the mountain began; a rushing creek at the foot of the hill made for a perfect boundary.

The sun was setting low in the sky, and he knew he should return to the ship before it got too late. Though his garb was unusually plain for a merchant, his ornate scabbard gave him away. He had noticed many eyes wandering to the scabbard, before casually looking him over.

Vitaeus had spent the night on the ship.Early the next morning, before he was even awake, the crew was already unloading the merchandise from the ship and loading it on carts to be taken to the marketplace. The seasoned crew knew their jobs well. There was a lot of excitement amongst them; knowing that they would be paid the rest of their salaries after the sale of the goods was made. Many Caminian merchants were already gathered at the dock as well, eyeing the goods as they were being unloaded from the various ships. Vitaeus watched as elaborate Permedian rugs were handled with care as they were unloaded. There were also furs from the Northern lands and silk and ivory from the Southern lands of savages. Beads of pearls, scented oils, myrrh, frankincense, and jewels from semi-precious stones were just some of the goods that they carried.

Vitaeus walked over to his carts of goods. The ship's crew flanked the sides to make sure that no quick thief could slip in and steal something. The crew was very protective of the merchandise, and most of the sailors had their swords unbuckled and ready to draw. But the sailors' dark menacing glares only kept a few of the young boys away. Skinny and dirty, Vitaeus could only guess that they were orphans living on the streets of Nitami.

A few boys tried to distract the sailors at the front by making it look as if they were going to rush in; prompting the sailors to brandish their swords. In the meantime, a small, skinny boy slipped in from the back and was about to make away with a sable robe and some pearls when Vitaeus stepped in behind him. Terrified, the boy dropped his treasure and scooted between the sailors; receiving a few kicks in the process.

The city looked remarkably clean with its cobblestone streets and buildings built with a mixture of white sand, crushed white rock, and yellow limestone. The buildings' stones were always light and bright, reflecting the sun's rays. Most buildings in the inner city were plain, square, three-story buildings, but as they entered the market plaza, the buildings were more ornate, with complex shrines dotting the city landscape to praise the Creator. High rises with rounded cupolas of gold and silver were seen throughout the rooftops. The people all seemed to be in a hurry to get to their day trades. The City Watch, dressed in silver and gold cloaks to symbolize the city's wealth, were visible strutting around on every corner of the city. It was as if the city flamboyantly sought attention for its wealth and majesty. The city was only 50 years old; it was born with the building of the Nitami Fortress and the securing of the harbor. Soon its ports were busy; as it was the only window that kept Caminia open to the world.

When the market officially opened for the day, Vitaeus was slammed with buyers. An overland merchant offered to buy all of the Permedian rugs for five pounds of gold. Another merchant overhearing the first offer quickly jumped in with an offer of seven. After some haggling, Vitaeus sold all the rugs for nine pounds of gold or 90 gold coins. He didn't imagine that the rugs were such a valuable asset. He had no doubt that with the sale of all the merchandise, he would split the profits with the crew and still have plenty of gold left over.

Another merchant came up and started to look at the trinkets and jewels, but shook his head when he realized that all of the rocks were only semi-precious stones.

"What goods are you looking for, sir?" Vitaeus inquired of him.

"The King told us to purchase as many precious stones as possible for a present that he wants to give to the princess from the Rok Isles. But these stones would be an insult to the King." The merchant said, as he waived at the jewels dismissively; which Vitaeus had laid out on the table.

"Well I do have these, but I am unwilling to part with them." Vitaeus said as he presented a small handful of gems, diamonds, sapphires and rubies.

The merchant's mouth dropped open. "Are they real?" He gasped slightly in a whisper.

"Of course, but I would need to see some payment first." Vitaeus prodded as he pulled his fist with the stones away. "How would you pay for these?"

"His Excellency Razim would pay you more than handsomely for all of it." The merchant replied.

"Describe handsomely, sir, because it's not a sum that I am familiar with." Vitaeus prodded, yet he knew that he had just struck rich. The merchant's despair was evident; which ensured that Vitaeus could bargain with the King himself.

"Sir," the merchant replied. "If you wish, his majesty has a private army to escort the merchant who has jewels to sell to him."

"What is His Excellency willing to pay? I'm a busy man and can't afford to waste time traveling on these overland routes unless I know how much it will profit me." Vitaeus kept his voice firm.

"Sir, his majesty has gold, land, and titles to hand out. Right now he is in urgent need of precious stones. I guarantee that you will profit handsomely. Caminia is rich in gold, but is lacking in precious stones."

"Very good sir. If it will be a service to the king and if as you have claimed I shall be paid handsomely, then I will accept your offer. Prepare the escort; I will see the king."

"Yes sir," the king's servant nodded excitedly. "My name is Nepides, and as I am His Excellency's most trusted servant. I will make sure that you will be well paid." Nepides bowed before leaving to prepare the escort.

"Captain," Vitaeus hollered, and the captain came over straightaway. His gaze fell on Vitaeus's closed fist; in which he held some of the precious stones. When he finally met Vitaeus's gaze, Vitaeus could see the glint of envy in his eyes.

"I have a proposal for you." Vitaeus continued. "I will leave the rest of this merchandise here, for you and the crew to sell, and you may keep half the proceeds for yourself. I shall be gone for about a month, but I want the ship here. See to any repairs that it might need. When I come back, I will reward you for your loyalty."

It was the first time Vitaeus had seen the captain smile; his black eyes that had always looked so fierce and angry actually seemed to melt as he beamed with happiness.

"Very good sir, the White Swan shall be waiting for you in tip top shape upon your arrival."

"Thank you captain, and you and the men enjoy yourselves. I feel fortunate to have come by a crew as legitimate as yours."

CHAPTER 17: SEREDINE

As the two rounded a hill, Achledis was amazed by the sight of Seredine. The bright morning sun gleaming off the white walls produced a halo around a city that already looked magnificent. Sitting on a slight hill, the city gave its defenders a decisive advantage. The white walls rose up to an astonishing 60 feet; with spiraling towers jutting out of the wall at certain intervals.

"She's beautiful," Achledis muttered under his breath.

Desiani smiled back with pride. "That's my home."

As they rode closer to the city gates, they could see the signs of life as farmers streamed into the city with fresh produce to sell; pausing for the guards to inspect their baggage and wagons one by one.

Desiani explained that they inspect everyone entering the city to protect it from weapon smugglers. The no weapons law was strictly enforced to ensure that the populace didn't start an uprising against Rakirian rule. Achledis was glad that Desiani had forced him to hide his weapons in the hills before they approached the city; especially after the long argument that they had where he tried to convince her that he might be able to sneak them inside. He could see now that it would have been a stupid thing to attempt.

Some covered wagons exiting the city barely received any attention from the guards. As the wagons approached them, Achledis locked eyes with a burly man walking on foot beside the mules.

"Aye there, young lad," said the man. "I hope you're not intending on staying at Seredine for too long." Without waiting for Achledis to respond, he continued in his cheery gruff voice. "They say that the Rakirian army has destroyed hundreds of villages. They burned everything to the ground as they went , and they left no survivors. Now that army is marching north, here to Seredine."

"No survivors?" Achledis smiled. "Then where do these rumors come from if no one is alive to tell them?"

The man was taken aback by the question, before recovering. "The scouts witnessed it. I guess." He responded; smiling now, proud of how he was able to think on his feet. "We are all headed to Caminia; scouts have been coming weekly now, urging the people to move there where they can be safe and protected by our army."

Achledis thanked the man for the heads up as he and Desiani continued on towards the gate.

"Well Desi, we might have to rethink leaving you here," Achledis said. They both stayed solemn as they approached the guards.

"What are you two doing here?" One of the guards snarled. "You don't look local."

"I live here; I was away for the summer to see my grandfather. And this…" Desiani paused as she looked at Achledis, than smiling she added, "and this is my new husband."

Achledis looked over at her, his eyebrows raised in surprise. The guard eyed the two suspiciously, allowing his gaze to linger on Achledis, than waived his hand for them to come in. The two entered through the gate and were faced with another wall in front of them that was about twenty feet high and extended alongside the main wall; at either end of the corridor, there was another gate. Any attackers who did manage to bust down the main gate would be forced to go through a gauntlet of boiling water, a hail of rocks, and other missiles from the defenders on top of the buffer wall, and at the end they would still be facing a gate at either end of the corridor.

Achledis was instantly disappointed once inside the walls; the city was run down and filthy, with a heavy stench of decay and human waste. The wooden buildings were in desperate need of repair. A burned out building further down looked desolate and abandoned, sticking out sorely.

"The city is being overlooked by a Rakirian Viceroy who doesn't share our pride for the city, nor does he care for its inhabitants," Desiani explained as if sensing Achledis's sudden disappointment.

A rounded keep stood 30 feet from the entrance on both sides of the buffer wall. Made of rock, it was a mini fortress inside a fortress. The defenders inside would rain a hellish fire of crossbow bolts on the invading force that would be trapped in the tight corridor, between the city wall and the buffer wall.

Inside the keep, the defenders could stay holed up for quite some time. One of the advantages of a rounded keep was that two defenders could keep a whole army at bay by using the sword in their dominant hand and forcing the attackers to attack to their left, while advancing up a narrow rounded passage that doesn't allow more than two men abreast.

As they advanced further into the center of town where the inhabitants lived, the stench of human excretion grew stronger and more pungent than before. The city was filled with flies and other parasites that seemed to feast on the waste that littered the narrow streets.

Desiani shoved him violently as she shouted for him to duck. A bucket of waste and slops was emptied from above, falling to the ground a few feet from where they stood; the spray ricocheting back to cover them in its mist.

"Sorry, I should have warned you; you always have to be on the lookout for that." Desiani said.

Achledis just shook his head in disbelief.

She didn't appear to notice the look he gave her, nor did she seem fazed by the horrendous sanitation as she carried on telling him about all the exciting parts of town that she still had to show him. First, they would go get something to eat though, at the inn that was operated by friends of her aunt and uncle.

Once Achledis was able to look past the busy, smelly, noisy, and dirty streets, he could see the splendor of Rosmir architecture in the magnificent buildings that were once the pride and glory of Rosmir ingenuity. He could see the high rise of the palace ahead with its many towers and conic roofs jutting out; it was a fortress on its own. The conic roofs seemed to be the theme, but further ahead he could see another beautiful building with many bright colors and onion domes sticking out. The domes that were once covered with gold were now gray as all the gold got scraped off. His mind wondered how onion domes like that could be built, and how long did it take someone to build them?

"What is that building?" Achledis asked.

"That's the theater where they perform plays and dance; we will surely go there sometime. Over there is the public bath house, with a dry sauna and steam room. It's a very popular place in the winter time." Desiani said as she pointed at a long building, made of gleaming white rock. "Remind me to show you the arena later. It's on the other side of town, but it's a place that you will love. Rakirian champions come and fight in front of large crowds; though the tickets to those events are very expensive."

As they walked past the numerous guilds and the expert craftsmen working, Achledis was dazzled. These guilds were by far superior to the ones in Pavanti. He watched for a moment as the shoemaker fashioned a pair of exceptionally fine boots and marveled at his work.

"The architecture and some of the buildings and towers are magnificent for sure, but everything else I can't stand." Achledis stated. "I don't understand how living here appeals to anyone, when the freedom of the open country, along with its fresh air and peace, is just outside these walls." He always imagined that he would love growing up in a city, with so many people around, so much stuff to do. Now he realized that he was wrong. He already missed Pavanti.

"Don't judge the city life by your first day here," Desiani protested. "Give yourself some time; look at some of the fine things you can buy here that you won't find in all of Rosmir." She pointed at a row of merchants, who were selling their exotic goods. They sell just about everything that you normally couldn't find anywhere else in Rosmir. Desiani held up a light cloth to her cheek and explained that it was called silk. She looked at it longingly and then quickly returned it to the table. She went on to point out spices, incense, and perfumes and even beautiful icons of Rakirian gods and goddesses.

"Over here young man," shouted a vendor. "I have something perfect that you can buy for your beautiful young lady." His accent betrayed him to be a Rakirian. Looking down the row of merchants and vendors, he noticed that they all looked Rakirian. They were dressed in very fancy and extravagant clothing; which made them stick out sorely in the gray and dirty city around them. Armed guards were stationed sporadically down the street for their protection.

"Here, this smells beautiful. It smells so perfect; let your lady friend try this one. Take a good whiff of that would you?" With that, he applied some of the perfume on Desiani, and the smell was extremely pungent and not pleasant in any way. "Well what do you think?" He asked as if the disgusted expression on Achledis's face didn't already show him the answer.

"I absolutely find that scent repulsive," Achledis said as he took Desiani gently by the arm and turned to go.

"Repulsive!? How dare you? That perfume is the biggest rage throughout the Empire and very expensive."

"My apologies. I meant no offense; I just didn't like the smell, that's all." Achledis continued walking.

"Hey stop! Where are you going? You have to pay for that application of perfume; it costs you ten din."

Achledis and Desiani continued walking; ignoring the ranting merchant, who had notified some of the guards nearby, accusing the two of theft. Desiani noticed as the guards started in pursuit behind them, shouting for them to stop. A couple of guards in front also moved to intercept their path.

"Why is it that when you're around I always get into some kind of trouble? Now with no money, to pay, they will probably throw us in the dungeons, and there is no escaping on this narrow street." Desiani complained.

"If you're thanking me for bringing excitement into your otherwise dull life, then you're truly welcome. Now, I think it's time for us to stop and acknowledge the celebration being thrown in our honor," Achledis said. "Besides, with me by your side you at least get to experience the thrill of adventure. It's a lot more exciting than fishing with an old man on a little boat. Trust me."

Achledis laughed at his own joke, but the scowl on Desiani's face immediately made him regret it.

As the guards approached them with the merchant following close behind, Achledis stepped out and asked what the problem was.

"Make them pay double and throw them in the dungeons. You simply can't allow these Rosmir dogs to keep getting away with this kind of theft. Make examples of them." The merchant raved, spittle flying out of his mouth, and his face was red with rage. A soldier with a purple plume raised his hand motioning for the merchant to quiet down. He was clearly the captain of the guard, and on his face he showed no expression.

"You two are being accused of applying the perfume without purchasing it first; according to our laws, that is theft. Either you pay double as punishment for the application..."

"That would be 20; no make that 25 din," the merchant yelled out.

The captain of the guard looked at the merchant; his eyes flashed angerly at the interruption. "Twenty din is what you owe the man, and you must either pay this amount or go to the dungeons to await trial. At the trial, the fate of your hands will be decided if you get to keep them or not."

Achledis waited politely until the captain of the guard was done speaking before he began to speak. "Captain, the lady and I were just walking by when this schmuck of a man ran up yelling about something that he wanted to sell and started applying the perfume on the lady without invitation. I told the man that his perfume reeked of dog piss, and he in turn demanded that I pay him for applying it on the lady. Now the lady's most beautiful scent is tarnished, thanks to this little runt. It is the lady who wishes to press charges against the merchant for assaulting her."

The guards in the back stifled their laughter at Achledis's choice of words to describe the merchant and his 'fancy' perfume. Even the captain had the faintest of smiles on his face; though he tried hard to suppress it. In the meantime, the merchant was madder than hell.

"He dares to insult me. I will personally go to Lord Lorne and demand that this man have his hands and tongue removed."

The captain looked at the merchant and assured him that he was well understood. The captain and the rest of his guards resented all of the merchants. They were all known to be pompous, and with their wealth they pulled a lot of power and influence. The captain believed Achledis's account over the merchant's. It was all very likely for his type to allow someone to sample a product and then charge them for it; forcing them to buy something that they didn't want in the first place. "Let me talk to this young man alone and counsel him of our laws." With that, he motioned for Achledis to follow him some paces away and out of earshot.

"We did no wrong, but if you must arrest someone then arrest me and allow the girl to go." Achledis said, but the captain shushed him.

"At first, I thought that you were simply foolish, but upon hearing you speak again, I realized that you're just ignorant. Your dialect betrays you as a foreigner to Seredine. How long have you been here?" The captain asked.

"Just got here."

The captain nodded. "A word of advice then, everyone that lives here knows that you don't cross these merchants. They wield a lot of power and influence. With their large pocket books, they can have the politicians do what they want most of the time. If he wants you to hang, you will probably hang. Even I wouldn't be able to intervene. My advice is to pay the man and next time steer clear from the likes of him."

"Then why are you wasting my time?" Achledis retorted impatiently, "Why are you talking to me if there is nothing you can do for me. Tell me captain, do you believe that merchant's claim that we applied the perfume?"

"Like I said, it doesn't matter what I believe. A Rakirian citizen is accusing you, a non Rakirian citizen, of theft. It's his word against yours, and he will win 100% of the time in court. With the size of his pocket book, he will make you regret this day for the rest of your life. Now will you pay him or not!?" The captain raised his voice at the end to make sure the others heard his question.

The other guards instantly started to move towards them again, their hands on their swords in anticipation.

"I don't have 20 din on me; I don't have anything on me." Achledis shouted; his frustration now fully surfaced.

"Then you're under arrest!" The Captain shouted, but he got no further as a commotion started behind him. He glanced back instinctively and saw the merchant's booth being looted and destroyed.

CHAPTER 18: TRAVELING FROM NITAMI TO CAMINIA

The road between Nitami and Caminia was slightly elevated and laid out with stone. Even in harsh rains the road was always clear of mud and slush. The villages they passed were set back from the main road; as Nepides had explained, it was due to the king's decree.

"His Excellency always has a good reason for everything, and this rule is just one of many that shows the king's wisdom."

"And what is the king's reason for such a decree?" Vitaeus asked.

"Simple, the King knows that if allowed, villages would sprout everywhere along the road, clogging the highway. Rather smaller roads from the highway lead to these villages and towns. If a traveler wishes to stop by an inn for the night or get some food before continuing his journey, then they may do so by taking one of the many smaller roads that deviate from the highway."

Vitaeus didn't say much as they rode on; on the way they also passed through a forest of pines trees that were as tall as any he had ever seen. The pine needles blanketed the road, and the stone was no longer visible. The high rising pines blocked the sun's cheerful rays, casting gloomy shadows all about.

"Are you hungry or tired My Lord?" Nepides inquired. "Should we stop by and get some rest? I know of a castle not far from here; the Duke residing there offers excellent hospitality to those with coin to pay for it."

Vitaeus chuckled. "Very good then, take me to this hospitable lord who craves my coin. I shall eat his grub, and he shall take my coin."

They came to a road laid out with cobbles veering left of the highway. A prominent sign nailed to a pine void of branches two-thirds of the way down, read 'Duchy of Hilam.'

"Not only is the Duke of Hilam good to those with coin, but he is especially devoted to those of His Excellency's court. His

Excellency has favored the Duke of Hilam; though no one knows why. He bestowed him with his title and these lands only in recent years. Yet in those years, the Duke of Hilam has grown in prestige and everyone knows of him throughout the land. It is a message to everyone how well His Excellency rewards those whom he favors."

"Hopefully the stones I carry will help me find favor in the eyes of his majesty as well." Vitaeus said.

"Perhaps. Rumors abound that the king is slowly replacing the old lords, whose loyalty he questions, with new lords whose devotion to him is firm. It is perilous times that are coming our way. Whispers and rumors of all sorts are floating around and are only growing louder as the king continues to age and is still without a male heir to succeed him. His first wife was barren, but he loved her too much to do away with her. The people of the kingdom sighed with relief in private and wept publicly when her majesty died of sudden illness. His second wife only bore him daughters, three of them, and all of them, along with his wife, had a sudden and unfortunate accident of falling off the cliff to their deaths. The king is in his seventies and needs a young wife who will bring his seed, a male heir, into the world. That is why his majesty needs these precious jewels to sway the Princess of the Rock Isles and to give a generous dowry to the Rok Isles King, with whom his alliance will then be cemented."

The sound of a steel axe chopping into wood rang louder as they approached; Nepides motioned for silence. Suddenly the sound of the axe stopped, and all they heard was the sound of their horses on a cobble road. Nepides raised his hand and the whole column stopped. All around was the incredibly loud sound of silence and the whispering of branches in the wind high above. Then there was a crack of a dry branch snapping and a sudden hush once more; Nepides's face grew stern as he listened for any more sounds that might come. After some moments had passed without any more sounds, he ordered the commander to ride and bring him the criminals. The commander, with a small entourage of men, rode out in the direction from where the last sound had come from and came back shortly with a young lad.

The boy could not have been older then fifteen, skinny, yet well-muscled. His clothes hung raggedly on his limbs, his face smudged with dirt, and his blonde hair tussled. Vitaeus saw fresh bruises on his face and arms; where the captain and his men had no doubt dealt him upon capturing him. The commander shoved the boy to the ground in front of Nepides.

"Here is the criminal boy, Sir."

"Yes, here he is the thief of his majesty's forest, and one who will learn quickly, without a doubt, why breaking laws is a bad idea. Though his majesty is benevolent, he is also just, and it's this justice that is marquee to His Excellency's wisdom. This is what keeps this kingdom straight and free from lawlessness."

"It was a dead tree laying on the ground My Lord, and I was simply cutting firewood for my family for fuel, Sir. How else can we cook without fuel, and without cooking the raw meat, how are we to eat it? My Lord, I beg that you impart on me the king's mercy for which he is in such abundance."

"Abundance of mercy? The King? Huh!" Nepides said. "The king is abundant in mercy because it's one thing he doesn't give away. Justice has no mercy; for then it wouldn't be justice at all. A world without justice is a world of lawlessness. The law is always just, and when a lawbreaker doesn't abide by the law, there are consequences. When mercy waters down justice, injustice abounds. Commander, in which hand was he holding the axe?"

"It was a big axe, My Lord," the commander said. "He had to have used both hands to hold it while chopping."

"Then both hands it shall require to recompense his crime."

"No!" The boy howled as he struggled to get free, but his struggling was useless. The boy finally stopped, panting from the exertion.

"My Lord, perhaps the Duke should be the one to administer his majesty's justice as the tree was on his land." Vitaeus said.

"Perhaps, but why trouble the Duke with a common dog such as this. I can simply deliver justice and not trouble the Duke."

"Then let the Duke do it." Vitaeus interjected more sharply than he intended.

Nepides gave him a surprised look before telling the commander to bind the boy; so they could deliver him to the Duke.

The boy looked at Vitaeus gratefully, but Vitaeus dared not meet his gaze as the column moved on once again. Soon they entered a grassy valley, speckled with small huts and gardens. The sun was already disappearing, and the view was a bit dark. But even in the gray sky, the rising smoke of a hundred fires was visible. Further in the distance loomed a castle, made of white and gray brick with golden banners flying from the castle wall that had three golden mountain lions emblazed as the Duke's family sigil.

"Sarik! Help me." The captive boy yelled out suddenly, and one of the peasants herding the sheep at the side of the road looked up. Sarik must have recognized the captive boy, and he responded by leaving his sheep and running to road.

"Let him go." He shouted.

"Boy, get out of the way before I have my men arrest you for impeding the King's justice, and that may cost you your head." Nepides declared.

Sarik looked long and hard at the captured boy, before turning his gaze at Nepides. "That is my little brother you have in your custody. Tell me why you have him in ropes."

"Get the dog out of my way." Nepides said casually, and the commander drew his crossbow. As Sarik realized what was about to happen, he turned to run, but the bolt had already struck him in the back before he could take two steps, sending him sprawling face first onto the road. The captive boy howled in agony as he saw his brother fall. Two of the guards dismounted and dragged the body into the weeds at the side of the road, leaving a red trail in its wake.

Vitaeus was shocked and angered by what he had just witnessed, and hate for Nepides's sense of justice simmered in his soul. He realized that his fingers were clutching the hilt of his Vulcan sword. *It's not my battle.* He reminded himself.

Nepides rode up to the gates and made his presentation to the guards of the castle, and the gates screeched in protest on their iron hinges as they slowly opened. In half an hour, the Duke met the party inside one of the banquet halls of his castle.

"Nepides, on another mission for our good king I presume?"

"Yes, as always, I'm doing His Excellency's bidding."

"No wonder the king keeps a man of such low birth like you around." The Duke said with an amused smile. "Will you eat before bed time?"

"Yes My Lord, we are famished from the long journey, but first I wanted to present to you a thief of His Majesty's trees." The boy was shoved violently forward by one of the guards; so that he went sprawling on the floor in front of the Duke.

The Duke looked down at the boy, and his face instantly grew grim. He looked at Nepides, then back at the sobbing boy, then back at Nepides. "What did you say his crime was?"

"He was found chopping a fallen tree for firewood in the forest, My Lord." Vitaeus interjected. "He was chopping it for fuel to keep his family warm as well as for cooking; it seems harsh to take a young lad's hands for the crime of trying to contribute to his family's wellbeing."

"And who are you?" He asked.

"A merchant, My Lord."

"Yes, I agree with you on that merchant. It is a grave thing to take a young lad's hands, especially over a dead tree. Who wanted to take the young lad's hands? Was it you, Nepides?"

"Yes Sir, the boy was caught chopping a tree in the king's forest; thievery, great or small, is still thievery. The law makes no distinction between a man who steals gold and one who steals wood; it only makes it clear that thievery of any kind is against the law. The boy was chopping a tree. He used both hands to hold the axe that struck at the tree, and so both hands must go to ensure that he won't steal with those hands again."

The Duke walked to a window and peered into the darkness beyond. "Nepides come here." He called. "Look, even in the light of the moon you can see the outline of the trees, and that tree line stretches as far as the eye can see. You would maim a lad for the rest of his life over a faggot of sticks? Since when did the king place you as the overseer of the law, especially on my duchy, and give you the right to maim my subjects?"

Nepides cast his eyes down as he spoke; his voice was more solemn. "His Excellency feeds me and my family. He does well by me, and so I always seek to help his cause in any way I can. The law is the law, and even you, sir, are not above the King's law."

The Duke turned on Nepides in anger; spittle flying from his mouth as he spoke. "Here on my duchy, you will presume to follow my laws; is that clear?"

"Yes sir, but what are your laws? Do they differ from the King's?" Nepides inquired suspiciously.

"My law for you is simple. While on my lands, you will not presume to think of yourself as the king's justice, and you will not lift a finger on my subjects. For crimes that are committed on my lands, I am the lord, and I will decide on what is the right justice." The Duke offered the boy his hand. The boy kept his eyes downcast as he mumbled thank-you. "Are you hungry boy?" A slight nod and sniffle escaped the boy. "Good, then you will eat. Tell me boy, does your family not have money to buy wood?" The boy's eyes swelled with tears once more.

"My Lord, my father has left for the king's army and has been gone for the past two years. My brother and I were the only ones to help our ma and our little sisters. The ration of wood given at the beginning of the year has been either used or stolen, and I..." His voice cut off suddenly, and he started to weep once more.

"In the morning we will ride to your family and see how we can help them. I want all of you to trust me as your lord and bring to me your hardships; so that we can try to fix them together. How old is your brother?"

"He was seventeen Sir, but now he's dead."

"Dead?"

"Yes, this man had him shot."

"The boy was impeding on the king's justice. I warned him, and when he didn't listen, I ordered for him to be taken out of the way." Nepides excitedly explained.

The Duke glowered at Nepides angrily, "With you around, one half of the population will soon either be dead and the other half will end up as maimed beggars rather than productive citizens." The Duke looked at his servant and motioned at Nepides. "Show this dog and his entourage to their rooms." Then looking at Nepides again he said. "I want you out of here at first light. I will not have you maiming any more of my subjects." And to the boy, "Will some mutton with potatoes be good, or would you prefer fish instead?"

"Either one sounds good My Lord."

"Feed the boy and give him the best guest room; oh and make sure you fill the bath for him."

"Sir, I need to go comfort my mother; if Your Majesty would excuse me?"

"Very well, I will go get your family this very night and find accommodation for you here. With your father serving the king, his family shouldn't have to starve while he performs such noble duty."

"Sir," Vitaeus interjected as servants tried to push him out along with the rest of Nepides's entourage. Duke Hilam looked at him questioningly.

"What do you want merchant?"

"Food Sir, and I have coin to pay for it as well."

"Nepides and his cronies will be supping on barley biscuits; will that not be sufficient for you?"

"No, Sir, I would much prefer to sup on a thick slice of mutton myself."

"Why should I offer you hospitality over the rest? Were you not a part of Nepides's party?"

Vitaeus held out a silver coin. "Because I am willing to pay for my food and bedding."

CHAPTER 19: DESIANI TAKES CHARGE

It took a split second for the reality of the situation to set in. Their accuser, the merchant, was being robbed while he and all the guards were preoccupied with Achledis. Achledis realized that Desiani wasn't around. With all of the attention on Achledis, she had managed to slip out, and with horror, Achledis realized that the person vandalizing the merchant's goods was Desiani. He could see glass perfume bottles being thrown around and smashed against the ground. The poor merchant was aghast as he tried to run on his short legs in an attempt to save the rest of his precious merchandise. He outpaced the guards back to his stand, and as he neared Desiani, she smashed a glass bottle of perfume across the merchant's face, sending him crashing back from the impact.

He screamed in pain and had a burning sensation in his eyes as he groped blindly at them. In his hazy vision, he noticed blood on his hands and only then felt the searing throb of a bloody bruise across his face.

A guard ran up to seize Desiani, but she held out a shard of glass to the merchant's throat. He went from an uncontrollable frenzy to being completely still, allowing only a whimper of fear to escape him.

"Step back!" Desiani commanded the guard.

"Take it easy lady," the guard cautioned. "It will go a lot easier for you if you surrender. What you have just done is unacceptable, but you don't want to make matters worse by taking this further."

"You should listen to him," the captain said as he approached, his face rigid with concern.

"When I did nothing wrong, I was to have my hands and tongue removed; now that I did this, what else will they remove, hmm let's see... my limbs as well?" Desiani replied sarcastically. Achledis shook his head in wonder. Desiani continued to amaze him with her fiery nature, and he was very proud of her.

"No, now you will probably stand trial and face an excruciatingly slow and torturous death." The captain's voice was now even, in complete control once again, and without a trace of emotion on his face.

"The law that I adhere to is an eye for an eye; if my life is forfeit, than I may as well kill this man here. Without his large money purse to convince Lord Lorne; perhaps a torturous death may be avoided."

"No! Please, don't do that! I will pay you and forget that any of this happened. Captain, Captain, do you hear me?" The merchant wailed.

"Yes, we all hear you," the Captain replied.

"I decree that this woman is innocent, and you with the host of other guards will be witnesses that I completely forgive the woman of all of her debt and for the damage done here today."

"And what of my friend?" Desiani asked sweetly.

"Yes, yes, the boy is pardoned of all debt and wrongdoing." The merchant eagerly replied.

The captain chewed on his lip thoughtfully as he considered what the merchant had just said. "Very well merchant, we have all heard you, and you can't go back on the oath that you have just made. You shall be bound to it according to the law. Are you sure you want to stick with it."

The merchant pumped his head back and forth enthusiastically. "Yes, yes definitely! You hear that young lady? You're free to go." He laughed with exuberance as he proudly proclaimed his pardon.

"Not so fast,! You forgot who is in charge, and I don't need you telling me that I'm free to go when it is I that is holding you captive! Now, I will have to press charges of 200 din for you splashing me with dog urine. A fine lady, such as myself, shouldn't be forced to stink in such a manner, and another 2,000 din for threatening my life and well-being."

There was a shock of silence for a moment, and Desiani pressed the glass harder against the merchant's temple.

"But 2,000 din I can hardly afford. I shall never recover from that. I am just a poor merchant," the merchant whined, suddenly dour once more.

"Silence!" Desiani commanded him. "Very well, I don't want to take all of your money and leave you with nothing; you are a merchant after all. How much din do you have?"

"I ah, have 2,700 din approximately, and you destroyed around 3,000 din worth of merchandise. 700 din will hardly be enough for me to have..."

Again Desiani cut him off.

"Ok so you have 2,700 din. "I will take 2,000 din for myself as previously agreed, and my friend who was also threatened by you shall take 650 din. With that, your accusations against us shall be righted."

"Now you can't do that; that's extortion." The captain said, and the merchant readily agreed.

"Like I said, you were planning to extort our limbs and tongues and possibly our lives from us. The law of our land, and you are on our land, is an eye for an eye and a tooth for a tooth. Because I am merciful, however, I won't take his eyes or limbs, not even his tongue. I only asked for a small monetary payment so that the wrongs against us could be righted. Now merchant, you're under oath. You tell the captain here what you are willing to pay me and my friend for your crimes to be forgiven." She pressed the shard harder yet into the throat.

Begrudgingly, the merchant agreed and made the oath; Desiani, seeing Achledis standing at the ready if anything was to go wrong, released the merchant and got up.

As soon as the merchant was safely far enough away from Desiani, he demanded that the captain seize her.

"For what?" The captain asked. "You have just pardoned her of all wrong doing, and you owe them a considerable amount of money."

"Surely you jest!" The merchant said. His voice wheezed as if the air had gone out of it before he began to speak.

"Surely, I don't. My guards, along with me, just witnessed an oath made by you."

"But I only made that oath because I feared for my life; you witnessed it."

"I witnessed you telling us that she was forgiven for all crimes against you, and then you promised to pay them for your crimes. I hope that I don't have to remind you that if you don't pay up, than you will be the one going to the dungeons for theft; as well as having all of your limbs removed." The captain's voice was harsh, and there was a steely look in his eyes that sent a tremor of fear through the pit of the merchant's stomach. He could hardly believe this was happening. How dare the captain? Didn't he realize that if he pulled some strings, this captain would be hanging before sundown?

The merchant looked at the other guards for support, but saw none. Their dislike for him was clear on all of their faces. "I will speak to Lord Lorne of this personally and have you whipped and scourged before your slow death. His lordship will be so disappointed that the captain of the guard that he appointed to protect the merchants of the city from these rats that abide here, has turned against me, a highly reputable merchant, and joined up with these scavengers that robbed me."

The captain's sword was at the merchant's throat in a flash. "Listen here, you are no longer a merchant. With 50 din in your pocket, you won't even afford a safe passage back to Rakiria, much less an audience with the Viceroy. Now, you pay up right now, or I will take you to the dungeons where you will rot, with all the other rats. I will strip all proof of your Rakirian citizenship and cut your tongue out. No one will ever be able to hear your dialect, and your face will be beaten beyond recognition. Now the money," and motioning to his men, he told them to take whatever else was left.

After all the money was received, and the disgruntled merchant was sent on his way, cursing and full of threats, the captain paced nervously. He considered if letting him go was a mistake. Perhaps no one would take him seriously.

One of the guards nudged the captain, and with his head motioned towards the pudgy merchant as he headed towards another booth, obviously to complain about him.

The captain instantly made his decision. "Seize him and throw him in the dungeons. Strip all of his identification and cut his tongue out." Two guards instantly responded by running in pursuit of the merchant. The merchant yelled out in protest as the guards seized him. The fat merchant started screaming and whaling as he was dragged away, begging the other merchants to speak to Lord Lorne on his behalf, and reminding them that their safety depended on it as well.

A tall merchant walked over to the captain and demanded to know the reason of the other merchant's arrest. The captain led him aside, just out of earshot, and after a brief conversation, the tall merchant grew pale and nodded his head in agreement, before turning around and walking back to his booth timidly.

The captain divvied up the money and handed Achledis and Desiani each 500 din.

"Captain, I'm afraid that I'm 150 din short, and my lady friend here is 1500 din short."

The captain's face grew pink at the boy's boldness. "Listen here, that merchant needs to be paid 1,000 din to keep him quiet; otherwise my head may very well be in peril for standing up for you two. I will keep the rest; for I risked a lot for the both of you today. Though I have respect for you, it may disappear quickly, and the only fortune I will bestow on you is to rot along with the merchant in the dungeon. It is your choice. Which one do you prefer?"

The young Rosmirians agreed without hesitation. Achledis had to admit to himself that he had just met the first Rakirian that he actually respected.

"Now go, and go quickly. Don't show yourselves for some time. I don't know what other friends this merchant may have in this city."

CHAPTER 20: CAMINIA CITY

Five days later, Vitaeus, Nepides, and his entourage of twenty men arrived at Caminia City. A beautiful lake with crystal blue water that sparkled in the sunlight lay at the foot of the hill just outside the city walls. The lake was fed by underground warm springs and was channeled into the city. Another small rivulet that left the lake flowed past the city and ran parallel with the isthmus before cascading down a waterfall into the bay below.

The outside walls of Caminia City were in sharp contrast to that of Nitami. They were a pearl white; while the inner walls were made of a dark, slate gray rock. The city itself sat on a large rocky hill adjacent to the cliffs overlooking the gulf between mainland Rosmir and Caminia. Another giant wall with a massive gatehouse blocked off the isthmus to Rosmir, and massive trebuchets sat on top of tall towers. Unlike the lush evergreens of western and southern Caminia, the land here was rocky and barren, with prairie grass and wild flowers covering the landscape.

The gates to the city were open, though guarded. The city watch of Caminia wore black and white cloaks to match the city walls. Putting aside his strong dislike for the man whom he had only recently found out was probably responsible for the murder of his grandparents, Vitaeus had to respect the wealth and the fortifications that the current king had built. Unlike mainland Rosmir where armed bandits were common on the roads, here people walked by themselves unafraid. They passed many travelers without escorts, and in general the people of the kingdom seemed prosperous. Nepides waved his hand impatiently, and the guards parted for the group.

Vitaeus dressed in his best clothing, a blue silk tunic and brown riding pants, also wore a gray cap with a white seagull feather. At his side was the Vulcan sword, and hidden at his ankles was the Vulcan dagger. He had the Vulcan journal hidden inside an inner pocket of his royal blue cloak; while the armor and some of his other personal belongings he kept on a separate mount.

The clacking sound of hooves against the cobbles echoed loudly as they rode through the gatehouse and into the city. Vitaeus's first impression was that the city was clean and built from Caminian rock; which was porcelain white. The buildings gleamed much like they did inside Nitami; except that Caminia was void of any yellow limestone. Everything was built with the porcelain white rock; which was in much abundance here. The white buildings contrasted neatly against the gray cobbled streets and the shimmering golden cupolas of shrines and elegant palaces against a blue sky. The King's Palace was visible almost at any place within the city. It sat atop a steep hill and was surrounded by gleaming white walls and red guard towers at all four corners of the fortress. As the group rode up to the gate leading inside the palace walls, the guards recognized Nepides and instantly opened the gate.

At the palace door, a host of servants dressed in fluffy white tunics and gray tights took the horses; while others took the luggage. "Take this man to the finest guest room." Nepides commanded one of the servants, and the servant made a slight bow to acknowledge the command as he handled the crate with Vitaeus's armor, clothes and gold. Though Vulcan armor is perhaps the lightest armor ever made, its weight, with the addition of nine pounds of gold, still took the servant by surprise, but he quickly recovered as he readjusted the weight in his arms.

"Follow me sir." The servant replied while keeping his eyes on the ground. Inside the palace, it was almost excessively decorated with frames of gold containing action pictures of Razim. In one, he was portrayed as if he was killing a wolf with his bare hands; another one showed a lion with a lance through it and three serpent heads peering through the golden mane. The carpets were a deep crimson red against white walls. The ceilings were covered in gold; which reflected light from the candles lit inside golden chandeliers.

"Here you are sir." The servant juggled the crate as he tried to open the door.

"Here, let me," Vitaeus said as he opened the door. "Just set the box down anywhere you please."

The servant seemed more than happy to oblige as he set the box down. "Sir, food and bath will be brought up to you right away." The servant did a slight bow before ducking out the door, closing it behind him gently.

Things had gone better than Vitaeus could have imagined. Here, he was inside Razim's palace, a guest under his roof. In a short time, he had acquired more gold and wealth than he could have imagined. He recited his alias and background story that he had made up for himself; everything had to go perfect. The room was as big as his house had been in Pavanti. It consisted of a small kitchen, a sitting area, and behind that was another wall separating the bed. From the sitting room, there was a door that led out to a balcony, and when Vitaeus walked out, he was stunned with the beauty. His suite was on the third floor, on the south side of the palace, where he had a magnificent view of the Caminian gulf before him and the Jade Lake to his right. He watched as the powerful waves of the Caminian gulf crashed into the cliffs over 200 feet below.

A knock sounded on the door, and Vitaeus hurried to open it. The servant who led him to his room now held a towel and a bronze key on top of it. "The key is for the room sir." Behind him, servants pushed a cart with steaming water, and behind them was a cart with a platter of food along with the servants from the kitchen adorned with white chef hats. "And this is your dinner and bath."

"Thank you," Vitaeus said as he handed him a copper coin as a tip. The servant accepted the tip but looked warily at Vitaeus.

"Sir, in two hours time, the king expects you up in his personal quarters on the fourth and fifth floors. I will come to escort you to His Majesty's quarters then." With a slight bow, he was off, and the rest of the servants followed on his heels.

CHAPTER 21: THE INN

The inn was a simple two story building, dull of color and with rotten wooden planks making up the exterior walls. A welcome sign dangled on a post by the doorway, with another sign right next to it, pointing in the direction of the stable.

"Is this it?" Achledis tried to mask the disappointment that crept in at the sight of the much talked about Inn.

Desiani ignored him and confidently pulled the door open. The aroma of roasted lamb, ale, and fresh coffee was strong, but inviting, in the muggy air of the inn. Achledis frowned at another smell, as it took him a moment to process, the stench of sweaty bodies.

As they stood at the doorway and looked around the room, a slight breeze followed them, blowing some of the dust inside. Achledis let the door linger open for a moment as he enjoyed the fresh air wafting inside. The inn felt like an oven; it was hotter inside by at least ten degrees than it was in the blazing sun outside.

"Shut that damn door! The dust is blowing inside." Called out the voice of a youth. Achledis looked in the direction it came from and saw a small group of men that ranged from middle-aged men to youth. They were talking in loud, argumentative voices that quickly hushed when Achledis and Desiani came in. Now they whispered suspiciously as a few of the men eyed the two newcomers.

Looking at Achledis, Desiani almost whispered, "Wow this place has changed a bit since the last time I was here."

Achledis deliberately closed the door slowly and glared the youth down, before taking Desiani by the hand. He led her to a table at the other side of the room.

"Don't worry, that's probably some of my uncle's friends. They come here and rant about their hatred for Rakirians. You will fit right in; I'm sure." Looking over her shoulder she studied the group of men, making no secret of it. "Well, I see Alrik; he is a good friend of my uncle's. They must have not recognized me."

Suddenly the young man, who shouted for the door to be closed, got up and started walking towards them. Desiani's face lit up in recognition. "Yurosi? Wow! I hardly recognized you."

The young man smiled pleasantly. His blond hair was neatly cut and combed to the side; his blue eyes were piercing with their intensity. "Let's not make this about me; you're the goddess, who blesses us with your presence."

"Oh stop with the flattery." Desiani said in mock protest, but the grin on her face showed that she was pleased with the praise. His eyes, the way he looked at her, and the way he seemed to take her in, made her feel beautiful.

"But really, you were so short, and I don't think your voice had changed the last time I saw you. Now look at you."

Yurosi chuckled in turn. "Well that was some years back before I moved to Caminia. Imagine when I came back for the girl that I had fallen in love with as a boy, and they tell me that she has moved away to only the Creator knows where." His eyes seemed to twinkle with humor as he spoke.

Then looking at Achledis, who had been giving him the dirty look, he apologized quickly. "I'm sorry, that was rude of me to yell out like that." Achledis gave a half nod to acknowledge the apology. "Well, I am Yurosi." He said with a bright smile on his face as he offered his hand.

"Achledis," Achledis replied as he shook his hand. Their hands grasped tightly as they surmised one another's strength and held the grip for a brief moment before Yurosi gave it a firm shake.

"Pleased to meet you Achledis."

"So what brings you back here to Seredine?" Desiani asked.

"I came back for you..." He let that hang for a moment as he turned over his shoulder and snapped his fingers at a young boy who was standing to the back watching him.

"Bring three glasses of the white Caminian wine." Yurosi ordered the boy.

With a nod, the boy turned to go, but Desiani stopped him with her hand. "I won't have any wine, perhaps some water instead."

"You must try it; it's made from grapes that are sour with a tinge of sweetness to it. I brought it from Caminia." Yurosi insisted. "Tiram, be sure to bring a couple glasses of water as well." He flicked his hand for the boy to go before turning back to Desiani. "Where was I? Oh yes, I came back here to see if you wanted to go with me to Caminia. It is part of Rosmir where we Rosmirians are actually free. Besides, we have had some decent fortune since moving out there. My father was made a count over an estate in Caminia, and I have been knighted. That's why I came here for you. I need a beautiful lady that will inspire me and cheer for me in my duels." There was an awkward silence as Desiani sat a little stunned and unsure of how to respond. "There is nothing left for us here; all that remains in Seredine is oppression. In Caminia, we are free men, our own masters, and no Rakirian can come telling us what to do." Seeing Desiani's discomfort, he glanced at Achledis and nodded understandingly. "I'm sorry; I should have known that you were with somebody else."

"Achledis and I are more like very good friends who went through a lot together." Desiani corrected.

"Yes, Desiani and I are not exactly a couple." Achledis confirmed quickly.

"Well that's excellent for me then; I will take advantage of the opportunity." He said with a grin.

Tiram appeared just then with a tray of three wine of glasses and two water glasses.

"Thanks Tiram," Desiani said as she gave him a sweet smile.

Yurosi handed a glass of wine to Desiani, and another to Achledis, before raising his in toast. "To life, prosperity and happiness." As their glasses clinked, Yurosi took an exaggerated whiff, before taking a sip. He looked at them for approval.

"Mmmh," Desiani said with a puckered smile. The wine was tinged with the slightest sweetness that entertwined with the sourness of the grapes. That seemed to stimulate her senses and forced her to pucker her lips as she took another sip.

"Though I usually try to abstain from wine or alcohol, this was very good." Achledis said as he placed his empty glass on an empty oak table.

Achledis excused himself from their conversation and walked away towards the bar. He usually didn't drink alcohol; as his father was opposed to it. He was always reminded of the one time when he tried it, back when he was just turning into a teenager. He had snuck into the tavern at Pavanti with some of the other boys at night. It had all started out in fun, but serious consequences soon followed, as someone said something about someone else. In the drunken atmosphere, everything escalated into a full brawl that left some of the boys seriously injured and the tavern in need of serious repair.

He shook the memory away, and his thoughts snapped back to Desiani and this new suitor. Her words echoed in the back of his mind. *"We're more like really good friends who went through a lot together."* She was right. He knew they were just very dear friends that went through a lot together and nothing more. Yet he wasn't sure about Yurosi. He was good looking, tall, and broad shouldered, with blue eyes and blonde hair. He was a knight, and his father was a count. By the clothes he wore, he obviously had money. He had a lot to offer Desiani, yet Achledis was unsettled by the prospect of Desiani going away with him. He wasn't sure why; perhaps he was jealous. No, he wasn't jealous, perhaps leery. Something about him made Achledis mistrust him. He remembered the way he treated his page, Tiram.

"What can I get you?" Asked a middle-aged woman startling Achledis.

"I could use some of that coffee." Achledis replied as he took a whiff of the pleasant aroma of coffee.

As the lady returned with the mug of coffee, Achledis went for his money purse, but the lady waved him away.

"It's been taken care of." She said.

"Oh no, I'll pay." Achledis insisted as he handed her the money, but the lady just pushed it away.

"It's rude to reject hospitality you know," came a male voice behind him. Achledis turned to see Yurosi standing behind him. He had a good humored grin on his face.

"Whatever you want to eat or drink, just order it. It's all taken care of."

"That's very kind of you, and no rudeness intended, but I insist on paying for myself." Achledis said as he handed the lady the coin.

Yurosi shrugged indifferently. "Come, I want you to meet some of the finest gentlemen in all of Seredine." Yurosi said as he prodded him towards the table where the loud group of men still sat talking. A few on one end of the long table had a game of cards going between them; while the others were busy conversing amongst themselves.

"Gentlemen!" Yurosi called out to get everyone's attention. "Meet my friend." He looked at Achledis for assistance, suddenly unsure of his name.

"It's Achledis." Achledis said, waving a hello to the group, "nice to meet all of you."

"Yes, Achledis. He arrived with our friend Desiani; I'm sure many of you remember her." At the mention of Desiani's name, a murmur went about the table.

Desiani approached just then, a bright smile on her face. "Hello everyone," she said.

"Hello." The men chorused at the table.

A man with broad shoulders, who was sitting at the head of the table, stood up and called for Desiani. "Desiani, dear child, you have become so beautiful; come sit by me. There is a lot you have to tell me."

"Alrik, it's good to see you!" Desiani said excitedly as she came into his outstretched arms and returned his embrace.

The men went around the table and introduced themselves to Achledis.

"Tell us lad, where is it that you come from?" A middle-aged man asked.

"I'm from Pavanti, a small village on the Southern border."

"I ran into a couple of guys some days ago, and they too were fleeing the Southern border. They said that they were headed for Caminia and urged me to do the same. They told tales of massacres taking place in the South."

"They weren't tales." Achledis said as memories of the nightmare flooded over him once more. He could see in slow motion as the spear impaled his parents, and the helplessness he had felt back then and still felt now. Achledis forced himself to brush the memories aside and realized that he was sitting with his eyes closed. Everyone around him was silent. When he opened his eyes, everyone was still looking at him with pity.

Yurosi stood and looked around the table before starting to speak. "I haven't been here for too long, but during the time that I was here, I have encountered a lot of refugees from the South. They are all telling the same stories of a Rakirian army making its way North, massacring our people as it goes. It only continues to make my case stronger that it is time for all of us to migrate towards Caminia. The Rakirian army can't breach our defenses there, and it is perhaps the only place where we will be safe."

Achledis stood and looked around the table full of strangers. "Gentlemen, as appealing as fleeing for the safety of Caminia may sound, it isn't the answer. The entire city won't be able to make it to Caminia; besides, what about the others in Rosmir. This murderous army needs to be stopped. We need to rise as one and confront it here at the city gates."

Rolen, a carpenter in Seredine, and a good friend of Alrik stood next. Achledis noted that Rolen was a quiet man and mostly reserved in opinion. "Not that I'm eager for a fight with a professional Rakirian army, because I'm not, but Achledis is right. Not everyone in this city will be able to make the trip to Caminia. Some of us have elderly family that we know for certain won't survive this journey, and I for one will not leave them here to be butchered."

Another man, who had introduced himself as Keltar, stood. "Achledis and Rolen are right. Most people won't be able to make the journey, and those are the people who are the most helpless of all. They are the elderly and the poor. It takes a lot of money to go on a journey to Caminia. Yet I'm very troubled by the idea of rising up to fight a Rakirian army. It would spell certain doom for all of us."

Achledis stood once more. "It may appear that we are doomed either way; however, doing nothing will bring certain doom. Fleeing to Caminia and leaving the helpless behind isn't an option to consider; it would be irresponsible of us. We are all staying here. Now we must consider if we will sit idly by and wait for the Rakirian army to come here and kill all of us like it did in the South. I watched the carnage and the massacre of my parents first hand, and I won't sit idly by. I will stand up and give them a fight, and I ask all of you to stand with me."

"Gentlemen," Alrik said as he stood. His loud voice instantly grabbed everyone's attention. "For over 50 years we have been ruled by Rakiria, and though there has been a lot of injustice towards us, we have never retaliated. This is why I am puzzled by stories of Rakirian aggression. Recently I have been hearing a lot of these stories. Initially, I wrote them off as tales being spread by advocates for Caminian immigration, but now I hear confirmation to those tales from trusted friends, who have witnessed it firsthand. It is clear that we have danger approaching, and we need to prepare ourselves in one way or another."

"Thanks Alrik," Yurosi said as he stood once more. His voice was calm and steady and he spoke as if he was addressing a roomful of scared children. "Gentlemen, the time of reckoning is upon us. We need to make a decision about our future. Do we want safety, or do we want pain? Will we choose suffering and death for ourselves, as well as our loved ones? Can an insurrection against Rakirian authority be the answer?"
The door to the inn opened, and a young man walked in. He was dressed in peasant jerkin and trousers, his face was slightly smudged with dirt, and his hair was tussled. There was nothing unusual about him as he stood and watched the group at the end of the tavern for a few moments, and then still unnoticed, he found a seat within earshot. He listened with keen interest to the

conversation taking place, but the last words out of Yurosi's mouth were all he needed to hear as he got up quickly and hurried back out.

CHAPTER 22: MEETING WITH THE KING

Promptly two hours later, Nepides appeared to escort Vitaeus to the king. As they ascended up the wide circular stairs, Vitaeus took note of the banisters made of hard, polished wood, painted white; which closely resembled ivory. At the top of the stairs, they walked through a vaulted archway a couple stories high that led to a double-door entrance. Nepides knocked on the oak door, and it instantly opened.

"Right this way," the servant said as he led them through a hall with a colorful teal floor and vaulted, arched ceilings of the purest white. The ceilings were supported by pillars painted in a rustic, yellow color. On all four sides of each pillar were white statues of the Creator's celestial beings. The male beings facing north and south; while the female beings faced east and west. They wore nothing except for the crowns of gold on their heads. The servant led them into a smaller room covered with a deep crimson red carpet. The walls in the room were light blue with dark royal blue tapestries. The ceiling was painted in a light golden yellow, and it had a chandelier made of silver that hung from it . On the south side of the room were glass doors from where the sunlight streamed in across the room and reflected off the golden ceiling, basking the room in its warm light. The servant told them to wait while their arrival was announced to the king.

Vitaeus made his way to the large glass doors; which led out onto a large balcony overlooking the Rok Sea. He could see the shoreline of the cliff as it rounded in a bend; this allowed him to see the entire city without walls or buildings to obstruct his view. He instantly felt the sun's scorching rays upon him. Right below him was the massive cliff leading to the crashing waves below. Even from all the way up here, he could hear the sound of crashing waves and smell the salty air. He watched as a flock of birds flew across a pale blue, cloudless sky and the sea gulls below as they circled above the water searching for prey. In the distance, ships could be seen as they sailed past the Caminian coast.

Vitaeus hurried back inside when he heard the servant announcing the King. King Razim was dressed remarkably unceremoniously, yet elegantly. There was no crown on his head, or a royal cloak to signify his rank. Dressed in white linen trousers and a yellow silk shirt, his clothes cost more than the average Caminian made in half a year. As Vitaeus walked up, the King stood straight. His white hair was combed neatly and trimmed, and it contrasted against his tanned and wrinkled face, which had seen a lot of sun throughout the years.

"Your Majesty," Vitaeus said politely.

"Bow before the King," Nepides growled under his breath, but Vitaeus pretended that he didn't hear him.

"Your kingdom is exceptionally beautiful; I was impressed as I traveled from Nitami to Caminia City with most of the things I saw. The wisdom of the King is evident from the laws to the fortifications and commerce that I have witnessed."

King Razim smiled. "You are very kind. I have been blessed with good subjects and excellent geography; which has allowed my kingdom to prosper in peace for half a century, even as other kingdoms have fought numerous wars during that time."

"I heard rumors of a wedding, Your Majesty. May I offer my congratulations?"

King Razim allowed a hearty chuckle to escape. "No secret is a secret for long, I suppose. Nothing official yet; so please don't go spreading it." King Razim glanced at Nepides who stood to the side of the room and waved at him with the back of his hand irritably. Nepides bowed and left immediately; his face having turned a dark maroon color.

"Your Majesty..."

"Please, call me Razim. This is an informal meeting, and I would like to feel normal for once. You not bowing to me was seen as a slight by my aide Nepides, but I rather enjoyed how human it made me feel. So please, let's continue to be informal as best we can. No need for titles but just names. I am Razim, and you are Vitaeus of the house of Konis. So I am told."

The king motioned to a plush chair with sable upholstery as he walked towards the wall and pulled on a rope that clanged a bell. Instantly a servant appeared.

"Bring me and my guest a bottle of golden champagne." As the servant left, the King took a seat across from Vitaeus on a chair with gray-wolf fur. A small table was between them, and that was where the servant placed their wine glasses as he opened the bottle in front of them.

"Tell me," Razim asked, "How does someone as young as you possess so much wealth? Where is it exactly that you come from?"

"I was born in Eastern Rosmir, in the woods of the north country by the sea. A trader used to stop by to purchase furs and furniture that our community made from cedar and pine. My father was the top guild master and was the one behind the designs and quality of the furniture; he was pretty much the front man of the company. Over the years, he and the merchant had become close friends; when my father was dying from an incurable disease, he asked the merchant to take me in and teach me his trade. My father had left me a small inheritance to help get my trading business started, but it was the merchant's death a few years back that left me to inherit all of his wealth. Today I am a young, wealthy merchant that has taken my business from fur pelts and furniture to more exotic and luxurious merchandise; though I grew tired of all the sailing and constant bargaining. I want to establish a base, a home that is safe from threats of piracy and an ever aggressive Rakiria. What I would like is a lordship from his Majesty."

"A lordship?" Razim asked, and as old as he was, he stood and paced the room. "A lordship is earned by proving loyalty and devotion to the crown. It is not something that I can simply give away to any merchant to whom I may have shown simple kindness to."

Vitaeus noted the sharpness in Razim's voice at the end but decided to keep pressing anyway. "Your Majesty, my loyalty and devotion I will show in a short time by becoming Lord of the Shield Islands. I will be able to wield a navy, rather than knights, to help protect Your Majesty's interests in trade. What good are lords with twenty knights when they have never fought in a real battle? They sit at home, never daring to venture outside the safety of Caminia. My ships will prowl the oceans ensuring Caminian interests, your interests My Lord."

"Let me see the rest of your stones."

Vitaeus took out five different pouches; one with diamonds, another contained gems, the third one had rubies, the fourth had sapphires and the last pouch contained a mix of semiprecious stones that were on the merchant ship. He spilled each pouch out individually, starting with the semi-precious stones and ending with the diamonds. The King's eyes were wild with lust as he studied these stones, holding them up to the light from the window. Vitaeus poured himself another glass of champagne, sat back and watched the king become bedazzled with the stones.

"Your Majesty, half of all this is yours at no cost of gold from the royal crown, and for that, I shall be named Lord of the Shield Islands and given all of the finest guild masters for hire to build my new castle, shipyard, and everything else I may need for defenses. I have seen plenty of poverty here in Caminia, along with its wealth I propose to take all the poor and those seeking employment and recruit them to come work and live on my lands, and have the young men become my sailors."

The King eyed Vitaeus suspiciously out of the corner of his eyes as he pondered his request. "I would almost wager that perhaps I am in luck. No proper lord wanted those islands. With the new defenses of Nitami Bay, we realized that we didn't actually need a presence there; so the islands were abandoned. Have you considered the isolation one feels being left on an island, away from the rest of the world?"

"Yes, Your Majesty, but with a navy, I won't truly be isolated. I will have a home in Caminia like I have always dreamed of. The navy will be offering my merchant ships and Caminia protection on the seas, and your kingdom will have more revenue from the taxes that the Shield Islands will produce each year."

Slowly the King started to pull the half piles of stones towards himself until he had a heap of stones before him. A small smile played on his lips as he nodded his head.

"Congratulations Lord of the Shield Islands," Razim said, unable to hold the mirth from his face as he held out his hand.

Vitaeus shook Razim's hand and then motioned at the remaining precious stones. "Your Majesty, perhaps with the rest of these I can also become Lord Duke of Nitami? It already has an established, safe harbor for my ships, and I can transfer timber for my new shipyards with more ease."

The amusement left Razim's face. "Do you know what you are asking?"

"Yes, for the title of Lordship of Nitami, My Lord."

"Do you know who the lord of Nitami currently is?"

"No, but does it matter?"

"If I can't produce a male heir before my death, the lord of Nitami will be your new king. He is someone you don't want to offend."

"Hmm," Vitaeus wasn't aware of that. But even though he couldn't say it, he believed he was destined to become the new king.

"Stay on your islands and don't make too many enemies. This kingdom isn't large, and envy among lords builds strife throughout the whole kingdom. I don't want wars among My Lords. I need the armies strong for possible conflicts outside Caminia's boundaries."

"Your Majesty is wise." Vitaeus said.

"Yes, I suppose you will need lots of gold currency to get your new castle built. Bring the gold!" Razim hollered.

Eight servants appeared carrying two chests, a man on each corner. They set it down before Vitaeus and opened the chests to reveal gold in one and silver in the other.

"Caminia may be one large rock, but it lacks precious stones. However, it makes up for it in its wealth of precious metals. Take this for the rest of your stones, and I will even provide you an army for safe transportation."

The gold and silver shimmered brilliantly, and now it was Vitaeus's turn to be stunned with the wealth of gold and silver before him.

"Thank you Your Majesty."

"Build me that navy you promised." Razim replied as he stood up. The servants stood up and closed the chests. "You will have your own guards at all times when you are here, but it is your responsibility to pay them. In a week, I will announce you Lord of the Shield Islands at a small ceremony."

Vitaeus bowed before Razim as more servants appeared with armed guards in tow. As Vitaeus left, followed by his escort, Razim stood and went to the window where he gazed across the bay to the other side of the city to where his new palace was in its final stages. Though only three stories, its grandeur was unrivaled in all of Caminia. It stood facing the ocean with not so much as a fence to obstruct the view of the magnificent waves smashing against the rocks below. In the center was a magnificent courtyard with a pool that had its mineral water piped from Jade Lake. The palace had been a project for the last ten years, and the building boasted close to a thousand rooms.

At his age, he had come to scorn the thought of going outside his current palace for the simple reason of having to come back up four flights of stairs, and though he was always carried up in his litter, the thought of being dropped frightened him even more. He was always reminded of his age and mortality by the growing frailty of his bones and joints.

Perhaps tomorrow he would take his new guest on a tour of the new palace. He was still trying to figure out the young man, who had shown his ambition, and his success was apparent by his great wealth. Can he rely on his fealty? He was pretty much a foreigner; being Rosmirian was not the same as having been born in Caminia itself. Besides, there was something else that Razim found unsettling; something about the face seemed hauntingly familiar.

In the week leading up to Vitaeus's ceremony, Vitaeus with Nepides's help wasted no time in hiring a council of some of the most prestigious men in their trades. He hired merchants, a former trade minister, builders, and masons, as well as knights and men-at-arms. He sent couriers to all of the towns, cities, and villages throughout Caminia, requesting workers and promising good living conditions for their families and great pay for the workers. Peasants without prior battle training were especially encouraged, with promises of sailing and adventure.

Vitaeus ordered that a new banner be made in time for his lordship ceremony. The banner had a silver snarling northern wolf, with its white fangs gleaming. Nepides chuckled when he saw the drawing made up for it.

"A northern wolf isn't so fitting for My Lord; a school of fish would be more fitting for the string of tiny islands, I think."

Vitaeus was quickly tiring of Nepides's dry and arrogant humor; his envy was obvious. Perhaps he had thought he would get a lordship for his loyalty; instead he just witnessed someone with enough wealth purchase it. Though his resourcefulness had helped Vitaeus seek out all the ministers and guildsman that he would need, Vitaeus was quickly coming to the conclusion that Nepides's usefulness would soon run out. Besides, he didn't like the King's closest aide being with him; it was one less spy that Vitaeus could do without.

Vitaeus needed to find someone that he could trust, whose loyalty he could always depend on, but he knew there was little chance of that. Suddenly he remembered Nepides's words at Hilam Castle, "His Excellency feeds me and my family. He does well by me, and I always seek to help his cause in any way I can." *Yes, that was it*, Vitaeus thought. *Give a man who had nothing wealth and gold, and he may grow more ambitious. But show kindness to a poor man, give him prestige, and provide his family with food, comfort, and security, and he will be loyal.* All noblemen had a heavy price for their loyalty, and their loyalty was only good as long as they kept their lands and titles. In time, he would reveal his true identity and make a claim for the throne, but first he needed a fortress, an army, and a navy. Most importantly, he needed a loyal council.

CHAPTER 23: COURSE OF ACTION

Desiani and Yurosi excused themselves from the table, stating that they needed to go do some shopping. Desiani looked down at her dusty dress for emphasis. "Perhaps a bath at the public baths will do me good as well."

Achledis stood up, "Perhaps I should go too; a bath sounds extremely nice."

"The inn has a bathhouse adjacent to it," Yurosi offered. "Tiram my squire will show you where it is."

"Enjoy your time with the boys." Desiani said with a smile, and as she walked past him, she gave him a playful pinch. "Perhaps you'll even miss me."

"Well," Alrik spoke up, breaking the silence that followed the duo's departure. "We are trying to figure out a way that we can protect our families from the Rakirian onslaught that is sure to come."

A farmer stood up. "Despite Yurosi's reasoning that we should move to Caminia, I want to stress that the road to Caminia isn't necessarily a safe one. The Rakirians don't go further north above Seredine to trade, and so they don't bother placing a lot of troops to protect the trade routes. Gentlemen, there are a lot of bandits on the roads from here to Caminia. Besides, how many of us could afford to buy enough supplies to last the journey? Are we willing to give up our possessions here just to start all over somewhere else?"

"I'm sure our cousins in Caminia will help us stand up on our feet." Another man spoke up.

"Yea right, sure they will," retorted the farmer. "Yurosi talks of how they are free men in Caminia. His father is a Duke, and Yurosi himself is a knight with a manor of his own. Those 'free men' who live in Caminia are poor farmers who live on their lord's lands and are taxed half of their income. Even I don't feel as oppressed by the Rakirians as the farmers up north are. Here in

Seredine, the Rakirians leave me alone to do my business as long as I pay my annual tax to them."

"There have been disturbing reports from Caminia about the plight of immigrants," said another man, "but perhaps Yurosi with his connections can ensure that we end up living in good places."

"I would rather take my chances here. This is my home, and here is where I stay." The farmer said.

"You better hope your chances are real good then because if the Rakirian army arrives here at Seredine, there is no telling what they will do with the populace. If Rakirian actions in the South are any indication of what will happen here, then your chances aren't good at all. May the Creator protect you." The man said.

"Well Keltar, what do you propose?" The farmer asked the man he had been arguing with.

"I suggest Marcus," Keltar replied as his eyes bore into the farmer, "that you sell the livestock that you can't take with you on the journey to Caminia. It's becoming pretty apparent that with this Rakirian army marching north towards Seredine, nothing will be safe here. We better start making plans to leave immediately."

"If we all put our money together, perhaps we can buy a parcel of land in Caminia where we can have our own community as free men and not be obliged to pay burdensome taxes to an arrogant lord." Alrik suggested, and the men around the table voiced their approval for the idea.

Only Achledis didn't voice his excitement as he sat and listened in sullen silence. He was hoping for a fight; he craved the chance to fight the Rakirians. However, these men weren't soldiers; they weren't fighting men. They were civilians with productive trades that sustained their families. They had a purpose in life; while his only purpose was vengeance against Rakiria. He looked about the table, saw their happy faces, and heard their excited chatter at Alrik's proposal. He wished that he could be a part of their excitement; however, his thoughts turned back to that fateful morning. He had felt the gratifying thrill when killing those three Rakirians at their doorstep, and he could still recall the adrenaline pumping through his veins when he saw a multitude of Rakirians coming over the crest of the ridge. He had felt no fear; he hadn't given any thought of the possible consequences or that he would lose his parents that morning. If he could relive that morning, would he do anything different? His mind ran through the various scenarios, but none guaranteed that the results would be any better, that his parents would still be alive today.

"Well mates, our next scheduled meeting is in a week." Alrik's booming voice brought Achledis's attention back to present. "However, I am scheduling another meeting tomorrow at 4:00 in the morning. We have a lot of planning and preparing to do if we are serious about making this move to Caminia."

The public bathhouse was a long one. It was a half story building that encompassed an entire block. The walls were built with yellow mortared brick, and white square pillars ran down in set intervals, supporting the extended roof around the entire building. This bathhouse, blessed with its proximity to the Seredine River, had its own aqueduct, and elaborate pillars supporting the water trough as it snaked its way to the building. The building had three entrances. On one end was the entrance for women, and on the other end was one for men. The center entrance was open to all, but only at night.

It was late evening, and most of the working crowd had left already. Desiani wanted to relax in the water for a bit, but she didn't want to keep Yurosi waiting. As if reading her thoughts, Yurosi inquired how long she wanted to bath.

"Take all the time you need," he assured her. "When I'm done, I will wait for you here by the door."

"Only an hour; so that I can soak my aching body."

"Ok, like I said, I'll be waiting for you right here." Yurosi said with a pleasant smile as he paid the attendant for Desiani's admission. He watched as she disappeared inside before heading towards the men's section.

Inside Desiani was escorted by a female attendant to a private warm shower room. She knew Yurosi must have paid a little more for her to get her own private room with a shower and spa. One end of the spa was lined with showers where women showered nude to get the dust and grime off before entering the large pool of water in the center of the building. Desiani felt the heat protruding from the furnace room as they walked past it; next was the sauna which stood adjacent to the furnace room. Though it was mid-summer, she knew that it would still be packed in there. Saunas were a significant part of the Rosmirian tradition.

The attendee stepped inside the private shower room to make sure that it had plenty of fresh towels and soap. Satisfied, she wished Desiani a lovely shower and left, closing the door behind her. Desiani had never before been inside a private shower room; she always had to use the public one outside where she showered in view of the women in the pool. She held up her new dress that Yurosi had bought for her on the way here and admired it for a moment before putting it aside. She took her dusty clothes off and got in the shower. She pulled the lever overhead and felt the warm water cascade down her body. The water was soothing, so relaxing, in fact, that she just stood and enjoyed the warm water before she took the bar of soap and started to lather her body. Next she reached for the little glass tube of shampoo. This wasn't provided by the bathhouse; it was something else that Yurosi got for her. She cringed as she remembered the expensive price tag on it, but Yurosi handed over the money as if it was nothing. She brought the glass tube to her nose and smelled the sweet fragrance of it before pouring a small amount onto the palm of her hand.

Once Desiani had finished her shower, she decided against the bath altogether. She was already hot, and the bath would make her hotter. Besides she felt clean. She smelled her hair and smiled at the fragrance the shampoo had left behind. She slipped on the new dress and wiped the steamed mirror off with a towel. Spinning on her toes in front of the mirror, she watched the dress twirl. The blue dress made of chiffon seemed to fit perfectly around her body, and she admired herself for a moment. She looked elegant.

Yurosi's jaw dropped slightly as he saw Desiani coming, and she smiled under his admiring gaze.

"I just stuck to the shower," she explained. "Thanks for the private room. I've never been in one of those before."

"You are so beautiful." He said, as he admired her for a moment. "You know, this dress was made just for you. It fits you perfectly, and the color goes really well with your blonde hair."

"You're so flattering." She smiled charmingly, fluttered her eyelashes at him, and then let out a giggle. "You bought it, so thank you."

She looped her arm through his and started to lead him away; so that he would stop gawking at her. It didn't stop the other men from admiring her though, as heads turned towards her as she walked. Yurosi still carried her old dress; which Desiani insisted that he should not throw away. They weaved their way through the throngs of people on the west side of town. Wooden buildings lined both sides of the street, with apartments upstairs and shops on the bottom. A young boy and girl sat on the edge with their hands out, asking for alms. Yurosi stooped down and handed the girl Desiani's old dress and gave them both a coin. The children smiled and thanked him profusely.

"That was very nice of you," Desiani said. "Giving your money is one thing, but being generous with my dress is another." Before he could protest, she held up her hand. "But it's ok; I'm glad you did. Besides, my new dress is prettier."

"Isn't it though? You don't need that dress. I'll buy you more dresses." He said, relieved that she didn't seem to mind him giving away her dress.

The clapping sound of horse hooves and wooden wheels on a cobble street grabbed Yurosi's attention, and he turned just in time to see a lavish horse drawn carriage approaching. Crowds of people dispersed in either direction quickly. With a protective hand around Desiani's waist, Yurosi guided her to the side.

"Where is that fool going? This is a narrow street designed for pedestrians only; no carriages are allowed on it." Yurosi fumed.

"It's a Rakirian; rules don't apply to them." Desiani said dismissively. "Even I remember that from childhood."

"Well, it isn't right." Yurosi muttered.

"Don't get worked up about it..."

The sound of horses approaching from the rear grabbed their attention once more. Looking back, they saw a cavalry of fifteen Rakirian guards on horseback approaching quickly. People scattered to the sides of the narrow street. They either ducked into shops or cringed alongside building walls as the horsemen took up most of the width of the street. Yurosi's hand grabbed Desiani's arm as he tried to pull her into a shop.

"Let go!" She shouted as she pointed at an elderly lady lying on the street with a boy of maybe five yanking on her hand.

Yurosi released Desiani's hand and sprinted in their direction with Desiani right behind. Desiani grabbed the boy in her arms and carried him to the side; while Yurosi stood next to the elderly lady and turned to face the oncoming horsemen. From the side, Desiani watched in horror as she saw the gap between Yurosi and the horsemen close quickly. She held the squirming little boy in her arms and closed her eyes not wanting to see what would happen next.

CHAPTER 24: VITAEUS'S LORDSHIP CEREMONY

The ceremony for Lord Vitaeus was small, given the short notice, yet news had spread like fire throughout the kingdom. Everyone was curious whom this new lord could be; given that no one had ever heard of him. Vitaeus dressed in his best to flaunt his wealth more than anything. He didn't want anyone to doubt his vast fortune; for the one with money often held the power. It was Vitaeus's intent to have those looking for work to gravitate towards him, and for the rest to seek his favor. He put on his Vulcan armor that was as smooth and shiny as silver, with the bluish tinge to the metal. On top he wore a fiery orange cloak made of silk; which flowed when he walked.

"You look magnificent, My Lord." Daenis, his new page, said. He was the one who had to carry Vitaeus's belongings and had shown him to his room in the palace upon his arrival at Caminia.

Outside his dressing room, while the guests were still arriving and settling in, mundane music played. It was quickly starting to wear on Vitaeus's nerves as he was forced to pace impatiently and wait for his cue to walk out. He felt nervous; since he wasn't sure what to expect. There had been no rehearsal prior to the ceremony; as if the King felt it was necessary to go through formal protocol but wanted to get it over with just the same. In the end, Vitaeus felt much the same, yet he knew this was an important time to seek friends and allies here at the King's court. The door opened unexpectedly, and King Razim entered.

"Your Majesty," Vitaeus said in greeting. "I did not expect a visit from you."

King Razim studied Vitaeus's garb and nodded approvingly. "The nobles may complain of your lack of noble blood, but hardly anyone can denounce your wealth."

"Thank you, Your Majesty."

"I have been thinking of your noble proposal to build a navy, and how you plan on taking on the expense yourself if need be. I decided, however, that the royal treasury shall help you. Your cause is noble, and I will also send my own engineers and builders as soon as this new palace of mine is built. I will also pay for the expense and help you with the logistics of sending stone for the building of your fortress. You are, after all, the Shield of Caminia. Serve me faithfully there, and I will promote you by giving you more territory inside Caminia."

"Your Majesty is very kind to me."

"Serve me well Vitaeus, and I will reward you."

"My sword is sworn to the Kingdom of Caminia and all Rosmirian people."

King Razim stepped forward and studied Vitaeus's armor. He let his hand run over the smooth metal and stepped over to the side as he watched the silver turn a bluish color under the light. "This is very beautiful armor. Where did you get it?" The King asked.

"I bought it from another merchant on the other side of the mainland, on the Chain Islands, Your Majesty."

"I must have it."

"I will look into finding one for you, Your Majesty."

"Very well, the commencement is about to begin. I must go take my place," the King said as he departed once more.

Daenis was beaming with a smile that stretched from one ear to the next. "My Lord, the King seems to like you very much."

"Daenis, I like you very much as my loyal servant. Serve me well and with loyalty." Vitaeus said.

"Of course, My Lord." Daenis replied.

Outside, the sound of a long trumpet blast signaled the beginning of the ceremony.

"And now I would like to present to you our newest lord, Vitaeus of the house of Konis, the Marquis of the Shield Isles." The orator proclaimed, and instantly trumpets blasted, and drums began to roll. Vitaeus stepped out of the room. A red carpet had been laid out for him that led all the way to the dais, where the King and his minister sat, and a place of honor was reserved at the

King's right hand side. Vitaeus was momentarily blinded by the bright light because every candle in every golden chandelier was lit, and the candles reflected off the gold trim. He noticed every eye gazing on him; people strained and shoved each other in order to get a better view of this new mystery lord. Vitaeus composed himself before he started his walk, taking large bold strides down the red carpet to mask his uncertainty to the clapping around him. His fiery orange cloak, emblazoned with the silver northern wolf snarling, flowed behind him as he walked. He noticed the fake smiles plastered on some, solemn uninterested looks on others, and envious scowls on the rest. Like King Razim had warned him, envy and strife were quick to follow in a small kingdom like Caminia.

Vitaeus was coached on protocol for this occasion and warned sternly to bow before the King, and so he did. He bowed low, letting his forehead touch the ground, and stayed there until King Razim arose and commanded him to kneel upright.

"Vitaeus of the house of Konis, will you promise to serve the kingdom and the crown as Caminia's newest lord?" Razim asked. A hushed silence hung over the hall as everyone strained to hear the new lord's reply.

"Yes, I promise."

"Arise, Vitaeus of the house of Konis, as Marquis of the Shield Isles and Protector of the Realm." The hall broke out in thunderous applause. The orator waved the guests to silence.

"Well, gentleman, ladies, we have a new lord amongst us. I present to you the great Marquis Vitaeus; please My Lord, tell us of your marvellous deeds that helped you earn your title."

"My fellow countrymen, I am afraid that I don't have any great deeds to speak of, yet I have ambitious ideas that I dream to accomplish. I voiced my desire to our noble King to build a navy in order to better protect our trade and interests on the seas, and he saw the wisdom of that. I am but a humble servant of Caminia and the crown."

"Well said My Lord," the orator replied. "Please tell us about your banner. It seems odd to have a snarling wolf on an olive banner. What prompted such design for the Lord of the Shield Isles?"

"The olive green stands for the peace that I desire, and the snarling northern wolf represents my eagerness to defend it from all who wish to take that peace from us."

The King stood, and everyone fell silent. "I want to congratulate our newest lord and thank him for his ambitious endeavor to build a fortress of Nitami to better protect our only port in the kingdom and to build a navy to protect our ships on the seas. I ask all of the lords to spare some knights, laboring peasants, and servants to Lord Vitaeus's cause, as well as gold from your coffers to the treasury; for this ambitious endeavor will also be a costly one."

Vitaeus saw a young page scurry up to the dais from the side and whisper something in the King's ear. The King's eyebrows narrowed, and he motioned impatiently to the orator and suspiciously glanced in Vitaeus's direction, letting his icy glare linger before being ushered out.

"Lords and ladies, please make your way to the banquet hall where the feast is about to commence. There we will get to know more about our new lord." The orator proclaimed.

The sound of a mass of people getting up at once and heading for the banquet door in an unorganized manner distracted most from seeing the King, surrounded by palace guards, slip out a side exit.

Being the lord of a remote region that wasn't even on the mainland may not have impressed everyone, yet the fact that an unknown man, who wasn't from Caminia, was suddenly awarded the title of Marquis and Lord and Protector of the Kingdom, meant that the man was in the King's favor. All of the lesser lords and insignificant nobles tried to make an impression by donating servants, money, and even material. Some of the significant lords that did show up promised to advertise that Vitaeus was looking for workers and threw some golden coins in his direction. They clearly didn't feel threatened by him or feel the need to impress upon him; that is except for one.

Duke Hilam seemed very interested in Vitaeus's sudden ascent in power and influence. He was the last lord to come up to congratulate Vitaeus at his table.

"Hardly two weeks passed since you were a mere merchant guest at my castle, and now you are a lord, a marquis none the less. This happened so quickly too. Usually the King gives a few months' notice, but with you, it seemingly happened overnight."

"See, I wasn't just a merchant, but a merchant with an ace up my sleeve." Vitaeus commented with a smile.

Hilam smiled back politely, "I never realized that the King even dreamed of a navy. I always figured he was content with the safety of Caminia."

"Our King is more ambitious than anyone around here gives him credit for." Vitaeus replied.

Lord Hilam leaned closer to try and keep his conversation more private. "It's just that the marriage alliance with the Rok Isles was supposed to be the Caminian protection on the seas. Perhaps the Rok princess, who is five times younger than our King, got cold feet; though she is rumored to arrive next week."

Vitaeus noticed that some of the nobility were casting curious glances in their direction and straining to eavesdrop on their conversation; he quickly changed the topic of conversation. "The boy that Nepides brought to you, how is he doing?"

"I gave him food and had his whole family dine at the castle, but the next day they went back to their house. I gave them some coin to purchase wood with; they were such sad company. With Nepides having the boy's brother shot dead, it was hard to make them happy. I think they blamed me for the boy's death simply because of my title."

"Send the boy and his kin to me, along with anyone else who is looking for work or adventure."

"Very well Lord Vitaeus, but I look forward to speaking with you again. You and I are the newest lords in this kingdom; which draws a lot of scorn from the older lords and nobility who think we have no place amongst them. I just want the two of us to look out for one another. In this court, especially, a man needs an ally."

CHAPTER 25: NOBLE YUROSI

Yurosi's face was slightly ashen when Desiani came to him. He had stood his ground, and the Rakirian horsemen had steered around him and kept going, not bothering to stop. He had saved the elderly woman's life because he had planted himself like a pillar in front of her. If he had not been there, there was no doubt that the old woman would have been trampled.

Desiani wept as she saw the little boy stooped down on the ground, hugging his grandmother who was very much conscious at this point.

"Thank you young man; that was very brave and very stupid at the same time." The old woman said as Yurosi stooped down to help her up to her feet.

"Are you hurt?" Yurosi asked the woman.

"I will be all right," the old woman replied with a grateful smile. "In the sudden madness of everyone trying to clear the street at once, I got knocked over, and if it wasn't for you..." Her voice broke as tears ran down her eyes. "My grandson would have been left alone to scavenge the streets for food."

Yurosi reached into his pocket and pulled out a silver coin; which he gave the old lady.

"May the good Creator bless you and your grandson." Yurosi replied as he took Desiani and led her away.

It was getting late in the day, and the sun has already set beyond the city walls when Yurosi and Desiani arrived at the inn.

"Thanks for taking me to the bath house and for the fine dress that you bought." Desiani said.

Yurosi gave her a broad smile; his white teeth showing in the darkness. He had the money to have the finest care, even for his teeth, Desiani thought. Products for teeth care were rare and expensive; whenever it was available.

"You are so beautiful." He replied as he reached out and tucked a strand of her hair behind her ear.

He leaned in closer, and Desiani thought he might try to kiss her. It would be too forward of him, especially for their first outing, but she wasn't sure that she wanted to resist as her eyes closed in an unconscious expectation.

"You smell so good." Yurosi spoke softly.

"What?" Desiani opened her eyes and noticed that his lips were slowly drawing closer to her; gently she pushed him back.

"Just saying," he said with a smile.

"I better get inside." Desiani said, suddenly feeling more reserved.

"Wait," Yurosi called out as Desiani turned to go. "I will come for you tomorrow morning. You need your beauty sleep; so let's make it 8:00."

"Okay, I'll see you tomorrow." She said, her dimples showing in the waning light.

Yurosi smiled triumphantly to himself as Desiani disappeared through the doorway. He always got what he wanted.

It seemed like Achledis had just closed his eyes to sleep when he heard an urgent rapping on the door. Swinging out of bed, he lit the lamp by his bedside and slipped some trousers and a tunic on. The rapping on the door sounded again. He peered at the clock on the wall, and the short and long hands were both just past one. *What could be so urgent at this time of night?* He thought to himself. He slipped a dagger under his sleeve, just in case, and hurried to open the door.

It was a young boy on the other side of the entrance, Yurosi's squire Tiram; Achledis recalled his name.

"I need help!" The boy stammered. "Master Yurosi has just been taken into custody by Rakirian troops. He is being charged with planning an insurrection, a crime punishable by hanging."

Desiani appeared from her room wearing a silk, light blue sleeping gown; her hair was tussled from lying down.

"Is something the matter?" She asked as her gaze traveled from Achledis to Tiram.

"Yes, Yurosi needs our help." Achledis said in a grave voice. "When was he arrested?" He asked the boy.

146

"About an hour ago. I came here right away. I had to tell someone." The boy explained.

"Yurosi arrested? But by whom, and why?" Desiani asked with a worried expression on her face.

"It was the Rakirian city guard. They accused him of being a knight from Caminia who had come here to start an insurrection. They also said that they have many witnesses who will testify to hearing Yurosi say that. He told me that Yurosi would hang for his crimes." Tiram said.

Desiani embraced Tiram and whispered gently, "Everything will be fine. Yurosi has a lot of friends here, and we will figure out a way to help him." Her voice was firm as she looked at Achledis; her eyes commanding him.

"Yes Tiram, we will help Yurosi."

Tiram didn't look very assured as he asked how.

"We will find a way." Desiani replied as her gaze met Achledis's.

"Tell me, what happened yesterday? What did the two of you talk about?" Achledis asked.

"It's not what we talked about; it's what was being talked about right here in this inn."

"I thought everyone in the inn were trusted men?" Achledis replied.

"Not everyone, there was a boy who came in. I thought he was just a curious boy, but it turns out he was much more than that."

"In that case, none of us are safe here. This inn has been compromised, and we need to get out." Achledis said. "Gather your stuff, and wait for me. The men have scheduled an urgent meeting for 4:00 this morning. They took Yurosi's advice about heading to Caminia and wanted to start planning the trip right away. If they come here, they may be walking into a trap. It all depends on what Yurosi tells them and how soon he tells them."

"Relax," Desiani replied. "Yurosi was with me; he wouldn't have known about your scheduled meeting."

"No? Not unless Tiram told him." Achledis replied, and he and Desiani both looked to the boy.

"No, I didn't; I had already fallen asleep when master Yurosi arrived late at night. But Master Yurosi has told me before that he believes that the city watch has been stalking him as of late. He thinks that his apparent wealth may have drawn attention in a city where only Rakirians have money."

CHAPTER 26: FESTIVITIES IN CAMINIA

The city was in a huge celebration of the much anticipated arrival of the Princess Raheena from the Rok Isles. Though Vitaeus had never seen her, he heard much of her fabled beauty from the singers who sang ballads and poets that recited their prose about her. Much was made of her dark hair and olive skin; that was only magnified by her turquoise eyes.

The King had announced a week of games and celebration for the capital city. Yet peasants were brought in from neighboring towns and castles to help with the labor that it took to keep the city running. Farmers were constantly pouring into the city with a fresh supply of meat, vegetables, fruits, and white wine for the great celebration. Magicians and entertainers from all over the realm seemed to descend on the capital of Caminia. Signs advertising a circus that had come to town hung all over town.

Vitaeus watched a tournament taking place as the knights competed with one another in one rink in a single hand combat. Another rink allowed anyone to challenge anyone, and so it was full of lowly men-at-arms and younger men from the country who sought their brief glory. Vitaeus had often dreamed of knighthood growing up. His dreams of honor that only chivalry could bring and the glory of great victories in battle often dominated his dreams. Now he watched this famous class of warriors take turns in fighting one another. Their fighting seemed more staged, and way too gentlemanly to be real. Soon his attention was diverted to the lower class of fighters in the other rink. Most of the crowd was slowly migrating in that direction as well; he realized, as the young men fought one another with nothing but victory at stake.

As Vitaeus made his way to get closer to the action, he was confronted by bawdy women who tried to get his attention with lewd remarks and promises. His escort of guards kept the women away as they cleared a path for him to the front row of the rink. A young man with old scars all over his body and surrounded by an entourage of women stood at the entrance to the rink awaiting his turn. In the rink, two men-at-arms fought one another with cheap swords. The battle ended with the blade of one man slamming into his opponent's shoulder blade and resting there as the loser fell face first into the mud; his blood spouting like a fountain from his neck.

A shout went up among the crowd as the winner stood in the center of the rink with his two hands raised in victory. He was covered from head to toe in gore and dirt. As the shouts continued to ring out, the winner was brought a flagon of water; which he chugged before looking towards his next challenger. The man with the old scars didn't appear too large, but his lean muscles were visible as he stepped forward, wearing a pair of brown trousers that were ripped at the knees. His chest and shoulders had been oiled by the women who stood shouting encouragement at him; even the rest of the crowd grew silent. The winner pulled his sword out of the corpse as he nudged the dead body with his foot, moving it to the side of the rink. The winner was a killer, and he looked like one. While the youth, even with his intimidating scars, appeared to be just a boy before him.

The killer braced his sword while the youth stood solemnly, holding just a dagger in his hand. The place around the rink grew eerily quiet as the onlookers held their breath in anticipation. Vitaeus wasn't sure he could continue watching this butchery take place and wondered to himself how men brought themselves to die as animals for the pleasure of other people's entertainment. This wasn't a battle that would decide the fate of a kingdom or bring glory to a nation.

"Aarrgh!" The killer roared as he drove his blade toward the young man's belly. The youth sidestepped the blade and sent a vicious kick to his opponent's hand; which held the sword. The blade clattered to the ground, and for a moment, all was silent. Then the crowd shouted in excitement when the killer lunged towards the ground, grabbing his blade. As he got up warily, he realized that the youth made no attempt to stop him from reaching his blade. Wincing in pain, he held the sword in his swollen wrist. He advanced slowly towards the young man who continued to stand there almost nonchalantly. This time, the killer was more cautious in his attack as he raised his blade and plunged it down, but the scarred man blocked the sword with his dagger as he stepped forward and delivered another kick into his torso. As the killer doubled over in pain, the youth's foot shot out again, delivering a blow under his chin, and sending him sprawling into the dirt. This time, the killer stayed down on the ground, and the crowd went wild. They had found a new champion.

A passing knight on his way to the knight's tournament paused long enough to witness the youth's victory over the killer, and along with his squire, he made his way to the rink. He stepped inside the rink where the youth was doing a celebratory jig to the crowd's amusement.

"What kind of a fight was that? Are you not man enough to fight with a sword? Take that sword from the dead man in the corner and fight my squire. He will show you how to fight with honor." The knight demanded with indignation.

"Your squire? I don't want to fight your squire; I want to fight you!" The youth declared, and the crowed howled their approval.

"I won't disgrace myself by fighting a dog like you; my squire will cure your insolence."

The youth took the sword and held it awkwardly in his left hand as he faced the squire who braced himself in a proper swordsman's fashion.

"It's in the feet boy," the knight said to his squire. "Remember what I taught you; a swordfight is much like a dance. Let the clang of metal dictate the beat for you, and let your feet dance to the rhythm."

"That sounds ridiculously stupid." The youth laughed, as the knight's face grew red with rage. But he contained himself from making a remark.

The squire was clad in chainmail but otherwise wore no armor; while the youth faced him with an oily bare chest. "How do we fight sir? Till first blood is drawn?" The squire's voice was that of a young man of maybe sixteen.

"Let's fight until you yield." The youth declared. "En garde."

The squire stood in a ready stance but didn't attack right away.

"Is this what you call chivalry? A knight who sends in a scared boy to do his fighting? I will piss on your honor; come and fight me." The youth declared.

The squire charged in, assuming that the youth was distracted, but he spun around, hurtling his body into the air spinning as his feet collided with the squire's body, dropping the boy to the ground. The youth stepped over the squire as if he wasn't there and advanced on the knight. The knight cleared his sword from the scabbard and braced himself for the youth's attack. The youth took the sword that he got from the dead men and tossed it in the knight's direction.

"Now you have two blades against my dagger; show me how you will avenge your honor."

The knight swung the blades in small tight circles, producing a hum, and the chanting crowd grew louder as they yelled in derision at the knight. The youth had no doubt become a favorite amongst the audience. As the knight advanced, the youth started doing a little jig to the excitement of the crowd; then turning suddenly, he threw his dagger at the knight. The handle of the dagger struck the knight's helmet above his eyes, leaving him stunned.

"Have you no honor?" The knight shouted as he attacked, keeping his right foot in front of the left at all times. The youth back peddled in retreat, then suddenly lunged forward, curling his body into a ball as he rolled under the knight's feet and sprang up behind the knight, grabbing his dagger from the ground. The knight whirled around to face the youth, and the youth knocked his helmet off and with his toes scooped the helmet and sent it sailing out of the rink. The knight set of a ferocious attack with multiple swords as the youth parried them with his dagger.

Vitaeus felt someone stand right next to him, surprised how they got past his escort; he looked to see Hilam studying the action in the rink.

"Savage youth isn't he?" He said without looking at Vitaeus.

"Incredibly quick," Vitaeus replied.

"You should recruit him."

Vitaeus glanced warily at Hilam, "For what purpose?"

"So he may train your guards, and perhaps the soldiers for your army that you're recruiting." Hilam replied nonchalantly as he continued to watch the fight below in which Vitaeus had suddenly lost interest. He was only aware of laughter and mockery that came from the crowd, as the youth continued to humiliate the knight.

"Why would you assume that I am trying to raise an army?" Vitaeus asked, a sudden edge in his voice.

Hilam looked Vitaeus dead in the eyes as he replied, "Because I know who you are, and be warned, the King has become suspicious as well. You are always being watched. Some of these guards in your escort may be the King's eyes on you."

"And who am I?" Vitaeus demanded his voice suddenly challenging.

"Quiet down!" Hilam hissed. "Why do you think the King was escorted out in the middle of your ceremony? It's because someone felt the need to show him a portrait of the late King Krepedes. Whispers throughout the kingdom voice that the King is still seeing ghosts fifty years after the royal family's death. You are that latest ghost."

Vitaeus was staring at the action in the rink without seeing anything, but Hilam's warning suddenly jarred him to the present. He saw the youth do another acrobatic maneuver that Vitaeus would have thought physically impossible. Yet, just the same, the youth had his dagger at the knight's throat.

"Sir, we never did clarify if you wanted a duel till death or first blood, or is it the same thing considering my dagger is at your throat?" The youth taunted.

"Let him go!" A voice commanded, and the youth shoved the knight to the ground as he looked at Vitaeus. Vitaeus realized that he was the one who spoke as all eyes were now on him.

"Ahh, our new lord," the youth made a slight bow. "Do you care to join our tournament, perhaps avenge the honor of this noble, whose dignity I have undoubtedly scathed?"

Vitaeus tossed him a gold coin. "Here, you are the official winner; this tournament is now over." The youth bit the coin and pocketed it contently.

Vitaeus tapped Daenis and told him to arrange a meeting with the youth; the boy was someone Vitaeus needed if he could be tamed. That was one thing that Vitaeus couldn't be too sure of.

When Vitaeus glanced to his side where Hilam had been, he realized that the Duke had already left. Everything had suddenly changed. Vitaeus felt vulnerable as Hilam's warning still rang clearly in his mind. What would happen next, he didn't know, but the princess was set to arrive tomorrow. He needed to get a lot of rest until then. The King had scheduled a week of expensive balls in the princess's honor, and all the nobles throughout the kingdom were expected to be there.

CHAPTER 27: PLAN OF ACTION

The diner at the inn was lit by a pair of candles, for too much light would attract suspicion. The candles' flickering light cast shadows across the expanse of the room. Each flicker from the candle made the shadows seem to dance like dark phantoms. The gloomy light was matched with the eerie silence of a dozen men as they sat in stunned silence at hearing Tiram's account of Yurosi's arrest.

"I don't get it." Keltar said. Achledis had come to know him yesterday as an outspoken supporter of Yurosi's plan for Caminian migration. "What exactly did Yurosi say that could incriminate him in trying to start an insurrection? He was the one vying for a peaceful migration out of Seredine to Caminia."

"That could be the insurrection they speak of; perhaps the Rakirians are trying to stem the flow of the fleeing population." Alrik said.

"But of course, if no one remains in this city when Viserate arrives, then whom will he have to slaughter?" Keltar spoke scornfully.

"There was a boy, who looked like a street beggar that came in to the inn when Yurosi was speaking. It could well be that he misinterpreted what Yurosi was saying; because he hurried out of the inn rather anxiously." Achledis said.

"What are we going to do for Yurosi?" Desiani asked as she stepped off the last step and walked towards the group huddling in a small circle in a corner away from any windows. All eyes stared at her, seemingly dumbfounded by her question.

"What can we do?" Asked a man.

"Orchestrate a rescue." Desiani replied curtly. "You can't just allow him to hang."

The men exchanged nervous glances amongst themselves. No one wanted to appear cowardly, not in front of this woman.

"It may seem like a noble idea my lady but not a prudent one." Keltar said.

"Don't call me lady as if I'm some fragile stem of a flower that will wilt away at the first sign of heat. I'm not the one shying away or cowering in fear. I'm the one advocating that we all stand as one in the face of Rakirian oppression. If they torture Yurosi and extract information about all of you and your families, then no one here is safe."

Achledis seized on Desiani's words; he knew it was an opportunity to make the men take action. "No uprising has been planned, but the Rakirians believe that we have planned it. They will more than likely torture any information that they can out of Yurosi. The only information that he has are the names of the men and the woman that he sat with at the table. Yes, we are all in danger, and yes, we need to plan Yurosi's rescue so that Yurosi won't give away our names as co-conspirators. But we need to do more than that. We need to revolt. We must take this city away from Rakirian authority. A Rakirian army is marching to this city, and when it arrives, chaos and terror will reign in this city. This city will be drenched with the blood of its citizens; unless we do something."

"The only weapons in this city are all Rakirian." Alrik spoke. As always, his voice was calm yet strong and commanded respect for the message it carried.

Desiani looked down, not sure what to say. It was true; they didn't have much chance at standing up to the Rakirians, regardless of what Achledis was saying. "I'm sorry, you're right Alrik. I spoke out of passion and not reason; my words were foolish."

"Your words were not foolish, heated and passionate yes, but not foolish." Alrik said reassuringly. "Like Desiani said, we need to have courage, now more than ever; we cannot wilt away with fear. We must stand steadfast against the enemy, and to do that, we need a plan, as much as we need weapons. To come up with a plan, we need information. Each of you will be assigned to scout a section of town. I need to know how many guards there are, where they are, and the time when guards change shifts. We will meet tomorrow, the same time as today, but we will meet at Rustab's stable. The inn isn't a safe place anymore."

The next morning, the group gathered together to discuss their findings. The lack of sleep was evident by the heavy bags under the eyes of all the men. No one attempted small talk, but rather they just sat there and sipped their coffee as they waited for Alrik to start the meeting.

"Well, let's take a look at what we gathered," said Alrik. "Achledis, you were assigned to scout the palace and the best entry point. Show us what you have."

Achledis took out the drawing of the palace entrance and the position of the guards. "There is no easy way to sneak up for the kill." He said. "The palace sits atop of that slight hill with a commanding view and a lot of open space around it, making it hard not to be spotted." He pointed at the two x's he had drawn by the entrance, "two guards by the front gate. Even then, if one of us attempts to sneak up on either one of them, the others will be alerted. That's why; I propose that bows be our weapons of choice. They are silent, and we can take the enemy out from a distance."

Alrik nodded in agreement. "Yes, that would be the idea if we had some decent bows and arrows here and men who knew how to shoot them accurately. If we botch the shots, then all that's going to do is give them notice of our arrival, and the whole attack will be doomed."

"With what are we to fight with?" Asked a man. He appeared to be a newcomer, whom Achledis hadn't seen him before.

The question was followed with a dismal silence. The lack of weapons was like boiling water poured on ice. Suddenly, it didn't matter what kind of intelligence they had because they still needed to address the problem of weapons, or else, all their plans would melt away.

Achledis's face lit up suddenly, "I did hide a crossbow with plenty of bolts, just outside the city gates. We can sneak them in. I have a nice sword as well.

"I will address the issue of weapons later." Alrik said evenly. "For now, let's finish discussing our intelligence."

They continued to look over all the positions that were guarded and planned on how they would take out the guards. Finally, all that was left were the two keeps by the entrance; it was Alrik's location.

"These towers would be almost impossible to take. The guards are always alert, and we would lose too many men if we attempt to storm it. We must make them surrender; to do that, we must conquer the palace and wrench control of the city away from Viceroy Lorne. Now let's address the pressing issue of weapons."

"Where do we get them?" Someone asked.

"We will have to start making them ourselves." Alrik replied. "I can smuggle some in, but not enough for the army that we will need."

"Can we find more people to help us build bows and arrows?" Achledis asked.

"Yes," said Alrik. "We will get Rolen, the carpenter, and a friend of mine to help. He can recruit others as well; he knows all the woodworkers and just about everyone in this town."

"And a blacksmith?" Achledis asked.

Alrik scratched his chin thoughtfully. "There are only a few of them in the entire city, and they are all paranoid. I tried to convince them to help out before, but they were unwilling to risk their careers. Their heads could also end up on the chopping blocks."

"We are all taking a risk here," Achledis replied hotly. "Just by discussing a possible revolt is cause for our heads to be placed on a chopping block. If they don't want to help willingly, then we will force them to help. Either way they will help. We are going to need arrow tips and swords."

"Achledis, where do you propose to get the metal for all of these weapons? They have a limited amount of metal. We might have enough for arrow heads, but swords I doubt," Alrik said.

"Let's gather all of the metal items in the city that we can get our hands on: pots, pans, shovels, hammer heads, nails, plows, and kitchen knives. Anything that's metal can be melted down and made into weapons. We can assign all the men that the blacksmith needs to help him hurry the work along." As Achledis finished talking, Alrik looked at him. There was a glint of a challenge in his eyes before he brushed it aside and nodded his head at Achledis.

Alrik cleared his throat loudly, and everyone turned to hear what he had to say. He took a deep breath as if he was about to reveal a big secret. "I know of a weapons cache outside the city walls. There are about 100 swords, shields, pikes, and bows with 2 dozen arrows per bow."

"And you didn't want to tell us about this before, why?" Asked one of the men in the group.

"It's an important secret, and there was no need for you to know until the moment came. The moment has just come." Alrik retorted hotly, as if stung that someone would question him and his authority. "Besides, I did say that I would smuggle in some weapons; however, we are still far short of what we will need."

"Hide it underneath all the hay; which we will be bringing in for the stables." One of the men suggested.

"And if it is discovered?" Alrik asked.

"There are two guards at the entrance outside. They are the only ones that are responsible for checking; we can overtake them and kill them," Suggested a man.

Alrik scoffed at the man, "None of you are trained to overtake a professional soldier. Besides, once you kill the guard, it won't take long before someone discovers that his post is deserted."

"Perhaps if we clear all the guards around the battlements and keep, we could sneak them all in at night." Marcus, the grizzled middle-aged farmer, suggested.

"Still, we lack the weapons and manpower to clear the keep and the battlements without taking heavy losses, and the warning bells will open up a hornet's nest." Alrik said, his voice sounding irritable as he busied himself studying the map of Seredine. He slapped his palm against the table and the chatter ceased. "The battlements on the west are narrow, and they only have two guards guarding that whole wall. We will take them out in the cover of the night and transport the weapons down the river and right up to the wall. Our approach won't be noticed, and we will hoist all the weapons up and over the wall, arming our entire garrison for the mission..." Alrik was cut short as Desiani ran into the diner wide eyed. She made for the group of men right away. Her breath came in short rasps as if she had been running, and the fear still ebbed on her face. Taking a deep breath, she tried to compose herself to speak.

"Yurosi!" Gulping more air, she continued. "He was charged with treason and will be hung at noon at the gallows in a couple of days."

"You are sure that his execution is set to be held at noon in two days?" Alrik asked.

"Yes, they are hanging banners all over town announcing it."

Alrik nodded his head thoughtfully. "Then we must move fast. Tonight, right after midnight, we will bring the weapons in, have the men assembled here and ready for action. In the meantime, here is the plan..."

CHAPTER 28: PRINCESS RAHEENA

The great hall of the old palace was a massive room; its ceiling stretched to the third floor. There was a small circular staircase on either side of the hall that led to a balcony upstairs. The walls, pillars, and ceilings were all white, with gold trim separating them from each other. At the far end of the hall was a dais with an empty golden throne. The stairs and the throne were covered in a crimson velvet tapestry with a golden three-headed serpent embroidered on the center of the throne. The king and the princess sat at a table in front of the dais; their table was raised higher than the rest of the tables.

Vitaeus had come in when the party had already started, and though the eating and drinking were already under way, the dancing had just begun. Vitaeus was dressed in a gentleman's clothing; which consisted of tan leather pointed shoes, white breeches, and his gray cloak with a blue surcoat on top. Atop his head was a black hat with a gray and blue feather.

Immediately, he headed in the King's direction, making a slight bow as he approached.

"Greetings to my King, and I am honored to meet his new bride." The girl of seventeen was beautiful; anyone could see that,. Her jet-black hair was pulled back into an elegant braid. Her dark olive toned complexion and a face as smooth as silk was set apart by her most beautiful feature, her turquoise eyes. The teal dress that she wore made the color of her eyes even more distinct. The dress hung limply on the edge of her shoulders; while around her neck, she wore a necklace of precious stones, stones that Vitaeus had sold the king.

"My lady, for once the singers and poets where correct, but even they couldn't portray your true beauty." Vitaeus accepted the hand that she held out to him and kissed it gently.

"And who are you My Lord?" She asked, revealing pearly white teeth that contrasted against her olive skin.

"I am Lord Vitaeus of the house of Konis, my lady." Vitaeus looked at the King, "Your Majesty, may I ask the lady for a dance."

Raheena looked at the King, who smiled back at her before giving Vitaeus a nod of approval; though his eyes suggested otherwise. Vitaeus took Raheena by the hand and led her to the dance floor. He was vaguely aware that all eyes were on him and the princess, though more on the princess. Their eyes of envy and resentment could be spotted as well. Like true royalty, the princess carried herself with her shoulders arched back and her chin up, but it was her smile that made her seem to glow. As they approached the dance floor, the song that was playing suddenly stopped, and the musicians took up a new tune with a more upbeat tempo just for them. They danced to the music with a lot of energy, spinning and floating across the dance floor. As their chemistry increased, their choreography also grew in complexity. Soon Vitaeus was feeling bold enough to dip Raheena. He would then lift and twirl her, letting her land nimbly on the floor. Her laughter and smile captivated him, and he could see that she was also enjoying herself. After the first song, they stayed on the dance floor for the next one, a song much slower than the first. Vitaeus was suddenly acutely aware of her warmth, the smell of her perfume, and the bliss he felt as he held her.

"My Lord, you are much too bold to dance with me the way you just did; it might arouse the King's jealousy."

"Nonsense my lady, you saw the King nod his approval to my request to dance with you, and if he isn't going to take his bride-to-be on a dance at a ball, then I should."

Raheena kept her eyes on Vitaeus. "Yes, I'm glad you did; for I was coming to dread my new life."

The music stopped, and Vitaeus saw the King approaching the two of them. Courteously, Vitaeus kissed Raheena's fingers. "Thank you for the dance my lady."

Raheena smiled back at him, "Thank you, My Lord," she whispered.

The King took Raheena by the hand, and everyone cleared the dance floor. With big beautiful eyes, she looked up at the king, keeping her smile plastered on her face. The king smiled when he looked down at her, and the two started a slow dance.

As Vitaeus watched Raheena dance with the King, a servant came up and offered him a glass of white sparkling wine. Vitaeus took it nonchalantly and continued to watch the young princess fulfilling her duty. He pitied her; even more, he felt as it was his noble duty to rise to the occasion and rescue her from her predicament. *Where was the fairness in this world? How can a young, beautiful girl be subjected to a marriage with an old man without a single protest from anyone around.* Vitaeus wondered. He suddenly realized that he was standing amongst Rok nobility.

"When is the wedding date set for?" He asked a Rok prince.

The Rok prince looked at him strangely, "It hasn't been set yet. It is for our princess to decide if she will agree to the marriage."

"Why would she agree?" Vitaeus wondered aloud.

The Rok prince smiled back at him. "Politics," he replied.

"When do we know if she agrees?"

The prince looked at him knowingly. "She will agree, but she will formally announce her decision at the last ball."

Vitaeus was aware of a few female eyes gazing at him, waiting for him to ask them to dance; as the general dance had once again resumed. His eyes wandered to the King's table, where the princess sat beside the King once again. He watched her down a whole glass of wine. A lord came up and asked her to dance but was instantly shooed away by the King. The lord walked off hastily, his eyes to the ground; his face portrayed a man with wounded pride. Princess Raheena glanced up at the King momentarily and quickly resumed her gaze across the room.

Vitaeus walked over to where his seat was supposed to be reserved, but instead he found himself surrounded by five palace guards.

"What is this?" Vitaeus demanded as one of the guards nudged him towards the door.

"We received orders to escort you out; your presence is no longer welcomed." The guard said.

"Fine, I will go on my own accord; just let go of me." Vitaeus said as he shrugged the guard's grip off him and hurried towards the door as onlookers gawked at him. Just outside the great hall, Vitaeus paced; suddenly very aware that his welcome in Caminia was quickly coming to a close. The palace itself felt like a prison where the King had his spies watching him, always. He had no one that he could truly trust. He still tried to figure out the King, who had initially appeared so hospitable, but was quickly making it clear that his welcome was overstayed.

Vitaeus remembered Hilam's words of warning once again. "Because I know who you are, and be warned, the King has become suspicious as well. You are always being watched. Some of these guards in your escort may be the King's eyes on you." Vitaeus's better judgment told him that he should leave and build himself a loyal army. From the Shield Isles, he could plan better; *yes*, he decided he would have to leave soon.

"Sir, perhaps you could show me where the garderobe is?" A sweet, feminine voice asked, a voice Vitaeus recognized. "Please excuse the rude question, but I really have to go." Princess Raheena continued as she stood at the crossroads where the hall split to the left and right.

"My princess, you shouldn't go to that garderobe beside the banquet hall. Come, I will show you another that would be more suitable for a princess."

She smiled back, "Thank you, I was wondering where you had left to. Are you bored with the ball My Lord?"

"No, I was notified that I was no longer welcome, my lady."

"The King did seem irritated. Somehow I fear that it was our dancing that put him in a sour mood."

"Well the king has no reason to be sour with me. Don't worry princess, I will be all right. Here is the garderobe."

She smiled. "Thank you My Lord, will you wait for me?"

"Of course."

Vitaeus relished the little bit of time he got with the princess. He was getting a sense that the King would make sure that he wouldn't be running into her anytime soon, if at all.

She came out smiling, "Thank you for waiting sir."

Vitaeus gave her a slight nod and smiled. "My pleasure. How does the princess like Caminia?"

"It's a beautiful city. Its streets are clean, and its gleaming white walls seem to shimmer in the sunlight." She replied. "Now I know why the sailers from back home always described it as having a halo around it. As our ship sailed up, we could see the glow of light reflecting off the walls far before we could see the actual city." She paused, a thoughtful look across her face. "Yet, I would love to see the city from a resident's perspective. I feel robbed of that experience when I have a whole entourage of guards riding next to my litter."

The two had walked in silence for a moment before Raheena asked him, "And you My Lord, have you come from far away, or do you reside in this city as well?"

"For the moment, I'm staying here until my castle is repaired; then I must leave."

"Hmm, too bad. I was growing fond of having a friend here." She gave him a sad smile.

"I have a feeling that the King doesn't approve of our friendship and will try to prevent us from seeing each other. I don't expect to receive another ball invitation from the King." Vitaeus said.

In the silence that followed, Vitaeus became fully aware that they were nearing the great hall, and he somehow wanted to extend his time with the princess, even if for a moment. He thought of what to say.

"Wait," Vitaeus stopped, and Raheena looked up at him.

"What is it?"

"I was just thinking of what you said about not getting a resident's feel for the city as you're always hidden away in a litter. I thought perhaps you could come with me tonight, and we could explore the city together. At night time, it may be more serene than the usual day life; so that may not make it as authentic, but..."

"I would love to, but what if we are caught."

"Let's not get caught. Dress up as a servant girl, in riding pants. I will see you outside the palace after one."

"Will we be safe? Should I take the Rok guards along?"

"No, that would be an instant giveaway. Servant girls don't take guards with them, but to answer your question, yes. You will be safe." By this time, they had arrived back at the banquet hall. "Farewell princess, I will see you at one o'clock, tonight."

She smiled. Vitaeus smiled back. Achledis would have been proud of his boldness just then. He was emulating his old friend more and more.

CHAPTER 29: PREPARING

It was a dreary night. Cool drops of rain spattered on the guard's armor, coupled with a chilling breeze; which seemingly found its way through the chinks in the armor to his skin. The guard cursed under his breath as he huddled on the battlement wall overlooking Seredine River. There hasn't been a threat of invasion to this city in over fifty years, and with the country firmly in Rakirian hands, it wasn't likely there would be one.

When he enlisted to serve in the Rakirian army, it was out of a sense of duty to an empire that kept his family safe and happy. He hadn't expected to be a sentry in this northern land. He had been dreaming of combat in one of the southern campaigns instead. A life of combat and glory is what he expected, but it never turned out that way. He sighed as he thought about it now. It no longer mattered where he was stationed; he just wanted to go back home. *Just have to finish out this year*, he told himself. *And then I can go back to my little Arsela and our child.* In a letter he received from his wife, she wrote him that she got pregnant after his last visit. He hadn't received any more letters since, but counting the months, he knew that by now she should have given birth. He prayed that the gods had honored him with a strong and healthy little boy.

Thoughts of home had warmed him significantly, but as the intensity of the rain increased, his thoughts were brought back to his bleary state. He glanced over to his left, where the second sentry was supposed to be patrolling further on. But with the rain coming down in sheets and the lights on the torches sputtering like they were, the guard couldn't see more than five feet out anyway. Just then, a flash of lightning lit up the world around him, and thunder struck close by, making the guard jump uncomfortably. With his nerves settled once again, the guard realized almost as an afterthought that he had seen something in the river that grabbed his attention even in that moment of shock. Thinking back, he realized that it resembled a raft. As his memory of it started to become more vivid, he realized that he must have seen the silhouettes of at least two people on board. His pulse quickened at the prospect, and the hair on his back seemed to stand on end. It instantly crossed his mind that someone was trying to enter the city undetected, and as the realization hit him, he shuddered involuntarily. The chilly air and the bite of the wind seemed to seep into his bones, and he couldn't stop his body from shaking.

Leaning his head over the battlement, he peered into the darkness below, "Is anyone out there?" He shouted. All he heard, however, was the continued pattering of rain. Then hearing some indistinct noises behind him, he spun around to where the sound had come from, his hand dropping to the hilt of his sword. Out of the darkness, a shadow formed as it came charging at him. The guard yanked at his sword, but it was too late. He was knocked to the ground, and a cool steel blade was at his throat. His life and dreams flashed before his eyes as the blade swiped across his windpipe, and he was left gasping for air that didn't seem to come.

With both guards on the battlement out of the way, Keltar seized the torch and started to wave it side to side, giving the signal to Alrik and Desiani that the battlement was clear. Desiani had decided to go with Alrik and retrieve the weapons that Achledis had hidden before entering the city.

"Well toss that rope down, you dimwit," he heard Alrik's snarl over the sound of the rain. In response, a rope thumped across his face, and Alrik busied himself tying it to the crate of weapons. Achledis, followed by five men, ran up the battlement to where Keltar was waiting for Alrik to tie the crate down. He had gone to ensure that the keep on the west side of town didn't pose a threat, and finding it empty, he returned.

The seven men hoisted up the heavy crate filled with iron weapons. After they had gotten the first one up, they dropped the rope down three more times, with the load being significantly lighter each time; as the weapons went from iron swords to wooden bows. Finally, Desiani and Alrik were brought up.

"Took you guys long enough. I thought I would have to wait till dawn," Alrik grumbled.

"Be glad you didn't," Keltar retorted.

Achledis gave Desiani a friendly embrace and whispered in her ear that he was relieved to see her safe. She gave him a playful punch in return.

"Leave the games at home!" Alrik hissed at them. "We need to get out of here."

"See, now Alrik is mad at me, thanks to you." Desiani said.

Achledis, seeing Alrik's irritation, decided not to say anything. Instead, he stooped to pick up one end of the crate, and Alrik grabbed the other end. They carried it down to a horse drawn cart that was waiting for them. This late at night, the streets were nearly empty, and with the heavy rain, the guards chose to stay someplace where it was warm and dry. The convoy of weapons made it back to the inn unhindered.

Inside the inn, the air was hot and heavy from the multitude of people working. Sounds of saws and chisels filled the pungent air which reeked of wood, sweat and... Alrik wrinkled his nose as he walked by where a man was stirring a pot of glue made mostly from animal tissue. In the next station, workers were chiseling and filing bone to shape it into arrowheads and spear points.

Rolen and his apprentices were walking around and supervising the work. Seeing Alrik, Rolen walked over to him immediately, relieved to see his friend's safe arrival.

Alrik nodded at Rolen with a smile of approval on his face. "Good work my friend; the turnout is better than I could have imagined."

"It's good to see you safe." Rolen responded. "Did we get the weapons?"

"Yes, Keltar and Achledis are in the stable arming the men."

"Alrik, the timing for this revolt couldn't be better. When I told my apprentices, they got so excited, and we started the word of mouth campaign, telling people we trusted. To our amazement, the people are as eager as we are to overthrow

Rakirian rule. Whom you see here are the most diligent of patriots working together for the common purpose of obtaining freedom for all and are willing to give their lives in the struggle to achieve it."

Alrik was stirred with passion. "When I leave, tell them how pleased I am, to have friends and countrymen like them."

Inside the stable, the air was charged with a nervous tension as the seventy Rosmirian rebels anticipated the upcoming battle. Some were silently inspecting the weapons given to them; others were practicing swinging the short swords in their hands. Achledis watched as most of the men didn't even know how to use the weapons that they held. Each man tried to swallow the lump of fear in his throat at the thought of what was about to face him.

The rebel force was by far short of the Rakirian forces, but Alrik believed that it would be enough if they maintained the element of surprise. Every man was armed with a short sword, buckler, and a dagger. Twenty men carried spears and shields, and the other fifty had bows with half a dozen arrows. The recurve bows were of a good quality, reinforced with ram horn, and carried a powerful propulsion of force behind the string. It would also require a lot of strength for the archers to pull the string back, and not all men present were physically able for such a task. In order to select the archers, Achledis ordered the men to string theirs bows. The ten that failed to do so were asked to step aside. Next, Achledis ordered the men to pull the string back to their ears. He grimaced when only about seventy-five percent of the men pulled the string the whole way back. Another ten were taken from the group. That left him with thirty archers, and twenty new short swordsmen.

Alrik came in, followed by Rolen and Keltar, looking around the stable at the men; his face grew grim at the sight of the recruits. Achledis noticed his expression and asked. "Well, what do you say captain?"

Alrik snorted. "As essential as surprise is to this attack, we will need lots and lots of luck to succeed."

Tonight Achledis had seen another side of Alrik; one that seemed to be in constant irritation with the burden of leading the rebellion. It was as if he was a completely different person than the one he met on the first day. The stable slowly grew silent, and the fidgeting and shuffling stopped, as the men noticed Alrik's presence.

"Men, it is with great honor that I lead you into the battle for freedom this night. The Creator seems to favor us by sending a storm; which will be a vital ally to us. I want to ask you if you are ready to fight." Alrik's voice boomed.

The men responded back with enthused shouting. Alrik raised his hand once more, and the chanting died down. Before Alrik could speak, a voice in the back called out, "We have weapons, but where is our armor for protection? Our enemies are sure to be better trained, better armed, and they will be protected by armor. Without armor for protection and fighting against professional soldiers, what chances do we have?"

"You're concerned for your protection?" Alrik boomed back angrily; his face twisting in rage as he looked around the room as if daring someone else to speak out. "If anyone here was under the impression that this job was safe, then let me dispel that notion. This is going to be a dangerous job, with a good chance that most of us are going to die. But that's what we all signed up for. If you're a coward and can't stomach that risk, then go and work with the women inside."

"No sir! We signed up to fight and die, if we must." A man in the front yelled, and there was a chorus of agreement.

Alrik held up his hand for silence, and the men grew quiet and got ready to listen intently once again. "Good, that's what I want to hear; those who can't stomach the risk should leave now. I need brave men who will stand by one another to the very end. Though outnumbered roughly five to one, stealth and surprise are our two biggest allies, and they are essential to our success." Alrik paused, allowing his words to sink in. "Gentlemen, we cannot afford to fail; for the consequence of failure is too great. In a month's time, a Rakirian army will be here. This army is rumored to be burning towns and villages as they march through our land.

They are killing the old, raping our beautiful women, and enslaving the rest of us. How would any of you like to serve in the Rakirian army, to fight, bleed and die for their empire? I would rather die than be captured alive or live with the guilt of knowing that I never stood up for our pretty girls and our beloved people as they were raped and killed."

The men shouted in agreement and stomped on the floor with their boots in excitement. Alrik knew that the time has come as he saw them charged with energy and adrenaline; they were ready to charge to their death if the command was given.

CHAPTER 30: MIDNIGHT ADVENTURE

The skies were covered with clouds; however, the light of the moon still penetrated through them, giving off enough light to make out the streets. The masses had long cleared the streets, leaving the city in an eerie silence; though only a few drunks were still sleeping it off on the streets, curled up against buildings in an attempt to merge with the facade. Vitaeus was going for a ride with the Rok Princess. Just thinking of her and remembering her beauty, her touch, and her smell gave Vitaeus comfort and made him smile, yet he felt uneasy. A sense of danger mingled with excitement; this was something his friend Achledis would usually do. Yet Achledis was nowhere around. This was Vitaeus's own adventure. If he was caught, he would become an instant enemy to the King, even more so than now.

The clopping of his horse on cobble streets echoed against the empty roads and stone buildings. His fingers wandered to the pommel of the Vulcan sword at his hip, and his fingers flexed around the handle reassuringly. Besides the drunks scattered across the city, he hadn't come across any patrols of the city guard; which seemed strange considering the recent festivities.

Vitaeus purposely didn't go straight to the new palace, but instead took a few detours as a precaution. Just in case he had a tail; so he would shake it off. After all, he had been warned that the King ordered a pair of eyes on him at all times. He hadn't gone far down a side street, when he thought he heard footsteps behind him. When he turned around, however, all he saw was darkness. Still he waited, hoping to catch a glimpse of some movement. Still nothing, his horse whinnied impatiently and stomped its hooves. As Vitaeus prodded his horse forward, it whinnied nervously as a shadow skirted alongside a building and disappeared into the blackness.

"Come out whoever you are; show yourself." Vitaeus called out.

The loud sound of silence was all that answered. Vitaeus nudged his horse into a trot and rode a few blocks before taking a left and riding a few more blocks; then he took a right and slowed down to a walk. Finally, he tied his horse in front of a large building on an open street and slunk away into the shadows.

He waited for a good twenty minutes before he first heard the soft padding of feet; the shadow peered in both directions before stepping out into the open street. At the sight of the horse, he instantly got down and edged closer to the buildings, staying in the shadows. On occasion, Vitaeus would lose sight of the stalker, but he always reappeared. Slowly, Vitaeus started to move in on the shadow. He had to hurry his pace after the stalker realized that the horse was without a rider, and the stalker started to look around uneasily. Vitaeus stayed low in a crouch position, moving slowly against the shadow of a building. Suddenly, a pebble skirted from under his feet, rolling and clattering as it went across the cobbles. The assailant looked right at him, and Vitaeus charged him. The stalker ran in the other direction, trying to get away, with Vitaeus in pursuit. The distance between him and the shadow closed quickly, and when the man realized that he was caught, he slowed down, yanking at his sword. Vitaeus barreled into him, knocking the man to the ground and held his dagger to the goon's throat.

"Who are you, and why are you following me?"

The man stayed silent; his face half hidden by his dark cloak. Vitaeus pealed the cloak aside to reveal his trusted aide.

"Daenis!" Even in the murky light of clouds hiding the moonlight, Vitaeus could see the fear in Daenis's eyes. "You have a minute. When it passes, so does your chance to explain yourself."

"Ahh, I, but," He suddenly drew his breath and exhaled slowly to calm himself. "I was commanded to follow you and report back on everything I saw, but I wasn't going to tell them the truth. I always make up a story for them; I never tell them what you actually do. Please," Daenis whispered, "I want to live."

"And who sent you?"

"Nepides sir. Sir, I haven't told you because I was afraid, but there are rumors among the servants of the palace that the King doesn't trust you. Very odd, considering he just gave you a lordship, but just today in the kitchen I overheard from the King's personal chef that he overheard the King discussing the new lord with someone. The King said that as soon as the Rok representatives leave, he has ordered that you disappear. For your own safety, My Lord, you should go to the Shield Isles and take me with you."

"Why should I take a traitorous spy with me?" He asked sternly.

"I'm not a real spy My Lord, but I had to obey because I'm afraid. The King has already condemned my father to a lifetime in the mines for disobedience, and I'm afraid of the same fate. I go to bed fearing that I have made a mistake that day, and wake up in fear that I might make one that day that would ensure the same fate as my father, if not worse. King Razim had said that hard work in the mines would be the just punishment for my father's laziness when he didn't complete his task. Please, My Lord."

Vitaeus put his finger on Daenis's lips to hush him. "Don't talk so loud. Now tell me what task was it that your father didn't complete that angered the king so?"

Daenis looked around nervously, then shook his head. "I shouldn't say My Lord; it's dangerous knowledge. If the King thought that I knew, I would be dead already; however, no one knew that the man condemned was my father. To everyone's knowledge, I was a bastard boy growing up in the palace whose mother died while giving birth to me."

"Very well, I will take you with me, and as long as you earn my trust, I will help you prosper alongside me. But if you keep anything from me again, I will throw you off the cliff, into the sea."

Daenis, with his big fearful eyes, raised his head and nodded.

"Okay, you can get up now." Daenis got up and hesitantly turned to go, but Vitaeus grabbed him once more. "How did they know that I was going for a ride tonight?"

"My Lord, I don't know where they got the information, but when I first entered Nepides's office, I overheard Nepides giving orders that a regiment be stationed outside the new palace."

"Is there anything else that you want to tell me?" Vitaeus asked as he glared at Daenis sternly.

Daenis thought momentarily. "Yes, I almost forgot; this was brought to me by one of the Rok servants." He reached into his pocket and withdrew a letter. "I was told to give this to Lord Vitaeus."

Vitaeus read the note, *tonight the horses rest,* was all it said.

"Did you show this note to Nepides?"

"No, My Lord, I received it right after talking to Nepides, and with the conversation I had with Nepides still troubling my mind, I forgot to give it to you."

"What will you tell Nepides that you saw today?" Vitaeus asked. His voice came off harsher than he had intended.

"You rode around the city and gave coins to the people sleeping on the streets."

"These drunks you mean? Good, you tell him that. Now go."

Vitaeus waited until Daenis had disappeared before he rode again. As he rode into the plaza in front of the new palace, Vitaeus could see the shadows of two guards at each entrance and men on horseback riding to and fro in front of the palace. The note Daenis gave him was clearly from Raheena herself. It would be close to impossible to sneak through so many guards, and certainly not worth the risk.

Vitaeus awoke, with morning light blazing in his palace guest room. He peered at a clock on the wall; it read 8:00. That's when he noticed Daenis standing to the side, looking rather hesitant.

"Sir, I didn't mean to wake you," he whispered, as if not daring to speak loud for fear of waking Vitaeus further.

"Speak up Daenis; I'm awake regardless of what you intended."

"I just wanted to let you know that I have received a summons to meet with Nepides, sir."

"Great, deliver something from me, will you?" Vitaeus swung out of bed and grabbed a parchment paper that lay on the table addressed to the King. Last night, in his irritation at learning of the spies all around him, he scribbled a letter to the King thanking him for his hospitality and informing him that he felt that he had already overstayed his visit.

"Sir, won't Nepides be suspicious if I bring a letter from you to him at this moment? Will he suspect that you have knowledge of my summoning?" Daenis asked hesitantly.

"I don't care what he suspects. Tell him that you don't have time to speak to him, and that I have other duties for you right away. You and I have a busy day today; so come right back." Vitaeus handed him the paper sealed with the silver wax and imprinted with his wolf sigil.

Daenis bowed courteously as he received the parchment and hurried out. Vitaeus stared after him long after he left. He had spotted a deserted keep on the other side of Jade Lake on his arrival to Caminia. Only now did he realize that it must be his base for the remainder of his stay here. His enemies were many, and his friends were few. The King himself, who just a week ago had rewarded him lordship, was quickly becoming an open foe. Vitaeus feared that if he didn't move swiftly, his time on this fair planet would soon run out.

Vitaeus donned on his Vulcan armor and put on his sword where the blade was free of its scabbard. Unlike most swords, this one wasn't oiled, and it didn't need to be. Vitaeus had read in the Vulcan journal that Vulcan steel didn't rust, and he witnessed that himself when he drew the dagger from a pool of water. Vitaeus had no way of knowing how long it had been there but close to half a century for sure. Vitaeus had read about many more miraculous inventions; which the explorer had documented in his journal. It excited Vitaeus to one day build them and use them when he became the ruler. He was Vitaeus, the first of the royal house of Arkonis, the rightful heir, and the destined ruler to the throne of all of Rosmir.

Vitaeus got the rest of his stuff ready and prepared to leave, yet Daenis still hadn't returned. Vitaeus started to pace impatiently as he waited and waited; after a couple hours went by, Vitaeus's patience was gone. He locked his room on the way out; though it hardly mattered because if Nepides wanted to snoop, he was sure he had a spare key to get inside his room.

Vitaeus barged into Nepides's sprawling apartment inside the palace. His officer at the door tried to block his path, but Vitaeus drew steel threateningly and walked passed him undeterred. Nepides's office was to his immediate left, with a large luxurious, waiting room for his visitors. At the moment, the waiting room was empty. The waiting area had plush leather couches and an ivory table between them. Permedian rugs sprawled across the stone floor, and the walls were covered with murals of nature, particularly birds. At the center of the far wall, the first thing that any visitor saw was a picture of a snake with three heads emerging from the same body; each head resembled a wolf, a lion and a bull.

"Who is out there? I said no visitors!" Nepides yelled from his office.

Vitaeus walked into his office and shut the door behind him. Nepides looked up at him startled. "What is the meaning of this? I am the King's most trusted servant. How dare you just walk in here like this?"

Vitaeus drew his dagger and held it in front of Nepides's face. "I dare, because my most trusted servant hasn't returned after I explicitly told him that I needed him right back; that is why I dare."

"Well, that's between you two; isn't it?"

Thump! Vitaeus slammed his dagger handle down on the desk so hard that the candle sputtered. "No, I fear it's between you and me; so I am going to give you a chance to explain quickly where he is and why?"

Nepides's eyes were fearfully wide as he eyed the dagger. "You wouldn't dare," he whispered.

"Wrong answer." Vitaeus pinned Nepides's hand to the desk and placed his dagger against his little finger.

"No! Fine I will tell! I will tell!" Tears shimmered in Nepides's eyes and sweat glistened on his face, but Vitaeus didn't let go of his hand.

"Then tell, quickly."

"He, he has been sent away on the King's orders."

"The King's, or yours?"

"The King's."

"Liar!" And the dagger bit into Nepides's skin.

"No! Please don't! Please, I will tell you; just let go of my hand, please sir."

"I need you to be more truthful and forthcoming. Tell me everything, and don't make me ask unnecessary questions.

"I was ordered by His Majesty to send him to the new palace to serve the Rok guests, and so I did."

"Why would the King request him, knowing that he is under my pay?"

Nepides shrugged. "His Majesty felt that he could be a trusted servant to his Rok guests; while they stayed in Caminia. Since he was a palace servant when you arrived here as our guest, his majesty felt that he was still the property of the palace."

"Well now I am short of a trustworthy servant," Vitaeus replied, his voice suddenly getting an icy edge to it. "But why should I worry when I have a trustworthy servant in you." His smile lacked politeness and humor, however, and Nepides stared at him wide eyed.

"You're not implying me, I hope?"

Vitaeus grinned. "I sure am."

"Sir, I will voice your concerns to the King, but I am a servant of the King. I can't serve you."

"No, Daenis is apparently a servant to the King. You were serving me on my journey here, and so you shall remain serving me until the King returns my own servant. Did the King receive the letter that I asked Daenis to deliver?"

"Yes sir."

"Good, get up. We have a lot of work to do, and we need to get started right away."

CHAPTER 31: LET FREEDOM RING

Sneaking up quietly, Achledis nocked an arrow in his bowstring and placed a couple more arrows on the ground beside him. As soon as Achledis shot the guards, Alrik and his twenty men would charge to finish the job; so the shots had to be perfect. If he didn't kill them instantly, the guards could yell out an alarm; which would be disastrous. Sneaking up any closer would be impossible, as the two guards had an open view of anyone thirty yards out. The breeze picked up just at that time as if daring Achledis to back out. A voice inside taunted Achledis, telling him that he was going to botch this shot; there was no way he could make it with this wind.

Achledis closed his eyes, letting his breathing slow. He pictured the arrows flying straight and true and ignored any negative thoughts. Without further ado, he whipped out his bow and shot the first arrow. While the first arrow was still in flight, he zipped off a second and notched a third. The first arrow slammed through the guard's face. The second arrow deflected off the second guard's pauldron, but moments later, a third arrow struck his gut, penetrating the tough leather vest. Alrik and his men were already charging halfway to the doors. Alrik threw out his spear at the second guard, and the spear slammed home through the chest.

Sword in hand, Alrik lingered by the door as everyone got into position for entry. The heavy door creaked in the stillness of the night as he pushed it open. Two guards appeared at the door instantly. Their eyes widened in disbelief, and they quickly scrambled to yank out their swords.

"Hands in the air!" Alrik commanded. "No need to die." The guards ignored him, however, and drew their swords, even as one shouted an alarm. Achledis and Alrik instantly engaged them, and the rest of the rebels quickly pressed the Rakirian guards from all sides. The clanging of metal and alarmed shouts coming from the guards reverberated throughout the stone walls of the hall that separated the barracks from the palace. The scuffle was short but loud, and it left everyone tense with worry that their advantage of a surprise had just been compromised.

The men looked to Alrik, who stood looking around the wide hall; not sure which door would lead to the barracks. Only a fraction of the torches lining the walls had been lit for the night, but even in the dim, flickering light, the elaborate grandeur of the hall was evident. A huge portrait of the Rakirian Emperor Duragino hung on one wall, and on the other wall was a portrait of Viceroy Lorne, Mayor of Seredine.

Alrik motioned to Achledis to inspect the door on the right; while he went to inspect the one on the left. Achledis turned the doorknob, but the heavy door wouldn't budge. Looking back, he saw Alrik motioning the men to his open door. He held a hand to his lips to motion for silence, and with his other hand, he motioned with a knife in front of his throat. The sound of twenty leather boots padded softly on a marble floor; as the men jogged towards the door. Achledis gave the signal for the other fifty men waiting in the shadows outside to come in.

Achledis walked to the door that Alrik had opened and found himself looking into a long hallway. It was wide enough to hold weapons and armor stacked for easy access. At the end of the hall was another door that led to a room where the soldiers slept.

As Achledis walked towards that door with his knife drawn, the last of the Rosmirian rebels were slipping inside. A Rakirian guard sat by the door in a puddle of his own blood. When a rebel asked him to surrender, he had shouted out, and his throat had been cut. Inside, Achledis froze at the sight before him. Columns of men walked from bed to bed, silently snuffing the lives of the helpless souls. It didn't feel right to take a man's life when he slept; they should at least be given the chance to surrender. Half the Rakirian garrison was already dead, and Achledis commanded everyone to stop. "Let's give them a chance to surrender," he half whispered; so that the men across the long room could hear him. They all looked at Alrik, who had given them the order to kill everyone, and Alrik motioned for them to continue before turning on Achledis.

"Don't you dare go against my orders; especially in the middle of an operation. If we wake them to ask them to surrender, and they refuse, then they will easily overwhelm us. Remember, we can't afford to lose tonight, and we are still heavily outnumbered."

Suddenly, a Rakirian soldier in the middle of the room sat up abruptly. His eyes were wide with horror at what he was seeing around him. It was worse than the nightmare that had jolted him out of his sleep. He heard a shrill yell, that seemed to add to the haunting scene around him, and it took a few moments to realize that the shrill sound was coming from himself. He noticed the men around him stirring awake and wondered if this was only another nightmare that he needed to wake up from. Just then, he felt something sharp slice into his back, and he watched in horror as the point of a blade protruded from his chest. But as the attacker pulled the blade back out from the Rakirian's heart, he brought an end to the Rakirian's nightmare.

Half the Rakirian army had stirred awake before the yelling Rakirian was silenced. Sitting up groggily and heavy with sleep, they were instantly sobered at the sight around them, and with shouts of alarm they quickly jumped into action. There were about 120 of them against 22 Rosmirians that were spread out throughout the room.

"I demand that the rest of you surrender!" Alrik shouted, but the sound of men jumping out of bed and screaming in alarm drowned him out. With a six to one ratio, they were emboldened to attack, and they charged as one, overwhelming the inexperienced Rosmirian swordsmen.

Achledis, who was already by the door, stayed his ground fending off the waves of Rakirians charging. Alrik took up a position to Achledis's left, and the two fought gallantly to make sure that no Rakirian slipped through that door. But the outnumbered Rosmirians, though initially better armed, were soon overwhelmed by Rakirian numbers. The Rakirians took the swords from the hands of the dead Rosmirians, and they joined the group that was pressing Alrik and Achledis at the door.

During a brief respite, as the Rakirians retreated to regroup, Alrik noticed some twenty Rakirians armed with the swords that once belonged to his men. The realization that the men that followed him into this room were all dead, with Achledis being the only exception, left him in a fit of anger. He shouted a command behind him, and Rolen and his men came in the room with their pikes out. They made a path for Alrik and Achledis to retreat behind them. Though their marching wasn't the prettiest military performance, it was still daunting as they marched in and spread out making two lines. Then, as Rolen ordered, they crouched with the right leg in front of the left; this provided power and a lower center of gravity. They held their ten-foot pikes out in front of them. The bottom part of the shaft was on the floor behind them, and the point protruded chest high in front.

The Rakirians were stunned as the two lines of pike men lined up in front of them. Though they still held the numerical advantage, they were all too aware that overwhelming an organized line of pike men would be suicidal, and in their case, only a small fraction of them were actually armed with swords.

Alrik shouted for Keltar next, and though the Rakirians didn't understand the new command coming from Alrik, they decided that they didn't want to find out. One of their officers, holding a short sword, raised the sharp weapon over his head and with a scream ordered the men to charge. The first line of Rakirians tried to bat the pikes away with their swords, and some even got through. But the second line of pike men were quick to jab those who evaded the first line of pointed pikes. The Rakirians' angry battle cry soon turned to one of dismay and panic. Rolen's voice kept shouting for the men to stay low and hold firm.

Keltar arrived with his small army of archers. With the pike men crouching, the archers lined up behind them. They could see the enemy perfectly, and in unison, they let their arrows fly, wave after wave after wave. The arrows broke the first Rakirian charge.

As the Rakirians tried to regroup, they were hit with another volley of arrows; which decimated their numbers. With their spirit broken, the 40 Rakirians that were still on their feet had retreated to the back wall and were all standing on their knees with their right hand in the air, holding the pointer and the middle finger together in a sign of surrender and vocally calling out for mercy.

Keltar held his hand up ready to bring it down and unleash yet another volley, but he looked to Alrik hesitantly for an order.

"Hold your fire!" Alrik shouted as he made his way through the pike men to the front where he could face them. His leather boots splashed through crimson blood; which having no place to seep into, pooled on the stone floor. Bodies lay pinned to bunks or cut down on the floor. He even noticed his men who had died before they got a chance to retreat. The floor was littered with broken bodies and wounded men as they lay moaning, and he heard a few whimpers as he strode past them. He stopped in the middle of the room and looked at the Rakirians in front of him. They held no weapons; most of them, if not all of them, were injured in some way. Some still had arrows protruding either from a leg or an arm, and others were doubled over from the arrows that had struck them in the chest or waist. They were dying slowly, but regardless they had enough.

"You should have surrendered right away. This massacre could have been prevented," Alrik said, his voice heavy with disgust. "But those of you who did surrender, I will see to it that your wounds are properly treated. Perhaps when this Viserate arrives, I will be able to strike a deal for a prisoner exchange." He pointed to one of the soldiers and summoned him forward. The man's left arm was bleeding, but he looked the healthiest in the group. "Come with me. Show me the door that leads to the palace."

CHAPTER 32: MOTTE AND BAILEY FORTRESS

The keep stood atop a small rocky hill with a courtyard below. It was surrounded by a small, stone wall that was covered in moss as well as other vegetation. Though the keep needed minor repairs, it mainly needed to be freshened up after years of abandonment. Nepides, though grudgingly, and after a lot of prodding from Vitaeus, organized a workforce that cleaned up the keep and got to work repairing the small huts in the yard below. Coal and metal were delivered for the forge, and hay was brought for the stable. The pinewood that was meant for the new palace that King Razim was building, was diverted to the keep. Fletchers and crossbow makers were recruited in large numbers. This was all done in a day's work, and Nepides, with his connections and resourcefulness, was a significant reason for the day's success.

The next day, Vitaeus took Nepides with him, and together they rode inside the city walls of Caminia. Vitaeus had a lot more planned. No words had been spoken between the two of them, except for Vitaeus to bark a command and for Nepides to agree, but after they had entered the city, Nepides grew bold enough to threaten Vitaeus.

"The King will have your hide when his guards come across us." He said.

"I doubt they would recognize you. You don't have your peacock cape on, and you look nothing more than a common servant riding with his lord. Besides, if you and I don't return together, it might be ill for your wife. I can't say what the brute will do; I found him beating up a knight fully clad in armor with nothing but his feet and fists. A real savage he is, but I have use for him."

Nepides looked at him; his face growing an ashen gray. "You took my wife?"

"No, I merely informed her of your new appointment as my new servant and told her that your new office kept you too busy to write her, but I invited her to come stay at the keep with us. I assumed you would miss one another and only did it out of courtesy to the both of you. I was informed, just this morning, that she was being escorted to the keep by my newly hired knights and men-at-arms. Perhaps if we can get our chores done quickly here, we can go back, and I will give you leave to attend to your wife."

"You, You..." Nepides seethed. He seemed to think better about saying more and clenched his jaw tight.

"Am very kind, generous, thoughtful; were those the adjectives that you were looking for? Well thank you, good servant, I do try to treat my servants well. I give my servants and their families shelter, food, protection, and most importantly, fair pay."

"The King will be enraged when he finds out."

"The King knows. I informed him of my departure in that letter."

Neither spoke as they approached the entrance to the armory. They were met by a large, grizzled man at the entrance, who introduced himself as the master guildsman of the armory.

"The new lord?" The guild master inquired, waving them in excitedly. "Can't say we expected you, but we are honored you came." His voice was gruff, his face scarred from burns, and his hands were well seasoned from hard labor. "We have heard much about you; well, mostly of your infamous silver armor that you wore during your lordship ceremony. Every knight, with enough money, has been requesting that I make one for them, but I haven't seen it. It's hard for me to design something I haven't seen before. However, it's the metal that sounds the most interesting. Tell me sir, is it plated with real silver?"

Vitaeus smiled at the guild master's enthusiasm, and as he glanced about the room full of breastplates and helmets, the designs were artfully and masterfully done.

"No, no silver, just steel." Vitaeus replied.

"Very interesting steel from what I hear."

"Do you have weapons and armor that you can sell me?" Vitaeus interjected, getting straight to business. Though he would love to talk, he had a busy schedule and didn't have the time to waste talking to someone about his armor.

"Yes, absolutely. What are you looking for exactly?"

"For a bit of everything, from armor, to weapons, to soldiers who can wield the weapons. Can you help me?"

"I can sell you the armor and weapons," the master replied with a smile.

"I am also looking to hire 50 experienced knights. Where can I find some?"

"Well, there are plenty of knights in the city; all coming down for the tournament that the King is throwing in honor of his new little princess." The master said smiling. "I'm sure there will be plenty of knights looking for a job afterwards. What, with their armor and weapons in need of costly repair, they may very well look forward to serving a wealthy merchant lord."

Vitaeus handed the master a silver coin. "Thanks for the advice; I may one day soon be looking to hire a master such as you."

"Thank you sir, I would be most honored."

"Now show me your crossbows. I think that everything else can wait until afterwards."

The armor master took him past a fiery hearth where an apprentice was hammering steel into shape; the hot air stank of steel and dust as they hurried past and into a separate room.

The master lit a torch and led them into a room lined with rows of crossbows on one side and bows on the other. "This is our bow and crossbow arsenal; there is enough to arm the King's army." The master pronounced proudly.

Vitaeus stooped to inspect the crossbows. The yew was covered in varnish, and the hemp string was waxed. This helped to protect the wood and string from moisture. All the crossbows were operated with a windlass crank. Vitaeus had to smile; this was the perfect weapon for his untrained army of servants. He hired some knights; which was expected. But to hire an army would certainly make the King suspicious. His servants were also his soldiers, and this would be their main weapon. It was easy to use, and most importantly, it required minimal strength and training.

Nepides was eyeing him warily, but when Vitaeus glanced in his direction, he looked away. *The perfect spy*, Vitaues thought. But with him hosting Nepides's family, he would be a good boy, no doubt. Vitaeus motioned for him to come over. "What do you think, nice crossbows huh?"

"Yes, they are." Nepides tone suggested that he was bored.

"You look bored; so I will give you something more exciting to do. Go and arrange for the wheat and barley to be brought into my stores. Also hire me another 200 workers; I have a lot of digging to do."

"How many crossbows will you be purchasing?"

"I was always fond of crossbows; I think I will buy myself one. Did you want one too?" Vitaeus asked.

"No."

"Well, you better be off then. Remember, if you're not home in three hours, your wife will have reason to worry."

"I can't get all of your errands in three hours." Nepides complained, "I need at least five or six."

"You have five hours then, but if I don't get my servants and food for my stores, I will be terribly disappointed. "

Nepides stared at Vitaeus's feet, not daring to look up. His lower lip quivered from either fear or anger; Vitaeus couldn't be sure. His cheeks were certainly flushed, and his eyes looked like black specks sunken into his sockets, staring like a corpse. Vitaeus waved him off with the back of his hand and turned his back to him, as he went to inspect the long bows made of yew. When Vitaeus glanced back, Nepides was no longer there.

The master came up to him smiling once again. "Your friend seems to have left in a hurry."

"He had business to attend to; now as to our business, I will give you 50 gold pieces for all of your crossbows, bows, and all the ammunition that you have."

"50 pieces?!" The master almost shouted his outrage. "You insult me with your offer. Get out of here! I was under the notion that I was working for a wealthy lord. Why should I risk selling you anything?"

"If you deliver it by the end of the day, I shall give you 300." Vitaeus replied calmly.

"500 and I will deliver it today."

"Look, I became a wealthy merchant because I don't allow myself to be ripped off. 300 gold pieces, or I will find another armory that will sell me the goods I need."

"No one can compete with my quality."

"But clearly just about anyone will compete with your value. If you are not interested in my deal, then decline, and I will go elsewhere."

"Fine, 400 gold and I will deliver it today."

"300." Vitaeus repeated firmly.

The master huffed and walked off. Vitaeus calmly turned and headed for the entrance, as well. There was no farewell, or even a second look at the master. Before he got to the entrance, he felt a hand grab him by the arm.

"Fine, you got your deal, but I want half now," the master said defeated.

Vitaeus took out his pouch of gold coins, "70 now, 230 when I get the rest." Before the master guildsman of the armory could say more, as he looked like he was about to, Vitaeus hurried out.

The master was right. Poorer men-at-arms, knights, and their squires had flooded the city. The tournament was set to take place on the Rok princess's last day, and that was only a few weeks away. When Vitaeus inquired about their service, most knights had already contracted themselves to other lords and couldn't break their contract, or else, their knightly honor would be stained. Vitaeus was walking through the market when he heard the sound of horses behind him. As he turned to look, he found himself surrounded by palace guards.

CHAPTER 33: HEROIC DEATH

The door leading to the palace was ironically the same one that Achledis had tried before and found to be locked. The Rakirian prisoner apparently knew this, because he didn't bother stalling them with mock pretense. Instead, he marched them straight to the headquarters of the palace keeper and told them that he would have all the keys for every door in the palace. The palace keeper woke up with a blade at his throat, and without any resistance, readily surrendered the keys, before allowing himself to be taken into custody by one of Alrik's men.

Alrik and Achledis proceeded through the heavy door that led to the palace where Viceroy Lorne resided and found themselves standing inside a spacious rotunda. Ornate chandeliers made of gold hung from the high dome ceilings above, the walls were made of white stone, and the floor of marble. A wide circular staircase with imported mahogany wooden railings spiraled upwards, to somewhere above and behind them, hindering their view to the hall where it may lead. Two wooden eagles sat perched on either railing, painted with such vivid detail that they appeared to be life-like.

Achledis took a step forward inside and instantly felt Alrik's hand grab his. "Hold it!" His head ducked behind the heavy door once more, and he motioned for Rolen and Keltar to proceed inside. Rolen entered with his pike men, followed by Keltar and the archers. Alrik and Achledis led the way in the front and started for the stairs at a run. The sound of a multitude of men running echoed against the rock walls and the ceiling above. Rounding up to the top, they came out into a wide hallway with mirrors in golden frames on both sides of the hall. Six guards stepped out to challenge the intruders; their spears raised waist high in a threatening posture. As they saw the mob that continued to pour into the hallway; however, Achledis could see them waiver hesitantly.

Alrik saw it too and seized the moment. "We have come to arrest Viceroy Lorne; step aside and surrender." At first, none of them responded but stared fearfully behind Alrik, and he allowed a quick glance back to see what it was that held their attention. The pike men crowded around each other; all crouched with their pikes held out. A mass of archers behind them had their arrows knocked and their strings pulled back.

"Do you surrender?" Alrik demanded once more and raised his hand as if ready to signal the archers.

The guards instantly dropped their spears to the ground and raised their hands in the air; except for one who stood a few paces to the side and suddenly charged Achledis. Instantly, the archers released their arrows in unison, and the palace guards all crumpled to the ground. They were all either dead or dying, with arrows sticking out of their armor and flesh in every direction.

Alrik cursed under his breath and motioned for the men to continue following him. They came to two large oak doors, and the men got in their position with the pike men in the front and the archers still poised behind, with their arrows knocked in the strings of their bows. Opening the doors, the men found themselves staring into the dark abyss of a banquet hall. Alrik waived the men to move on once again. The men grew frustrated after they stopped to search a couple dozen rooms and found them all empty.

Once the whole floor had been thoroughly inspected, they made their way to the third floor. Two guards came charging down the stairs. It happened so fast that Achledis didn't get a chance to respond with anything other than sidestepping the spear that was aimed at him. He heard a yelp behind him before an angry mob devoured the attacker, kicking and stomping him to death. Alrik didn't get as lucky as the second guard speared him through the shoulder. Achledis quickly responded to Alrik's attacker by pulling out his sword and running it through him.

Alrik, refusing assistance, managed to stumble the rest of the way up the stairs and collapsed; a pool of blood forming under him. Achledis pulled off his jerkin, tearing it into strands. He bound the wound tightly. Rolen and Keltar demanded that the men step back, as they too came to Alrik's side. Both men had known Alrik for a long time, and it pained them that they couldn't help.

"Go on, finish the mission." Alrik's voice rasped; taking a quick breath, he began to urge them once more. "I'm fine right here. I will only slow you down; leave me and go." When no one responded, he seized Rolen with his good hand and looked into his friend's teary eyes. "Stop being such a wuss and go, damn it."

When no one moved yet again, Alrik shook his head and attempted to rise, but the three instantly pressed him back down. "Out of my way! damn you all! Let me get up!" With surprising strength, he pushed them aside and rose up. "I'm fine. I told you that already; I just needed to catch my breath. Now let's go."

"Alrik, take it easy; you're losing a lot of blood." Rolen began, but Alrik hushed him by placing his hand on his mouth.

"Let's move," his voice boomed. The army started down the long wide hallway once again, stopping in front of another set of heavy oak doors in front of them. Achledis quickly stepped forward to open them, and they walked into yet another lobby that split off in different directions. On Alrik's orders, the army stayed in the lobby with Keltar and Rolen; while Alrik and Achledis scouted the floor.

As soon as they were alone, Alrik slowed his pace down considerably, and his breathing became heavy. Achledis suggested that they stop and rest, but Alrik rejected the suggestion angrily. Not wanting to hurt his friend's pride, Achledis let the matter drop, and the two pressed on for some time. Alrik was visibly growing weaker.

"Alrik, let's be frank; tell me how you're really doing. You lost a lot of blood, and I'm seriously concerned."

Alrik stopped and looked at Achledis; his jaw was clenched tightly. Besides that, he showed no pain or emotion. After a pause, he sighed and nodded his head slowly. "I'm losing blood."

"Keltar can take command and see it through the end. Some of the men can carry you to a doctor." Achledis suggested. "I will personally carry you to a physician."

"No, the men must not see my weakness. We are almost finished here, and I can't afford to have them lose morale. We can request the palace physician as soon as we get Lorne."

They grew quiet at the sound of whispering voices coming from a chamber and peered around the corner carefully to see who was there. The chamber appeared to be the royal family's dining hall, much smaller than the spacious banquet hall, but just as elegant.

A Vicereine sat at the table with two younger girls and a young lad who she held against her. She was telling them a fairytale to occupy them, but her eyes were constantly scanning the room. A palace guard came through the doorway, and after he whispered something into the Vicereine's ear, she got up angrily and waved him away.

"Go get the troops; while I stay here and keep a lookout. Leave Rolen with ten archers and ten pike men to guard the staircase." Alrik's voice was slightly strained as he tried to bear the pain in his shoulder. Achledis noticed that the cloth wrapped around his shoulder was soaked with a deep crimson red fluid and couldn't help but worry. The wound was undoubtedly severe, and the pain had to be a lot worse than Alrik let on.

"Hide yourself until I arrive with the rest of the men." Achledis whispered back as he tiptoed away."

Alrik waived a hand dismissively at him. When Achledis disappeared around the corner, Alrik inhaled a deep breath, and through gritted teeth, he released the air out of his lungs slowly. The pain had seemed to diminish, but dizziness came over him that brought him to the edge of unconsciousness. As the looming black cloud threatened to overwhelm him, he fought to stay awake.

The sound of men marching carried well through the stone corridors, and the children looked at their mother questioningly.

The oldest girl stood up suddenly. "What's happening mother? Why is everyone on edge tonight? Tell me why you awoke us; you said we had to go somewhere right away. But after a guard shared a secret with you, we have been sitting here listening to your stories. You never tell us stories anymore."

The mother stood up too; she embraced her eldest daughter and tears welled up in her eyes. "Nothing escapes you my dear. I need you to be a big girl tonight and help me. Take your sister and brother and go back in the room."

A tall man came out of the door and hurried them inside. Though he was balding, he appeared rather youthful. Only his speckled gray and black hair that wrapped around the backside of his head hinted at his real age. He wore a purple gown, and his wife held his embrace, allowing tears to come for the first time. The Viceroy had received reports from the guards that the Rakirian garrison had fallen and that the rebels had infiltrated the palace itself and were slowly making their way up.

He had just woken up his family a bit ago in an attempt to get them out, but a guard had just reported that a rebel force was stationed not too far from the courtyard and that it would be too risky getting them there. The courtyard had a hidden passageway; which led to an escape chute that came down into a hidden tunnel. It was fabled that the Rosmirian King himself had used it when he evaded Rakirian capture. Now the clamor of men coming down the corridor sounded closer and closer, and Viceroy Lorne knew that he had run out of options. His eyes roamed the room; he had the look of a rabbit that was cornered and had nowhere to go. Sadly, he kissed his wife and whispered reassurances in her ear, and then she turned and went into the same room where the children had gone.

The Viceroy made a visual inspection of the room, and the guards remained, armed with crossbows waiting for the enemy to arrive. With a hopeless look on his face, he turned and went through a separate door from the one where his family had gone into.

Alrik saw it all and noted the doors where the family and Lorne himself had gone through. He glanced anxiously towards the sound of his men approaching, but they were not yet in sight. Finally, one after another, the men filed around the corner, and Alrik stood to wave them over. He swayed dizzily.

"Hurry!" Alrik's voice croaked as he waved for the men impatiently.

Achledis was at the forefront, and though he couldn't make out Alrik's words, his gesturing was clear. He trotted to meet Alrik, who was visibly weaker now, and Achledis had to be at his side when they went in to demand the arrest of Viceroy Lorne. Alrik, seeing Achledis approach, nodded at him and started inside. Achledis hadn't even rounded the doorway before chills ran down his spine as he froze at the dreadful sound, the sound of a crossbow's release. Alrik's body staggered backwards through the door, and he fell flat on his back, his eyes wide and staring into nothing.

CHAPTER 34: MEETING WITH THE PRINCESS

The party of palace guards, with Vitaeus in tow, galloped into the plaza of the new palace, sending the masses scattering to get out of their way. An army of guards was still entrenched around all exits and doors that led into the grand palace, providing heavy security for the Rok royals. The commoners, who had been celebrating the princess's arrival for the past week, were all eager to see the fabled beauty but had thus far been disappointed. Even when the princess did leave the palace, she was always hidden inside a carriage with knights all around.

The guards and Vitaeus dismounted in front of the main entrance and handed the reins to awaiting servants at the door. A guard led Vitaeus inside the palace where they were met by the princess herself, as she happened to be descending down the grand staircase with golden rails.

"My Lord!" She exclaimed. "How good of you to come and on such short notice."

"Your men gave me little choice; yet I am honored to be your guest." Vitaeus said, as he bowed and kissed Raheena's hand, forcing the guard to let go of him.

Raheena led Vitaeus to the west end of the palace, to a sitting room next to her apartment. A small table with ivory legs and a marble top stood in the center of the room, and plush, soft chairs covered in velvet stood on either end. The room itself was small, designed for a more intimate setting, where the king and his queen could have a meal together. As soon as they were both seated, a couple of maidens, close in age with the princess, brought two glasses of sparkling yellow Rok wine and small salads.

"How has your stay been so far, princess?" Vitaeus asked once they were both seated and sipping their wine.

"The King has been very hospitable." She said smiling. "As you can see, the palace has been comfortably furnished for my stay. Staying in a separate palace from the King has also helped me feel more at ease."

"Have you had a chance to go for a ride and see the city, or the countryside at least?" Vitaeus asked, "Or have they kept you confined inside these walls, beautiful as it is inside here?"

"That's part of the reason I asked to have this meeting with you, My Lord. I wasn't sure if you received my note regarding our last appointment."

"I received it on the streets as I was making my way to your palace, actually."

"What?" She said with a nervous laugh. "How could that happen?"

"Apparently, the person who was supposed to deliver the letter to me didn't, and instead decided to follow me during my midnight prowl."

"Someone followed you here? At night?"

"Yes, I am being followed and spied on just about anywhere I go. Apparently, I have fallen out of the King's favourable graces." Vitaeus said with a mocking tone.

"Does that concern you sir?"

"Yes and no," he replied.

"Sir, I also heard rumors about a growing rift between the King and the new lord he appointed, but kidnapping the king's personal servant? Isn't that a bit far, My Lord? Are you not asking for a war?"

"Kidnapped? Please, tell me who told you this strange tale. Nepides felt that the King had been cheating him and offered to run a few errands for me. With him being so resourceful, I was seduced to accept his offer."

The smile on Raheena's face seemed to stiffen a bit. "Lord Vitaeus, sir, I am making an appeal to you to be sensible. The King seemed very agitated yesterday at the ball. Please return Nepides to him, or you will almost certainly have a war on your hands."

"What did the King say exactly?" Vitaeus asked.

Raheena shook her head and turned her sorrowful eyes at Vitaeus. "I can't say, but there has been a lot of secret orders issued. Just last night at the ball, it seemed that there was a constant flow of messengers coming and going, and I knew they all had to do with you." She paused, as her eyes studied him intently. "I missed your jolly prescence at the ball, and without your charm, the balls are rather dull and loathsome." Suddenly tears sprang into Raheena's eyes, and as she tried to brush them off, Vitaeus quickly stood and wiped her tears with a handkerchief.

"What's wrong princess?"

With teary eyes, she clutched his hand and drew it near herself. "I am afraid." She whispered. "I am young, and the thought of being alone with the old King for even a night frightens me more than I can say. Yet, out of duty as a princess, I am expected to marry an old man who happens to be King; so that by bringing in the King's seed into the world, my father on his Rok throne would in essence rule Caminia through me once King Razim is dead." Raheena sniffled, and with her dove eyes looking at Vitaeus pleadingly, she continued in her small voice. "My marriage is political, and I'm expected to be dutiful. Since I was a little girl, I was taught that my role in life would be to one day marry a powerful lord that would strengthen my father's power." In a sudden explosion of tears, Raheena broke down and started sobbing; her chest heaving and tears rolling freely. Vitaeus, forgetting all protocol between lords and ladies, pulled his chair next to Raheena and held her close to him, letting her weep against his chest.

"I never expected my father to arrange a marriage with a man who is so old that his arthritis pains him to walk."

Vitaeus sat next to her and took her hand, "Don't be sorrowful princess. I am Lord of the Shield Isles, and I plan to make many trips to the Rok Isles. Besides, I own some vineyards in your country. Openly refuse the King's marriage, and I will ask your father for your hand in marriage. I will make an offer that he won't be able to refuse."

Raheena looked at him with sad eyes and smiled. "Sir, you are wealthy by all accounts, but a few rocks on the sea won't impress my father. Even among the lords here, you are viewed as a petty lord who bought his title. You lack nobility, and that is something my father can't overlook."

"It seems silly that a man's prestige would depend on something that he has no control over. I mean, I believe that prestige is something that should be earned, not given to a man on a silver platter. Don't you agree princess? If something of worth is given to a man that he has not earned, then he will never fully appreciate it."

The princess smiled. "I think that sounds really admirable."

"Of course, you're a princess; you were of the highest nobility since your birth and never knew anything different."

"My Lord?" Vitaeus heard a familiar voice, and as he turned around, there was Daenis standing before him, looking ridiculous as ever wearing green tights and a fancy shirt while holding a tray with their main course.

"Oh look, it's my runaway servant."

"My Lord, I heard you were here and had to see you. You have to know that I wasn't allowed to return to you. Nepides had guards escort me here; so that I wouldn't have contact with you. But I would love to come back and serve you once more if you will have me sir?"

"I will have you if the princess will release you to me." Vitaeus replied, trying to contain his happiness. Daenis was definitely more trustworthy than Nepides.

"They kidnapped your servant too?" Raheena's tears dried, but her eyes glistened as she suddenly had a smile on her face. "Definitely take him back; the poor guy is out of sorts being surrounded by young maidens. He hardly knows what to do with himself." Raheena said giggling. "He should have told me sooner. I would have reunited you two much earlier."

A few days later, back in his private chamber of the keep, Vitaeus tried to read more of the *Vulcancrat Journal,* but his mind kept wandering back on Raheena's dilemma and his own. There was no doubt in his mind that he would ever stand by and allow the princess to marry his mortal enemy. He had assembled an army of 200 peasants to shoot crossbows for him, not nearly enough to stand up to the King. Besides, Caminia was flooded with knights who were seeking the King's favor. If it was true that the King suspected him of being a relative of Krepedes Arkonis, then why he still has not been arrested and accused of treason puzzled him. Yet something was going on, and Raheena confirmed that much by telling him of the constant barrage of messengers and orders being issued during a ball.

It occurred to Vitaeus that if he stayed much longer, the chances of being headless increased significantly. A tempting thought occurred that perhaps he should retreat to the Shield Isles. Out there, he would be out of Razim's reach, but if he did return, he could never hope to regain a foothold in Caminia to retake his kingdom. Right now he was staying in a small fortress with a small army right outside Caminia; no doubt that alone was putting Razim on edge.

After a bit more deliberation, Vitaeus sat down and started to write some letters. The first was to the captain of his ship, asking him to bring the ship around the Caminian coast to his fortress; where the olive banner with a silver wolf was displayed.

The second letter was to King Razim regarding Nepides. Vitaeus had deliberated long and hard on the matter and came to the conclusion that he had little choice. If he released Nepides, then he would go and tell the King his version of being forced into Vitaeus's service. On the other hand, if he allowed Nepides to continue serving, then the King would request him back any day now, and he would be forced to give him back. The same result would occur of Nepides recounting of being forced into Vitaeus's service. Vitaeus decided that his only real choice was to imprison Nepides and accuse him of plotting treason against the King.

In the letter to Razim, Vitaeus recounted how he had requested assistance from Nepides and Nepides's eagerness to help. *Nepides was full of advice, but his first advice was for me to relocate to this old motte-and-bailey castle,* Vitaeus wrote. *His advice made sense; for I needed headquarters as a base for recruiting workers, farmers, knights and sailors. Then Nepides wrote a treasonous letter rejecting you, My Lord, as King, and I had no choice but to imprison him. I write this letter asking for your advice on what to do with this subject.*

Vitaeus called for Yolif, the fighter who was able to defeat an armored knight in the ring with nothing except his bare hands and a dagger. Vitaeus had been so impressed with Yolif that he had Daenis hire him after the match. Yolif could do a lot more than just fight; Vitaeus had soon learned. He watched as the youth scaled a stone tower up to his keep. The mortar between the stones barely allowed for a finger hold, yet it had been enough for Yolif.

There was a gentle knock on the door, and Daenis popped his head inside. "My Lord, Yolif is here to see you."

"Let him in."

The youth came inside, tall and lean with a similar build to that of Vitaeus. His sandy brown hair was cut short, and his grayish blue eyes looked Vitaeus over warily before giving a courteous bow.

"You may go Daenis." After the door had closed, Vitaeus motioned for Yolif to sit on a wooden chair across from him. Yolif took in his surroundings seemingly inconspicuously as he sat down, but Vitaeus noticed it. "I'm afraid that wooden chair is the most comfortable thing I have to sit on; as you can see, my furniture isn't very lavish in here." Vitaeus remarked.

Yolif continued to look at him, showing no emotion. His steely grayish blue eyes set Vitaeus slightly on edge, knowing that he was defenseless against this man if he chose to kill him for whatever reason.

"You seemed livelier in the ring than you do now; somehow I assumed that it would make you a great conversationalist." Vitaeus remarked. "I have some sparkling golden Rok wine or some imported red from the Four Nation Island, as well as some dried and peppered sausages with cheese, if you would like." Vitaeus got up, poured two glasses of wine, and brought over the tray with the sausages and cheese.

"Thank you." Yolif mumbled as he picked up a sausage and bit into it hungrily. Vitaeus waited to let Yolif eat before he continued the conversation. Yolif was tall and lean, and his strength was tremendous. Though you would never guess just by looking at him; Vitaeus could only imagine how strong the boy truly was.

"Tell me Yolif, where are you from?" Vitaeus asked.

"From the Orel Mountains," The boy replied.

Vitaeus had heard the name somewhere before, but his geography was poor in relation to Caminia. "Where is that exactly?"

"They are mountains in Western Caminia, My Lord." The boy replied in a condescending tone, but Vitaeus pretended not to take notice.

"Tell me then, what is it that brought you here to Caminia?"

"The life of a shepherd didn't appeal to me; so I moved out here hoping to find something more exciting."

"Do you know why I asked you to come into my service?"

"I impressed you at the tournament." Yolif replied without hesitation and a thin smile on his face.

"Well that's true; I was impressed. I wanted you to be my bodyguard, yet I'm not sure if I should fully trust you with my life. Tell me Yolif; what do you think of me? Tell me the truth."

"What does it matter what I think of you sir? Word has it that you are a new petty lord, with a few rocks in the sea for land and lots of wealth. A couple months ago, I never heard of you, and now you're all I hear about. For one, I hear of a growing rift between you and the King. Rumor has it, it's because you started courting the Rok princess; even though she arrived for an official engagement with the King. That either makes you noble or immoral; I'm not sure which. That would depend on which side of the argument you fall on; I guess. Is it right for an old man like the King to wed a young girl like the princess? If not, then I guess you would be noble for trying to prevent that from happening. But if it is right, as everyone in the Caminian and Rok courts seem to think, then you are an immoral womanizer and every man should be extra careful and protective of their women when you are around."

Vitaeus was so taken back by Yolif's bold yet philosophical response, that he sat stunned for a few moments after Yolif was done speaking.

"Is this really what the commoners talk about?" Vitaeus finally asked. It would be over for him sooner than he believed if the common people in Caminia seemed to think that he and Princess Raheena were having romantic encounters.

"It's all they seem to talk about sir. You and the princess have added a lot of intrigue to a kingdom that has little to talk about."

He had only been seen with the princess publicly a few times, yet it was true that they had started exchanging letters frequently during the last couple of days. He would get as many as two and sometimes three letters from the princess in the same day. But how could the commoners know of their growing relationship? Vitaeus never spoke of it to anyone, and the two always used aliases when writing to one another.

"Yolif, where were you educated?" Vitaeus asked, changing the subject suddenly.

"At home, by my parents." Yolif replied.

"If your parents were educated, then what were they doing in the mountains of Western Caminia?"

"Let's just say that you're not the only one with a mysterious family tree." Yolif replied.

Vitaeus stood suddenly, sending his chair scooting back. "Mysterious family tree? What are you implying?"

Yolif stayed calm as he continued. "The commoners have their rumors, and the nobility have their own. I have heard of your resemblance to the late King Krepedes. Suddenly, you show up with wealth galore, posing to be a merchant, and buy yourself a title. But the only lands that you're granted are a few islands off the coast of Nitami. Tell me sir, is that not a bit odd?"

"How do you know all of this?" Vitaeus demanded.

"I hear talk, bits and pieces, here and there."

Vitaeus shook his head as he started to pace. He had totally underestimated Yolif; he was less sure of him now than when he first recruited him. How could he possibly ever trust this man? He was an enigma, a mystery that Vitaeus knew nothing of, well almost nothing, yet he had learned a lot in this meeting alone. Yolif was an educated peasant from the Orel Mountains, with a mysterious family that he didn't want to talk about. He knew of an exotic way of fighting, and he had an apparent wealth of information. A man who appeared to know nothing yet seemed to know everything.

"If you are wondering if you should keep me employed, then the answer is yes," Yolif said. "I will be a great asset to you. For one, I will do what you hired me for, and that is teaching you the art of Bezo and being your personal bodyguard. You and I both know you need one. And most importantly, to win the throne against this King, you need an army who can defeat his knights. I will teach you the military techniques to do so."

Vitaeus didn't reply at first; he just looked at Yolif apprehensively as he pondered the many questions he had about this man. "I need a bodyguard I can trust. Tell me, why should I trust you?"

Yolif blinked in mock amazement. "Didn't you learn anything from our conversation? Yes, I can protect you from physical harm, but I can also be your eyes and ears. That alone is critical for your survival."

CHAPTER 35: BORN TO LEAD

Achledis stared into his new friend's unblinking wide eyes with horror. *This didn't just happen; it couldn't have. Alrik must be alive. He needs to be alive; we need him.* His thoughts of disbelief didn't matter. The reality remained in front of his eyes, and as the truth sank in, it seemed to cut him on the inside. Achledis wasn't mindful of anything around him at the moment, not even of the danger or the closeness of the enemy. He didn't even notice that the Rosmirian rebels had stopped their march behind him and were standing there frozen in shock; as they too saw the body of their dead leader.

"Aaaargghh!" The sound came out as a helpless cry, echoing down the corridors of the palace. As Achledis turned to face his countrymen, the expression on his face sent chills down everyone's spines. His expression was that of a madman as he crouched in front of them, his eyes roaming angrily.

Out of the stricken group of men, Keltar emerged, shortly followed by Rolen, and the two men both came and stood at Achledis's side, their hands on his shoulders. The three men stood in silence for a moment before Keltar, who was the most composed, spoke softly so that Achledis and Rolen where the only ones able to hear his words.

"We must all be strong. He died for the cause of freedom, and he would have wanted you to be the one to see it to the end."

"No, you two were his closest friends. Keltar, the men need a strong leader they can all believe in, and that's you."

Rolen grabbed Achledis and turned him towards himself; so that he was staring into his steely eyes. "No, Achledis. Keltar and I may have been his close friends for many years, but you instantly became his right-hand man. Why do you think Alrik chose you to scout with him?"

"It was because of the greatness in you." Keltar interrupted. "The same greatness that we all sense, and which is the reason that you are the man to lead. The men have already seen your bravery and courage, and with Rolen and me standing behind you, they will follow your lead without hesitation. Now lead."

As Achledis pondered their words, he realized that they may be right. He always led, and in the wake of Alrik's sudden death, someone had to step in to make sure that this rebellion succeeded. He sensed the truth in the words of Rolen and Keltar and realized that it was up to him. Taking a deep breath, he composed himself before turning slowly to face the men. He found himself staring into faces of broken men who were demoralized to the point of defeat. Slowly, everyone's attention shifted to the youth who stood before them; their faces were void of any expression. With Rolen and Keltar standing on his right and left, it signaled to the men that he was now their new commander.

"Today we have all seen and experienced death. Today we have felt a great loss, but I tell you, do not despair. For we are on the brink of a great victory. We have come this far, and we will not waiver and be defeated. Our leader Alrik wanted to bring freedom to Rosmir; even if it meant giving his life in exchange. So, we must all ensure that he succeeds, even in death; for he would be crushed if he would see that his death had demoralized all of us to the point of defeat. These bolts may have killed him, but the truth is that he was already dying since the moment he got speared. He knew that he wouldn't come out of this palace alive. He only wanted to live long enough to see that the victory and freedom that he paid for with his life had actually been obtained." He paused for a moment and looked at the faces before him. The morale was still low, and some of the men still had doubtful expressions. His youth was a big reason for some of these grown men to lack trust in him. The only way for them to respect him was for him to lead. "Now, I only see six bolts buried in Alrik's body. Which means that they are greatly outnumbered, and another reason why they haven't engaged us yet. This is yet another reason why we are on the brink of victory."

"So the first in line are almost surely going to get shot and killed." A man in the front said.

"Getting shot at, you can bet on, but not necessarily killed. Now I have a plan, and it will require that we use those shields to build a fortress if you will. It will require that you all work and move as a team."

The idea had been forming in his mind, and though the tactic wasn't a new concept, it was for these men. They had never practiced it, and it required a lot of coordination between them. He would have to show them. With Viceroy Lorne trapped and the Rakirian garrison imprisoned, he decided that there was plenty of time for them to do it right and be safe.

The first three men in the front crouched low, with their shields overlapping one another and their pikes protruding out. The second row had their shields overlap the shields below them, and their pikes sticking out of the shield wall, as well. Very slowly, the wall of six pike men marched toward the entrance, with the archers and the other pike men eagerly waiting to charge in on the action. It would be a lot easier for six men to coordinate with each other, than for a multitude to create confusion.

The six pike men rounded the entrance and taking two steps inside the dining room stopped, but no shots were fired. Achledis, who was inside the shield wall, studied the layout of the dining room through a small opening between two shields. Initially, he didn't see anyone, just a bare room. As he let his gaze swing through the room once more, however, he noticed three guards on either side of the room standing next to white pillars with crossbows ready. Achledis nocked an arrow into his bowstring and aimed the arrow through a slit in the shield wall. He got this arrow from the Rakirians when he was making his getaway with Desiani. The arrowhead was made of iron, and its long and narrow body was designed to pierce armor. The Rakirians noticed the arrow protruding out of the hole, right before it was fired. The arrow pierced the guard's metal vambrace and stuck into his forearm; the Rakirian guard dropped his crossbow and yelled out in pain. Achledis had another arrow knocked and sent it to the other corner where it hit the second guard right above the breastplate, through the chain mail, and stuck in his neck. At this, the other guards responded by firing their crossbows at the shield wall where Achledis took refuge.

As they struggled to reload their clumsy weapons, Achledis broke free of the shield shell and charged them with the six pike men following close behind. The pike men in reserve, seeing that the battle had broken into hand-to-hand combat, also came storming in so that they too could get in on the action. The Rakirian guards on the right saw the wave of men with pikes charging towards them and instantly abandoned their clumsy crossbows and reached for their swords, but they couldn't draw quickly enough before the pikes were upon them.

Achledis's charge took the guards on the left by surprise, and they quickly went for their swords. But two lost their heads before the third was able to pull his free and engage. Achledis attacked instantly, hammering in some hard blows as the guard stumbled from the force of having to block them. Achledis pressed the attack harder and raised his sword overhead. The Rakirian guard seeing the overhead attack coming quickly, brought his sword up to block the blow. Achledis's sword whistled downward in an arc, missing the Rakirian guard's sword and curved sharply to the side, striking the Rakirian in his exposed side right under his armpit. Keltar, who watched from the side, shook his head in wonder at how smoothly Achledis pulled it off. Achledis yanked his sword out forcefully from the Rakirian's ribcage, and the Rakirian slumped to the ground blood oozing from his mouth.

At the sight of the last Rakirian defender killed, ecstatic shouts of victory rose all around. The air was charged with an excited sense of triumph, and Achledis bit his lip to hide the smile that threatened to show on his face. He pumped his crimson stained sword in the air, and the shouts of men became deafening. Achledis watched Keltar and Rolen approaching from the side, broad smiles across their faces.

"Congratulations! It might seem like a small victory, but the confidence that the men gained in you is enormous." Keltar clasped his hand on Achledis's shoulder and shook him roughly. "From this moment on, they truly believe in you, and so do I."

"Thanks friend, but our mission isn't over. We don't have Lorne yet." Achledis was interrupted as the two heavy doors before them started to open, and everyone instantly went silent in nervous anticipation.

"Archers prepare to fire!" Keltar shouted, and the archers from every corner in the room nocked an arrow and pulled the string back.

"Truce!" The call came from behind the heavy doors as a white cloth protruded from the narrow opening.

"Release the tension on your strings, but stay alert," Achledis commanded. Two Rakirian guards appeared as they opened the doors wide open.

"Who is the leader?" One of the guards asked, and Achledis stepped forward, his blood-stained sword hanging in a loose grip.

The guard looked him over quickly, before meeting his eyes. "My Lord Viceroy Lorne would like to discuss terms with you, please come." The guard turned on his heels and started to lead the way back through the doors without waiting for a response from Achledis. Achledis, followed by Keltar and ten archers, followed the guard through a short hallway, which came to another door. The guard knocked on the hard wood.

"Come in." A strong voice beckoned. The guard opened the door, and Achledis stepped forward through the entrance. The chamber was dimly lit, and Achledis had to let his eyes settle in before he could see the man sitting on a throne atop the dais. Achledis let his eyes wander the width of the room quickly; relief flooding him to see that this wasn't a trap. The two Rakirian guards quickly came up to the dais; after a curt bow, they stood on either side of the throne. Achledis came forward slowly, studying the man on the throne; as the man on the throne studied him. The man's gaze lingered on the bloody sword that Achledis held in his right hand, before allowing his eyes to lock with the youth before him.

"Who are you?" The man asked.

"You are in no position to ask questions," Achledis retorted. "Are you Lorne, the governor of Seredine?" The man stayed calm, allowing a brief silence to linger before responding.

"Yes, I am Viceroy Lorne, the governor of Seredine and the surrounding provinces of the Rosmirian territory."

"Viceroy? Not anymore you're not; you're under arrest." Achledis drew his sword and stepped forward; the two guards instantly jumped to block his way.

"Young man, you are committing treason; which is the worst crime anyone can commit. Now I can show leniency, but you must surrender immediately."

Achledis, flushed with anger, lunged forward, flicking one of the guard's spear aside and running his blade through him before turning and slicing the throat of the other guard. He brought his sword gently to Lorne's neck.

"Do you surrender?"

Viceroy Lorne's face had turned an ash gray as he nodded his head timidly.

"Take him to the dungeons; while the people decide his justice," Achledis ordered.

As they led him away, they encountered his wife and children in the dining hall. The Vicereine and her children wore expensive clothing that signified their rank in society. She stood tall and dignified with cool and steely eyes. She stared at Rolen as she blocked the path of the men who were leading her husband away.

"Are you the leader of this rabble?" She asked him.

"No, ma'am." Rolen said, pointing at Achledis who had just come out of the throne room and was studying the situation. He met the Vicereine's stare coolly and walked towards her.

"I demand that you release the Viceroy of Seredine, who is the governor of all the lands of Rosmir." She said, her voice menacing.

"Take him away." Achledis ordered. Rolen instantly gave the Viceroy a shove forward; so that Viceroy Lorne stumbled.

"How dare you treat a Viceroy like that?" The Vicereine gasped; her voice slightly louder than a whisper.

"Your titles mean nothing. You are now under Rosmirian jurisdiction, and the people of this city have a whole list of crimes that they claim your husband has committed."

The Viceroy started to struggle and breaking free momentarily, he crawled to Achledis's feet, seizing them and holding on as Rolen and another man grabbed him and tried to pull him away, but he held on fast. "Please, my wife and children are innocent; please don't harm them."

"Their innocence is for our courts to determine; now be gone." With his foot, Achledis kicked the Viceroy away.

CHAPTER 36: TREASON

Vitaeus woke up the next morning feeling like he had barely slept, yet filled with excitement. He had stayed up late the night before just talking to Yolif, and he had learned so much from the youth that he felt like he finally had a real trustworthy friend. Their conversations went from exchanging stories of their youth growing up, in their own circumstances, to Yolif sharing ideas of military doctrine, leaving Vitaeus impressed. Vitaeus had gained a brother and a trusted ally in one night. Yolif had shared his vision with Vitaeus to build a small band of elite warriors, who could infiltrate anything and get to anyone. Yolif had been interested in acrobatics since his childhood. He was inspired when he saw some acrobats performing incredible stunts at a circus that came around. He was lucky enough to meet the acrobat after the circus was over, and the man shared with Yolif the training that he undertook. From then on, Yolif took his training seriously. On top of his core body strengthening, he started to study on how to develop a technique to fight without weapons. It was similar to performing a new stunt. One must first envision performing the spectacular act before doing it; so he had to envision making the perfect kick, the perfect swipe of hand, or delivering the perfect punch. No motion was to be wasted; every movement had to have a purpose.

A loud commotion outside brought Vitaeus to the window, where Yolif was assembling the peasant workers. He watched as a peasant mouthed of to Yolif and ended up lying flat on the ground. From that point, everyone seemed to take Yolif seriously as they lined up at his command. Vitaeus smiled as he turned to dress. With Yolif at his side, he felt confident enough to walk into a den of vipers and be unscathed. It was time to meet Razim once more.

The party of horsemen rode up to the gates of the city, kicking up dust as they went. A small crowd of onlookers stopped near the gates and watched the party ride in; looking especially at the banner of the silver and white wolf displayed and at its leader, wearing a silvery bluish armor, polished to the extent that the metal reflected like a looking glass. A city watchman blew his horn in the distance, sounding a signal or warning to the city guard. Vitaeus had five knights as his escort. Yolif rode beside him in plainclothes, and Nepides followed in chains.

The loud rumbling of approaching horsemen sounded from the front and behind him; turning around, Vitaeus saw a group of the city watch dressed in white and black cloaks appearing from a side street and turning in his direction. From the front, another troop of the city watch approached as well, as if to cut off his escape. His knights no doubt sensed the same as they all reached for their swords.

"Stay calm men. No need to draw your weapons." Vitaeus commanded as they reigned in and waited for the city guard to approach.

As the guards rode up, they instantly circled around Vitaeus's party. The commander of the guard rode up with a golden sash displayed from his left shoulder down to his waist on his right.

"Sir Vitaeus, you have been ordered before the King."

"That's where I am headed," Vitaeus replied. "If you want to ride along, you are more than welcome to do so."

"You alone must come; the others may go." The commander replied with a steely voice.

"My men are coming with me." Vitaeus replied

"That isn't an option sir. Now come along of your own free will or be dragged in chains before the King."

"Lord Commander!" Nepides cried out. "Demand my release. I have been kept prisoner by this man."

The lord commander of the city watch studied Nepides for a few moments and nodded his head in recognition. "Release this man; he is the King's servant who has gone missing."

Vitaeus turned to Yolif. "Go back to the castle; you're in charge until I'm back."

Yolif gave a nod and waved the escort to follow him as they turned around and galloped back in the direction of the city gate, leaving Vitaeus alone with the city guard.

The city guard escorted Vitaeus inside the throne room, and two guards gripped him firmly on either arm. King Razim sat on his elaborate throne that had the head of a giant viper baring its teeth and was posed to strike its prey as it protruded from the backrest and over Razim's head. Two viper heads on either side of the throne served as armrests for King Razim where he sat delivering judgment when they approached. The guards, along with Vitaeus, waited. Razim hadn't so much as lifted his eyes to acknowledge them.

"For the crime of stealing from the crown, I will give you two options." Razim was saying to the prisoner. "Either you lose your hand and serve five years in the dungeons, or you may serve a lifetime in the mines to recompense for your crimes."

The man let out a whimper as he closed his eyes and wept openly. "Mercy my King, have mercy I beg you."

"My sentence is merciful and just; your crime cannot go unpunished. If every man in this city was to steal a loaf of bread from me, what would happen to me, I wonder? I would most likely starve." Razim answered.

"It was stale bread and had to be tossed out anyway."

"Take him to the mines." Razim commanded and made a swiping gesture with his hands.

Instantly, guards grabbed the man and dragged him away as he kicked and screamed for mercy. Vitaeus felt the guard's grip on him tighten as he too was suddenly brought before the king. The guards then applied pressure behind his knees with their heavy booted feet. As his knees buckled, the guards shoved him forward so that he fell prostrate before the King.

"My Lord, you wished to see me." Vitaeus said as he raised his head to address the King.

"Yes, that's why I had you dragged here." Razim said irritably. "It disgusts me to look at your traitor face. I should hang you off the cliff and allow the vultures to clean it for me; then it would be more bearable to look at."

"Traitor? My King, you are known to be just; please tell me why I am accused of treason."

"Yes, treason is your crime, but I wanted to know exactly what your plan was. You can either tell me here or tell me in the dungeons as you're put to the question under threat of having your limbs pulled apart on a rack."

"It was your servant Nepides who was treasonous, and I have his letter that he wrote and signed."

"Nepides? Is that why you kidnapped my most loyal servant so that you could implicate him in your own crime? I trusted that man with everything, and you repaid my kindness by kidnapping him. Bring him to me." Razim growled, and the guards grabbed Vitaeus under the armpits and dragged him up the stone steps of the dais until he was right before the King. Razim pulled his arm back and slapped Vitaeus with all of his strength across the face. "There, that's for insulting me." Razim said as he clutched his hand in pain.

Vitaeus struggled to keep his face free of mirth; so he kept quiet for fear that even a word would break his laughter loose. "My King, in my jacket pocket is a letter written by Nepides himself. Perhaps you should read it and decide for yourself. I wrote a letter and had it delivered to you regarding Nepides. Did you receive it?"

Razim reached for Vitaeus's jacket and pulled out a neatly folded letter. He opened it up and read it, not saying anything for some time as he pondered the words and the writing on the paper.

"The handwriting and the signature are unmistakable." The King finally replied. "Where is Nepides?"

"I was escorting him to you, my King, when your guards arrested me and freed my prisoner."

The King looked at the lord commander of the city guard; whose face had paled at the implication of allowing a prisoner charged with treason go free.

"My King," the lord commander came and bowed. "I recognized him as your servant who had gone missing. I wasn't aware of his crimes."

"Neither was I," the King replied as he moved his gaze back to Vitaeus.

"He will be questioned regarding that letter; I only hope he was forced to write that with a blade at his throat because it will go worse for the man who coerced such a letter out of him. Tell me, is treason why you kidnapped him from me in the first place?"

"No, my King, my servant was away assisting in the service of the Rok royals; so Nepides volunteered to help me get started with recruiting my workers."

"Is that why you fled my hospitality?" The King demanded angrily. "Don't try to deceive me. I have heard too many vile whisperings of your evil deeds lately, and I won't be slighted further."

"My King, please allow me to explain. There has definitely been a lot of murmuring about me lately, and I too have heard the disgusting rumors that my enemies have been spreading about me."

"Go on then, tell me your tale."

"When I approached Nepides, asking for his assistance, he was very eager and insisted that I move to the castle as a base. From there, I can come and go unimpeded, and anyone looking for employment would know where to go. His advice was sound, and I took it. In the last few days, he helped me recruit a couple hundred workers and the numbers grow daily. Yesterday, I thanked him for his help and offered that he return to your service; afraid that he may be missed. But that is when he gave me the letter my King, renouncing you as King and implicating an innocent man such as myself in his crimes. I had no choice, but to lock him up even after all of his help. I will not be tainted by his filth as I assume that he has been the one responsible for spreading all these rumors about me; which my King is all too aware of. They are the reason your suspicions have grown against me My Lord. Though my ambitions are as pure as when we first spoke, is there any way that I can prove my innocence?"

"Proving your innocence will be difficult I'm afraid; for I have seen you and the princess during the ball. I was insulted by a petty lord, who came in and pompously swooped my lady right from under me. I am your King, not your equal, and I will not be slighted."

"Sir, the princess and I have been friends for a long time. I have visited the Rok Isles and sold them valuable Permedian rugs for their palaces and dishes made of pearl and ivory. She has been very comfortable with a familiar face, and if My Lord permits me to speak freely, I must tell you of new developments. But I don't mean to offend you, My King."

"Go on then, speak." The King commanded gruffly, as he motioned for a servant girl standing to the side holding a flask of wine. She came and offered him the flask, and the King drank heartily. The wine spilled around the flask and down his chin; which the servant girl quickly wiped for him."

"The princess is seventeen, My Lord, and just a young maiden; you, My Lord, are five times her age; so please try to imagine her anxiety about this union. I am trying to reassure her and council her to accept your engagement."

"She is contemplating on refusing?" The King gasped in mid-swallow. The wine went down the wrong pipe and sent the king into a frenzied coughing spell. Everyone watched anxiously as the King's face went red, but no one moved to help him. The King looked at Vitaeus with fearful eyes; as he still couldn't draw a breath. It was terrible to watch an old man dying right before him. This man was Vitaeus's enemy, and he was dying right before him. Without Vitaeus so much as touching him. The King rasped for a breath and pounded on his own chest. His fists beat feebly as his eyes stared into the distance; the realization of the inevitable settled in. He was going to die.

CHAPTER 37: YUROSI THE HERO

Achledis mulled over his decision to imprison the Viceroy's family and staff in one of the large guest rooms. The Vicereine's attitude had not improved for the better, but he ordered that she be treated humanely and with respect. His men had instantly disagreed and argued with him to throw them all into Seredine's darkest dungeons. In their eyes, the Vicereine was just as guilty as the Viceroy himself. Deep down, Achledis's sentiment was with them. He had no love for these foreign occupiers and wanted revenge, but thoughts of his father and the way he always acted nobly reminded him of what it actually meant to be a man. His father would never subject a lady to such treatment simply because she was the wife of a guilty man. The Viceroy was the ruler, and he would be the one punished. If charges were brought up against the Vicereine, then she too would be tried. But in the meantime, he would make sure that she was treated with dignity. Besides, perhaps he could strike a deal for them when Viserate arrived at the gates of Seredine. In the end, he had made his decision, and the men had obeyed him. Now he must concern himself with governing the city and preparing its defenses.

Hurried footsteps interrupted his thoughts. He looked up and saw that it was one of his men. Saluting quickly, the man instantly began to relay his message. "Captain Keltar is asking you to meet him at the eastern keep. He said to tell you that it's about Yurosi."

One of Keltar's men met Achledis at the entrance and led him inside. A steep, narrow, circular staircase made of solid stone was immediately to their left, but the guard walked around to the other side of it, motioning to a small door that led underneath the stairs. The small entrance forced Achledis to stoop low to avoid bumping his head across a beam. A lit torch from somewhere below provided barely enough lighting, and Achledis had to pause in order to see where he was. He appeared to be on a ledge, and right below him was a ladder that descended into the cool darkness below.

Achledis found himself in a small tunnel. He had never been claustrophobic, but he felt as he might be at that moment. The rock walls were so narrow that his shoulders brushed against a rough rock on occasion, and the dirt ground was uneven and cold. A faint light was somewhere in front of him, and though it didn't radiate enough light for him to see right in front of him, the sound of rodents scurrying out of his path was enough to send goose bumps up and down his spine. The air seemed to suddenly get that much colder. His hand closed around the hilt of his knife in his belt for some reassurance. If a rodent decided to attack him in this darkness, however, he knew that fighting back with a knife would be foolish and dangerous. It was a good way to stab himself accidentally. He smiled at the silliness of trying to fight rats in the darkness and shook his head as he took his hand off the hilt of the knife. He came to a small chamber; the light from a small torch that hung on the wall seemed to dance across the walls. The air inside was musty and hard to breathe.

"Over here," came Keltar's voice. "He is unconscious, and his breathing is shallow. But he is alive." Achledis looked in the direction from where the voice came and saw Keltar stooped over the body of a man. "How long have you been here?" He asked.

"A little bit before you. I got Lorne to fess up the location and sent word to you right away, but instead of waiting for you, I hurried to investigate by myself. I hope you don't mind."

"I don't mind; you did the right thing. Looks like we found him while he is still alive." Achledis said, as he stooped to get a closer look at the wrecked body in front of him. Even in the shallow light, he could see the bruising on Yurosi's face and the tatters of his shirt as it hung loosely around his frame.

"He has a fever, but if we can get him to a doctor, I think he should live."

"Let's get him out of here." Achledis agreed.

Upon bringing Yurosi to a nice clean bed in one of the rooms in the palace, a doctor was summoned. When the doctor entered the room and saw Yurosi, his expression was similar to that of many others who saw him; though the doctor was able to compose himself quickly. Whatever thoughts had raced through his mind, he kept them to himself. First, he checked the pulse, and after making sure that it was there, he checked the forehead with the back of his palm. With worry, he shook his head involuntarily and asked that the room be cleared.

"Will he make it, doc?" Keltar asked, his brows heavy with concern.

"I can't say for sure. He is in a very serious condition. One thing I can tell you is that today will be a big battle for him. I need lots of water, alcohol, and clean rags. We will kill the infection and hopefully beat back his fever."

"We will get those things right away." Keltar said, and looked at Achledis who was standing beside him.

"Yes, right way." Achledis agreed.

As Achledis and Keltar were leaving the room, Desiani appeared huffing angrily. One of the guards, whom Achledis had posted, was right behind her in pursuit. Seeing Achledis, she scowled at him, "Tell that idiot behind me to leave me alone; he keeps trying to block me from coming through."

"Sorry sir, she ran right past me." The guard apologized as he tried to grab Desiani's hand. She swatted his arm away and smacked him with her palm, leaving a pink imprint on the side of his face.

"Stay away from me!" She yelled angrily. The guard jumped back, glancing at Achledis hesitantly.

"Let her be. She is fine." Achledis reassured the guard. The guard nodded and flinched at the sight of Desiani as she raised her hand to strike him again. He hurried away. Achledis chuckled aloud as Desiani glared at him.

"It's not funny! That idiot wouldn't let me through for several hours, and eventually, I lost my patience and kicked him where it mattered. Then I ran past him while he rolled around on the ground," She said that last part proudly with a smile on her face. Achledis and Keltar looked at one another and winced.

"Remind me not to get on her bad side." Keltar joked.

"Never mind that. Where is Yurosi? I heard bits and pieces from your "guards" that you guys couldn't find him at first, and then excited rumors that he was found."

"He is in the room with the doctor, but you can't come in right now, doctor's orders."

"Bull, I'm going to see him right now." She pushed past Achledis defiantly, and right before she walked through the door, she turned as if she just remembered to say something. "Oh and congratulations on your victory here." She flashed a quick smile and walked through the door. A moment later, they heard her gasp at the sight of Yurosi's battered and bruised body.

"Good thing she didn't see his back." Keltar said.

Achledis shook his head at the thought of the grotesque image of Yurosi's scourged back. Though his initial impression of Yurosi wasn't positive, he had acquired a newfound respect for the young man who was flogged within an inch of his life, went through endless torture, but never gave up his comrades. They all owed him for the successful revolt. If he had given in to their beatings, the rest of them would have been arrested and gone through something similar.

CHAPTER 38: TO SAVE A KING

Vitaeus grabbed the King and smacked him on the back a few times, clearing the airflow once more. The King sank back on his throne, closed his eyes, and breathed deeply; while his body continued to tremble.

"My Lord, are you well?" Vitaeus asked politely.

The King looked at him briefly and closed his eyes once more. "Of course not, I thought I was going to die."

Everyone stood shocked, not daring to say anything. The servant girl finally asked in a small timid voice. "Can I get you some more wine My Lord?"

"No, don't get me any more wine! Are you the one trying to kill me?" The girl paled at the King's accusations, but the king only shooed her away with his hand.

"Get out of here! Everyone get out!" The king shouted.

As Vitaeus turned to go with everyone else, the King grabbed his arm. "You stay." When the throne room emptied and Vitaeus was alone with the king, Razim looked at him and whispered, "You proved your loyalty. When everyone stood around and waited for me to die, you were the one that saved my life. I will reward you for it."

"Thank you my King, but I only did what any loyal subject would do for his king."

"If that is true, then you were the only loyal one in the room I suppose, and everyone else should be tried for treason. Why did you save me?"

"You are my King and a fellow person. How could I let you die my King?"

King Razim looked him over apprehensively before giving a slight nod. "I suppose you had a reason; either way, I will reward you for it. Now you were telling me about my young princess. Please tell me, is she seriously thinking on refusing me before my realm?"

"She voiced her concern, but she didn't actually tell me that she would. I believe that she is feeling anxious My Lord."

"Yes, I suppose that is understandable. Lord Vitaeus, you have proved your loyalty and are now back in the King's graces. Please accept my invitation to the ball tonight and persuade the princess to accept my engagement. If she were to refuse, it would be a humiliation that I may not recover from in my old age."

"Yes my King." Vitaeus bowed. "If I may have your leave, I will prepare to do just that."

"You may go." The King said, and as Vitaeus bowed and turned to go, the King called him back. "Not sure if you heard the good news from the mainland, but there has been a Rosmirian revolt against Rakirian rule that took place in Seredine."

"No, I haven't, but that is very good news." Vitaeus replied.

"Don't be so sure about that," the King warned. "It was the Celesta rebellion in the North that brought Rakiria's wrath and caused this army to invade and murder so many of your countrymen. I can only assume that with this insurrection in Seredine that Rakiria's response will only get more heavy handed. The fools overthrew their Rakirian masters; even as a Rakirian army of 10,000 marches on toward the city. I'm troubled by this revolt in Seredine; it might cause Rakiria to go to another war with us. Then it will be more knights that I will need, not ships."

"Your Majesty, in the case of war, the isthmus that borders Rosmir is heavily defended, and it will be my ships that can transfer our troops to strike the enemy from the rear. The navy will be more valuable than ever."

"I don't need to strike them from the rear. I simply need to show them that invading Caminia is futile."

"Your Majesty, perhaps if we sent an army to help Seredine drive this Rakirian army back, then we can reinforce the defenses on the Rakirian and Rosmirian border. Then Rosmir and Caminia will once again be joined together as one nation."

"No, I will not expose my army to wager a war outside Caminia. It is too small to withstand a war with Rakiria."

"Your Majesty-"

"Enough! I will not hear more on the matter. You're not my general; you're a merchant. So, what would you know of planning a war? I will send my advisors and engineers to you today. Tell them what you need, and they will ensure that it gets done. Here is my seal. Put this on any work order and document. It will ensure that your work order goes through twice as fast, and the crown will pay for it."

"My King is too kind, thank you My Lord." Vitaeus replied humbly, even as he fumed inside at the King's unwillingness to help Seredine.

"No, your King is gracious and wants to reward you. Make sure that you send Nepides back to me in chains." Vitaeus bowed once more and left.

The next morning, Vitaeus thought back on the prior day; which was filled with so much blessing. Not only was he back in the King's favourable graces, but he had met with chief engineers, builders, and masons. Together they had outlined what his new fortress and shipyard would look like spanning the Shield Isles. Starting today, work crews will be traveling to begin their work on his new castle. He sent purchase orders for fifty ships from the Island of Five Kingdoms, with Razim's seal affixed to it, and a promise to pay in Caminian gold.

His mind then wandered to the ball last night; it had been magical. He was honored by the King in front of the court for saving the King's life. During the feast, Vitaeus sat next to the princess; while on her other side sat the King, and it was Vitaeus who entertained her for the majority of the night. During the dancing, the King apologized to the princess and told her that his old legs were too tired from a weeklong of balls, but he offered that she dance with Vitaeus, stating that Vitaeus dances with far greater grace than he could muster.

Daenis came in suddenly, interrupting his daydream, "My Lord, are you awake?" He asked tentatively. "You have a visitor."

"Who is it?"

"It is the princess's servant girl. She says she needs to see you urgently and wouldn't listen when I told her that you were sleeping and that she must come back later."

Vitaeus was instantly alert as he got up and slipped some clothes on. "Tell her that I will see her."

"She is waiting for you in your sitting area, My Lord."

Vitaeus washed his face from a basin and combed his hair neatly; he wanted to make sure he looked sharp as he checked himself in the looking glass. This wasn't Raheena. But the servant girl undoubtedly would relay his negligent appearance; if he showed himself in such manner.

"I present Lord Vitaeus," Daenis announced as he opened the door for Vitaeus. The servant girl was beautiful. She had a dark complexion of olive skin, dark hair, and blue eyes; which were defined by her long eyelashes.

"My Lord, a note from the princess," the girl kept her eyes down as she handed him a letter.

Vitaeus opened it and skimmed its contents. "Daenis, bring me a fresh piece of paper and ink."

Daenis bowed and disappeared.

"Did the princess sleep well?" He asked.

The servant girl smiled shyly and nodded.

Raheena's plan was to go for a ride outside the city, along with her brothers. She invited him to perchance have a run in. Vitaeus wrote his reply, inviting the princess and her brothers to stop at his castle. No sooner had Raheena's servant girl left, along with her escort of two knights, when he had another servant run in panicked and out of breath.

"Sir, a letter addressed to you from the palace of the King. The messenger who gave it, stressed its urgency to you."

Vitaeus read the letter; which contained only one alarming line. Addressed from a 'friend,' the script was more of a scribble as if written in haste or inconspicuously written in a public place. Vitaeus wondered at its implication and what it meant for him as he reread it, "Nepides has been cleared by the King."

Vitaeus went to a window in the tower that faced the city of Caminia and overlooked Jade Lake in the distance. As he looked past the water, which glittered in the sun, he noticed a rising dust cloud far in the distance. A multitude of knights seemed to appear from the dust cloud as they approached with the King's banners waving. Somehow he doubted that this was Princess Raheena's escort. This was something more foreboding, and he felt it in the pit of his stomach.

CHAPTER 39: SUN RISES TO A NEW DAY

As the first rays of daylight broke unto the horizon, the last of the storm clouds were disappearing on the other side of the sky. A bell was clanging away, pronouncing the arrival of a new dawn, a new era of freedom from Rakirian rule. Throngs of people had already gathered at the palace square as news of liberty traveled swiftly throughout the city and was making its way into the countryside. Young men ran through the streets, pounding on people's doors and shouting the good news of the victorious rebellion against Rakirian rule.

Achledis stepped out on the balcony facing the crowds; a smile crossed his face at the sight of the jubilant people below. At the sight of him, the crowds went into an exuberant chant, some shouting out Yurosi's name and others shouting for Alrik. It was a beautiful day, he thought as he took a deep breath of fresh air. After the thunderstorm, the foul smells of the city had subsided a lot. In the distance, he watched as an eagle circled in the air high above, before swooping down to catch its prey. To see an eagle was always a good omen, he thought. He felt the presence of someone behind him and turned to see Desiani, enthralled by the sight.

"It's so beautiful today; isn't it?" She asked.

"Yes it is, and the air is actually pleasant and fresh as well." Achledis replied, and Desiani smiled at that. She remembered how disgusted Achledis had been with the smells when he first had entered the city. After a moment, her mood turned serious once more. "I heard about Alrik's death; that's so sad."

"Alrik was a true leader and patriot. He knew the risk, and he took it willingly. He was encouraged by the fact that we were closing in on Viceroy Lorne, and that victory was imminent. I only wish he could have lived long enough to see it to the end; he was so close."

"Me too," Desiani said with a sigh. "He was definitely a good man."

The two stood in silence, watching the crowd below them grow around the gallows.

Achledis knew that as the leader he had to go address them, but the thought of speaking to a large crowd seemed daunting, even to him.

"I better go address the crowd." Achledis said.

"That would be a good idea." Desiani replied with an encouraging smile.

As Achledis turned to go, the dread he felt must have been apparent on his face because Desiani took his hand.

"I'll go with you." She said cheerfully.

On the platform, Achledis raised his hands up in a gesture for the crowd to quiet, but he was largely ignored as most of the people in the crowd were looking towards the palace. Achledis shouted for silence, but his booming voice was only heard by the people right next to the podium. Otherwise, his voice was swallowed by the loud buzz of people all conversing at once. The people closest to the podium, upon seeing the tall youth with shoulder length blonde hair flowing in the breeze and piercing blue eyes, sensed his authority and chimed in with him, shouting for silence. Eventually, more and more people took notice of him and took up the chant for silence. Once all the attention was upon him, Achledis raised his hands, and the crowd fell silent. Achledis let the silence linger as if to make sure that he had everyone's attention before he began to recount the events of the past night.

"I am Achledis, son of Kalim, and I want to thank all of you who volunteered last night and helped to make this victory happen. If it wasn't for all of your support, Rakirian oppression would still be upon us this morning. Last night we lost 21 of our country men, and amongst them was our great leader Alrik." At the mention of Alrik, a murmur went through the crowd, and again, Achledis raised his hands in the air as a gesture for silence. Once he got the crowd's attention again, he recounted how Alrik got injured, and how the men lost the morale to keep going without him. He told of Alrik's inner strength to stand up and keep going, pretending that the wound was minor; even though it was slowly killing him in order to make sure that the men didn't falter after coming so far. Achledis wrapped up the story by telling them of Alrik's death and the men's courage to finish what they started, even with their leader dead. The story ended with the capture of Lorne and his family; at which the crowd shouted out in jubilation. After a few moments, Achledis had to plead for silence once more, and again the crowd grew quiet.

Someone in the crowd shouted, "Hang Lorne, hang that criminal!" And the rest of the crowd shouted in agreement.

"I share your desire to have revenge on Lorne and all of the Rakirians, but we must remember that if we believe in justice, then we should practice it. We will put Lorne and his family on trial, where they will get a chance to plead their defense. If we prove him guilty, then we will punish him."

Angry shouts of protest rang out, and the crowd started to turn hostile. A burly man close to the podium jumped up on it and started shouting, and the people grew quiet in order to hear him.

"Bring him out to hang! That is the only justice he can expect from us. After everything he has done, he deserves nothing short of death."

"Listen to me!" Achledis shouted, but he was drowned out by the man next to him, who continued to get the crowd worked up. Achledis's anger brimmed to the top, and he stepped toward the man and shouted, "Be quiet! Can't you see I am trying to address the crowd?"

The man pushed Achledis away from himself, and with fire in his eyes, he lunged at Achledis with a flurry of fists. Achledis deflected a couple of the blows, but also took a couple of blows to the side of his face. He then stepped up and delivered a shot at the man's jaw, wincing at the sound of a bone popping. The man got up gingerly but didn't dare attack Achledis again. Taking a deep breath, Achledis apologized to the man and to the crowd, but the damage was already done.

"A Rakirian army of an estimated 10,000 men is on the march towards Seredine and should be here within a month. This army is headed by a vicious colonel who is pillaging the land, butchering the elderly people, and taking the young captive. I would like to try and negotiate with him for our people in exchange for Viceroy Lorne. It would be foolish for us to hang one man who could help us get our countrymen back from captivity."

There was a murmur of assent from the crowd that was quickly blotted out from others in the crowd who didn't buy the argument. Some even shouted accusations, suggesting that Achledis was a Rakirian agent. Keltar, Rolen, and Desiani made their way through the crowd and joined Achledis on the platform. Keltar nodded at Achledis, but neither one said anything to one another. Instead, Keltar and Rolen faced the crowd.

"I am Keltar, the best friend of Alrik, the man who gave his life. Though I was Alrik's best friend and most trusted confidant, he made it clear that Achledis was his right hand man and next in line of command. After Alrik's death, it was obvious why Alrik chose him. For Achledis is a natural leader who rallied us to victory even in the wake of Alrik's death, when morale was down, and the men's fighting spirit was broken. Now Achledis is by no means a politician. He is a warrior through and through, and one with little patience for nonsense. He showed that to us when he punched the instigator, who was being rude and trying to turn all of you from the good sense that Achledis was trying to present to us. Next to me is Desiani, and she has a personal story to share with all of you."

Desiani stepped forward and told the crowd her story of how Achledis had first defended her against the Rakirian guard and later of his daring rescue. By the time she was done with her story, the crowd's opinion of Achledis was positive once more, and some were even clearly in awe of him. It took a few people in the crowd to start, but soon everyone joined in on chanting Achledis's name. Desiani turned to Achledis, and the two embraced.

"Thank-you so much for coming to my rescue. I thought the crowd was going to lynch me." He whispered in her ear.

She smiled back. "Now we are even," she replied sweetly.

Keltar winked at him. "I don't doubt that my friend. That was a crazy stunt you pulled by breaking that man's jaw," he said with a chuckle. "If it wasn't for beautiful Desiani pleading for you, you would have been a dead man. Look at how she turned the crowd around, who just moments ago wanted to lynch you, but now they adore you."

"Achledis look," Rolen said as he pointed at a stranger on horseback making his way to the platform as the crowd had cleared a path for him. The man's horse was weary and covered with white foamy sweat, and the man himself looked almost too exhausted to ride and seemed to be on the verge of collapse. His long hair was plastered to the side of his face, and his eyes were dark from the lack of sleep. As he rode up to the platform, Achledis, Keltar, and Rolen helped the man dismount from the horse and helped him up on the platform; where he was instantly given a canteen of water. Rolen took the horse and assured the stranger that it would be placed in the palace stables where it would be groomed, watered, and fed. The man nodded graciously, before turning to address the crowd; which had grown quiet in anticipation of this man's story.

After introducing himself, the man started to tell his tale. He was on one of the wagon trains heading to Caminia. One night after they set camp and had gone to sleep, they awoke to the sound of horses galloping. Quickly running out of his tent, he witnessed a Rakirian cavalry swooping down on their campsite. In graphic detail, he recounted how the people were either cut down by a blade or trampled underneath the hooves.

"I managed to run and hide in the bushes," he admitted as giant tears flowed down his face. "Like a coward I hid myself and watched my family and friends get hacked down." His whole body shuddered as a big sob overtook him; he couldn't speak for a moment before he was able to regain his composure. "They didn't spare anyone, neither women nor children; everyone was murdered. They just wanted us all dead."

Desiani and Keltar led the man to the palace where he could be fed, and the man's story had suddenly unnerved the crowd. People started asking what would happen to them when Viserate arrived. More and more grumbled against Achledis. Some started to blame him, saying that after their rebellion, Viserate would kill them all in punishment.

"If Viserate gets a chance, he will kill most of you, and it doesn't have anything to do with us overthrowing Rakirian rule in Seredine. His army has been marching through Rosmir murdering and killing our people for a month now. I am a witness to this because I lived through the attack on my village of Pavanti. I watched as my family got murdered. That was why it was so urgent for us to overthrow Lorne; so that we as citizens could prepare to defend ourselves. If Lorne was still in power, he would have allowed Viserate to march right through our walls and kill us all, but now we have the power to defend ourselves. We will organize an army for our defense. Our engineers will devise ways to help us. As for the rest of you, I am asking you to help by donating all of your metal to the forge, where we will cast new weapons. Volunteer at the guilds by helping to make weapons and armor for the army. Help us bring in food and supplies to withstand a long siege. It is all of our duty to assist, and I ask all of you to stand with me to fight for us and for our country."

CHAPTER 40: TO SPURN A KING

Vitaeus rode outside his walls to personally meet the host of the King's knights as they approached his castle. At the sight of him, they instantly reigned in, and only the lead knight proceeded the last 100 feet.

"Sir Vitaeus, I am Sir Yousel, the commander of the King's palace guards." Sir Yousel took off his helmet and offered his hand in greeting.

"Good day Sir Yousel, and what is it that the commander with nineteen of his fellow guards is doing so far away from the palace? Who is guarding the King and his royal bride-to-be in your absence?"

"Following the King's orders sir; we were ordered by His Majesty to give you a safe passage to his palace."

"The King is generous to offer an escort; however, I wasn't aware of an appointment there," Vitaeus mused with a broad smile on his face. "Tell me sir, did the King give you a time for when he wanted me there?"

"My understanding is that he wanted you there right away sir."

"No offense sir, but I didn't ask for your understanding of the matter. I asked if the King requested a specific time."

"No sir, His Majesty did not state a specific time. He merely asked me to escort you to him; which to me always means right away."

"Sir Yousel, your concern of wanting to keep the King content is understandable. It's just that I have pressing business at the moment; however, I will be delighted to see him tonight after I attend to my business."

"Tonight the King will be busy and won't want to be disturbed. You sir will be coming with me right away. I'm afraid that you don't have a choice in the matter."

Vitaeus raised his hand in the air to signal his crossbowmen behind him. He didn't need to see that they were there; Yousel's eyes told him that they were.

"Tell the King that I will see him tonight." Vitaeus reiterated.

"To threaten the King's personal guards is treason sir. I hope you know what you just did; for your own sake, be warned."

"Get on your way then, or my threats will prick you more painfully than words ever could." Vitaeus retorted.

Sir Yousel turned his horse around and galloped away; as he passed his guards they fell in behind him. Vitaeus watched until all he could see was their dust settling in the distance. He had just raised the ante in his open feud with the King, but Vitaeus was aware of his many mistakes that he had already made. There was no going back now. Vitaeus knew he had to tread carefully. But he was more determined than ever to take back his throne, and to do that, he had already formulated a plan.

Vitaeus was met at the gate by two Rok dignitaries. They wore yellow cloaks on top of their white tunics, and medallions around their necks to ensure their rank was clear. They bowed politely when they came to his makeshift dais.

"My Lord, Princess Raheena regrets that she won't be able to make it to your castle today, but asks that you join her and her brothers for a bit of sailing on Jade Lake. She is there now My Lord."

"Thank you for your message. Please tell the princess that I will see her there." Vitaeus replied.

Sir Yousel strode through the palace, followed by the other nineteen guards who had ridden out to Vitaeus's castle with him. He was still fuming at being rebuffed the way he had been by Vitaeus, who ignored the King's request and then threatened him with crossbowmen. It was more than his dignity allowed. Vitaeus was also the same lord who kidnapped the King's most trusted aide and brought about the King's ire. Yet Lord Vitaeus had showed that he wasn't to be cowed, and this he knew would displease the King a great deal.

Yousel paused by the throne room as he heard the King shouting angrily inside; he drew his breath and strode in. He felt the King's eyes fixate on him immediately and heard the King shoo away his next petitioner by shouting vulgarities at him. Then there was the loud sound of shattering glass as the king threw his wine glass at the retreating figure. Yousel bowed before the King, "My Lord and my King."

"Stand up! Why are you here without the merchant?" The King growled.

"He refused to come, claiming that he was busy at the moment and could only come later this evening My Lord."

"He actually refused to come?" The King asked; surprised by what he heard. And under his breath he muttered to himself, "That insolent fool; he only proves his own guilt." Then looking at Yousel once more, he addressed him sharply. "Commander, did you let him believe that this was something he could turn down?"

"No, Your Majesty. When he refused, I told him that he had no choice in the matter, and that he was coming with us. Then on his signal, a host of crossbowmen appeared on his battlements, aiming their weapons at us. We were shooed away like mere bandits."

"Then why are you coming to tell me of this? Are you incompetent? Take every guard and knight in this city and bring him to me dead or alive. I don't care, but I want him here.

CHAPTER 41: YUROSI'S RECOVERY

"Achledis, Achledis, you must come with me right away!" Desiani ran into the room; her face aglow with excitement. "It's Yurosi! His fever has broken, and he has regained consciousness. He said he wants to talk to you."

"That's great news," Achledis replied. He focused his attention back on his sword; which he was sharpening. He smiled at the thought of Desiani's excited face; he hadn't seen her this excited in a long time. He remembered the time he spent with her as they traveled north to Seredine, and he realized that he had missed spending time with her. Since overthrowing Rakirian rule in Seredine, they had both been busy, preparing the city for the siege.

"Why are you smiling? Are you really that excited for Yurosi?" She asked him.

"Would that be a bad thing?"

"No, I just didn't expect it from you. Frankly, I suspected a bit of jealousy on your part."

Achledis arched an eyebrow at her. "Jealousy?"

"Yes jealousy." Desiani concluded.

"Being beaten and left to die by the Rakirians is hardly something to be jealous of. In all honesty, I'm glad it was him rather than me."

"Oh stop," she pushed him playfully. "You know what I mean. You were jealous of him that first day; I could see it in your eyes."

Achledis shrugged. "Not jealous, I just thought his act was a little excessive."

"What act?" Desiani asked, her voice instantly turning defensive.

Achledis never seized to be amazed that even when angry, her face maintained its angelic appearance; she couldn't look angry even if she wanted.

"He likes to flaunt his money and has his servant or 'squire' serving him all the time."

Desiani arched an eyebrow at him. "Wow, I didn't realize you were that jealous."

"I just don't care for his cavalier attitude."

"You only met him that first night. How can you pass judgment so quickly?"

"Bad first impression." Achledis stated.

"He acts just as cavalier as you do. You should see yourself. Granted you have become more serious and less pompous since the revolt took place."

Achledis gave her a wry look. "Whatever." He replied.

"Look, give him a chance. He has a lot of great qualities, and he is very brave. I personally witnessed him risk his life to save the life of an old woman from being trampled by a Rakirian cavalry on the street."

"Hey, I didn't say that he wasn't brave. It was his attitude, oh never mind. Forget I said anything, okay? I will do my best to hold my feelings to myself."

"Please do, the poor man is recovering in bed with deep scars on his back from the beating he's taken, and here you are criticizing him."

Achledis wiped the oil from the blade with a towel and placed it on the bench beside him as he stood.

"I think you should go talk to him," she said, as she turned to go. "After all, he's a hero."

"Des," Achledis called after her, and she paused in front of the door at the sound of his voice. "I just wanted to thank you for all of your help yesterday."

She scrunched her nose at him in a cute way. "I know, you owe me your life."

"It's just that there is so much to do, and you seizing the opportunity and organizing the labor yesterday was a lot of help. This city appreciates it, and so do I. I admit that you surprised me a little. I mean, I knew you were a capable organizer; I just didn't realize that you were on a whole different level of good."

"There is a lot about me that you still don't know," she said, her eyebrow arched.

"Yes, you are a mystery which I intend to solve." He replied with a wink.

She smiled at him as she left the room. As the door closed behind her, Achledis picked up his sword and stared into the blade; his reflection stared back at him. He thought of Desiani and realized that she was the only real thing he had left from Pavanti. She was the only beautiful thing he knew in his shattered new world, and even then, he never actually knew her until after the Rakirian attack made them both prisoners. Together, they had gone through a lot, and Achledis realized that with Vitaeus gone, she was now his closest friend. Yet he felt as if he was competing for her friendship with Yurosi. Desiani was right. He was even more jealous than she realized, and it just now hit him.

Achledis knocked softly before entering the room where Yurosi resided. He looked towards the bed where the skinny, pale occupant of the room sat up rather quickly to see who his visitor was. A bright smile dawned on his face as he looked over to see the tall visitor. Achledis smiled back and tilted his head in a slight nod, but inside, he cringed at the sight of Yurosi's weak and battered body.

Yurosi's bed was set in the midst of what appeared to be a botanical garden. For Achledis, it was his first time in the room since bringing Yurosi's unconscious body in yesterday morning, and he was taken with how beautiful the room looked. Desiani had told him that she would make sure that the room would be a comfortable sanctuary for Yurosi to heal in; it appeared more like paradise. The all-white furniture and walls of the room maximized the brightness of the sunlight streaming in through the window, and the splash of various colors of different flowers that seemed to be arranged carefully throughout the room brought a pleasant aroma of lavender, roses, lilacs, and many other flowers. Achledis drew in a deep breath to capture the wonderful fragrance and held his breath for a moment before exhaling.

Yurosi had an all-knowing smile on his face. "I woke up thinking I died and went to heaven." He joked.

"No kidding," Achledis said, giving the other boy a smile. "Desiani did a good job in here making you comfortable."

"Her face was the first thing that registered in my vision when I came to," Yurosi laughed heartily. "I thought she was the Creator's angel."

Achledis smiled politely, "Good to see you're recovering."

"Is that what you call it?" Yurosi asked, as he looked down at himself for emphasis. His voice croaked as he spoke, "because this recovery burns worse than dragon's breath.

Achledis handed him a pitcher that stood on a table. With eager hands, Yurosi grabbed the pitcher tightly and drank, taking deep gulps. "It may not be water, but the effect is the same, if not better," Yurosi said as he wiped his mouth with the back of his wrist. The stench of liquor from his breath made Achledis realize what he had just, in fact, handed him.

"Hopefully the doc wasn't staying hydrated on that."

"He may have taken a swig. It's good medicine to deal with stress, as well as pain from open wounds."

The tension in the room had gotten considerably lighter between the two, and soon they were engaged in conversation like old friends. Yurosi told Achledis of the treatment the doctor used which included an antibacterial honey that was used to cover his open wounds. Supposedly it would help the wounds heal in record time. The antibacterial properties in the honey would fight any bacteria that may still exist after the doctor's thorough cleaning of the wounds. The honey provided a clean and moist environment that would help the cells heal and prevent any more germs from entering the wounds. "The doc says that my fever should disappear within a few days, but it will take two to three weeks for the wounds on my back to heal."

In turn, Achledis related every detail of the battle that took place to capture the palace and the events of the day following their victory. He recalled that after he had finished his speech at the gallows, Desiani got on the stage and called for all the master craftsmen of the guilds up on stage. From there, people came to volunteer their labor for the various jobs such as wood cutting, helping the blacksmith in the forge, and helping at the tannery and the butcher shop. The butcher shop was used to make glue from animal byproducts, shape ram horns into a birch frame that made the frame of the bow, and preserve meat to last them through the siege. Women volunteered to go pick berries and help out in the fields by gathering hay and other vegetables. Everyone wanted to help somehow, and they were overwhelmed with volunteers. All the young men have been asked to report for military training.

Achledis had sent a letter to the King in Caminia, explaining the events at Seredine and asking for assistance to defend the city against Viserate. Yurosi, who had more knowledge of the King, told Achledis not to expect too much assistance from him; for it was a well known fact that the King never engaged Rakirian armies outside Caminia. He preferred to stay in the safety of the natural defenses of the Caminian Peninsula; defenses that the Rakirian armies have never been able to penetrate.

Yurosi recounted to Achledis his harrowing story of the interrogation he had to go through. "They were stuck on the idea that I was a knight from Caminia, and that I was planning an insurrection. I kept telling them that there was no planned insurrection, but they didn't believe me and continued to press me for information that I didn't have. Some homeless kid came in during an interrogation once, pointed at me, and said that he personally heard how I was urging people to start a rebellion. I tried explaining that I was urging people to move to Caminia, but either they didn't believe me or they didn't care. Every time they tortured me to the point that I couldn't take it anymore, I would give them a fictitious location and make up names of the co-conspirators. A story like that would buy me a meal, and at times some sleep. However, I always awoke to a whip. Then the investigators would be furious at the false story, and the process would start all over again. The last 24 hours of the interrogation that I can remember, I didn't sleep at all and went through more whippings. They would hold my face in a tank of water until I started drowning, then yank me out. I remembered wanting to die; so when my face went in the water, I would purposely swallow water. That forced them to stop that technique, and they resorted back to the whipping."

"Clearly you weren't aware of a plot; so you couldn't give that away. But why didn't you give up our names? Since there was no plot, then there should have been nothing for you to worry about, right?" Achledis asked.

"I feared that it would start a domino effect. If I gave away your name, and you got arrested, then you might somehow implicate Desiani. Then she would be forced to go through the torture that I was going through. I wasn't going to risk that." Yurosi said.

The door swung open interrupting their conversation, and a boy, roughly around the age of fourteen, ran in. His blue eyes wide open from excitement; he tried to speak between gulps of air. "Sir Keltar and Sir Rolen are calling for you. They are by the barracks," he said, addressing Achledis.

"Tell them I'll be there soon." He told the boy.

The boy turned to go and hesitated, then turning around again he said, "It's kind of urgent; a cache of weapons has been found."

Achledis was instantly up on his feet. "Well I better go," he said rather excitedly. "Heal quickly my friend. We need you."

Yurosi nodded with understanding; a wistful look plastered on his face.

"Achledis?" Yurosi's voice stopped Achledis before he went out the door. "Keltar and Rolen told me that in the wake of Alrik's death, it was you who took control of the situation and ensured a victory over Lorne. Your account of the battle differed slightly from theirs; I noticed you didn't mention much about yourself in that battle. You have my respect."

"Thanks Yurosi, I'm honored by the praise, but actually, it's you whom we owe thanks to. If you would have broken under Rakirian interrogation, and I know most people would have, and given us away, then we never would have succeeded. You're the hero." Achledis turned towards the door, but Yurosi's voice stopped him again.

"Achledis, one more thing before you leave, I want you to keep me informed daily, and as soon as I'm on my feet, I want you as my right hand man. I have sent a request to my father to send as many men-at-arms as he can to aide me. I wrote to him of what happened here. He will have to understand that I wanted us to move to Caminia, but fate kept us here. As a Caminian knight, I have sworn to defend Seredine, using all of my military training."

Achledis was slightly dumbfounded; though he didn't let on, maintaining the stone face as cover. "I'm sorry Yurosi. It's not your fault you didn't know, but I'm in charge of Seredine. It's my city now, and the garrison is under my command. But I'm grateful for your assistance; we can always use your father's men."

Yurosi's eyes hardened briefly before he composed himself. He sighed and even smiled. "Of course, you were made commander." He held up his index finger, "A, because Alrik died," his middle finger flicked out alongside his index as he counted, "B, I wasn't there," ring finger up, "C, There was no one else."

"And here I am as your commander, and there you are under my command." Achledis replied, his voice had suddenly chilled.

Yurosi retained his smug smile, but his lips were pressed tightly together as if trying to maintain his emotions. The upper part of his cheek twitched on occasion as he studied Achledis as if for the first time. The tension was heavy between the two as all pretenses and sly maneuvering evaporated, replaced with the bluntness of words spoken from their hearts.

"Hmm, I didn't expect you to hold on to power so zealously," Yurosi finally replied. "But I am a knight, and you aren't. The chain of command automatically goes to me. I guess they never taught you this back on the farm, or wherever you're from. I only have to request direct orders from the King, and we shall have them. So don't piss on the hand that keeps you, or I will find another loyal dog. Remember, I am the only man of armor here, the only true knight."

With steely eyes, Achledis glared at Yurosi, and it was all he could do to maintain his control.

"Look tin man," Achledis said with gritted teeth, "I will throw you outside these walls regardless of your condition if you don't learn the first rule of military doctrine, and that is respecting the chain of command."

Yurosi smiled, defiance in his eyes. "I'm glad you know it then. As soon as the orders from the King arrive instating me as commander, I will hold you to your words."

CHAPTER 42: JADE LAKE

Princess Raheena, along with her two brothers at her side, met Vitaeus as he rode up to the lake where a sailboat was moored. There were few boats on the lake; as only the nobles could afford to own boats and have the leisure to go sailing. Princess Raheena was all smiles as she proudly presented her two brothers; who stood a head taller than her.

"Meet my oldest brother, Refal, and my younger brother, Meral."

Their skin was the color of bronze, and their jet black hair was done in a thousand thin braids that fell to their shoulders. But they shared their sister's turquoise eyes. They both had visible scars on their bodies, where a blade left its mark on them. He had once read that Rok boys were taught to fight and sail from an early age, and when they trained, they trained with steel rather than wooden swords. Their arms were like massive trunks, their chests were well defined, and the muscles ran down from their necks to their shoulders and down their backs in well-defined strands.

"The much spoken of Sir Vitaeus," Refal said with a grin, as he shook Vitaeus's hand firmly. Meral shook Vitaeus's hand as well but stayed quiet.

"I am honored to meet the two Princes of Rok," Vitaeus replied and exchanged a kiss on the cheek with Princess Raheena.

Meral was the last to board the boat as he was the one to push the little skiff away from shore before jumping on board. The boat skirted out into the deep blue waters of the lake. The shore on the other end was a mere speck on the horizon as they set sail towards the center of the lake.

"Your country has a lot of beauty, but few places where one can take a boat and go sailing like this. It is good that this lake is so close to Caminia City where my sister will be staying. A Rok princess needs a boat; so that she can continue to sail." Refal said.

Meral, who had remained quiet thus far, spoke in a heavy Rok accent. "The saddest part about your country is that it is technically on the sea, yet the people have no access to the water. My sister will have to change that. A lake is not the same; you can't sail very far without hitting land."

"I grew up beside a lake myself, and it is the only sea I ever knew." Vitaeus said smiling, "But in the coming year, I will have to rectify that and do more sailing."

"And yet it was enough for you to become the Lord of the Shield Isles." Raheena offered.

"The King has built an elevator at the new palace for easy access to the ships below; perhaps the princess can take full advantage of that as well." Vitaeus replied.

"Yes, but the height is something that we Roks aren't very comfortable with, and if those ropes were to break, then it would be certain death below." Refal replied.

"My Lord, you must excuse my amusement, but your country is in a sad state if they offer the Shield Isles to a man whose sailing experience is limited to lakes."

"It is Caminia's weakness, yet that is why I plan on building a navy and will be looking to hire experienced sailors and captains for my ships. Perhaps the two princes of Rok will be able to assist me with finding the right talent."

"You will need good ships first." Meral said. "Our shipwrights are the best in the world. We build the fastest boats; which are capable of sailing even in the shallow seas and rivers. It has allowed our navy to raid deep into Rakirian lands. We caused so much attrition, that they were forced to beg for peace."

"Yes, I will need sleek fast ships, but my vision for my navy goes much further. I want to build floating fortresses on water. The true shield of the Isles will be my powerful ships, that can withstand anything on the open water."

"We can build those too." Refal assured him quickly. "Like my brother said, our shipwrights are the best in the world."

Raheena squeezed his hand. "Look over there," she pointed to the sky above where the sun was beginning its descent, leaving the sky painted in a floral of many colors ranging from streaks of orange, pink and purple.

"It's very beautiful."

"Let's go for a swim Lord of Shield Isles." Refal suggested, as he stood in the small boat, causing it to rock violently in the water. He dropped his pants and jumped in the water. Meral followed right after him, and the boat rocked from side to side with such violence that Vitaeus grabbed onto Raheena.

"You sissy boy, are you afraid?" She teased.

"No, I just don't want to fall in and get all wet." Vitaeus said. Meral and Refal swam away from the boat and further into the lake with effortless strong strokes that caused their bodies to seemingly skim on the water.

Raheena splashed water in Vitaeus's direction, covering his face and shirt from the first stroke. "Now you're wet! No more excuses, get in the water." She said, as she stood suddenly and pulled his hand eagerly.

Vitaeus laughed as he stood. "Though I don't want to get any wetter, princess, I also don't like being called a sissy by you."

"Then prove it. Prove to me your courage as Lord of the Shield Isles," she said, even as her delicate fingers undid the buttons on his tunic. Raheena had turned away when he was undoing his own trousers. His face reddened when she glanced back, and she laughed upon seeing him blush, even as she pushed him in the water. As he came up sputtering, he wiped the water from his face before opening his eyes. His jaw dropped subconsciously at the most beautiful image he had ever seen, Raheena's slender figure in her camisole, and then she dove in. She came up out of the water right next to him and wrapped her arms around his neck. "Not afraid of water after all." She let out a giggle before bringing her lips to his ear and whispered, "Now I think you're brave." Her breath send a shiver down his spine, and he pulled her into his embrace with one hand and grabbed the side of the boat with the other.

"And you are the most beautiful creature in the whole world." He replied

She was about to kiss him, and he pulled away. "What's wrong?" She asked.

"You can't marry the King. I won't let you." He whispered in her ear.

"Oh yeah? Tell me what is it that you plan to do to prevent my marriage to that old man?"

He looked her over and smiled at the look of amusement on her face. "I will either kidnap you and take you with me to my rocks on the sea or ensure that the King is in no place to get married."

"You speak boldly, but I wonder if your actions could possibly match your words."

Vitaeus smiled, "Let's just say that I have a plan, princess, to ensure that you and the old man don't get married."

Raheena stared somewhere into the sky beyond, allowing her thoughts to roam freely before she spoke. "I really enjoyed that last ball with you." She finally said dreamily.

"Yes, I got to share your company with the King that night; it was very generous of the King." Vitaeus said teasingly.

"I thought about it all day; it was my favorite day in Caminia." Raheena confessed.

"It's all I thought about since then too," Vitaeus confessed.

She kissed him. "Now you can think about this," she whispered huskily. His lips met hers in the most tender kiss; as their tongues intertwined, he felt one with her. He had never felt such magic in all his life. His senses were so keen to her warm body pressed to his; it made his head spin. Somewhere in the back of his head, a voice screamed no, but it was such a small voice compared to the rest of what he felt. When her lips touched his, and he felt the wet exchange, his nerves, his heart, and a large portion of his brain said yes. Vitaeus returned the kiss, sweetly, lovingly. This turned into another kiss. This time it was a fierce one, and one full of longing and desire. As her legs wrapped around his body, he felt his whole body stiffen with yearning. He felt ecstatic, and yet the small voice in the back of his head screamed for him to stop. This went against everything he had been taught. Helplessly, he looked around for assistance, for someone besides himself who could stop this before they reached the point of no return. He was weak and powerless to stop, and Refal and Meral had seemingly vanished and could no longer be seen in the expanse of the lake. Raheena stared deep into his eyes; her eyes fixated on his with intense desire.

CHAPTER 43: LOSING CONTROL

The next three weeks went by rapidly as the whole community worked hard to prepare for the siege that was sure to come. Enough weapons had been obtained to support an army of two-thousand foot soldiers, five-hundred archers, and a hundred cavalry, and the army has been drilling hard ever since. Desiani had become a very respected figure in Seredine as she was in charge of organizing all the labor for gathering food and other essential supplies. Achledis, meanwhile, was left with the task of ensuring that the archers, infantry, and cavalry were being trained and drilled to respond as one unit.

Achledis rode up to the training grounds where Rolen was training the infantry. Rolen, being a carpenter by trade, had designed the pikes for his men himself. Meanwhile, the city crafts men had been busy fashioning pikes of ash and poplar wood, with iron tips on the ends. The pikes were ten feet in length; whereas the Rakirian standard spear was only seven feet long. Most men had some sort of armor that was taken from Rakirian stores. The men wearing the metal breastplates were at the very front ranks, followed by the chain mail, and then by the boiled leather. The last ranks didn't have any armor, but they were also the reserves and not as likely to see battle right away.

Even though Rolen lacked any military background, he had been studying the Rakirian manual on Phalanx maneuvering, and it showed. He had the infantry responding as one unit. Two quick toots of his horn, and the infantry started to move. They build up on both ends, while leaving the middle looking thin and vulnerable. When a long toot sounded from a horn, the men in the front put their left foot forward, and the right stayed planted slightly behind as they crouched shields, interlocking with each other as they braced for impact.

Achledis marveled at the job Rolen had done, and it gave him renewed confidence for the battle that was to come.

"Good day sir," Tiram said, as he tried to catch his breath.

"Morning Tiram."

"Master Yurosi has requested that you come see him at once. He said that he will wait for you inside the throne room."

"Throne room?" Achledis asked puzzled. "Why there?"

"I'm not permitted to say sir."

Achledis frowned at Tiram's response and puzzled more at the odd request.

Since that confrontation with Yurosi on his sick bed, Achledis had hoped that perhaps Yurosi had given up his plans on being in charge. Achledis tried to involve him as soon as he was walking. He placed him in charge of intelligence, and he had scouts reporting directly to Yurosi. Yurosi was also named chief engineer, and he and Desiani had been supervising the work on building up the city's defenses.

Yurosi still tried to show his importance as a knight every chance he got and had a habit of trying to manipulate circumstances when he was in charge. Though it was irritating, Achledis had tried to brush it off and keep his calm. This time, he had been summoned by Yurosi, yet another example of Yurosi twisting a situation where he would place himself in control. Achledis swung on top of his horse and started for the palace. He would meet Yurosi, but it would be on his terms.

Yurosi patted the King's letter; the seal still intact. He wouldn't break it; not until Achledis was there to witness it for himself. He already knew what the message read, and it was hard for him to keep the smirk off his face.

"Bring me some of that honeyed berry wine from the Rok Isles," Yurosi commanded one of the peasant foot soldiers that arrived from his father's garrison.

The boy hesitated. "Um, where is it stored?" He asked.

"I don't know. You were supposed to bring it here. I specifically requested it in my letter."

Sir Kerwan stepped forward; he was just a peasant boy who used to work on his father's estate. Why his father made him knight, he still didn't understand.

"Your father sir," Sir Kerwan began, "said that it is weapons and soldiers you need if you are to fight, not wine to sip."

Yurosi was up in a flash; his steely blue eyes flashed angrily. It was just like his father, always trying to curtail his lifestyle. *What is it with him? Nothing wrong with enjoying the fine things in life.* Yurosi composed himself once more; he shouldn't show weakness by showing his emotions. He climbed the dais once again and sat on the bronze throne. It would be his first order of business to make sure it was polished. Achledis had never used it. This room was always empty, and it was where Yurosi could always escape to be alone. He would sit here on this throne for hours at times, pondering and strategizing. Somehow he seemed to draw strength from it. It always reminded him that soon he would be the one in charge, and not Achledis. Now that time has finally come.

His father had sent him a total of 200 men, 150 men-at-arms and 50 peasant cavalry. Sir Kerwan led them here and transferred command to Yurosi. Yurosi studied Kerwan and watched him shift uncomfortably under his gaze. He wore cheap armor, and the metal in his long sword was something that was used more for training than in actual combat. It was made out of heavy steel no doubt.

"Kerwan!"

Kerwan jumped to attention nervously. "Yes, Sir Yurosi!"

"Were you not my father's stable boy?"

"Not necessarily, sir. I was in charge of your father's servants."

"How does one go from being a stable boy to a knight?"

"Your father promoted me sir. He organized a banquet, and during the banquet, in front of everyone, he knighted me. Then he pulled me aside and told me that I would lead his men here to you."

"Did father run out of knights that he had to promote a stable boy?"

"No sir, but the King requested men from the manors for a tournament, but I believe that there might be trouble brewing as well."

Yurosi smiled, more to himself. *Even a pig dressed in silk is still a pig,* he thought. He was sure that the last time he saw Kerwan, he was running the stables, but he did have a beautiful sister who had been the household maid. His father had promoted her to be in charge of all the servants at the castle.

"I'm glad your sister pulled through for you," Yurosi said with a glint of humor in his eyes. Kerwan's face went red, but Yurosi continued on as if he hadn't noticed. "Serve me loyally, and I will see to it that father rewards you with a small tract of land."

Kerwan nodded.

"Smile, Sir Kerwan; you and I are the only knights in this city." Yurosi said with exuberance, and Kerwan did smile. "Perhaps you and I can even duel for the good people of this city; they could use some entertainment." Kerwan squirmed uncomfortably at that thought. "Then again, perhaps not, I fear we won't have time for tournaments." Yurosi smiled at the flush of relief that swept over Kerwan's face. "I'm sorry to disappoint you; I know you're itching to be in your first competition."

Tiram entered and made a slight bow at the foot of the dais.

"Well, did you call him?" Yurosi asked impatiently.

"I did, and he has arrived at the palace. But now he waits for you inside the war room. He said that you are to see him there."

Yurosi frowned as he looked at Kerwan, "Well, my orders were clear. I did say that I want him here in the throne room, not the war room. Sir Kerwan, could you please go bring the subject in question to me. Tell him it's about a message from the King..." Yurosi's eyebrows bunched together as he thought for a moment. "Take ten men-at-arms to make sure your words carry more weight. Now go!"

Desiani clenched her fists in frustration. No one knew the whereabouts of Yurosi, and as for Achledis, only the Creator knew where that boy was today. She had just found out about the arrival of a small army from Caminia, and it disturbed her that they only found out about them when they had arrived at the city. *How did the scouts not report their movements earlier? How could they miss a force as large as that,* she wondered. *Thank the Creator it was only allies. If it was the Rakirians, then we would be in a lot of trouble.*

Desiani stopped when she heard the distant sound of men in iron marching. Could this be the Caminian force she wondered about, and why were they inside the palace? Something had gone wrong, or someone didn't do their job as they were supposed to. She would find out who allowed these men inside and wring their necks personally.

The procession rounded the corner and came into Desiani's view, ten men-at-arms led by a lowly knight. She could see that by his cheap armor; it wasn't even fitted for him. Still the knight held his head high and his gaze straight ahead, but as he neared Desiani, he signaled the men behind him to stop. He bowed slightly in her direction.

"My lady, how do you fair?" He asked.

"Just fine, but who are you, and what are you doing inside the palace? How did you get in?" Desiani demanded making no attempt to hide her anger.

The knight was surprised by the response and took a moment to gather his thoughts. He wasn't quite used to speaking to a lady of high birth, like this girl clearly was.

"I am Sir Kerwan, a knight from Caminia, and I have been sent to offer my services to Lord Yurosi. My men and I..."

"Lord Yurosi?! Take me to him right away" Desiani commanded.

"I cannot at the moment. I am on assignment."

Desiani shook her head in frustration; then looking at the knight, she tried to put on her fiercest face. "Fine don't take me to him, just tell me where he is hiding."

The knight hesitated before speaking, not sure if he was supposed to tell anyone, but at the same time, not sure whom this assertive young lady was. "He is not to be disturbed..."

"Where is he!?"

"He is in the throne room about to have a meeting."

That's peculiar, Desiani thought as she turned and walked off in a hurry. She heard the knight behind her wishing her a great day, but she made no attempt to acknowledge that she heard him.

Yurosi sat on the bronze throne atop the ornate dais with ten men-at-arms on both sides of him and scores of men lining both sides of the wall. He wore his fine knightly chain mail, all polished and gleaming with a crimson tunic on top, and a rounded hat with a red, yellow, and green plume that adorned his head. He looked magnificent, and Desiani had no doubt that that was the point. Like Achledis had once pointed out to her, Yurosi could be extremely showy. The men at the door stopped her before she could get any further.

"Let her come!" Yurosi's voice bellowed, and the men instantly let her pass. Her shoulder hurt from where one soldier had grabbed her. Yurosi sat on the throne, with his arms relaxing on armrests; he sat upright but had just a hint of a slouch to show that he had made himself comfortable.

"My lady, you're not hurt are you?" Yurosi's voice was suddenly soft and concerned. His eyes flashed angrily at the two soldiers by the door, and his voice grew sharp once more. "If you hurt the lady, then I will personally flog you."

Desiani came up the dais boldly, right up to Yurosi, and stared at him in anger. "What is all this!?"

"My father sent me some of his men to assist us."

Desiani cut him off. "What are you doing in the throne room?"

"Got a letter from the King," Yurosi's voice was steady and soft. He looked into her eyes earnestly, trying to read them to see if she was impressed. "I am waiting to open it when Achledis gets here, but I'm glad you came too. It will be good for all of us to hear what the King commands us."

"So, why are you playing King?"

His eyebrows rose in surprise, and he quickly smiled. "Playing king? No, not a king, just a lord, and it is only the beginning." He motioned her closer to him and whispered in her ear. "I believe that when I defeat the Rakirians, and I am confident I will, the King will reward me with the title of Duke of the Duchy of Seredine. You will be my duchess. We won't have to move to Caminia. We can stay here like you always wanted. Won't that be great?"

Desiani closed her eyes, put her hands over her face, and held them there. *This can't be happening, not right before the Rakirian army arrives.*

"Des, aren't you happy?" Yurosi asked, his voice slightly hurt.

"I take it Achledis doesn't know anything of this yet?"

"He will when I read the letter."

"Last thing we need is division amongst you before the Rakirian army arrives. Show me the letter." Desiani demanded.

Yurosi brought it out of his tunic pocket, careful not wrinkle it and gingerly handed it to Desiani.

She stared at the seal, a three headed serpent. She supposed it was the King's seal. She heard that a three headed serpent was on the King's coat of arms. "It's still sealed." She blurted out.

"Of course it is; I need Achledis to see it. I have also summoned for the war council. Keltar, Rolen, and Marcus should be coming here soon as well. Everyone must witness the King's seal before I break it."

"So why are you so sure that you are in command without having read the letter?" Desiani asked.

Yurosi looked at her incredulously, "I am the only knight here; so naturally, I am the one to take command."

"Still, Achledis was chosen by his peers."

"My dear, the King makes the law, not we the people."

Desiani heard men coming in behind her and turned to see Achledis coming in, followed by the knight she saw earlier in the hall, and lastly, followed by the ten men-at-arms.

"Glad you made it Achledis; we are still waiting for Keltar, Rolen, and Marcus before I begin."

"What is this!?" Achledis demanded loudly, holding no pretense of his displeasure as his eyes took in the scene around him.

"When everyone arrives, I will begin the meeting, but not just yet." Yurosi said, his eyes steely as he stared down Achledis.

Achledis glanced at Desiani, but her eyes were downcast. And she didn't make eye contact. Slowly, he looked around the room and made a quick count of the men. Halfway up the first wall he got to thirty; so he estimated that there must be sixty on each wall. Plus the ten that escorted him here. Another twenty were up on the dais. A hundred-fifty men-at-arms and he never heard of their arrival. *What a fool I have been.* Achledis thought, *placing a traitor in charge of intelligence, without any oversight. Did Desiani know of this?* He wondered. Why would she not look at him?

Yurosi stood, and with two hands forward, he signaled for the three commanders to come in. Keltar, Rolen, and Marcus walked in hesitantly and looked around the room. Achledis noticed their grim faces, and they all gave him a nod as they approached him. Achledis stood before the dais; while Yurosi stood in front of the bronze throne. The crimson tunic he wore over his gleaming armor certainly added to his majesty.

"I'm glad that everyone has finally arrived. I have a letter from King Razim himself." Yurosi took out the letter and stepped off the dais to show the King's seal. "The three headed serpent, the sigil of our King." Carefully, Yurosi broke the seal and opened the letter. He skimmed the letter's contents and then called Desiani. "Please read this letter my dear. I think it ought to come from your lips; so that everyone could see that I haven't added a single word to this letter. And that it would be clear what our King commands us."

Desiani snatched the letter from him with irreverence, and her eyes skimmed the words. Then without another word, she tore it in half. Then she tore that in half again and was about to rip it a third time, but Yurosi snatched it away from her.

"How dare you?" He asked.

"That gibberish doesn't apply here." Desiani said defiantly.

"Take her away!" Yurosi commanded, as his eyes flashed angrily.Instantly, two guards appeared on both sides of her, to escort her away, but not before she slapped Yurosi, leaving a red mark on his face.

Yurosi bit his lower lip and watched as Desiani was ushered away before returning his gaze at the four pieces of the letter. "This letter from King Razim orders me to take charge of the garrison here at Seredine; as the highest ranking knight in this city, it is my duty to defend it. Keltar, Rolen, and Marcus, you will keep your posts. I have seen a lot of progress in the training and know of no one better who could fill those posts as well as you have done. Achledis, you will work with Sir Kerwan. He is a knight, and you will report to him. The two of you will be in charge of scouting and defense; though I will continue to work closely with the both of you. Any questions?"

"More of a statement." Achledis said. "That letter means nothing here. This King has never been my King. He wasn't here when we overthrew the Rakirian garrison, and his army certainly won't be here when we defend it from the Rakirians."

"You speak treason!" Yurosi said, his eyes cold, and his finger pointing at Achledis accusingly.

Achledis's sword was out instantly, and Yurosi drew his. The sound of swords sliding from their scabbards resounded with a metallic ring throughout the room.

"Put it down my friend; there is no need to die so pointlessly." Keltar whispered, as he placed his arm gently on Achledis's shoulder, and Rolen took the sword from him.

Instantly, four men-at-arms had Achledis from every side, ensuring that he couldn't struggle. Yurosi's steely gaze didn't leave Achledis as he folded his arms over his chest. "Flog him twice then lock him up."

"My liege," Keltar made a bow, "Give me the honor of scourging a traitor."

Yurosi studied Keltar suspiciously. "He is your friend. Why would it honor you to flog him?"

"He spoke treason." Keltar replied.

"Then do it, but my guards will accompany him the entire time." Yurosi said as he sat back on the throne. "Everyone dismissed." And he gave a curt wave with the back of his hand for emphasis.

CHAPTER 44: TIME TOGETHER

The desire was intense, and his body screamed in yearning, but Vitaeus pushed away from Raheena allowing the cool water to separate his body from the warmth of hers.

"We shouldn't do this," Vitaeus's voice came out in a barely audible whisper.

Raheena's dark lashes swooped down in hurt and shame to cover her beautiful eyes. Vitaeus instantly reached out and squeezed her hand in reassurance, but she pulled her hand back from him.

"I'm okay, I'm sorry for putting you in such an awkward position. I mistook our friendship for more." Raheena replied.

Vitaeus let out a deep sigh. "You didn't mistake anything, but I didn't want us to do something that you might someday regret."

At that Raheena turned and swam to the little skiff and Vitaeus followed, the two climbed back inside, and wiped themselves with linen towels before getting dressed once more. Being together had suddenly become awkward. He gently placed a wool blanket over Raheena's shoulders and sat next to her.

"Raheena, I won't let you marry that old king."

She turned towards him suddenly, her eyes dancing, looking into his eyes as she seemed to search his soul to see if he was being honest.

"Why not?" She finally replied.

He stared deeply into her greenish-blue eyes before responding. "Because you're meant to be with me."

"That's sweet," she replied her voice void of emotion and pulled the blanket up a little more tightly around herself. "Then tell me is the rumor true?"

"What rumor?" Vitaeus asked.

"There are whisperings about court that the king pronounced you a traitor and the next moment the king was choking on an actual grape that was in his wine. And no matter that the king was about to sentence you to death, you rescued him from an almost certain death."

Vitaeus was slow to reply, and finally nodded his head yes.

"Why?" Raheena cried out. "If the rumors swirling about court are true that your grandfather was murdered by this madman then why would you allow him to live?"

"I had a reason."

"Was your reason greater than forcing me to marry that old man? How can you even dare to tell me that you will make sure that I don't marry that old man, when you prevented fate from doing so?" Raheena demanded as tears sprang in her eyes and she shoved Vitaeus away in her anger.

"Wait, let me explain," Vitaeus grabbed Raheena's hands as she attempted to shove him again, and pulled her close. "Believe me I wanted to let him die, but right before the king was about to die I realized something. If the king died, and everyone in court already knew that the Duke of Nitami was to become the next king, then the Duke of Nitami would dispose of me just as quickly. It would be easy to fabricate the lie since I was already accused of planning treason that I was the one to have poisoned King Razim. I would be sentenced to death and killed perhaps even that same night. Instead I came out looking like a hero, instantly got on the king's good side and even got to share another ball with you."

"I'm sorry for getting angry with you. I just couldn't imagine why you would allow that old king to live, but now it makes sense." Raheena said.

Vitaeus pulled her close and gave her a squeeze, "I still meant what I said, about making sure that you don't get married to that old man. Return to the Rok Islands and stay there until I come and ask your father for your hand in marriage."

"Father will kill you on the spot if he thinks that you're the reason I turned down the Caminian king's offer and cost him access to the Caminian throne." Raheena said in a quiet voice.

"Razim is only a usurper, I'm the rightful ruler with our marriage we can guarantee an alliance with our two kingdoms."

"You're silly," she laughed nervously. "You're not suggesting overthrowing Razim's rule, are you?"

"No, I'm insisting on retaking my right to rule. I'm the rightful heir to the throne."

She kissed him before resting her head on his chest, "And yet I'm afraid, afraid of my father and afraid of your king. They were both hell bent on this marriage, my acceptance was supposed to be a mere formality for the sake of our laws, but I won't accept, never." She replied as she rolled off to the side and pulled a wool blanket around herself to keep off the evening chill. "It's not fair that I was cursed to be the Rok princess so that I could go through the nightmare of marrying someone five times my age. I've been pressured for too long, and whether it's only a few years or even a few hours I won't do it, the very idea repulses me."

"Worry about no one my dove, don't tell anyone that you're planning on rejecting the king until you get up and do it publicly. That way no one will talk you out of it, but they will have to accept it when you have proclaimed your decision in front of everyone. Will your brothers be there for your support after you make your announcement?"

"Refal will, he has always looked out for me like his little sister, but Meral is too loyal to father and he might be angry."

In the distance, two small objects appeared and seemed to be getting closer as Vitaeus sat in the boat with Raheena by his side, staring across the expanse of water.

"Let's go meet them." She said as she stood suddenly.

"Wait," he called. But she had already jumped into the lake gown and all and was swimming towards her brothers. Without further hesitation, he jumped in behind her, swimming hard trying to catch up to her, but was surprised how fast she was, especially for a girl wearing a gown that created so much drag.

Before he could say anything to her; however, Refal and Meral met them. Refal grinned as he looked at Vitaeus. "So my little sister did get him to swim after all, very good Lord Vitaeus."

"Yes, but only after I splashed him and he was too wet to care," Raheena said laughing.

Meral looked at him, then at Raheena, and back at him suspiciously, before swimming on.

Refal and Meral had already got on board by the time Raheena and Vitaeus arrived. Vitaeus helped her onto the boat, and she pushed him away with her foot in a playful manner.

The younger prince offered Vitaeus his hand, "My sister is playful by nature and can go too far," and then looking at Raheena he chided her. "This is Lord Vitaeus sister, be courteous like a proper lady."

Vitaeus looked at Raheena and made a silly face mocking her brother so that only she could see it. Raheena giggled aloud so that both her brothers looked at her curiously, but before anyone else could comment Vitaeus diverted their attention to shore.

"Look over there." He pointed to the shore line, where a large cavalry was approaching as a storm of rising sand stretched a mile in their wake.

"I wonder where they are going." Raheena asked.

"They are headed to my castle to bring me before Razim by force, however, I'm not there, and Daenis has been charged not to allow anyone inside while I was gone."

"I don't think that those men are going to take no for an answer." Refal replied.

"That's what I'm afraid of." Vitaeus replied.

CHAPTER 45: A CHANGE IN HEART

Keltar, followed by Rolen and Marcus, stayed a few steps behind the men as he escorted Achledis to the public square. They all wore grim expressions, but they didn't say a word to one another. They all felt betrayed. Eyes cast down, Keltar stared at the cobblestones at his feet as they marched Achledis out towards the center of the public square.

A trumpet blasted, and everyone stopped and turned at the sound. On top of the balcony stood Yurosi with a trumpeter next to him.

"Bring the prisoner back!" Yurosi commanded.

Instantly, the men-at-arms turned Achledis around and started to head back inside. Keltar, Rolen, and Marcus stopped and waited for them to pass before they fell in behind them.

When they walked into the throne room, Yurosi was no longer sitting on the throne; rather, he stood in a nonchalant pose, to the side of the room, his fancy hat and crimson tunic were also off.

"Release him, and get out!" Yurosi commanded the men-at-arms.

Achledis raised an eyebrow in surprise and waited patiently as the shackles were undone.

"Keltar, Rolen, Marcus, please step out for a moment."

When everyone left the room and the door closed, Yurosi and Achledis were left alone. Achledis was itching to start the fight but forced himself to wait patiently, mostly out of curiosity, to see what Yurosi had in mind.

"I owe you an apology." Yurosi began. "I do have anger issues, as well as you do from what I hear. I heard the story about you breaking a man's jaw that interrupted you when you were addressing the crowd the morning after the revolt." Yurosi tried smiling, but when he didn't get a response from Achledis, he continued. "Anyway, just saying that you and I are a lot alike. You are a great leader. It's no wonder that men are drawn to you, but you saw the letter from the King and his command."

"I grew up on the mainland of Rosmir, a conquered land. I grew up without a King. And this King who hides on his peninsula of rock is no King of mine. People are being butchered here, but he makes no move to come to our aide."Achledis said.

"Though your thoughts are treasonous, I can understand how you would feel differently than I do. You, Keltar, Rolen, Marcus, and I are brothers. I overreacted, and I am sorry. With my father's men present, I felt I had to act a certain way, and when you didn't come as I asked for you to, I became upset."

"Your betrayal is inexcusable." Achledis replied. "You've been plotting this the whole time."

"Achledis the Lion, some call you," Yurosi smiled. "My father's coat of arms has two lions."

Achledis stared back at him blankly.

"Anyway, I guess that you and I both have a lion inside of us, and we both feel destined to be in charge. I am no fool; I know Keltar, Rolen, Marcus, and even Desiani are loyal to you and not to me. We can't afford to have our house divided as the enemy approaches. I am putting my own pride aside and asking for a truce." Yurosi offered his hand.

Achledis ignored the outstretched hand. "Will you submit under my command once more?" Achledis's voice was as firm as iron.

Yurosi said nothing. Instead he stared at Achledis, studying him for a weakness, even a slight crack in his resolve, but there was none. He noticed that Achledis had his sword unbuckled, and his hand seemed to be itching for it.

Finally, Yurosi spoke. "I propose that both of us be in charge. You have enough charisma where you can lead the men; I will continue to work on the defenses."

Achledis instantly shook his head in rejection. "No, that won't work. We only need one leader during a war."

"Let's call in our friends." Yurosi said, as he strode towards the solid oak doors.

Achledis watched as he waved them all in. Everyone cast a dirty look in Yurosi's direction as they came in to stand next to Achledis.

"I never realized what a rotten person you are." Desiani said. Achledis had never seen her as angry as she was just then.

"May I say something?" Yurosi asked, as he held out two fingers pressed together in a sign of surrender. Without waiting for their response, he continued. "I am sorry. This is how I should have brought up the letter in the first place; I got carried away and had to put on a show. To me it only seemed natural to take command, as I am the only knight here, but I realized how that letter from the King meant nothing to any of you and neither did my title of knight. Seredine laws are different from the ones I am used to. The King's law hasn't applied here for a long time, but when we defeat Viserate, we must become one with Caminia once more. We are one nation with one King; we need to get used to that reality. The King's law will reign here again one day."

"As of today, it doesn't, and the King's word doesn't mean a thing." Desiani said.

"Aye" everyone chorused.

"I realize that you feel that way. I first realized it with shock when Desiani said it the first time, and then Achledis repeated it later. I didn't know how to respond to that. I acted out."

"I will pardon you, but you must have all of your father's men submit to me. You are no longer in charge of intelligence, but Desiani will continue to work with you on building the city defenses." Achledis said.

"That won't be possible. My men are loyal only to me, and my loyalty is only to the King. Yet I don't want us to be divided when we all should be united against the common enemy."

Achledis's hand was firmly resting on the hilt of his sword, when Desiani gently pulled it away.

"Yurosi, you were appointed by the King, and Achledis was appointed by his peers. Yet the two of you won't trust the other to rule; so I suggest that we rule by council. We will elect a councilwoman or a councilman to preside over the council, but all crucial decisions will not be made by one person." Desiani spoke with finality in her voice; which provoked no argument from either man.

"Now shake hands." The two reluctantly reached and grasped one another's hand. "Good, now that this is done, we can move on. Tomorrow at four in the morning we will meet in the war room to vote on the council presider, but first Yurosi will call in his men and address them. They will swear allegiance to the council presider whoever that may be."

Yurosi looked at Desiani hesitantly, but the look she gave him made him only nod in agreement.

CHAPTER 46: RAZIM'S KNIGHTS ATTACK

Vitaeus urged his horse to go faster. Even in the dimming light of the sunset, Vitaeus could see across the great expanse of plains that the battle had already begun. He watched as a flurry of crossbow bolts flew into the King's charging knights, and the entire front row was taken to the ground. A domino effect followed, as more horses stumbled over the fallen; the rest reigned in and turned around. Vitaeus also reigned in and trotted over to a lone tree; as hope began to swell that perhaps his crossbowmen could hold off the knights tonight. Tomorrow they would request for siege weapons. The only ones Vitaeus had seen around here were in defensive positions, mounted on towers, and those were unlikely to be used.

The knights yelled their battle cry as one. "For the King and his kingdom!" They charged up the hill towards the wall all at once. This was a motte and bailey, with a keep sitting on top of a natural rocky hill up against the cliff; an eight foot high rock wall surrounded the perimeter of the castle grounds. Though the perimeter walls were relatively short, they were high enough to keep horsemen, laden down with armor, out. So Vitaeus puzzled over what the knights planned on doing when they got to the wall.

As the mass of knights reached the walls, they tried to stand on top of their saddles and pull themselves up on the walls. However, it all ended in complete catastrophe for them as the horses would move before the knights were set, causing the knights to fall sometimes headfirst, instantly breaking their necks. The ones who tried to pull themselves up and over the walls weren't strong enough to accommodate their heavy armor and had to give up on that as well. Many more were merely shot with the bolts from the crossbows; their bodies rolling down the hill and into the ditch below. A retreat didn't need to be sounded; the knights who had survived the terrible ordeal thus far turned around and retreated. Their horses stumbled in the dark, over the bodies of men and horse alike, going aground and sending their knights flying. Many horseless knights were either running or limping in their attempts to escape the range of the bolts.

After the King's knights had retreated back to the safety of Caminia City, Vitaeus continued to ride towards the gates of his castle. The haunting scene around him caused an odd sensation to spread across his flesh. *Fear.* He rode past the broken bodies of men and beast, listening to the sounds of the whinnies of horses and the whimpers of men, calling out to him, begging for mercy. Like a vision from a nightmare, the scene was etched into his mind.

From inside the castle came the lively sounds of pipes and stringed instruments playing a lively tune, as men sang and shouted in celebration of their victory.

"This is Lord Vitaeus, open the gates!"

A watchman appeared and studied him momentarily before calling for the gate to open. A trumpet announced his entry, and the men who were celebrating stopped and cleared a path for him while chanting, "Lord Vitaeus, our true king!" It was a strange feeling, but men bowed towards him as he rode through their columns. He was met by a smiling Daenis, who bowed before him.

"My Lord, we have won a great victory for you tonight."

"Yes, you did well." Vitaeus said without smiling, "but what did you tell these men? Why are they calling me king?"

"Because you are our true king, My Lord; which is why they shouted it. After you left, Yolif displayed a picture of King Krepedes and a picture of you and told the masses that this is why King Razim wants your arrest. Razim is the real usurper, and you, My Lord, are our true king. His speech rallied the men to your cause; everyone here was willing to die tonight. Farmers, peasants, and mere street beggars believed that they were the true knights tonight, and they fought and defeated those knights."

Great, now I'm branded as a traitor for good," Vitaeus thought. "Where is Yolif?"

"My Lord, he addressed the men, then numbered them all into five groups, and instructed them to memorize their number. He said that he had something urgent to take care of but instructed me to have the number ones shoot their crossbows first, wait five seconds, then instruct the twos to fire, and all the way down the line until the five's fired. By then, the ones were reloaded and ready to go as well. That is how we managed to keep such a deadly rate of fire on the enemy." Daenis explained excitedly. "But I haven't seen him since; I hope he is all right." His voice suddenly turned to one of concern.

Vitaeus stood on top of the hill next to the keep to address the men. "Tonight all of you men proved who the real knights are. It is not those with lots of money, or those who can afford an expensive battle-horse or even armor. A true knight is one who fights with what he has, fueled with righteous indignation and the courage to face down all injustice. I thank you all for your courage and your steadfastness in battle, but most of all, I thank you for your loyalty." Vitaeus waited until the men's jubilant shouting died down before he continued. "Outside are men who are either dead or wounded that fought against us, and they are in serious need of compassion. I want all of us to go out there with torches in hand and bring those whom we can help inside." The excitement turned to grumbling, but Vitaeus encouraged them by saying, "We are all countrymen, and those who were once our enemies are now our allies."

Daenis organized those who would hold the torches, and soon the perimeter was well lit. The knights who were still alive were brought inside; the dead ones were placed neatly in a line. Vitaeus helped alongside his men to carry in the wounded, and as he knelt beside a knight, he instantly recognized him. "Yousel!"

The knight turned away from him, and Vitaeus sensed his humiliation.

"Go ahead and kill me," Yousel said. "I don't expect any mercy."

"Why would I kill you like this? You're clearly injured, and your leg is trapped against an armored battle horse. You're in no condition to fight."

"It's better if you kill me," Yousel muttered. "I would have killed you if given the chance and collected the reward that the King has offered."

"If you're sorry, then I will forgive you and show you mercy. If you will fight for me, I will reward you, but if you won't, then I will keep you as my prisoner. Either way, you have no reason to fear me." Vitaeus said, as he called another man to help him get Yousel's leg from under the dead horse. A crossbow bolt had pierced the horse's armor and sank through its chest.

"Why are you being so merciful?" Yousel asked. "It's a weakness that may be the end of you."

"Let me ask you sir. Why were you so intent to risk your life like this to bring me to the King; though I have done no wrong?"

"You are accused of treason, and earlier today you demonstrated your rebellion against the King. As a sworn knight and commander of the King's palace guard, it was my duty to bring you to justice."

"Are you aware that my grandfather was the King of all Rosmir?"

"I have heard the rumors, but King Razim has sworn that you're a liar. 'A clever usurper' he called you. One who used his similar image to the old king, seized on an old and false legend of the king's heirs being alive, and twisted it to your advantage in order to seize the throne."

"Razim is the real usurper, and even in his old age, the old man continues to look over his shoulders with paranoia. For the sake of peace in the kingdom, I wanted to avoid a civil war and wanted to wait until Razim died to lay claim for what is already mine. Yet Razim has been paranoid ever since he noticed my resemblance to Krepedes, and now he has openly declared war on me. I have no choice in the matter."

Vitaeus grunted as he pulled Yousel's leg from beneath the horse.

"Thank you," Yousel said. "I can see why men would follow you. Your chivalry inspires loyalty, even from a man like me. But for your own safety, Lord Vitaeus, I ask you to bind me and keep

271

me in your dungeons, or better yet, kill me. For I have sworn an oath to King Razim; whether right or wrong, I will serve him until death parts that oath."

"Very well sir, I thank you for your honesty. When Razim dies, I would love to have you in my service." Vitaeus stood and commanded some of the men to bind Yousel and to take him to the dungeons.

"Lord Vitaeus," Yousel called out as Vitaeus hunched next to him to hear what he had to say. Yousel stayed quiet as if summoning the courage to say something before he spoke. "For your own safety, get out of here quick; for you can't win for long. Razim may be old, but he is determined to rule and have another offspring to rule after him. He won't be at peace with his rule of this kingdom as long as you're alive to threaten it. Either tomorrow or the next day, this place will be surrounded by a large army and powerful trebuchets will be set up around it. By the time Razim is done, not a rock will be left standing."

"If you're loyal to Razim, then why tell me this?"

"On the field of battle I will kill at his command," Yousel replied. "But in the future, after Razim dies of old age, I would wish for you to be my king."

"Thank you sir." Vitaeus replied.

CHAPTER 47: SEREDINE UNDER SIEGE

Achledis was already up when he heard the bells ringing the alarm of the approaching Rakirian army. Wasting no time, he hastily got dressed and ran to the stables, where the stable boy had his horse saddled and ready to go.

"Can I go into battle with you sir?" The stable boy asked, his young eyes pleading for an opportunity to have a slice of adventure.

Achledis looked at the scrawny orphan. His eyes shone with excitement; which only made it harder to say no. "The fighting will be left to the men that have been training for it. Your duties are here; this is where we need you."

Achledis had gotten to know the boy exceptionally well over the past month and knew him to be diligent. The boy admired him, and Achledis was well aware of the fact that he was the boy's role model in many different ways. That's why Achledis never wanted to disappoint the boy, but he had no other choice. At eleven, the boy was much too young.

The soldiers were already filing out of the barracks and onto the plaza in front of the gate when Achledis got there. Dismounting, he didn't bother to tie Ronen; rather, he instructed him to stay put. Achledis bounded up the steps to the battlements two at a time. A few archers were already standing there; seeing Achledis, they jumped to attention.

"At ease," Achledis instructed them as he looked into the valley below where he could see the crimson tide of Rakirian uniforms marching to the cadence of drums. Besides the Rakirian army, there was still a handful of civilians, rushing to get behind the walls for safety. He saw a small family galloping on horseback; further behind them, he could see an abandoned wagon still harnessed to the oxen that the family had left behind in their bid to beat the Rakirians to Seredine. The bells continued to clang to ensure that those in the countryside were aware of the pending danger. Achledis felt a strong hand on his shoulder, bringing him out of his thoughts. He turned to find Rolen standing there.

"The men are assembled below," he said as he gestured in their direction. "They are overwhelmed with fear." Achledis took one look at his army below; most had their heads cast down and were talking in hushed tones to their partners on the left or right of them. They looked like an army that had just been humiliated and defeated in battle and were waiting for their enemies to pronounce judgment on them.

The morale, which seemed to be flying high all week as they trained, had suddenly frizzled, and the sight of these men was enough to dampen anyone's mood. Achledis knew that the situation had to change quickly; otherwise, it was all over before it could even begin.

"Men of Seredine," Achledis shouted in order to get everyone's attention. "A month ago, we were all celebrating our independence from the enemy; we had just lifted off the yoke of Rakirian bondage and tasted the sweet flavor of freedom. On that day, we all felt brave and courageous; for we had gained our freedom with the sword. We swore an oath that when the day came to protect that freedom, we would do so with our lives if we must.

Today that day is here, but I don't see any strength and courage in you. I don't see any wrath from you. Wrath that would prompt you all to take action against an enemy that has been committing genocide against your people. Rather, the enemy arrives at your doorstep, and I see you shaking in your boots with fear. It is Rakiria who should be awaiting our wrath; for we have been oppressed by their tyranny for far too long. Now, should we allow that tyranny to continue?"

"No! We will never let them into our city," a man shouted from somewhere in the rear ranks.

Achledis walked down the steps of the battlement to where Ronen stood waiting for him. As he was mounting his horse, he heard a low murmur go through the troops as they all started talking together in hushed tones.

"Silence!" Achledis shouted. He rode right in front of the first line, making eye contact with a few of the men, who would instantly break eye contact and look down.

"You!" Achledis pointed at a man.

"Yes, s-sir" the man stuttered.

"Who are you fighting for soldier?" Achledis asked.

"I fight for you, sir," the man replied.

"And you?" Achledis asked another soldier.

"For you sir!"

"And you?" Achledis pointed at a man a couple of rows back.

"I fight for you too, sir," the man shouted.

"Good. Fight for me, but also fight for the men around you, for the women and children of our city, for your countrymen and your country. For this is the land that holds your city; which a month ago all of you swore to defend. Now it is time to make good on that promise. Fight with courage! Your wives, your mothers, your sisters, your daughters, today they all look to you for protection. If you turn yellow and betray your loved ones to a life of slavery and bondage all because you didn't want to risk losing your life, remember, that is exactly when you lose your life. You may live to die another day, but your cowardice, and the day you betrayed your country will live with you forever." Achledis paused and looked at the faces of his men. They were tense with determination, but most importantly, they all looked proud.

"As you fight, remember whom you are fighting for. You are fighting for our mothers and sisters, for our wives and daughters, and for our fathers and brothers. Tell me, for whom are you all willing to put down your lives?!" Achledis shouted.

"For our mothers and sisters, for our wives and daughters, and for our fathers and brothers!" The men chorused.

The men, who had just a moment ago stood shaking with fear, were now alive and confident; their fear was swept away by euphoria of swelling patriotism and adrenaline.

Riding back and forth in front of the lines, Achledis pumped his sword into the air and shouted hurrah. The soldiers all joined in, and in a loud chorus, they chanted their hurrah. The shouting was so loud that the sound carried across the valley to where the Rakirian army was marching to battle for Seredine.

CHAPTER 48: VITAEUS UNDER SIEGE

When morning came, Vitaeus found his castle surrounded by an army of a thousand men-at-arms and a large host of knights. The King's banner of the three headed serpent was posted at the highest point with the banners of the other lords who came to join the fight below. As the morning drew to noon, the size of the army outside his castle walls had quadrupled as more lords arrived from the roundabout regions, bringing their armies with them. By evening, tents were set up, and wood, as well as other building materials, were brought to build the siege weapons. The King was preparing a possible siege, rather than pay a heavy price in casualties by storming it.

On that first day, no riders came to discuss terms; rather they made more effort to demonstrate their superior force and allow the defenders to see how futile any resistance would be. But on the second day of the siege, a rider carrying a white flag arrived with the King's terms for surrender. They were simple, yet generous for a King like Razim. The lives of all men in rebellion against the King would be spared but condemned to the mines for life. The King's message even clarified that the offer was also extended to Vitaeus, if he chose to surrender immediately.

Vitaeus reread the terms to Yolif and Daenis to get their advice on the matter, but for the most part, his mind was already made up. He would ask the men to surrender; resistance would only prolong the inevitable, at the cost of a thousand lives.

Daenis spoke first, "My Lord, may I speak freely?"

"When I ask for advice, I always expect you to speak freely."

"Thank you My Lord, though I try to refrain from being negative, the simple fact remains that we are surrounded and completely cut off from any retreat. These terms are the most generous that you can ever expect to receive from the King."

Vitaeus gave a slight nod in acknowledgement before returning his gaze to Yolif. Yolif stared into the distance but made no reply. Vitaeus didn't rush him; he had come to know that this was simply Yolif in meditative thought. He could sit unmoved for an hour or longer without moving a muscle. However, Vitaeus didn't have an hour.

"I too have thought on this, and I think you're right. These are the best terms that we can expect from Razim. Considering that Razim is known to deliver harsh punishments to deter others from attempting the same crime, this punishment does seem light. Daenis, you have served in the King's palace for a long time, and so I will trust your advice regarding the King. My question is, can we trust King Razim to follow through on his promise to spare everyone's life, or is that an empty promise?"

"Yes My Lord, the King may be treacherous in dealing punishments, but he believes it is necessary to deliver 'justice.' He believes himself to be noble, and to my knowledge, he always does exactly as he says."

It's what I expected from someone who believes himself to be so just. Vitaeus thought. "Daenis, I want you and all the men to surrender." Vitaeus paused, as he closed his eyes momentarily, drawing on some inner strength. "I only wish I could repay you for your service and the sacrifice that you have made. I'm sorry for taking you out of your comfortable life in the King's palace and for being the cause for your sentence of hard labor in the mines." Vitaeus pressed his lips tightly in an attempt to hold the tears from rolling down his face, but as hard as he tried, they came anyway.

"It was an honor to serve a man like you, My Lord, no matter my fate. I don't regret it, and if it's the mines, then so be it. I still have my life." Daenis replied softly. "My Lord what will you do?"

"I will do what I will do, but the rest of you need not go along with me any further."

"I will follow whatever you do My Lord," Daenis replied.

"No, you do as I command, and I command that you surrender along with everyone else." Vitaeus replied, trying to keep his voice firm.

"I can't, I won't My Lord. Please don't ask that of me. I will serve you as long as you or I am alive. Please allow me to go where you go."

Yolif snapped out of his trance and looked at Vitaeus. "The crossbowmen should surrender, but the three of us, along with the ten knights, will hold out inside the keep. We have enough provisions to last us at least a month, and with all the crossbowmen gone, we will have fewer mouths to feed. During that month, we will look for an opportunity to escape."

"No, Daenis is right. Escape will be futile; your only chance is to surrender." Vitaeus replied.

"And you will hold out until you are too weak and tired and then be captured or simply die?" Yolif asked. "What will you prove? What purpose will your death serve?" Yolif glared at Vitaeus, but Vitaeus gave no reply. "No matter how small the card is in your hand, even with just a two of hearts, you're alive and in the game. Who knows? Perhaps tomorrow will be the day you draw the ace of spades." Yolif stood over Vitaeus, his eyes pleading. "I'm just asking you to stay in the game and not give up. You may be a draw away from a reversal in fortune."

Vitaeus didn't say a word for some time as he pondered Yolif's words, then he stood abruptly. "I'm going all in with my two of hearts, but I can't ask the rest to gamble with their lives. I'm going to address the men and request they surrender. You two should make preparations to surrender as well." As Vitaeus approached the door, he turned to look at his two most trusted companions. "Thanks to both of you for everything you have done for me, and most of all, thank you for your undying loyalty. I am sorry that I have failed, and that it had to end this way."

That day, all the crossbowmen surrendered as ordered, but the ten knights refused to do so, saying that they swore an allegiance to him and if they went back on that oath, they could never be knights again. "To live as knights, to die as knights," said one knight, and the rest echoed him.

"A knight would prefer an honorable death in combat versus slavery in the mines." Yolif whispered to him afterwards; so Vitaeus didn't press the point on their surrendering further.

But with all the crossbowmen surrendering, there were not enough men to keep the fort secured; so the knights retreated into the safety of the keep. The King's army wasted no time in moving into the castle grounds and surrounding the keep.

When the King's knights started ramming on the keep door, nine of Vitaeus's knights retreated to the second floor; while one knight stayed to guard the circular stairs leading up. The steep, narrow stairs of the keep spiraled upwards in a tight clockwise direction, giving the defenders the advantage of holding the higher ground, and the ability to use their right sword hands unrestricted while the attackers would be forced to attack with swords in their left hands. The narrow staircase allowed only one man up at a time; so one knight could hold the entire King's army at bay. The knights switched guard rotation every hour, but when the fighting got intense, they switched every twenty minutes to stay fresh. Even with all of those disadvantages, the King's knights were not to be held back from trying, as they fought their way up with determination.

CHAPTER 49: THE COUNCIL

Desiani rode up to the eastern battlements with Yurosi, Tiram, Keltar, and Marcus in tow. They dismounted and ran up the steps to the battlement where Achledis and Rolen stood watching the Rakirian army take their positions below. Desiani walked with a purpose in her step; her shoulders thrown back and a few paces ahead of everyone else. She wore an elegant white gown with a low neckline and a blue trim around it; Her hair was made in a single braid; which reached the small of her back. She was beautiful as usual. Achledis couldn't contain the small smile at the sight of her, but she only scowled in return.

"Did you two forget about the vote that was to take place this morning?" She asked, as she looked from Achledis to Rolen; her eyebrows bunched in anger.

"That meeting got cancelled when the bells clanged the call to arms." Achledis stated, and Rolen nodded in agreement.

"How can we meet when the enemy is at the doorstep?" Rolen asked.

"Well, we almost voted without the two of you, but Yurosi insisted that your voices be heard." Desiani stated, "So we came to you."

Achledis looked up at Yurosi in mild surprise, and the young knight met his gaze and gave him a nod.

"Well, the enemy is getting in position, and we don't have much time. I wish I could say let's vote and get this over with, but this vote will have an impact on the upcoming battle. The men below know nothing of our little plan to elect a new leader; they simply know that their leader is me. So whoever is elected as presider of this council, I ask that I may remain to lead these men."

Desiani looked at Achledis and nodded her agreement. "Achledis is right. The military chain of command should remain as it currently is; though the commander, or Achledis, must submit to the presider of the council, who will always speak on behalf of the council." Desiani was looking at Achledis as she spoke. "We will go around, and everyone may nominate someone for the role of presider of the council. But you may not nominate yourself. Now, if no one here has questions, then I will begin."

"We are pressed for time. Let's skip this nonsense nomination process, and all in favor of Desiani as presider, please raise your hand." Achledis said, as he raised his hand, and the rest raised theirs in unison. All but Yurosi, who hesitated momentarily before raising his as well.

"There you have it, Miss Presider of the Seredine Council, congratulations." Achledis said and gave Desiani a salute; the rest followed suit and saluted her too.

Desiani looked around at all of them, her face beaming. "This is not how this was supposed to work. We were all supposed to make a case why we believed someone was worthy, and as a council, we were all supposed to be heard. Our votes were to be recorded in secret on paper and then read aloud. As flattered as I am by the result, we need to revote. Otherwise, how am I to know that you are all serious about your vote?"

"Miss Presider, this doesn't have to be very formal, not yet anyway. Our government is still in the process of being formed, and you're the first part." Keltar said.

"Agreed," Achledis said. "Now the majority of us were absolutely serious about you as our presider. You were in the role before the vote, and you should maintain the role now. I lead the men of war, and you have been instrumental in leading this city for the past month. Let's not kid ourselves, you were always the leader here, and the people of Seredine always knew that. I was simply a face, but you were the voice." Achledis embraced Desiani and whispered in her ear, "Don't act surprised. You certainly dressed the part with that elegant gown. As always, you look beautiful."

"Thank you, you don't know how much this means to me. You are truly the best friend I ever had." Desiani whispered in Achledis's ear; then she turned to face the rest. "Thank you all for entrusting me with this responsibility. I accept the vote, and I promise that I will always strive to keep your trust by being fair and honest."

Desiani's words were met with applause from the remaining council members.

"Now, as I have stated earlier, the military chain of command will remain as it was, with the only exception being that I have the final authority." She looked at Achledis with a thin smile on her face. "That means you report to me now."

"Yes, Miss Presider," Achledis replied.

Desiani gazed over the battlement wall and motioned for everyone else to come take a look. Below them and a good three-hundred yards away from the city walls, just outside a bow's range, the Rakirian army stretched the entire length of the Eastern wall, five ranks deep. Viserate and his officers stood in the front center, watching the city with a spyglass, presumably trying to find a weak spot in the wall's defenses.

"I will go address the people; while you get the men ready for battle. I will be back soon, and if the battle begins before I'm back, then I need to be notified immediately."

"Very well Miss Presider," Achledis confirmed.

Desiani glanced back with a scowl. "You can stop calling me that; it's gotten annoying."

"They have raised a white flag," Yurosi called. "Viserate and an officer are riding out; they want to discuss terms. My lady, as head of security, I will accompany you to see what terms they have to offer."

"Sir, you will call me by my title; I am not a lady to you!" Desiani snapped. "The only terms acceptable to us are the ones where they, the Rakirians, turn around and head back for Rakiria. Achledis will ride out on my behalf; the rest of you be ready." Desiani turned on her toes sharply; so that her gown swirled as she headed for the stairs, with Achledis in tow.

CHAPTER 50: TRAPPED

Vitaeus looked out over the water from the window of the lord's chambers on the fourth floor of the keep with longing. Sounds of sporadic fighting coming from the stairs of the first floor were not heard all the way up here. Vitaeus had watched as his one knight held the entire King's army at bay; more fresh bodies were being sent up, only to get defeated. Vitaeus's knights had rotated every twenty minutes during the fighting to keep fresh, yet the battle had lasted several hours. Every attempt the King's men made to storm up the stairs, Vitaeus's knights had rebuffed them each time, and they did so with ease.

It only took one trained knight to effectively hold the King's army at bay, but still Vitaeus and his men were trapped. The courtyard outside was teeming with the King's army, and they had nowhere to go. On occasion, a bolt from a crossbow would fly through the window, and so as a general practice, they had learned to stay clear from any windows looking out into the courtyard. The spy holes for the archers were available however, and they would use those anytime they wanted to observe whatever was happening below.

Vitaeus's conscience troubled him incessantly. He was the cause of 300 good men being sentenced to the mines and twelve more were now resolved to die with him inside these walls. He had come to Caminia with a bold intention of taking his kingdom back, but his close resemblance to his grandfather had instantly made him a target of suspicion. He had planned on working inside Caminia by networking and building allies, yet he had barely got started before earning the ire of the King. Now he was resigned to await his doom inside these stone walls.

Daenis had been pacing, going from floor to floor, and checking on the knights and their status before coming back up to report. Sometimes he would leave to wander the desolate keep for hours at a time. Vitaeus had been trying to read the Vulcan journal, hoping to find an idea that might work to help them escape, but he couldn't concentrate on the words as his mind raced with all of the possible nightmarish outcomes to this siege.

A rock missile slammed into the keep where the window was located, causing a crack to run from the corner of the window and down the wall at an angle. The walls of the keep were a solid two feet thick, yet the brick laid out around the perimeter of the window was crushed in the area where it had been struck. Another missile slammed in the area where Yolif had been stationed, causing the keep to shudder as sedimentary dust rained down from the ceiling above.

"Here, I found some rope," Daenis shouted over the noise of the missiles hitting the keep as he ran in, holding some hemp rope in his hand.

"What are you planning to do with that rope?" Yolif asked, even with all the mayhem going on, he managed to have a bemused smile on his face.

"We need to get out of here, or else we will get buried."

"The only use you have for that rope is to hang yourself before the King gets a hold of you alive. It's not bloody suitable for much else. The rope will reach the ground out front, but if that's where you want to go, then just walk out that door. Razim's soldiers have fallen back shortly before the trebuchets started their bombardment. Perhaps you can make it a few feet before someone rides up and cuts you down, or maybe an archer's arrow gets you before a knight gets his chance to hook you on his lance."

"Then I can walk out with a white flag and ask for terms, they wouldn't dare kill me when I'm holding a white flag." Daenis replied.

"There will be no more terms. The time for terms ended."

"Aren't you concerned even a little?" Daenis asked.

"For you guys I am; however, I can get out at any time." Yolif replied confidently.

"And how is that?"

"I'll climb down the wall facing the sea. From there, I will scale the cliff across until I'm a safe distance away from any soldiers. At that time, I will simply climb back up and be on my way. With all the prisoners being taken to the mines, it leaves no one to recognize me, and I will once more be a free man."

"Yes, we should try that," Daenis gasped. "We have nothing to lose."

"Except your life," Yolif muttered. "You wouldn't last thirty seconds holding onto a narrow ledge of rock with a few fingers to grasp a ledge. Besides, climbing that cliff will require flexibility and immense core strength; two things that you are greatly lacking."

"We need to do something; perhaps at night, we can try to escape in the dark."

"Best plan you've had so far." Yolif replied, as he got up from the floor where he was reclining and slapped Daenis across the back. "Send me a letter once you are safely on the other side of them soldiers, will you?"

Yolif's words were cut off as a rock landed on top of the flat roof of the battlements above. They could hear it rolling across the surface, and suddenly there was a violent splintering of wood followed by a gentle thud, as it fell into the trap door leading to the battlements.

Daenis started laughing hysterically, and Vitaeus and Yolif stared at him in disbelief.

"What is so funny?" Vitaeus finally demanded.

"Here I'm sitting and wondering when their supply of rock will end," he pointed at the protruding rock in the ceiling with mirth still on his face. "And now my answer is before me." He started to laugh once more. "They aren't getting the rock supplied; they are mining it right on location. After all, we are all sitting on layers and layers of Caminian rock."

The rocks did stop raining as dusk approached, but not before the window was enlarged from a rock that smashed the upper left hand corner, dislodging a large stone. Without its support, more damaged stones from above came loose and crumbled down. The ones that didn't fall, threatened to fall as the integrity of the cement between the stones was jeopardized with large cracks spiraling in the cement between the rocks. When the missiles stopped falling, Razim's army pressed in around the castle once more.

"There goes your plan of escaping in the dark." Yolif commented. "You certainly won't get far now, not even a few feet outside that door really."

As Vitaeus sat down to read the Vulcan Journal, Yolif sat next to him and pulled the journal away gently. He pointed at Daenis. "Have you noticed how pale and skinny your loyal servant has become the last few days? He can't even stomach any food. Yes, we all chose to follow you into this hell, but you're the leader. You need to lead and not read a book while we are in the midst of chaos."

Vitaeus looked at Daenis and then back at Yolif. "I will think of something; I won't let you two be captured."

"Unless those pages contain wings for us to fly away from here, I don't find it likely." Yolif said as he waved his hand dismissively in Vitaeus's direction and left down the stairs.

Daenis looked at him momentarily and followed Yolif downstairs. Vitaeus couldn't help but catch the disappointment in his eyes. He also noticed that Daenis didn't excuse himself, as he had been accustomed to doing, before leaving. Vitaeus suddenly felt at a loss for what to do. These were grown men that were beginning to panic around him, and Yolif was right, he wasn't leading. How could he plan on ruling a kingdom one day, when he couldn't even hold a small crew of men together inside a keep?

Thud!

Vitaeus stared at the crossbow bolt imbedded into the oak tabletop with a letter wrapped around it, mere inches from his hand. His first reaction was to glance to the gaping hole in the wall, but all he saw was a black void. He picked up the bolt and hastily untied the hemp string holding the letter to the bolt. With nervous fingers, he smoothed out the letter.

The northwest corner of the keep is being mined. The rocky ground is causing some delay, but the crews are working hard and are progressing much faster than expected. You have until noon tomorrow before the keep comes down. Surrender today; so that you may live tomorrow. The letter was simply signed – *Friend.*

Vitaeus stared at the letter, dumbfounded by the message it contained. The clock was ticking to their doom. He couldn't bet on still being alive by noon; it could be a lot sooner. Again, his conscience reminded him of the sacrifice of Yolif, Daenis, and the ten knights, as well as the archers who had been condemned to the mines. He had destroyed hundreds of lives, broken countless families. Now there are wives and children who would never see their husbands and fathers because they were either killed or sentenced to a lifetime of labor on his behalf. Something had to be done, Vitaeus decided. He would surrender on the condition that everyone else would be free to go.

CHAPTER 51: REUNITED FOES

The blustery clouds had cleared, and the sun burned hot overhead. Sweat gathered into small drops before it rolled down the face of Viserate. He eyed Achledis as if trying to recollect why the face looked so familiar to him. There was a lingering silence as the two sat on horseback, studying one another, waiting for the other to speak first.

Viserate's eyes widened ever so slightly in recognition before he composed himself back to the disdainful look he had maintained. "Tell me boy, why does your face look so familiar?"

"I'm the face that has been haunting you in your dreams at night." Achledis said tauntingly. "I'm your biggest nightmare." The men on both sides of Viserate slowly put their hands on the butts of their swords as if sensing the sudden tension. "If you surrender now, then I will show you and your men mercy." Achledis continued casually. "Just order your men to come and drop their weapons on the ground, and in turn, we will allow all of you a safe passage back to Rakiria.

Viserate's eyes flashed angrily as he blew air out his nose. "You insolent fool. I will personally cut out your tongue when I get to you, but not before I skin you alive and listen to you scream."

"First you need to get to me, and I will present you a clear chance to do that. We can settle the matter the old-fashioned way, the way of a duel; winner takes all. If I kill you, then all of your men will surrender to me and vice versa if I lose." "I'm not going to fight you personally; why would I? I have a whole army at my back. By not surrendering now, you offer me a show. I will sip wine and watch as my men tear your city apart brick by brick, before slaughtering all of your people. I will have your guts spread out before me; so that I can piss on them."

"Spoken like a true coward." Achledis said with disgust. "Well, the time for talk is over. Send your men to their death if that's what you wish, but know that these 10,000 corpses won't be able to stop me for coming after you." Achledis said as he gestured at the Rakirian army.

Viserate felt his blood start to boil, and he wanted to knock this disrespectful kid to the ground. The memories of the boy's escape still tormented him at night; he had felt humiliated in front of his army. Even now, he spoke with such insolence that Viserate wanted him dead, and he felt like he could arrange it too.

"I will offer you one more chance to spare the inhabitants of that city from the massacre that is sure to come. Fight my champion; winner takes all."

Achledis whipped out his sword and pointed it at Viserate, fury burning in his eyes, "When will men, such as you, who start the fights actually have the guts to fight in the battle themselves? I will see you on that field soon, and when I do, I won't be so merciful. I will take your head!"

Achledis whipped his horse around to gallop back to Seredine, then stopped short. "I accept!" He yelled at Viserate who had his back to him and was riding back to his men.

Upon hearing Achledis yell out, Viserate turned towards him to make sure he heard him.

"Bring out your hero. I will kill him, and as agreed, your army will then surrender their weapons and leave Seredine, back to your accursed country." Achledis shouted.

A gleeful smile crossed Viserate's face. He had succeeded in getting the fish to bite on the bait; now he had to reel the prize home. He was sure that his hero, who was almost seven feet tall, could defeat this boy. From what his best scout had told him, Achledis inspired his men. Without him as their leader, the garrison here at Seredine would quickly fold in battle, if they didn't surrender without a fight.

Achledis rode back inside the walls of Seredine where Desiani and the other councilors were waiting. He told them about the deal that he had struck with Viserate, expecting them to respond excitedly; instead their faces turned grave with concern.

"Achledis, you can't go through with this!" Rolen said.

"We all know of your skill in combat, but this is a Rakirian champion. He is trained for moments like this. We are surrounded by high walls. Yurosi has booby-trapped the surrounding area; I say let's take our chances. Don't risk your life on the first day. If you die, it will be a major blow to the whole army."

Achledis raised his hand to silence Rolen. "I think you have forgotten what it is that we have a chance at achieving here, a quick victory. With a stroke of my sword, I can spare thousands of lives and ensure our conquest."

"It won't ensure anything, whether you win or lose." Desiani replied. "Because if you lose, I won't surrender the city, and if you win, I doubt that Viserate will surrender his army. This is an unnecessary risk, and as presider, I want to motion against it."

"I won't lose; so there is no harm in trying." Achledis replied.

"What if you do lose, and under this agreement we are forced to surrender?" Keltar interjected. "Surrender, just like that? Allow them to come into our city and massacre all of us? Do you know what they say about this guy? He is almost sure to exact revenge for the rebellion."

"Even if you do win, Achledis, how do you know that Viserate will stay true to the agreement and surrender?" Rolen asked.

"Okay, okay," Achledis replied and threw his hands up. "I concede that you guys are right. There is a reasonable chance that Viserate won't surrender, and if I'm dead, none of you will surrender either. But with my victory, that will raise the morale of our men and diminish the morale of the enemy."

Rolen had never seen anyone so sure of their victory, especially before they even saw their opponent. Achledis was youthful and reckless, and they had nominated him to lead. Yet it seemed dangerous to go along with his decision. "Achledis, I just don't feel right about this; everything about this whole situation makes me very nervous. I can feel it in my gut, and at my age, you learn to always trust your gut."

"Let's put this up to a vote." Desiani said.

"I'm not voting on this; this is my decision. I am only endangering myself with this, no one else. As I already said, I have to try, and if Viserate has any nobility, then he will stick with the agreement and surrender his army."

"The point of a council is to vote on all matters." Desiani replied angrily.

"No, not about this, this isn't up for debate." Achledis replied coolly as he turned and walked away to prepare himself. He had not expected his most trusted friends to have so little confidence in him. He put on his helmet, leaving most of his face uncovered except for a slit that went down the length of his nose. A tough leather vest was all that Achledis had on his body for protection. He declined all the offers for chain mail and heavier garments. Knowing that his fighting depended a lot more on speed, than on sheer brawn, he wanted to stay light.

Word had gotten out about the duel, and all the people inside the city wanted to watch. There had been a lot of tales floating around, about Achledis's heroics, and they all wanted to witness it for themselves. Some said that he was invincible. If that were true, then it would have to be a good show; especially when they saw the Rakirian champion.

The Rakirian hero rode out on a black, bay horse, stopping a hundred yards away from Seredine's eastern gate. He sat for a long while appearing impassive, looking in the direction of Seredine, but eventually, he got off his horse and started yelling at the top of his lungs, calling for Achledis to come out and fight him.

You could hear gasps of awe and fear, from the people of Seredine; once they saw the stature of the Rakirian giant. He was bigger than any man that they had ever seen. Even from a distance, they could see the heads of most men being even with his shoulders; his large arms looked like tree trunks, with rolls of muscle rippling down his biceps. He swung the long sword with ease, singlehandedly in circular motions, showing off his incredible strength at keeping the long and heavy blade in perfect balance. When he shouted his challenge, he would stretch out his arm, holding the long sword perpendicular to his body, pointing it straight towards Seredine. It was a feat most men struggled to do with both hands, and for the Rakirian giant, it was a show of superiority and intimidation to his opponent, who was undoubtedly studying him, even now. By getting into his opponent's head, he could get his opponent to start doubting his own victory. With his opponent's confidence shaken, he knew the battle was half won.

Rolen and the others once again tried to persuade Achledis not to go, but to no avail.

"Look," he said. "I can see the man, and no matter his size, he is just a man. He bleeds just like all of us." Achledis tried to sound indifferent, but inside he felt nervous jitters.

"Come out and fight!" The giant continued to shout, stopping when he finally saw the gates of Seredine opening and a lone horseman riding out.

The Rakirian giant studied his opponent as he rode out on an impressive gray horse. A simple leather vest and helmet was all he wore for protection, and his weapons consisted of a round buckler, a short sword, and a lance made of ash with an iron tip. As the rider got closer, the giant saw his youthful face and threw his hands up in rage.

"What is this? A boy! You bring out a boy to fight against me?" The giant was red in the face. He felt disrespected because this went against his honor. "Come out you cowards; don't send a boy against me to steal my honor. Send a man that I can fight."

He turned around to look towards Viserate; surely this isn't what he had in mind. He was let down yet again, as Viserate signaled for him to kill the boy. This was humiliating. Never in his life was he asked to be someone's executioner. He wanted a fair fight. He was a soldier, however, and had to obey orders. When he realized that there was no way around this, he was determined to do this quick.

Achledis was dismounting, when out of the corner of his eye he saw an object flying towards him. He fell to the ground just in time as a spear blurred by where his head was a moment ago. Rolling over quickly, Achledis was up and charging the giant with his short sword in hand. The giant braced himself for the attack, with his feet squared just outside his shoulders. He crouched with his left hand holding a large shield and his right hand holding a long sword.

Achledis came in low and spun, his shield caught a glancing blow from the giant's sword, but it wasn't enough to knock Achledis back. As he spun, his short sword cut through the chain mail, just enough to give the giant a nick in his left arm that was holding the shield. The giant roared with anger and swung at the boy but missed.

Achledis backed off fifteen paces and studied the giant, who was now all too aware of the boy's quickness. He also realized that the long sword wasn't going to be as useful as previously thought; for the boy got in close and rendered the long sword's advantage useless. Achledis charged again, running straight for the giant, but at the last possible moment, he lunged to the right and stabbed his sword into the left bicep. The large shield dropped to the ground with a thud, making the earth shake underfoot.

Achledis was quick to spin around to see the giant turning to face him rather slowly. His left arm hung limply at his side. The rage he felt was covered with the agony he felt. The giant came in swinging wildly at Achledis, and it took Achledis off guard. He quickly tried to shield the blows. Each blow felt like it would rip his shoulder from its socket, and his buckler was a mangled mess. Achledis tried unsuccessfully to get away from the blows, but they just kept coming. Until finally, a blow knocked him to the ground. Achledis's arm was trapped in the strap of the buckler, and he had to yank it hard, ignoring the searing pain from the strap and metal scratching and cutting his flesh as his arm came free. Achledis quickly rolled to get up, but the giant's foot slammed into his behind, sending him sprawling once more.

Rolling on his back, Achledis tried to hop up, but the giant put his foot on his chest and the tip of his sword to Achledis's throat. A look of triumph was on his face. "You have my respect boy." The giant said, as he applied more pressure with his sword. In a blur, Achledis's left hand knocked the sword to the side and with his right, he stabbed the giant in the leg with a dagger.

The giant's foot, with the dagger still stuck in the leg, quickly left Achledis's chest, leaving him free to get up. Achledis scampered quickly to grab his lance before facing the giant once more, who stood awkwardly on one foot, his left arm hanging limply at his side. Achledis abandoned the tactic of attacking the giant straight on. Rather, he started to circle around the giant slowly, forcing him to hop on his one foot to keep facing Achledis, who circled him like a hungry wolf does to an injured bull.

The concern on the giant's face was now clearly evident. He was hurt and hobbling and already getting dizzy. Trying to keep his balance on one foot was quickly sapping all of his energy. Then he saw the boy burst into a sprint; grabbing the ash pole in both hands, the boy hurled his body towards the giant. His arms brought the lance forward in a savage thrust that pierced the gorge plate and stuck in the giant's throat.

Achledis let go of the lance, but it stayed in the giant's neck. The giant swayed for a moment, as blood seeped between the cracks in the armor, before falling at Achledis's feet. In a display of triumph, Achledis picked up the giant's own long sword with two hands and cut his head off. Then he picked up the head by the hair and waived it for all to see. A roar of approval rose from Seredine; while the Rakirian side was deadly quiet.

To see their giant hero fall dead was something hard for them to wrap their minds around. A rebel youth had just defeated a well-trained Rakirian hero; who killed for a living. Even Viserate was paralyzed with confusion. He had watched this giant kill countless men, and his men were inspired by him. Now with him dead, he knew that his men could lose heart quickly; so it was necessary to get their morale back.

As the gates of Seredine opened, he watched foot soldiers run out in perfect unison and move into formation in front of the city gate. A cavalry rode out and broke to the side of the phalanx; while five riders continued to ride in Achledis's direction. He knew they were waiting for him to come out and make good on their agreed surrender.

What fools, he thought to himself. There stood the leader himself, surrounded by his five closest in command, right in the middle of the field; they were easy pickings for his archers. Better yet, the rebel army stood exposed outside the walls. He smirked to himself; this was going to be a lot easier than he had planned. No need for the siege weapons that he had been building. Without further hesitation, he sounded the bugle blast for the archers to aim and then fire.

Achledis and his friends were looking towards Viserate, who wasn't coming forward.

"That sly rat, I told you that he would never surrender." Rolen spat out bitterly; his words were cut off by the bugle.

"Run!" They all shouted in unison as they whirled their horses around and raced back to their lines; as the shadow of a multitude of arrows blotted out the sunlight. Achledis felt the impact of arrows sticking to the buckler strapped to his back. As they rode up to the front line of foot soldiers, they turned around to see the field covered in arrows.

CHAPTER 52: SURRENDER

The King had agreed to a parley on the first floor of the keep. Knights from the King's royal guard stood blocking the exits and the stairs. The entire back wall was lined with crossbowmen; while the King himself sat behind a crude wooden table, on an elaborate wooden chair. The chair was covered with a majestic moose hide, and smaller mink pelts dressed the arm rests.

Vitaeus kept his eyes fixated on the King and forced himself to breathe as he made his way to the wooden stool across from the King. He knew that the King wouldn't have to agree to anything. He was literally at the King's mercy as the entire first floor of the keep was flooded with the King's men; while his own men didn't even know that a parley was taking place. With great concentration, Vitaeus maintained his poise as he sat on the stool across the table from the King.

"At first I thought you were attempting some sort of a trick." Razim mused. "Yet here you are, helpless as a lamb in the midst of wolves. I commend you for your bravery and scold you for your foolishness boy."

"I know you to be an honorable King; one who stays true to his word. That is why I am here, alone, with only your honor to guard my safety." Vitaeus replied.

Razim stared at him, making no initial reply, but when he spoke, his words were as cold and hard as ice. "Should I act honorably with a traitor? A man who came to me as a guest, and whom I heaped with honors, riches, land and titles." Razim pointed a shaky finger at Vitaeus. "I even offered your life if you had surrendered, but now I shall see to it that your death will be a slow and a painful one. It will take you a month to die."

"My King, I must remind you that this is a parley, and your reputation for being trustworthy is at stake. Though your men serve you, they will still talk if you act with treachery towards me. I have not yet surrendered but will do so on some conditions."

The King slammed his fist on the table and stood glowering at Vitaeus, "Who are you to offer conditions to me? Even if you leave from this parley, you will still be mine by tomorrow."

"Perhaps you will acquire my corpse, but I won't give you the satisfaction of taking me alive. I will rob you of the pleasure of torturing me, but if you agree to my conditions, then I shall surrender, even now."

"Speak then, what is your request?"

"I only ask that all of the men that served me be pardoned. They were only following my orders and had no desire to be part of any insurrection against you, My Lord."

King Razim smiled for the first time. "I will pardon all of those men that surrendered on the first day, but everyone that stayed with you will be condemned just as you are."

"No deal." Vitaeus whispered, fighting against the lump growing in his throat. "Either spare them all, or I will jump off the cliff. That way, you won't even have my corpse to hang on display." Vitaeus stood, "I will be expecting your answer within the hour." Vitaeus turned and walked back towards the stairs rigidly, expecting at any moment to be cut down with several dozen crossbow bolts. Rather, it was King Razim calling out that stopped him in his tracks.

"You have a deal." Razim called out, and as Vitaeus turned to face him, Razim motioned for the palace knights to seize him. Almost instantly, Vitaeus felt powerful hands seizing his shoulders from both sides and forcing his wrists to his midsection, as cold, heavy shackles snapped around his wrists. A couple more knights held down his legs; while other palace guards fixated iron shackles around his ankles.

Razim motioned with his hand irritably. Suddenly, the chain shackled to his wrists jerked, and he felt himself being pulled away. Vitaeus was seized with fear of what awaited him next, as goose bumps covered his skin.

On the fourth floor of the keep, Yolif watched the activity below with bewilderment. He had refrained from disturbing

Vitaeus so far; who seemed to be reading that book incessantly. Yolif decided that it would be best for Vitaeus to finish reading. There was not much else one could do around here but wait for their pending doom. Yolif watched the neat columns of foot soldiers and knights outside slowly moving towards the only gate of the motte-and-bailey. He had to tell Vitaeus of this new development; perhaps in the midst of the bombing, they could make their getaway.

The sound of approaching footsteps on the stone stairs echoed from below, and Yolif stood. It was unusual for any of the knights to come up here. They usually kept to their own camaraderie, yet it was a knight who appeared.

"The King's forces are pulling back," the knight stated bluntly.

"I noticed. You should notify Vitaeus instead."

"Vitaeus has surrendered himself and is in the King's custody; the King has pardoned the rest of us."

Yolif shot up and grabbed the knight by the shoulders. "Vitaeus did what?"

"Vitaeus made a deal with the King. He surrendered himself, and the King agreed to pardon all of us."

"Why didn't you stop him?" Yolif demanded through clenched teeth.

"We didn't know of his intentions. He said that the King had agreed to a parley; so we thought that he would ask for terms."

"But why would the King agree to allow the rest of us to go free?"

"It was part of the bargain that Vitaeus presented to the King. Vitaeus threatened to jump off the cliff, so that not only would the King not get his chance to torture him, but he wouldn't even have a body to present on the city walls."

"Vitaeus surrendered in order to spare us? Doesn't he know what the King will do to him?" Yolif muttered as he looked about the stone walls.

"From the conversation we heard taking place below," the knight continued, "Lord Vitaeus understood what kind of torture awaited him, but he ensured that the King would pardon all of the crossbowmen, as well as all of us. It seems the King was willing to allow all of us to go free for the simple satisfaction of torturing Vitaeus."

Yolif looked the knight in the eyes and whispered. "Sir, go tell the other knights to gather here immediately. We will locate our crossbowmen and reorganize our army. Then we will free our future king."

CHAPTER 53: THE FIRST HURRAH

Desiani stood next to Achledis on the battlements, along with Yurosi, and watched the Rakirian army prepare for battle. Roughly 1,000 Rosmirian men stood in front of the eastern gate into Seredine, baiting the 10,000 Rakirians. Achledis was still fuming at Viserate's treachery; it had happened just as his friends warned him it would. But no one even mentioned it to him. Though his recklessness had, in fact, placed him and all of his friends in danger when they rode out to meet him after his victory.

"Hopefully the bait will appear to be so good that he sends all of his men in, and we can give them hell in turn," Achledis mused out loud.

"And at the same time, I'm nervous as hell. What if something goes wrong?" Desiani replied. "Yurosi, as the head of defense and military strategy, how well would you say we prepared for this event?"

"I am confident. If Viserate takes this bait, then he will receive the most hellish welcome of his life." Yurosi replied. But he was also chewing his lower lip nervously, and his eyes were glued to the scene below.

Achledis glanced nervously to his side where the archers sat patiently behind the walls, out of sight of the unsuspecting Rakirian army. "Yes, and that's what I intend to give him." Achledis said, as he scanned over their quivers to make sure that they all had about two dozen arrows. Satisfied, he turned his attention once more to the advancing Rakirian army. He had rehearsed the battle plan dozens of times with his captains, and they all assured him that their men were ready. He expected everyone to play their role; whether they were infantry, cavalry, or archers, they all had to be perfect. The captains would do their parts, and he as commander would fight alongside his men.

Achledis pulled Yurosi aside, away from Desiani's ears, and told him his plan. "You will be in charge to make sure that the operation goes as planned. You are the military mind. I'm the soldier, and so I will fight alongside the men. You may relay this to Desiani after the battle is already under way. I will join Marcus and the cavalry, and you can look for me there."

"Are you sure you want to do this?" Yurosi asked.

"Yes."

"Well the Presider won't be happy about this when I tell her, but I will take command as you requested. We will be keeping an eye out for you." Yurosi placed his hand on Achledis's shoulder and looked intently into his eyes as spoke in a very serious tone. "Achledis, be careful."

Achledis gave a good natured slap on Yurosi's back. "Will do," he replied, as he walked away.

Viserate smiled haughtily as he looked out at the Rosmirian forces standing in formation in front of the city gate.

"Take a look, and tell me what you see," said Viserate, as he handed the spyglass to his lieutenant.

"Sir, I see roughly a thousand Rosmirian peasants standing in battle formation outside their city wall." The Lieutenant replied.

"Yes, a thousand raggedy peasants," Viserate confirmed. "The fools should have stayed in their city walls." Viserate remembered how angry he got when he first learned of the Rosmirian revolt in Seredine, but now he looked at it as an opportunity. Today he would put his name in the history books. Glory and honor would be his. He was ready to destroy these Rosmirian rebels with one sweep of his army.

His father had high hopes for him to become a famous general one day. But for now, he was colonel, given the task to come through and loot the Rosmirian countryside and put down the rebellion in Celesta; a task that almost guaranteed that he would not taste glory for a long time. No general, or colonel, for that matter, considered putting down a rebel uprising as being worthy of their rank. Everyone sought glory in the Southern campaigns, but today, opportunity was knocking on his door. He had to seize it. Viserate turned to his lieutenant and ordered him to send all the men in.

"All of them sir?" The Lieutenant asked.

"Yes."

"Sir, is it prudent to send them all now?

"If you presume to question me again, then I will demote you to the kitchens." Viserate replied with menace in his voice.

"No, n-n-no Sir," the lieutenant stuttered. "I was merely wondering, what if it's a trap of some sort. They could be baiting us."

"Baiting?" Viserate's voice grew sharp with anger. "My spies tell me that they have no more than 2,000 men, and if they want to throw half of them out to bait me to engage, that's fine. I will take the bait. Five to one in my favor is a hell of an advantage for me. They are untrained peasants; I will crush them. Send ladders with the rest of the divisions to attack and take the city."

After a moment, a bugle sounded a few short blasts, signaling a full attack. Viserate watched as his army slowly set into motion and started to march. Goosebumps ran up and down his spine as he continued to watch them. He could hardly wait for the action to begin, and the slaughter to start. His mind wandered to how he would proceed; once he took the city again.

Yes, more than likely, they will surrender after only a few of them die. After he disarmed them, he would not be merciful. He will set an example of them for all of Rosmir to know that treason has a high price, and if you revolt against your Rakirian masters, you will be brought to justice. Yes, he will hang them all. Every man, woman, and child would be hanging from these city walls for any passerby to see what happens to those who oppose Rakiria. He would leave the city a barren ruin.

The City of Seredine lay nestled around the bend of the Seredine River on its south and west sides; so that the river flowed right up against the city walls, offering an excellent water-barrier. The rolling plain of the northeast made it most vulnerable to attack, and so the walls on those sides were much more heavily fortified to withstand siege weapons for longer periods of time. However, the city sat on a hill, and its defenders benefitted from the advantage of controlling the high ground.

Viserate's army was marching at a slight and steady incline towards the city. In the last hundred yards, the hill got considerably steeper; which presented another challenge for the attack. If it was a professional army that he faced, then he would have taken a lot more caution in attacking them, but this was a rebel army of farmers and peasants. And they barely knew how to use the weapons they held; so it was hard not to be arrogant.

His army was still a considerable distance from battle, but he was losing his patience. He ordered the charge. Once again, his lieutenant tried to reason with him.

"Sir, that hill will sap the men's energy before the battle even begins." The lieutenant shut up and gulped as he felt a dagger at his throat.

"Lieutenant! If you question my orders again, I will cut your tongue out. After this battle, you may report to the kitchens. Perhaps there you will remember that I am in command of this army, and you are a mere lieutenant.

The bugle sounded, and the Rakirian army responded with a roar as it surged towards the awaiting rebels with their backs against a wall. Through the looking glass, Viserate watched with a grin on his face as the gap between the two armies closed quickly. This would be a crushing victory. Viserate's joyous thoughts were suddenly interrupted; however, as he watched in alarm as a thousand Rosmirian archers appeared on the battlements with fire arrows. Before the arrows were even launched, Viserate had a sinking feeling. He heard a shrill blast of a horn from far away and then watched helplessly as a thousand tiny missiles made their way high into the sky before starting their descent towards his unsuspecting army. Flames shot up from the pitch soaked earth as the fire arrows hit the ground. Even from where he stood, he could clearly hear the screams of agony and terror. At least 2,000 of his men were burning alive, and more yet were being pushed into the flame by the forces behind them. Some three-hundred more of his men must have been pushed into the fire before his army came to a halt; another 700 were trapped on the other side of the fire, where the Rosmir archers continued to use them for target practice.

There was panic in the ranks, and the disorganization only continued to grow as the men closest to the fire were turning and trying to push back. There was nothing for him to do but signal a retreat.

Instead of being an organized retreat, it was chaotic as men pushed and shoved one another in an attempt to escape the arrows. His army should have built a tortoise or a wall to deflect the arrows, to allow a more organized retreat, but the panic proved to be contagious as it swept from the front all the way to the rear of his ranks. Viserate continued to watch with disgust through his looking glass as his men shed their weapons and shields as they fled.

The horror only continued as 250 horsemen appeared from around the wall of fire and gave chase to his fleeing men from behind. Another trumpet sounded, and the thousand Rosmir rabble that had stood in front of the gate charged ahead to finish off his men that were trapped on the other side of the fire. Viserate flung his spyglass to the ground; a quarter of his army had just either been routed or destroyed on the first day of battle.

The day was lost, and he was humiliated. He couldn't even begin to imagine how he could explain the loss of a quarter of his army, nonetheless in a single day. He looked to see where the lieutenant, who had advised him not to attack so boldly, was and saw him sulking angrily. Viserate was made even angrier that the lieutenant had been right.

The Rosmirian cavalry, headed by Achledis, came out of the east gate and charged the side of the Rakirian phalanx, who had their shields and spears now aimed straight ahead to stop the charging Rosmirian foot soldiers and to deflect the raining arrows. The Rosmirian cavalry had closed in before the Rakirians had a chance to notice them. There was a panicked rush to adjust formation to protect their flank, but it only led to more confusion among the soldiers. Their panic only grew when they recognized the blue and yellow plume; for the man leading the charge was also the one who slew their hero.

The blue and yellow plume attached to Achledis's helmet flew majestically in the wind as he galloped. He let out a fierce war cry as his horse hurdled over Rakirian soldiers, trampling them to the ground. His sword was flying left, then right, as he cut the enemy in front of him with ease. The Rakirian phalanx, trapped by the fire, had regrouped after the initial panic and were now trying fiercely to push this Rosmirian horde back. The man with the blue and yellow tail was cutting them down, however, and the courage of his men only continued to grow.

Achledis's senses were always heightened to an extreme in battle, but right now, it was as if never before. He could almost see his next kill before he even swung his sword. But suddenly, he found himself on the defensive as a short stocky Rakirian turned out to be remarkably proficient with his short sword and seemed to fend off every one of Achledis's quick blows. He surprised Achledis by turning up the heat on him. In a blind turn of events, Achledis felt himself being dragged off his horse from the back, leaving him momentarily stunned to find himself lying flat on his back, but he quickly recovered as he saw the short stocky man over him with his sword raised.

Achledis kicked the short Rakirian's legs out from underneath him, sending him sprawling on the ground. Achledis yanked his knife out with his left hand as he sprang up and slashed the short man across his unprotected neckline. The thick warm liquid sprayed across Achledis's face. He wiped the blood from his eyes and turned to face another Rakirian; who at the sight of him turned and fled. Achledis's entire body seemed to be covered in the crimson color of blood, and when the Rakirians saw his red face spattered with blood, they fled from him in terror.

The Rakirians were trapped. Behind them was an inferno, and from the front, the confident Rosmirians, led by Achledis, pressed them towards the flames behind them. As the onslaught continued, more and more Rakirians decided to retreat through the flame.

CHAPTER 54: IRON SHACKLES

Vitaeus had been placed into an iron cage atop a cart pulled by a large black horse. As the cart made its way through the city gate, it was instantly met by throngs of people.

The town crier shouted through the noise of the crowd, "Hear ye, hear ye, the traitor Vitaeus of the House of Konis has been captured alive. May the King's judgment on him be just; according to the crimes that he has committed."

The cart turned right onto a street lined on both sides with crowds as far as the eye could see. Vitaeus was suddenly blinded with a flurry of objects being thrown at him. The objects ranged from pebbles and stones to rotten fruit and horse dung. All sorts of vitriol was directed at him by the crowd as they shouted for his crucifixion. The boys and youths of the city were especially enamored with the idea of making dung balls and throwing it in his direction. Soon Vitaeus was covered with animal and human feces, as well as rotten fruit, and had welts that he was not even yet aware of. Within minutes, his body had gone numb, to the point that though he still felt something when struck by a stone, he no longer felt the sting or the pain of it. His headache was far worse.

The cart made its way through the streets and veered down a side street a few times. Every time it did, Vitaeus would get a moment's reprieve from the constant harassment of the crowd, but it didn't take long for the crowd to catch up. The crowds had lined up on the roads that would have taken him directly to the old dungeon. It quickly became clear to Vitaeus that either he was being taken elsewhere, or they were deviating from their course for another reason. Though he couldn't figure what that reason may be.

The reason for the detour soon became clear as the cart rolled from the rough small streets that they had been on and onto a main highway. To the left was the new palace. There were plenty of onlookers lined up on the balconies, and some were looking from the windows high above. As the cart headed down the street, town criers on every corner read out loud the proclamation against him. "Hear ye, hear ye, the traitor Vitaeus of the House of Konis has been captured alive. May the King's judgment on him be just; according to the crimes he has committed."

Vitaeus searched for a glimpse of the princess on the balconies, but he didn't see her anywhere. He gazed up at the windows but still saw nothing. The driver took the cart up along the walls of the palace where people emptied their latrines on him, and once more Vitaeus was covered with fresh human feces. He endured the mockery the entire stretch of the palace with eyes cast down; it shamed him that the princess might see him like this. Just when the cart was about to clear the palace, a bouquet of roses fell on top of the cage, and a few red petals floated down and landed on his lap. Vitaeus looked up to see a face vanishing from a window above. It let him know that there was still someone inside this city who cared about him, and the thought gave him comfort.

The cart drove through a stone archway and into the dungeon courtyard entrance. A large, heavy iron gate with rusted orange, iron spikes protruding upwards slammed shut behind them. The dungeon stood on a massive rock, surrounded on three sides by cliffs. The dungeon itself looked like a giant fortress, with dark stones and ivy running up its walls. As the cart continued down the winded path, they passed a heap of skulls on full display. The cart came to a sudden stop before the dungeon's main entrance, and the prison guards ran out and surrounded the wagon immediately.

The torturer and the jailor walked out to meet them; both wearing black tunics and leather vests on top. The palace guards unlocked the cage, and the jailor grabbed the chain and yanked Vitaeus out.

"Yet another who has earned the King's ire." The jailer said, and then his eyes fell on the rose petals lying inside the cart. Looking up, he saw the roses lying on top of the cage. "Well look at this one, not only is he covered in filth, but he also has some roses to go with it." The jailor laughed. He was a stocky man with broad shoulders and a protruding belly; the result of a life of leisure. The torturer was slightly taller, with shoulders just as broad as the jailor's, but he also had lean muscles running the length of his biceps and forearms.

The torturer scowled in the jailor's direction, clearly not sharing his amusement. Prison guards took the chain and led Vitaeus into the dark entrance sparsely lit by torches. The jitters in Vitaeus's stomach increased after walking through endless hallways and down countless winding stairs. Was he to be taken to a cell, or was he to be tortured first? One thing was clear, breaking out would be nearly impossible as he was already lost in this stone maze.

Soon Vitaeus found himself being escorted through a tunnel. The lighting here was poorer, and the air was clammier than in the other parts of the dungeon that he already walked through. He could see a light coming from the end of the tunnel. The jailor led the way, followed by a guard, and then Vitaeus, and two more guards behind him, with the torturer following last. They walked out onto a wooden balcony overlooking a grand cave. The floor was a good thirty feet down, and a steep staircase chipped out of stone led the way down to the floor. The cave was well lit, and Vitaeus got a good view of the layout of the cave and all of the torture devices located throughout. Chills ran down Vitaeus's spine, and goose bumps crawled over his flesh as he realized why he was here. On one end of the cave were prison cells where prisoners were placed in between torture. As they continued to make their way down the stairs, Vitaeus could hear prisoners moaning in pain. The sound disturbed him.

"Where do you want him?" The jailor asked the torturer.

The torturer was eyeing the rack, a wooden frame with rollers on either end. A prisoner's arms would usually be tied to the rollers on one end and his legs to the other. The rollers would then turn in opposite directions, stretching and eventually dislocating arms and legs out of their sockets.

"He has a month to die; so you may want to start him slow. Kill him too soon, and the King will be coming after you."

The jailor reminded the torturer. "Besides, you're the artist, do it with taste and make this one your masterpiece."

The torturer grunted and pointed at two posts connected by a beam with a hook hanging from the center of it. On the side was a crank to turn the beam. Next to the post was a rack that held an elaborate whip with several dozen leather strands all ending with jagged hooks. Next to it was another whip, six thick strands of rope with big balls of knots strewn throughout the length of the strand.

The jailor looked at Vitaeus, a disquieting smile on his face. "You're in luck boy. I'm supposed to keep you alive for a whole month; which means that you get the whole torture tour. Every day you will experience something new and more excruciating than the day before. Considering it's your first day, we will start you with something simple; a few lashings to get you used to the pain. Then we will walk through and give you an introductory of every device in here and what you can look forward to."

The chains on Vitaeus's wrists were then attached to the hook hanging from the beam; so that Vitaeus's body was stretched upwards. The torturer started to turn the crank. The chain wrapped itself around the turning beam, and Vitaeus felt his arms stretching more and more. Soon his toes had cleared the ground, and he was dangling helplessly. Vitaeus thought he heard popping sounds but wasn't sure if it was only his imagination or not, but the pain he felt at the joints in his arms was real. Suddenly, he realized that the pain that would come next would be far worse, and the image of the whip with several dozen leather strands all ending with barbed nails came to mind. Subconsciously, Vitaeus started to mutter a prayer under his breath; even as he realized that he was sweating from the blow to his back. He heard the torturer taking his place behind him and the whistle of the whip as it sliced the air, as the torturer whirled it around for emphasis. The psychological torture had already started, and Vitaeus was in full panic mode. What could he do? He wondered, and every time the answer was the same, nothing.

"Wuh-psssh!" The whip snapped, and Vitaeus instantly felt the air leave his lungs as the burning pain across his back seemed to suck all the oxygen from him. Just when Vitaeus sucked in some air through clenched teeth, it left him instantly; as once more, the blinding pain settled across his back. The pain continued to repeat itself until Vitaeus was at the edge of unconsciousness, and only then did the whipping stop. The chain was unwound; so that the tips of Vitaeus's toes touched the ground. This was the position that he would remain in for the night.

Every time Vitaeus's eyes closed in exhaustion, water would trickle over his face, primarily over his nose and mouth, stimulating him awake and leaving him gasping for air.   When morning came, Vitaeus was beyond exhausted; he was delirious. He hadn't slept all night; since he was being kept awake by the constant dripping of water on his face. The torturer unwound the chain; so that Vitaeus could comfortably stand on his two feet. Then what followed made Vitaeus scream in anguish, jolting him wide awake. The sound of chortled laughter announced the jailer's presence. The man conducting the torture only gave the jailer a wry look before turning his attention back to sprinkling the liquor across the open wounds on Vitaeus's back.

"Good to see that he is wide awake once more; for he has another busy day today." The jailer said, as he came up to Vitaeus and slapped him across his raw back, making Vitaeus cringe in pain. This only brought about more laughter from the jailer. "Yes, today your schedule is packed. We skipped your tour yesterday and got right down to the down and dirty; so today we will back up a little and give you your tour. But first, you will need to get some sleep; boy you look like a mess."

The torturer held a wooden mug filled with water to the brim and gave it to Vitaeus, who grabbed it with shaky hands and brought it to his mouth. Vitaeus started to drink eagerly with water dripping from the sides of his mouth. He had only managed a few gulps before the jailer knocked the mug from his hands. Vitaeus scrambled down to pick up the mug, but the torturer kicked it out of reach. In the midst of the jailer's laughter, the torturer yanked the chain around his wrists, sending Vitaeus crashing face first onto the rocky floor. Vitaeus felt himself being dragged across the rocky terrain. Every time he attempted to get up, the chain attached to his ankles would be yanked by the jailer, and Vitaeus would find himself on his face once more. When the dragging finally stopped, Vitaeus looked up warily as the torturer and jailer walked away. He found himself lying on a wet, musty carpet of hay inside a prison. The jailer left the door to his cell wide open, but Vitaeus didn't even notice as sleep instantly overtook him.

"Aaaugh!" Vitaeus cried out in panic and fear as he shot up wide awake two hours later as the torturer held a red hot iron rod to his upper left arm. His skin sizzled, and Vitaeus, even in his delirious state, smelled the vapor of burning flesh.

The torturer led Vitaeus out to where the jailer stood waiting by the rack, eating a fat drumstick of chicken. Vitaeus watched hungrily as the grease shone on the meat. The jailer would take a big bite and chew slowly, watching Vitaeus eyeing him hungrily. The torturer shoved him on the rack, and moments later, Vitaeus's arms were attached to the roller above him and his legs to the rollers below.

Creator please, not this, not till later, Vitaeus thought.

"I thought I was promised a tour first; the rack was supposed to come later." Vitaeus's voice came out more pleading than he had intended.

"We will introduce you to some more minor pain and then give you a tour of the rest of this facility." The jailer said, smiling wickedly the entire time; grease dripped down his ragged beard as he spoke.

Vitaeus felt his body stretching steadily until he grunted in pain as the ligaments started to hyperextend. The torturer would then leave him stretched for a bit before cranking the rollers a bit more. Vitaeus was grinding his teeth in pain; while the jailer stood over him eating his chicken, watching in amusement. Vitaeus was somehow finding the courage in his bleak state. The panic he had felt the previous day was no longer present. He was determined to bare all the pain without giving the jailer and the torturer anymore satisfaction in hearing him scream. But with the next crank of the rollers, his resolve melted away, and he screamed.

In the midst of his screaming, Vitaeus heard a man's voice commanding them to stop, but instead of stopping, his tormenters continued to crank the rack. The searing pain of muscles straining and of joints on the verge of popping brought him to the edge of unconsciousness. That was when he realized that he must be delirious. He had imagined the voice commanding his tormenters to stop. It was all in his head.

CHAPTER 55: MAKING A STAND

Early in the predawn morning, Seredine was rocked with missiles from the trebuchets and catapults. The assault continued for two hours, well after the sun had risen to light the day. Desiani, Achledis and Yurosi watched as the Rakirian infantry advanced in a steady, disciplined line, from the northeast, towards the city. Seredine sat on a hill, nestled around the crook of the Seredine River on its south and western walls. The banks of the river were steep, and no army in history had ever successfully mounted an attack on Seredine by crossing the Seredine River and scaling the steep banks on the south and western shores. The only sides the defenders of Seredine had to worry about were the north and east, but even here, the approach to the city was a steady incline, with the north side being considerably steeper than the east.

Achledis felt the wall shudder from the impact of a rock hitting nearby and watched as the men cowered behind the parapets of the battlements. Even with the heavy losses that Viserate's army incurred the day before, he was still able to field an overwhelming army. Achledis had put the bulk of the infantry on the eastern wall with another large force on the northern battlements. The south and the west side had fifty men guarding the wall; just in case Viserate tried to infiltrate saboteurs or spies from that direction. They were to sound the alarm in the event they needed reinforcements. Marcus had left with a cavalry of a hundred men. They were to follow the Seredine River north and then cut east, in an attempt to flank Viserate's infantry from behind.

As rocks from Rakirian trebuchets continued to pummel the city, the women and children had cleared the streets and retreated for the relative safety of the southwest side of town. With each collision, Achledis could see the men before him chattering nervously. A bugle sounded in the distance, and suddenly, the Rakirian infantry, which had marched in such perfect cadence, even with occasional arrows falling around them, charged, screaming their war cry. Achledis stepped away from the parapet and shouted for the archers to fire at will. Even when the waves of arrows dropped many Rakirians, it didn't stop the tide of crimson uniforms as they converged on the city.

Viserate sat on top his horse and watched through a spyglass as his men charged towards Seredine's northeastern corner. The defenders on the battlements naturally drifted towards that corner in anticipation of the oncoming attack, and Viserate signaled the engineer next to him to fire the trebuchet. He watched as the long arm swung out and threw its projectile. The rock crashed right on target, into one of the parapets in the corner of the northeast battlement, sending shards of rock onto the crowded battlements. At the same time, part of his attacking force split east and rushed towards the main gate; while the rest pressed the eastern side of the northern battlements.

Today he would crush Seredine's defenders; he was sure of it. Yesterday he had been naïve and perhaps overly excited to see the Rosmirian rebels standing outside their walls, and his attack had ended in failure. Now his whole army was attacking in force, with all the siege weapons an army needed to take a well-defended city. He closed his eyes briefly and imagined that he was commanding the attack in a Southern campaign, against a more prominent foe. He smiled at the thought and turned to a commander to signal the cavalry platoon forward. With a whoop, the calvary raced towards the eastern gate, carrying ladders and battering rams in tow. His smile broadened as he saw that the first of the siege towers had reached the northern wall, and his attack was now well under way.

Achledis had hoped that the archers would be able to keep the Rakirians at bay, but even the archer's numerous arrows wouldn't stop the crimson tide as it slammed into the northeastern corner of the city. Seredine's defenders were instantly overwhelmed with the sheer number of siege towers and ladders that kept popping up. Their infantry was busy trying to push them off, but when the siege tower approached and the bridge was dropped to cross onto the walls safely, the task became even more overwhelming. The tower had brought a fresh flood of Rakirian attackers, and the tower's wooden walls gave the Rakirians excellent protection from the arrows, allowing them to scale the tower's ladders untouched. Now Seredine's defenders met a determined attacking force, and as long as that tower stood there, a steady flow of Rakirians kept coming through. More Rosmirian defenders were forced to confront the ever growing number of attackers, leaving the rest of the wall more vulnerable as ladders kept popping up with incessant persistence. There was simply not enough men to knock them all down.

Achledis was in the middle of the fighting that was taking place on the battlements when a messenger ran up and shouted for his attention. "Sir, Rolen asks for your assistance at the eastern gate. He says that it's just a matter of time before the Rakirians break it down. All of our attempts to disable the battering rams have failed."

Achledis swore under his breath as he tried to collect himself; so that he could think more clearly. Looking around, he could see that he didn't have many options left. His situation was bleak, and his men were simply being overwhelmed by the Rakirian's vast numbers. If they got through the main gate, then the entire Rakirian army would be inside Seredine in a matter of hours. He had to stop them.

"Let's go," he told the soldier. "Lead me to Rolen."

"Yes, Sir," the man replied.

Rolen spotted Achledis first and hurried towards him. "I need help over here; we already ran out of the boiling pitch and are now boiling water to dump on the men manning the battering ram. With every one of their soldiers that gets disabled, another one steps up and the ramming continues. The framework around the gate has been significantly weakened, and it won't be much longer before the gate comes crashing in." Rolen paced back and forth nervously. He couldn't stand still, and something had to be done. "Perhaps I could lead a small cavalry force around and try to scatter them from the gate." Rolen suggested.

Achledis studied the gate that shuddered violently with every hit it took from the ram but didn't answer Rolen immediately. Instead, he stood nonchalantly and pondered what to do. To Rolen it looked like Achledis didn't understand the grave situation they were in and reiterated his suggestion to send a cavalry around, but Achledis shook his head no and still gave no further response. Rolen was losing his patience and wondered if Achledis could be counted on. Every hit from the ram sounded like a clock ticking the time away before the explosion of Rakirians burst through their gates.

Still seemingly unnerved by the gravity of the situation, Achledis finally replied. "We should have more pitch in our storage somewhere; send some men to look for it."

"Yurosi has gone to look for it, but even then, I'm not sure it will help." Rolen said his voice sounded defeated.

"It will help," Achledis answered coolly. "Bring lots and lots of hay, and when Yurosi arrives with the pitch, we will soak it and spread it in the corridor between the main wall and the buffer wall. Once it is done, shut the gates in the corridor and unlock the main gate for the Rakirians; let them come in. The gates on both ends of the corridor will hold a multitude of foot soldiers. Once the corridor is filled with Rakirian soldiers, we will light them up."

Rolen nodded his approval for the plan, and said he would execute the plan immediately. As Rolen galloped off, Achledis pressed his horse into a gallop back to the northern wall to see how his men were faring. As he approached, he could see that Keltar was managing a lot better than when he left him. The Rosmirian infantry had retreated into a defensive position on the battlement and had their long pikes extended to keep the Rakirians at bay, and the archers were shooting into any Rakirian that attempted to cross from the siege tower to the battlement. Hundreds of flaming arrows were stuck in the siege tower, and it had finally caught fire and was burning. Relieved, he turned back towards the eastern gate, comforted that Keltar didn't need him and was doing well on his own.

Only later would Achledis find out that it was Marcus attacking the Rakirians from the rear that saved Keltar on the northern wall. It forced the Rakirians to turn and defend their back, giving Keltar a much-needed break from the hard-pressed Rakirian attack. The brief respite in the Rakirian attack allowed him to set up his defenses better.

At the eastern corridor, the men were busy spreading out the pitch soaked hay between the main wall and the buffer wall. The iron hinges that the gate sat on were slightly bent, but it was the wooden framework around, that was splintering and breaking from the punishing blows it received from the rams outside. Achledis had been watching anxiously as the iron hinges were slowly coming out with every blow. Afraid that the gate would crash open at any moment, he ordered the men to get behind the buffer wall before the hay and the pitch was fully spread throughout the corridor.

Suddenly, with a load groan, the gate swung out, teetered, and came crashing in. The defenders manning the gates on either end of the corridors instantly started shutting the gates before their comrades could get through, trapping them inside the corridor, but ropes were dropped to haul them out before the Rakirian infantry got to them.

The Rakirian infantry came inside in a disciplined fashion. As one unit, with their shields interlocking with one another, they had formed a tortoise, and arrows and rocks wouldn't penetrate the shield as the missiles either stuck to the shields or bounced off harmlessly. The battering ram was well protected as it came to the end of the buffer corridor and started ramming the gate. But the defenders waited patiently as the corridor filled up in both directions and both gates at either end of the corridor were being pounded by Rakirian rams. The Rakirians were confident, until the Rosmirian archers appeared over the buffer wall with flaming arrows...

CHAPTER 56: MARCHING PRISONERS

A cloud of dust followed the beleaguered prisoners; every single prisoner marched with heavy iron shackles around the wrists and ankles. Their shirts were tattered, ripped, and bloodied across the back, with fresh dust settling on the wounds. The shouting of taskmasters and the crack of whips, as they urged the stragglers on, was the constant noise, and the air itself was full of fear. Their energy had been sapped long ago; rather it was the dreadful anticipation of the bite of the whip that kept the adrenaline running through their veins and carried them on. Those, whose adrenaline had failed them, fell to the dirt, mindless of the whips that lashed across their flesh, leaving raw flesh gaping out of the cuts. Their bodies were then picked up and tossed as corpses on the wooden carts pulled by mules that followed the prisoners.

The prisoner had sustained a few lashes already, and the fear of another urged him on. He walked despite the fact that he was severely dehydrated, despite the pounding headache, and despite his tight muscles that threatened to cramp at any moment. He had seen many of his fellow companions that he had come to know get seized with a cramp and fall to the dirt helplessly. That was when the taskmasters, like vultures, converged on them and beat them until not a muscle moved. Only the labored breathing of their lungs was seen as their chest rose and fell with a rhythm.

With every step he took, reality set into the prisoner's mind; he was doomed to die. His determination wouldn't carry him another twenty miles. His muscles were tight and would seize up at any moment, and without water, he wouldn't last another five minutes. No one would arrive at the mines alive; they would all die before they got there. Though Razim promised to spare their lives and confine them to the mines, it was clear that their execution was the most horrible of all. This was a horrible way to die, and yet the idea of death suddenly felt like the best alternative. The more the prisoner thought about dying, the more he liked the idea. When he would fall, he would suffer for a bit, and then he would be left in peace for eternity. There would be no more pain, no more anger, no more heartache, or feelings of betrayal; only eternal nothingness, without happiness and without sadness. *Life in this world brought about more sadness than it did happiness,* the prisoner thought. Feeling nothing for eternity seemed like paradise.

The prisoner's left foot seized suddenly, and he staggered briefly before falling into the dirt face first. The excited shouts of taskmasters and the crack of their whips sounded through the air as they made their way towards him; however, what they didn't understand was that their whips no longer intimidated him. Rather, he waited in eager anticipation for them to end his life and send him into eternal tranquility. As the prisoner lay on the ground in his beleaguered state, he felt the ground tremor and heard the sounds of horsemen approaching. It did nothing to peak his interest. He had set his mind on dying, and he didn't want anything or anyone to interrupt that from happening.

The prisoner lay and waited for the whips to start falling on him, but they did not come. Everyone's attention rested on the new arrivals, mainly on the man who sat on a large white destrier; his armor shimmered with a bluish glint, as did the buckler strapped to his back. An ornate scabbard hung at the side. He was undoubtedly a lord. A squire sat at his side, and ten more knights were behind him. The lord handed a letter to the officer in charge and commanded the taskmasters to unshackle the prisoners and to give them water. The taskmasters jumped to comply without waiting for orders from their commanding officer. The commanding officer, a short little man, jumped in infuriation and shouted for his men to stop.

"I did not command you to release anyone!" His voice rasped hoarsely as he yelled. "Now carry on with your duty of moving this rabble to the work site."

Even in his vexed state, the prisoner's interest was suddenly sparked. This new lord had demanded that they be given water and released from their chains; certainly he was someone to root for. The prisoner sat up as apprehension dawned on his face. The armor that the man wore was the same armor that the man that he had sworn service to had worn. His lord came for him after all; he did not desert them to die. The sword sang with a steely zing as it was removed from the scabbard, shining with a bluish glint. The lord put his sword at the commanding officer's throat and demanded that he comply with the orders in the letter.

"You are the traitor, and these are your men. The letter you gave me means nothing." The officer said defiantly.

"The letter I gave you are your orders from your King himself." The lord stated. "And you will either comply, or you shall die. That is your choice."

"The letter is from no one important, and the seal is a bad counterfeit." The commanding officer retorted. "My orders came from the mouth of the King himself. You sir, are no lord, but a mere traitor."

"The reason I stand here before you with this letter is because the King has pardoned me and all of my men. Your men have thirty seconds to start passing out water, or I will personally execute you for disregarding your King's orders."

The officer's countenance faltered, either at the realization that what the lord said made sense or at the threat, but his voice was timid when he gave the orders for his men to give water to all of the prisoners and then to unshackle them.

The prisoner's desire for death dissipated when his lips first made contact with water. As he drank heartily, the shackles on his feet were unfastened, and the weight dropped off. Then the shackles around his wrists were taken off, as well. Though his whole body still ached, and the muscles in his legs were tight, he knew that he would live.

Yolif rode up to the prisoner; who stood on shaky legs, with exhaustion displayed on his face. Yolif swung off his destrier and reached into his riding bag. The prisoner's eyes never left him; even as Yolif took some dried mutton and gave it to the prisoner. The prisoner refused it.

"More water," the prisoner croaked.

Yolif took his water pouch and gave it to the man. All around him were more men just like this man, in grave need of water.

"Daenis, get more water from the supply wagon and see to all of the wounded on the wagons." Yolif commanded, before turning to the commanding officer who rode up behind him. "You and your men better make sure that all of these men are seated on the wagons, then have your men go and get more water. You will help me escort these men back to the fortress."

The officer looked like he was about to argue, but the look Yolif gave him instantly made him reconsider. He simply nodded in compliance. As he left, barking orders to his men to get the prisoners on the wagons, Yolif looked at the prisoner before him.

"Thank you for helping us." The prisoner whispered; his voice still hoarse. He handed Yolif's empty water pouch back to him.

"You are Sir Vitaeus's men; it is my duty to make sure that you are all healthy and able. Sir Vitaeus will have need for all of us, and we must be strong and ready to serve.

The following morning, the crossbowmen sat at the dining hall of the keep, eating their hearty breakfast of potatoes, with poached eggs, and thick slices of ham. Two pigs had been roasted for the occasion, and farmers had herded more of their animals to the keep. Yolif had paid them handsomely with Vitaeus's gold. The merchants headed to Caminia to sell their wares were also relieved of their goods and paid. Yolif had waited until the men had finished eating before he told them their mission. All 129 of them, who were well and able, were to infiltrate the new palace where the princess was staying, and where the final princess's ball would take place.

The prisoner, dressed in the clothes of a pig farmer and leading a herd of twenty swine, along with five other assistants, made his way inside the city walls of Caminia City without a single question being asked of them by the city watchmen. Underneath their ragged cloaks were daggers and crossbows strapped tightly with a quiver of bolts. Following not far behind them were more of their companions dressed as merchants, laden with silks and other goods. Farmers were also driving their carts filled to the top with vegetables and hay. Ranchers herded cows and bulls inside the city, and even some of the finest horses were brought inside to showcase for all the lords of the kingdom that would surely be here this day.

Of all the festivities since the Rok princess arrived that were in her honor, this was to be the biggest. Already entertainers of all sorts had arrived to the city, and more were pouring in. The main entrance to the palace had continuous traffic coming in and out; even the doors to the kitchen and stables were in a constant hub. The prisoner and his assistants herded the swine to the palace butcher shop. The place was packed with racks of venison, mutton, and pork drying, roasting, or smoking on the rack. Chopped up animal carcasses lay on bloodied oak tables everywhere.

"What's all this swine doing here?" Demanded the gruff voice of the butcher. A large man with a protruding belly and a sleeveless jerkin appeared. Splatters of blood were all over his clothes and body, including his face and bald shimmering pate.

"We are here to sell it to you; you don't want to run out of pork on a festival like today." The prisoner replied.

"I have all the meat that I will need. Now get your dirty swine out of this place before it contaminates the meat."

"Whether you have enough or not is not my concern. The palace ordered twenty swine, and so here they are. Now I want the payment."

"Well you won't get your payment because the palace hasn't ordered these pigs." The butcher waved the cleaver threateningly. "Now I order you to get out; you are not authorized to be here."

"Wait!" A foreign voice sounded from behind. "Twenty swine were indeed ordered. For there will be a lot of guests, and the princess wanted to make sure that the food doesn't run out." The man's stylish clothes made of silks and fine linen and his thick accent gave him away as the Rok prince and brother to the

Princess. "Butcher, won't you please take the swine to the pigsty where they belong."

The butcher, with a look of bewilderment, complied instantly as he herded the pigs together.

"The rest of you, please follow me." The Prince beckoned.

The prisoner and his companions followed the prince through a side door that led to the servant's quarters of the palace. Though brand new, the quarters were ordinary. The walls were made of yellow brick, and the floors of gray cement. The doors to the various apartments were thin and made of pine. The prince led them into one of the apartments with 'Uniforms' labeled above the door and gave them the palace liveries to wear.

"This garb will distinguish you as servants in this palace, and your presence won't be questioned by anyone here. You will be free to do your job in preparation for the feast."

The prince then led them to the banquet hall where already many of their companions, also wearing the palace uniforms, were making last minute preparations for the feast. The banquet hall was opulent and colossal. The main floor was open for dancing, and at the far end was a dais with an elegant table. There was a doorway on either end of the dais where the King's personal guards stayed out of sight yet ready to serve and protect the King at a moment's notice. The doors were still in the process of being installed.

The prisoner took in the vastness of the banquet hall, with wrap around balconies four floors up. Elegant stairs leading up to the balconies were at all four corners of the hall. The walls of the hall were a deep maroon. The trim was made of pure gold; just as the banisters on the stairs were. The stairs were made with a dark blue marble. Above the King's dais was the King's banner with the three headed viper. On one side of the banner was a portrait of the King; he appeared some thirty years younger than he actually was. The portrait of the princess was on the other side; her beautiful features and elegance were accentuated by the artist.

Yolif approached them; dressed in a elegant linen suit, he addressed the prince. "Any trouble on the way up?"

"No, everything went smooth, but be sure this succeeds. And above all else, make sure the princess is safe." The prince said sternly as he looked at Yolif.

"Absolutely, her majesty's safety will be our top priority." Yolif responded as the prince turned on his heels and walked away.

The prisoner had been so busy looking around that he hadn't noticed Yolif's approach. He was fond of the youth who had saved him and his companions from not only a lifetime of hard labor in the mines, but quite possibly their lives.

"I'm glad the rest of you made it here safely." Yolif said with a smile. "Sir Vitaeus is lucky to have a special group of men such as you. He knows it, and he will reward you all greatly."

CHAPTER 57: FIERY FURNACE

The fire in the corridor was like a large oven cooking the Rakirian soldiers alive. The shrill screams of dying men in agony were enough to send chills down the spine of any man. It was enough to make Achledis feel shame; even though he knew it was perhaps the only way to stop the Rakirian attack. He knew that he had succeeded before the first report came to him; that the Rakirians at the gate had fled back to their camp with hails of arrows cutting many of them down.

Achledis hurried away from the haunting sounds of tormented men; even though the sound quickly diminished as death overtook the Rakirians one by one. He tried not to think of what had just happened and ran up to the northern battlements, where the Rakirians were mounting another charge. He could see the tides of retreating men were being intercepted by cavalry; who forced the men to turn back around and charge once more. More battering rams were being brought as well, and Achledis knew that they would try to break down the gates of the corridor on the east side.

Through his spyglass, Achledis looked back at the eastern corridor, and he could see that the flames were pretty much all gone and that the Rosmirian infantry was filing through the corridor from both ends, their long pikes extended. Rolen too must have seen the Rakirians returning with another charge, and knowing that the gates in the corridors wouldn't last long against the Rakirian battering rams, he had to stop them from getting to the corridor gates. As the Rosmirian infantry filled the corridor and blocked the eastern gate, with their pikes extended out to meet the Rakirian charge, the gates on both ends of the corridor shut to ensure that there would be no retreating by the Rosmirian defenders.

The Rosmirian infantry stood guarding the eastern gate, waiting for the screaming Rakirians to come. They marched through the smoldering Rakirian corpses in the corridor, and as gory as it was, it also gave the men renewed confidence upon seeing the multitude of Rakirians that had perished in that attack. With the Rakirians returning for a renewed attack, however, there was no eastern gate to hold them back, and no more pitch to burn them with when they started to hammer at the weak gates at the corridors. They were the last line of defense as Rolen had told them that the only way the Rakirians would enter through the eastern gate was if they allowed them to. Retreat was not an option for them. If they retreated, then all was lost. They would be forced to fight until they could fight no more.

As the rushing Rakirian army approached, it was apparent that they were exhausted, and the Rosmirian men who saw this were renewed with confidence. But then that confidence dissipated as horses emerged, harnessed to a frame; which carried long logs of battering rams coming straight for them. Instantly, the Rosmirian ranks split down the middle as men rushed, yelling and screaming, to whichever side in order to avoid the oncoming torpedo.

The ram was supposed to destroy the Rosmirian orderly ranks, but the hail of arrows managed to bring down the horses before they reached the Rosmir infantry and served as a hindrance to the Rakirians who were attacking. This forced them to break their neat ranks and to go around the massive lump of horseflesh and ramming framework between them. The rushing Rakirian infantry quickly ground to a halt; as they encountered hundreds of long pikes extended out protecting the entrance inside the city. The Rakirian infantry regrouped into formation, and with their shields interlocking, they pressed into the extended pikes with their comrades helping to push behind them. The Rosmirian pike men felt themselves being pushed back as the Rakirian phalanx pressed into their pikes, but the men behind them stepped in and slammed their pikes into the wall, as well. Both sides maintained their formations and pushed against one another, but the beleaguered and exhausted Rakirian side soon started to give way. An occasional pike would slip through a crack in the shield wall and nick a Rakirian, weakening the spot in the shield wall.

On the northern battlements, the Rakirians were beaten back, and there was a pause in the fighting. Achledis took advantage of the respite in battle by preparing for the final Rakirian assault.

"Haul it up boys!" He yelled as the weary men started to haul big balls of hay soaked with pitch onto the battlement. Achledis jumped in and helped a group of soldiers pull on the rope, feeling it cut into his hands before the tension in the rope suddenly gave way. Achledis and the men flew back. Fwoop! Came a sound above Achledis's head, and one of the men yelled out and shoved Achledis down, as another arrow flew by where his head was a moment ago and stuck in the hay. Achledis jerked his head around to look in the direction the arrow had come from and saw a man disappearing into the growing darkness. It was impossible to see who the shooter was, but his men had scrambled in pursuit of the assailant.

"Are you all right?" Keltar asked.

"I'm alive; the assassin needs to learn to shoot. Now let's focus on the Rakirians. They are preparing for another assault." Achledis retorted hotly, but inside he felt jittery at being the target of an assassination. He tried to shrug it off and focus on the enemy that was marching once again; the crimson line clearly visible as dusk settled.

Keltar nodded, but just the same, he had men flanking Achledis on all sides. He would not allow the assassin to kill their leader; which would cause men to lose morale just as they were on the verge of securing another victory. He ordered his men to light their arrows and shoot ten feet from the wall; hundreds of tiny lights immediately appeared on the ground before them. With a roar, the men launched the balls of hay below; which instantly turned into massive balls of fire as they rolled over the burning arrows and down the hill towards the attacking Rakirians. With shrieks of panic, the Rakirians who saw the balls of fire coming down towards them, turned and fled. Soon the entire attacking Rakirian army on the northern wall was in full retreat. On the east, Viserate was suffering heavy casualties and barely making any headway; so he was forced to sound a general retreat.

CHAPTER 58: ANXIETY

The new palace where the princess had been staying had initially seemed comfortable enough. She had always felt at ease and at home there, but now it felt like it had become a prison. It was a constant reminder of the imprisonment that would soon follow if she accepted King Razim's marriage proposal. She had finally found the courage within to make the decision to turn the King down, yet when she heard of Vitaeus's capture and the torture that he would go through, her heart had ached. She had arranged a personal meeting with the King and had begged for Vitaeus to be spared. It had come down to a deal, and she made it without any hesitation.

She was still tormented at what she had witnessed when she came down to the torture chamber, and the scream. Good Creator. The scream was unearthly. She shuddered at the memory; even as she forced the memory away. At least she had made sure that the torture stopped, and tonight she would pay the price for making it stop.

The door opened softly, and her maid, Keness, appeared. She seemed hesitant as she entered, knowing that her lady demanded time alone.

"We must finish getting you dressed my lady. The ball will start in a few hours, and there is still a lot to do until then." Keness, at sixteen years old, was hardly a year younger than the princess. Raheena had personally selected her because she was more of a friend than a servant, and Raheena loved her dearly.

"I know." Raheena stood as she met the girl's embrace. "I'm scared, that's all."

"You are still the bravest person I know." Keness replied. "The way you went to that King and forced him to do your bidding." A small smile played on the girl's lips. "Well, let's just say that you will be an excellent queen. Besides, the common folk of this country have fallen in love with you from what I have heard."

Raheena sat on a stool in front of the looking glass as her maid tended to her hair. "Yes, but how long before he dies?" She wondered aloud.

"Princess, you shouldn't say such things, at least not out loud. You never know if the wrong person will hear you and report it to the king that you are eagerly awaiting his death. You may even be locked up for treason."

"Do you think that old fool actually believes that I want to spend my life with him; for me to lie and await him eagerly every night?"

"Just be careful with your words princess; remember, we are no longer on the Rok Isles."

"Ouch!" Raheena winced as the maid's brush got caught up in some tangled hair.

"I'm sorry my lady." The maid apologized, and when Raheena didn't reply, she continued brushing her hair. "You have a palace all to yourself, far from him; so it may not be all that bad."

"He will demand an heir." Raheena replied. Her voice and her gaze were distant as if her mind was elsewhere.

"There is a great opportunity in all of this for you, my lady. If you give birth to a son, then he will be next in line to rule after Razim passes on. You will rule as a Regent Queen until your son is of age to begin to rule on his own."

Raheena stood suddenly before her maid was finished with her hair and rushed to the window, looking out to sea.

"My lady, we really need to finish getting you ready. The ball is scheduled to begin soon."

"I just want to go home." Raheena replied. "I don't want power, status, or prestige; I just want to be a little girl again. I want to be free of all these expectations. I want to be my daddy's little girl again. There was a time when I believed that he would abdicate his throne if I asked him to. My father never said no to me before. Yet he was adamant that this marriage take place. He said that I was of age to do my duty for the Rok kingdom." With deep sadness in her voice, Raheena whispered, "Why did my father stop loving me?"

"Your father loves you, my lady; you know he does. He always has. It's just that we all have a role to play in life. My role is to be your servant, and your role is to become a wise and powerful queen. I am excited for you my lady; though you may not see it now, you are extremely lucky."

"I am lucky to marry an old man?" Raheena looked at the maid angrily. "Are you kidding me? Get out."

"But my lady..."

"Get out! I don't care if we are late for the ball. I need to be alone right now."

The maid turned and left, closing the door gently on her way out.

Raheena lay down on her plush bed and closed her eyes. The stress and anxiety from the last couple days had really worn her down; she hardly slept anymore. She drew a deep breath and let it out slowly, and she continued to repeat the process until her beating heart stopped pounding in her chest. A few moments later she had fallen asleep.

The sound of sharp knocking woke her up, and she turned over in her bed before choosing to ignore it and closed her eyes once more. But moments later, there was another round of knocking, and this time it was even more urgent than the first time. Raheena rolled off the bed and walked to the door. She glanced at the clock on the wall and gasped. She only had a little over an hour before the ball would begin. She also got a look at herself in the looking glass and was horrified to see her hair. Keness's work had gone to waste. She frowned as the knocking started up once more and hurried towards the door.

"Who is it?"

"It's your brother; we must speak now."

CHAPTER 59: THE FINAL PLAN

Yurosi, Rolen, Marcus, and Keltar, sat in Achledis's chilly chambers, but none of them seemed to notice the penetrating chill. They were stunned by Achledis's command. They had barely slept more than a couple of hours before messengers were urging them all to Achledis's quarters. Achledis seemed completely unperturbed as he told them to go and wake the men for the attack.

"Tonight we will deliver the final blow," Achledis said as he looked at their astonished faces.

The silence lingered long enough for the shock to thaw off Rolen's face. "Are you mad?" He objected.

"No, not at all, they are tired and weary, and it will be the last thing that they expect from us." Achledis said.

"Achledis, this is madness; we can't attack," Marcus interjected. "Our men are just as weary as they are. Besides, why should we attack when we have the advantage of defending ourselves behind these great walls? They lost half their army, and the plain to the north and east is littered with Rakirian bodies. They still haven't penetrated our defenses, and by now, we have sowed doubt in their minds of their ability to do so."

"Tonight I had a troubled sleep," Achledis began. "But after I woke up, it was clear to me what we must do. I dreamed of a fox that was holed up. It initially had a chance to break out but was too fearful of getting caught by the hunter's hounds; so it decided to wait out the danger from the safety of his burrow. Eventually, out of necessity, the fox came out of its burrow and right into the hunter's well prepared trap.

"Are you saying that we are the fox?" Keltar asked.

"No, we are lions, and we will not stay caged in. To cower behind our walls forever will only bring death. Our provisions are low, and if Viserate decides on a siege, we will not be able to hold up for long before the food is out. Then we will be forced to face him, and we will be too hungry and weak to put up a strong resistance. We must strike now."

"Let's wait a day and do it tomorrow night." Marcus suggested.

"Tonight is our best night to surprise them. They are battered and exhausted, and their guard will be down. Tomorrow night their camp will be much better guarded."

"Why are you so sure that he will try to lay a siege? So far he has proved to be too impatient to lay a siege." Keltar said.

"Because another attack like yesterday's would pretty much leave him without an army." "Where is the Presider? Is she aware of your plans?" Yurosi demanded.

Achledis glared back at him. "Yes, she will join us soon."

The deep silence was interrupted by the opening of the heavy oak door and the creaking of rusting iron hinges. Desiani walked in wearing knee high boots, a brown leather skirt, and a long sleeved shirt with a leather jerkin on top. She looked over the men with her green eyes and nodded her head in greeting, letting her gaze rest on Achledis.

"I want to go too." Desiani said.

"You are the presider; your place is here." Achledis replied gently.

Desiani looked at Achledis. "Does that mean I can't go?"

"Yes it does," he replied.

"Yurosi, I want the scouts reporting back to me every fifteen minutes." Desiani said.

Yurosi nodded. "They will Miss Presider."

"Here is the plan." Achledis pointed at the table where Yurosi laid out the Rakirian camp with wooden chips and icons. "The cavalry will split into two sections. One will be north of the Rakirian prison camp, and the other one will be just due east. At 3:00 am, both cavalries will charge through the camp. The east cavalry will be be responsible for taking out all opposition, and the north will be in charge of setting all captives free and arming them with wooden lances. All captives are to be directed south at that point where our main army will already be fighting. The Rakirians should be concentrated on their southern flank where we will attack with our infantry and archers; which should leave the cavalry free to sweep in on their rear, with the freed prisoners following on the flanks of the cavalry. Any questions?"

"When will the infantry strike?" Rolen asked.

"At precisely 2:45 am; so let's make sure that our watches are all in sync."

Desiani called Achledis aside. "Are you sure about this? Because I am a nervous wreck. I won't be able to sit still while the battle is in progress; I have to come with."

"Yurosi and his scouts will keep you updated." Achledis replied. Then he lowered his voice and spoke in a hushed tone so that only Desiani could hear him, "This operation will carry a lot of risk. There are no guarantees, but I want you to promise me that no matter what happens, you will keep yourself safe."

"Same goes for you." Desiani replied as she took Achledis's hand and gave it a squeeze.

When the Rosmirian army marched out, the cold rain was only sprinkling, but now it was pouring down in torrents. The troops marched miserably to face an enemy that they all feared; cold, wet and weary. The memory of beating that enemy just a few hours before seemed like a fading dream, rather than a memory. The cold mud was ankle deep as they sloshed through it; to the cadence of mud sucking their boots every time they picked up their feet to take another step.

Achledis sensed the low morale of the troops but was determined to crush Viserate once and for all. Even with the woeful premonition pressing against him, Achledis believed firmly that they would rise above all the odds and win. He wanted to be sure of it, and he wanted everyone else to believe that too. As much as Rolen, Marcus, and Keltar disagreed with Achledis, they followed him. Once they saw that he wasn't to be moved from his decision, they tried to embrace the plan.

For one, things were turning out much better than anyone expected. The scouts had been reporting that the Rakirian camp was quiet and asleep so far. It turned out that Achledis was right. The Rakirians were tired and comfortable in their belief that

Rosmir would never dare to attack them outside their walls. The element of surprise, which was so important for this attack to succeed, had been obtained.

The cavalry headed by Marcus had already left; they would circle around north of the Rakirian prisoners' camp, from where they would commence their mission of freeing the prisoners. Their horses were loaded with lances, with which they would arm all the males and direct them into battle. All the women would also be given an opportunity to join the battle, but those who decline would be shown the direction to Seredine and hope that they would make it there safely.

The Rosmirian army crept up quietly until they saw Achledis's torch light up. It was a signal for them to stop. A small ridge separated them from the Rakirian camp and hid them from view. Every foot soldier carried a bow and six arrows; one arrow they had already knocked into their bowstrings. The torch lowered to a 45-degree angle, and the soldiers drew their bows. Once the torch dropped, the archers let their arrows fly and instantly reloaded. Instant sounds of men crying out in pain and alarm sounded, and with each new volley of arrows that were sent over the ridge, more panicked cries would answer in return.

A bugle from the Rakirian camp sounded a long and dreadful note into the night, followed by a shrill blast from Achledis. With a roar, the Rosmirian army charged into the Rakirian camp; which was quickly filling up with dazed Rakirian soldiers. The Rosmirian raiders grabbed the torches that had been lit throughout the Rakirian camp and rushed to set everything flammable on fire. Sounds of steel crashing on steel echoed in the night air, and the sight of tents burning lit the night sky.

The initial charge was easy, and Achledis and his army butchered their way through the disorganized Rakirian resistance. But further north they struck a solid wall of an organized Rakirian phalanx. The sound of a Rakirian bugle sounded and in the fire lit sky, Achledis could see the silhouette of a Rakirian army forming on top of the ridge on either flank.

A dreadful feeling hit Achledis as he realized that he had just entered a trap. Bewildered, Achledis couldn't understand how Viserate could have organized a counterattack so quickly. He didn't have time to ponder on that for long as a blood curling scream came from all sides. The Rakirian army appeared from every direction, screaming their war cry as they charged the bewildered Rosmirians.

"Form the triangle!" Achledis yelled, but his command seemed to get swallowed up by the sounds of panic all around him. He could see Rolen on his horse galloping back and forth, waving his sword and ordering the men to make a formation. The fact that they had nowhere to run helped him contain the chaos as the Rosmirians quickly ran towards the center and huddled together. Achledis, Rolen, and Keltar managed to get most of the men to form the triangle as they stood waiting for the first line of Rakirians to hit them. Equipped only with swords, they lacked the pikes to hold the enemy at bay. Achledis had expected to catch the enemy asleep; so he opted for the sword. But that turned out to be a grave mistake.

As the Rakirian tide hit, it penetrated deep into the Rosmir formation, and soon chaos reigned on the field of battle once more. A sense of doom seemed to hang over every Rosmirian soldier as he fought for his life. It motivated them to fight harder and better than they ever knew that they were capable of. Though grossly outnumbered, they seemed to fend off the Rakirians much better than expected.

There was no clear formation that Achledis could see. The battlefield was littered with Rakirians and Rosmirians fighting one another, with the Rosmirians outnumbered three to one. He had to find Viserate. Every time he was confronted by Rakirians, he would dispose of them quickly. He was fueled with a vengeance, as the memory of his dead parents drove him on.

Achledis sensed that they might all die today; for they were surrounded from all sides and escape was impossible. His only desire was to make sure that he took Viserate, and as many Rakirians out as possible, before he was killed.

Viserate sat on his white stallion and watched the shadows and silhouettes of men fighting below. It was a fearsome sight; he thought. For the first time since he attacked Seredine, a battle was finally going his way. He was almost giddy with excitement, but he was reminded of his first objective and that was to capture Achledis. So far, he had proven to be elusive, and in battle, he seemed invincible. The feelings of doubt and defeat that had plagued Viserate just earlier this night were now all but gone.

Viserate had been watching the battle below with an umbrella over his head to protect himself from the rain. He had noticed a figure that seemed to be killing scores of men but had assumed it to be one of his commanders. Lightning struck nearby, and the night became like day for a split second. Viserate gasped as he saw the bloodied warrior more clearly; the long blonde hair was unmistakable. The eyes that stared back caused chills to run down his spine.

Achledis spurred his horse into a gallop towards him. Viserate took out his sword and braced himself for the attack.

"Get him!" Viserate yelled at the troops by his side. Seeing their hesitation, he shouted again. "He is flesh and blood just like all of you; now get him!"

Achledis braced his sword as he galloped up the hill towards the charging Rakirians. He took the heads off the first couple with ease, but the third one ducked at the last moment and stabbed Achledis's horse in its side. His horse stumbled, and Achledis felt himself flying into the dirt. He didn't even get a chance to get up before three Rakirians came at him from different directions. He managed to fend off the blows, but soon he was surrounded by more and more Rakirians.

Viserate shouted an order, and the Rakirians suddenly stopped attacking and just held their spears towards Achledis to keep him at bay. Trapped with no where to go, Achledis watched Viserate ride towards him, a triumphant smile plastered on his face. Achledis looked down the hill where the battle still raged and smiled, seeing that no one had noticed his capture.

"Not as immortal as you thought you were, are you now, hero?" Viserate sneered. "As promised, I will skin you alive and listen to your screams. You will die a very slow and painful death for all of the pain you caused me." He nodded at the man on

Achledis's left, and suddenly Achledis felt a missile penetrate his neck and his body sagged to the ground.

CHAPTER 60: PAINFUL RECOVERY

The echoes of laughter coming from down the hall sounded as the guards continued to exchange crude jokes with one another. A rat ran across the floor and scurried in a crack between the wall and floor. Somewhere in the distance, Vitaeus heard the piercing scream of a prisoner being tortured. The sound made him cringe. The memory of the pain he had gone through was still fresh, and yet he hadn't been tortured for over a day. The physician handed Vitaeus an herb for the pain, but this time, Vitaeus rejected it since all it did was make him want to sleep. After he had passed out from the pain of being pulled apart on a rack, he had awakened in this cell. He hadn't seen the torturer or the jailer since; most of the day yesterday he had to lay around trying to recover from the pain, both physical and psychological. A physician came in and gave him some herbs for the pain; which contributed to his drowsiness. When he fell asleep, he dreamt of the rack and relived the torment all over again. He awoke to a guard shaking him awake. He had been soaked with cold sweat; Vitaeus remembered. The guard had been a youth, and his face showed concern and even understanding. He had given Vitaeus a large flask of water and had urged him to drink it.

Half an hour later, the physician had returned and gave him more herbs. "To take away the dreams." He had claimed.

Sure enough, when Vitaeus fell asleep again, he didn't dream at all and must have awoke in the middle of the night; as the only sound he heard was the occasional scurrying of rats and the moans of prisoners. There were no footsteps of guards outside, nor voices of any kind. A faint light flickered from a torch in the hallway and protruded through the bars in the door to his cell, giving him just enough light to see around his dank cell. He tried to get up in order to make his way to the latrine bucket. But his knees had buckled, and he had fallen to the ground. Vitaeus gingerly touched the inflamed bruise on his forehead at the memory. He had half rolled and sometimes crawled to get to the bucket. Every time he stood, the pain was excruciating. He felt it in every joint and muscle in his body, from his shoulders to his wrists and from his neck, down his spine, his hips, knees and ankles.

That night, Vitaeus had been wide awake, and to pass the time, he would force himself to stand and endure the pain. Initially, his body would shake from the pain and exertion of standing, but soon he had grown accustomed. He would gingerly take a step and then some more, until he was walking around his cell in circles. The exercise had taken a lot out of him, and Vitaeus had slept once more, waking up to the guard bringing a wooden bowl of oats in mush and a cup with water. The physician had made a few visits to give him more herbs for the pain. Each time they would make Vitaeus drowsy, but he would fight the urge to sleep.

On the physician's last visit, Vitaeus told him that he had been exercising, and to prove his point, he had walked around his cell taking every step carefully and gingerly. Vitaeus could tell that the physician had been impressed; though he hadn't said anything. Rather, the physician had left and returned within half an hour with a roll of linen wrap. He had first wrapped his ankles tightly for extra support; then he did the same with his knees. The added support around the joints had taken a considerable amount of the pain away. The physician simply smiled when Vitaeus thanked him.

As of yesterday, Vitaeus had been in too much pain to wonder about anything, but this morning, he had become suspicious as to all the care he was receiving from a physician. Summing up the courage, Vitaeus finally asked the physician that exact question.

"Why am I being cared for by you? You are constantly giving me herbs to help subside my physical and psychological pain."

The physician looked at him oddly; the heavy wrinkles on his face drooped even more than usual before replying. "I am here because you are in pain."

"The torturer and jailer took my torture too far I think; perhaps they feared that they almost killed me. King Razim has mandated that it take a month for me to die, and if they kill me sooner, then Razim will torture them in my stead. I think that now that I am feeling better, I will be tortured once more."

The physician smiled at that and shook his head. "Those two are very talented at inflicting the greatest amount of pain; all the while ensuring that their subjects are alive and conscious to feel it. I suspect that the reason that they put you on the rack on your second day was because they heard the rumor of the bargain that the Rok princess had struck for you. They decided to have their fun before the official order from the King arrived to make them stop. The King's official was already yelling for them to stop, when they suddenly cranked up the rack, and you passed out. Normally you wouldn't have been so lucky."

"What kind of bargain?" Vitaeus asked, unable to keep the fear from his voice.

"There had been rumors floating around that the princess was going to turn Razim down on his marriage proposal. But when she learned of your capture and the month of torture you would endure, she went straight to Razim, and in front of his advisers, publicly begged to have you spared from torture. With a room full of witnesses, she had promised to accept Razim's marriage proposal at the final princess's ball. Sadly for you, your life itself wasn't part of that bargain. While Razim has ordered that your torture be stopped, your execution date has been shortened from a month to a week. You have five days from today." The physician said, as he stood and left without another word.

Vitaeus sat on his cot, numb from the revelation. He had remembered how Raheena had told him that she would turn the King down, and yet she had made the ultimate sacrifice in order to give him an easy death.

The last meal of the day was brought in by the same young guard who had cared enough to give him a flask of water and notified the physician of his nightmares. Vitaeus had always been grateful to the youth, but this time, the youth avoided making eye contact as outside the other two guards were taunting him, calling him "a craven youth with a woman's heart." Their chortled laughter was suddenly cut short. The youth left the tray with the meal and water at the foot of Vitaeus's bed, ignoring Vitaeus's thank-you and hurried out the door. Almost instantly, he staggered back inside and fell flat on his back, his eyes staring at the ceiling and a crossbow bolt through his chest.

CHAPTER 61: MOMENTOUS

The first rays of light peered through a sliver of storm clouds on the horizon as light overpowered the darkness, and as the night turned to day, so did the tide of the battle. The sounds of steel ringing as it struck against steel, the screams of anguish, and the angry battle cries of soldiers who were transformed into savages from the blood lust were still being heard as morning arrived. The maimed lay in the mud, cowering and crying; unashamed as they begged for mercy, even as Rakirian swords drove them through. The Rakirian attack seemed to get spurned on by the shrill blast of a trumpet. The fire that had been set on the tents of the Rakirian soldiers raged undaunted by the torrent of rain that was coming down from the sky. Orange tainted streams of blood, as it mixed with mud, rushed down the hillside.

With a blood curdling scream, the freed prisoners armed with wooden pikes and flails rushed into the fray of battle below. Marcus and his cavalry attacked the Rakirian's left flank with a vengeance, swinging at the Rakirians on either side, heads rolled and bodies dropped as they rode through. As they rode further in; however, the Rakirians from the sides closed in.

The battle raged as the encircled Rosmirians fought with sheer adrenaline. There was nowhere to run, nowhere to hide. They were fully surrounded by Rakirian forces and were forced to fight to the death. The battle for survival transformed the ill-trained warriors of Rosmir to an elite squadron of gladiators. They fought fearlessly, and pretty soon, they were starting to force the Rakirian forces back.

The toot of a bugle sounded, and the Rakirian army started to retreat, with the recently surrounded Rosmirians giving chase. Suddenly, the soldiers of Rosmir stopped their chase abruptly as a gasp went out among them. An eerie silence followed, broken only by the pattering of rain and the crows circling overhead. They all noticed the spectacle on the ridge above. It was their leader and hero Achledis, being held up high for all to see that he had, in fact, been captured and killed. His lifeless body hung limply between two large Rakirian soldiers, and Viserate sat triumphantly on his white stallion. Every Rosmirian stood in disbelief, their momentum deflated, and the air left their lungs as they stood in shock.

Rolen looked about him, as tears of utter helplessness flowed from the eyes of grown men. He too, was at a loss, as his eyes showed him the reality of what his mind could not accept; that their hero was dead. It had to be a Rakirian trick; anytime now, he expected Achledis, the mighty lion, the king of all beasts, to emerge and to urge them on. Achledis didn't emerge; instead, a horde of Rakirian archers appeared on top of the ridge to blast them all from existence. All eyes were on the bugle as it rose to the bugler's lips. An eerie silence loomed as men condemned to die awaited the signal to announce their end.

The sound of approaching horses was heard in the distance, and Viserate took out his looking glass to look. Beside him, the bugler suddenly toppled off his horse with a quarrel through his mouth. Astonished, Viserate looked at the body lying at the feet of his destrier, and then he looked in the direction from where the missile had come from and squinted his eyes to make sure he was seeing correctly. Up against the riverbank was a girl with a blonde braid, sitting on a white horse, and dressed in black leather; she was almost done reloading her crossbow.

"Get her," He screamed; his index finger pointing at the girl with the blonde braid. But her crossbow was already reloaded and was pointing at him. Her horse walked in his direction, and the girl sat atop the saddle with poise, all the while keeping the crossbow trained on him.

Viserate's men started toward her. But she jerked the crossbow in Viserate's direction for emphasis, and Viserate ordered his men to back off.

"Order your men to drop their weapons in a pile." The girl commanded, and the Rakirians complied without waiting for the order from Viserate's lips. One by one they dropped their swords and halberds.

"Stop!" Viserate shouted. "I didn't give the order to surrender." In a fluid motion, he drew his sword and pointed it at the girl; who continued to come in his direction undaunted by his sword. The sound of horsemen galloping was much louder and closer. Viserate looked back to see a Caminian peasant cavalry dressed in green approaching from the north. From the east, the Rosmirian army was marching in his direction once more. His archers still stood on the ridge with their bow strings slack and arrows nocked but pointed at the ground before them. Suddenly he made up his mind. He would not return to Rakiria in a humiliated defeat; he would rather die.

"Kill them all!" Viserate shouted.

Suddenly, a powerful arm grabbed him from below and yanked him off the saddle, knocking his sword free from his grasp in the process. He found himself looking up into the eyes of the youth, the lion as he was called

"It's over." The youth whispered. "You have been defeated."

"How are you awake? The dart was supposed to keep you sleeping for hours." Viserate asked in dismay.

"Does it matter?" Achledis asked.

"The rain water must have diluted the sedative on the dart; I should have simply killed you." Viserate said, as he looked around wildly.

"I do recall suggesting that to you." Achledis replied. The Caminian cavalry had reigned in and were looking on as the Rakirian army surrendered their weapons.

Achledis looked up as Yurosi and Desiani approached; both had triumphant grins pasted on their faces. Achledis started towards Desiani; he was so relieved to see her alive and well. He had already been conscious, but still delirious, when Desiani had shot the bugler. She alone had won this battle. Suddenly, Achledis was full of emotion as he met Desiani in a deep embrace.

"Achledis watch out!" Yurosi shouted.

Achledis turned around, sword drawn at chest level, and felt his whole arm jar violently. In disbelief, he watched Viserate stagger backwards and fall to the ground, with the sword impaled through his chest.

Desiani embraced Achledis, still shaking from relief at the near miss. "That was a close one."

"He is dead."

"Yes, and you killed him; now I will officially recognize you as the Hero of Seredine." Desiani said.

"No, we all did it, and you are the one who saved the day: Heroine Desiani, the Defender of the People, the Savior of Seredine, the Vanquisher of the Rakirian horde."

Desiani pushed Achledis playfully. "Stop mocking me. If it wasn't for Yurosi's private army from Caminia, all would have been lost."

"Look," Achledis pointed at the sun breaking the zenith; the storm clouds were all but gone, leaving behind clear blue skies. "It looks like the dreadful night has come to an end, and the day looks promising."

CHAPTER 62: THE COUP

All the guests on the floor and on the three stories of balconies stood and clapped politely as King Razim made his way down the center aisle to his dais to the music of Giordin's Symphony. Raheena, seated at the table on the dais, also stood and clapped along with everyone else. She looked up at the banner of the three headed viper above the dais, the sigil of King Razim, and frowned in disgust. She was going to be married to this viper.

Though King Razim tried his best to hide the limp, it was clearly there. For Raheena, it was a constant reminder of how fragile he truly was at his age. Tomorrow, her brothers would be sailing back to the Rok Isles to make the formal announcement to the kingdom, and her father, along with the rest of the elite nobility, would sail back here for the occasion of seeing her marry an old man. She could see them all now, planning and scheming on how they will profit from the riches that Caminia had to offer them. Her father would have an ally on the mainland; whose armies he would use in his quest to threaten Rakiria. Caminia, as well as Rosmir, was rich in lumber; which would be excellent for Rok ships, as well. And of course, most importantly, the yellow metal that has always driven men mad. Caminia was rich in gold. Even the rock mined here was growing in demand. The bedrock on the Rok Isles was slated gray, but Caminia's was a pearl white. Every lord dreamed of building a majestic palace with pearly white stone. Yet when she became the regent queen, all the deals that they made she planned to undo.

Razim was more than half way down the aisle now, and the clapping was already halfhearted at best. She looked at the elite nobility of Caminia; their tables were on the first floor, closest to the dance floor. Once Razim walked past, many of the ladies would simply sit back down, with the men glowering at them to stand. The high ranking generals were on the first floor as well; closest to the dais where the King and Raheena would sit.

The smaller lords and the army officers were on the second floor; whereas the third and fourth floors had mostly chiefs of staff and lesser relatives who attended. They had a smaller dance floor on the fourth floor of the balcony. Raheena could see the lower ranking officers in uniform milling about on the fourth floor balcony.

She forced a smile as Razim took his first step up the three step dais. Already she was plotting for her own power, and a world without this viper. Razim stood before Raheena, a thin smile on his face, and kissed the back of her hand gently. Raheena looked away, giving the King her best bashful look. It must have worked because the King looked delighted as he turned around to face the crowd. With as much regality as he could muster, he sat down on his throne. Instantly, servants ran up and helped move him closer to the table. The crowd followed suit and sat down too. All of the tables were covered with purple linen, and the chairs had coverings of light violet. On each table stood a bouquet of white and purple lilacs mixed in with lavender.

The servers rolled out their carts and served Razim and Raheena first, with an assortment of cheeses and crab salad on thin wafers, followed with a bowl of salad. As soon as the bottle of champagne was opened and poured, Razim stood and held his glass up in the air for a toast, and all rose with him, holding their glasses out.

"I propose this toast to the princess, for her beauty, elegance, and wisdom." Razim shouted in his powerful voice, and the crowd chorused the toast as the sound of clinking glasses sounded throughout the room.

Raheena smiled at the King. "Thank you Your Majesty. That was a very nice gesture."

"It wasn't just a gesture princess; I meant it." He said, as he sat down. "You are very beautiful, and I consider myself to be the luckiest King in the whole world."

"Luck had nothing to do with any of it, My Lord. I was simply placed in a position where I couldn't refuse." Raheena replied, all the while maintaining a pleasant look on her face.

Razim looked up and smiled back at her as he placed a fork full of green leaves and vegetables in his mouth.

Suddenly the music stopped, and the doors at the far end opened up to reveal a lone man standing in the doorway. As Raheena watched, the man stood there for a solid thirty seconds, taking in his surroundings. Already a lot of the guests had noticed the stranger; Razim certainly had.

"Where are the guards?" He growled. "Who dares to disrupt this occasion."

Gasps from the crowd could be heard from all four stories as the stranger made his way. Razim's eyes weren't keen in his old age, but Raheena could see the man clearly. Wearing silver armor, which shimmered with a bluish hue; the armor was unmistakable to anyone who had ever seen it. Even the cloak on his back brought about memories of the man crowned Lord of the Shield Isles. The insignia of the silver wolf looked back on the crowd as he passed.

Razim stood suddenly and pointed his finger at the approaching figure. "Seize him!" He bellowed.

But there were no guards about; even the servers had seemingly disappeared. Razim looked at the table of Captain Yousel, the lord commander of the King's palace guards.

"Captain, you have orders, obey!"

Instantly, Captain Yousel, the general, and the colonels at the tables behind him stood and made their way to the approaching figure.

"Guards!" Razim yelled at the arched doors next to his dais. His guards were to be stationed out of sight but available at a moment's notice. On the King's orders, the doors swung open, and a troop of ten men ran out from each door. They stood in a line in front of the King with crossbows aimed and ready.

At that point, Vitaeus was only twenty yards away from the dais and well within sight of Razim. He drew his sword, and Captain Yousel drew his. A trumpet played a long sad note, and Captain Yousel looked up at the balcony from where it came from and froze. Lining both sides of the fourth floor balcony railing were men holding crossbows, and they were unmistakably aimed at King Razim.

"Put your sword down." Vitaeus commanded and gestured behind Yousel. When Yousel turned around, he saw that the line of crossbowmen had their weapons trained on Razim, as well. A man walked through the arched door on the right and walked up the dais. He paused in front of the banner of King Razim. He took hold of one of the golden braided ropes that hung on either side of the banner and yanked on it. The banner fell from the wall, unfurling itself over the King's table and covering his face. The crowd gasped. In place of the King's banner hung a large portrait of the late King Krepedes Arkonis. The King who ruled some 50 years prior, before the rule of King Razim.

The man then came up behind Razim, who was unraveling himself from the banner, and yanked him roughly out of his chair. Another gasp went throughout the crowd as Razim's hands were brought behind his back and cuffed. Razim looked at Raheena, revealing anger and betrayal, but her eyes were on Vitaeus. A mixture of relief, surprise, and adoration were on her face. Vitaeus walked past Yousel, who stood with resignation and disbelief on his face, and mounted the steps to the dais. He smiled in Raheena's direction and turned to face the crowd. Those closest to the dais in the crowd gasped, and the murmuring grew in chorus. The strong resemblance between the image of Krepedes and Vitaeus were unmistakable.

Vitaeus glanced at Razim, who was on his knees at the foot of the dais, looking up at him, with fear in his eyes, and his lower lip was puckered and quivering. Vitaeus stood straight and regal; without any indication that he had been placed on a rack only a few days prior. His face was shaven and clean, and his armor and clothes were every bit majestic and kingly. On each side of the dais stood five of his knights; in full armor, they clenched the hilts of their swords tightly in their fists and against their chests, with the blade pointed straight downwards. When Vitaeus motioned downwards with his hands for the crowd to be quiet, the knights slapped the pommels of the hilt on their swords against their steel plated chests, and they repeated the pommel to the chest four more times. Each time, the sound of steel clashing resounded, like a drumstick on a cymbal. The crowd was on its feet, quiet, and straining in excitement at what would come next.

"Vitaeus Arkonis, the true King of all Rosmir." Announced the man who had pulled down Razim's banner and now stood to the right of the dais.

Another excited murmur went through the crowd, but as the sword hilts pounded against steel chests five more times the room was quiet once more.

"I am Vitaeus Arkonis, and the portrait above me is my grandfather King Krepedes Arkonis, the last true King of Rosmir. A King who was treacherously deposed of by the usurper who kneels before me now. A true viper, he struck my grandfather unsuspectingly when my grandfather came to him for refuge after Seredine had fallen to the Rakirian enemy. Razim had then commenced to rule Caminia as its king, preaching justice and the rule of law; all the while being the most unjust in this whole kingdom, the only one with the King's blood on his hands. Today I stand in judgment of this man and proclaim him condemned.

Razim rose suddenly, but before he even took a single step, a knight was on either side of him. With powerful hands, they grabbed his frail shoulders and delivered a kick to the knees.

Vitaeus grimaced at the popping sound as Razim's feet stayed planted on the ground; while his knees crashed inwards. With a yelp of pain, the old man fell face forward and lay flat on the ground.

"Even now, Razim proclaims his venomous justice against himself; as a viper, he shall cling to the ground where he belongs."

Distant clapping from the fourth floor started, and the chorus grew slowly as it spread across the remaining of the fourth floor balcony, then to the third floor, finally to the second, and to a select few tables at the very bottom. Raheena could see that most of the nobles on the first floor were still bewildered and unsure if it was yet safe to throw their support behind Vitaeus. Raheena, however, was one of the first to stand and clap. The table with her brothers, and the rest of the Rok royals who came, stood and joined the thunderous applause.

Finally, Vitaeus raised his hands and motioned for silence; his knights clapped their hilts to their chests five times, as they had done before, to quiet the room.

"Today you have all come to see the proposal of marriage that would seal an alliance between Caminia and the mighty kingdom of the Rok Isles, but I want to propose more." Vitaeus looked at the princess who sat in her chair beaming at him. "Princess, I fell for your beauty from the first time I laid eyes on you; then after our dance, I fell for your charm and elegance. After our walk down the palace hall, I had fallen for your courage and wisdom. In the past month, since your arrival to Caminia, my feelings of love and affection for you continued to grow. And right now, more than anything else in the world, I would like to dance with you." Raheena accepted Vitaeus's outstretched hand graciously and nimbly followed him to the dance floor.

The orchestra started to play Giordin's *Symphony of a Swan on a Frozen Lake.* The melody was soft and flowed with a harmonic rhythm. Vitaeus guided Raheena with his right hand, holding Raheena's hand gently, and with his left on her hip, the two swayed and moved, rising and falling to the cadence of the music. Vitaeus pulled Raheena closer and looked down into her beautiful eyes and her excited smile, and it was all he could do not to weep at that moment. His biggest fear of the last couple days was that he would never get to see her, hold her, or feel her warmth again. Even worse than that, she would share a marriage bed with a snake.

"I have dreamed of this." She confessed when the music stopped. Vitaeus smiled in return as he kneeled on his right knee and held out a ring between his fingers.

"Then you know you should accept."

Raheena let out an excited giggle as she held out her hand. "Yes," she whispered. Vitaeus slipped the ring on her finger, and it fit perfectly. He then kissed her finger with the ring.

This time, everyone clapped, including the nobility on the first floor, and a chant went out among the crowd. "King Vitaeus, the King of all Rosmir."

Vitaeus and Raheena made their way back to the dais, hand in hand; both beaming excitedly. Razim still lay on the ground, but he had slithered to the side and out of their way as they walked up the dais. The Rok grand prince, Raheena's oldest brother Refal, as well as Prince Meral, both approached the dais; they both bowed before him before rising once more.

"King Vitaeus, I am honored that you will be the one to become our new brother-in-law. A big congratulations to Your Majesty on your success of reclaiming your throne." Refal said, and Meral echoed his congratulations.

"The honor is mine." Vitaeus replied with a smile.

"You knew that this coup would happen, didn't you?" Raheena asked Refal. "You only warned me to be careful this night."

"I told you what you needed to know for your protection; in case the coup failed. I wanted you to be safe."

Captain Yousel approached the dais next. He stooped to one knee and bowed his head in humility, low enough for his nose to touch his knee. "Your Grace, I once told you that I would be honored to serve you one day, and that day has arrived. You are indeed My Lord and My Liege; my life is yours to do with as you please."

Razim snapped his head up and stared at Yousel, anger and betrayal clearly written across his face. "You traitor!" He croaked. Then his gaze settled on the growing line behind Yousel. Duke Hilam, along with the other lords, great and small, were eager to show their undying loyalty to the new crown. Even the Duke of Nitami, who should have been the next in line to be King after Razim died was sulking at the very end.

Duke Hilam was next, and he bowed in deep reverence. "Your Majesty, I'm happy to see the Arkonis line restored to the throne. You should know that my father had once served your grandfather; as I hope to continue serving you. I was happy to see you act on my warnings and even happier to see you before me now, as My King."

"So it was you." Vitaeus replied warmly. "I will remember your kindness and make sure that you are rewarded accordingly.

Razim rose slowly so that he was on his knees. His face twisted in pain and anger as he glanced at all the lords who deserted him so quickly. With a determined effort, he stood on shaky legs as he looked at the crowd. "Have you all so quickly forgotten me? Have all of my accomplishments meant so little to all of you? When I got rid of the fool of a king before me who lost Rosmir to the Rakirian occupiers, I did so to preserve the Duchy of Caminia from the Rakirian invasion. I turned Caminia from a duchy to a kingdom and became its king. Most of you are too young to remember what this place was like 50 years ago. It was a scraggly rock jutting out into the ocean, the wasteland of Rosmir, with hardly a proper beach suitable for ships to land on and for trade to prosper. It was my wise and watchful guidance that has allowed Caminia to prosper, and for its economy to boom. Today Caminia is an emerald kingdom, the jewel of the world. I have ensured justice and the reign of law."

"And is it justice to condemn a man to the mines for refusing to poison your wife, and then to proclaim her death as due to an illness?" Daenis said, as he stepped before Razim. "That's right; I know your murderous secret, of how you disposed of your first wife. That first doctor who refused to listen to you was my father, and you stole him from me."

"You're a bastard; you don't have a father." Razim said, his voice brimming with rage. He tried to find the only ally he could count on, but he spotted Nepides slinking away into the crowd.

Suddenly more guests and nobles started to throw accusations at him. It was like a dam had broken, and everything that he had ever done to wrong anyone was being thrown into his face. All these people that had once sought to please him and to win his favor were now in open opposition to him. He felt the spit of those closest to him in the front, and his anger grew. He was helpless, however, the ligaments in his knees were torn where the traitorous knights had kicked him, and the pain he felt was like a soothing sedative that had kept his anger in check. He turned away from the crowd and wiped the spit off his face as he looked at Vitaeus. The youth who had come into his court and had stolen everything from him, his bride, his kingdom, his life, and even his legacy; it was now all gone. He took a step forward, his knees shaking from the effort it took to support his weight. Instantly, Yolif and Daenis stepped out to block his path, but Vitaeus motioned for them to step aside.

"Let him speak." Vitaeus commanded. "What do you have to say for all the crimes that you are being accused of by the people before us?"

"Hateful lies, all of it. I am the King, me!"

With that, Razim attempted to lunge at Vitaeus, but his knees buckled, and he fell forward. He managed to wrap his arms around Vitaeus and pulled him down with him. Razim felt the dagger that was buckled to Vitaeus's ankle when he fell, and he pulled it loose and stabbed it into Vitaeus's rib cage. The dagger jarred violently as if it had struck a rock. Razim was quick enough to realize that Vitaeus must be wearing chain mail and scrambled to get to his unprotected neckline. But his momentum was suddenly cut off by a diamond necklace wrapped around his neck. Raheena gave the necklace a firm tug, and Razim went sprawling backwards. Raheena held onto the necklace as if her life depended on it. Razim grabbed it with one hand and was pulling it free from his throat, and his other hand was trying to slash at Raheena behind him.

The edge of a bluish-silver blade at Razim's throat made him stop struggling, and he looked up as Vitaeus stood over him. "Lock this man up. He will stand trial for all that is accused against him, and we will ensure that justice is served."

"Blood!" Someone shouted out in panic from the back, followed by a loud, piercing shriek of a woman.

A gasp went through the crowd as they saw the assailant on the fourth floor balcony. The lifeless body of a crossbowmen hung over the banister with his throat slit, and his blood draining to the first floor. The assailant had taken the crossbow and aimed in the direction of the dais.

"Everyone drop your weapons to the bottom floor, or Vitaeus dies." Shouted the assailant.

Only a few complied with the demand and dropped their weapons. As everyone's attention was on the assailant on the top balcony, Razim jumped away from Vitaeus's reach and got behind Raheena.

A wicked smile crossed his face. "My faithful Nepides." He announced. With his dagger out once more, he grabbed Raheena by her hair and pulled her close to him to use as a shield from any of Vitaeus's crossbowmen.

"Vitaeus, command your men to drop their weapons." Razim ordered.

"Drop your weapons." Vitaeus said without hesitation.

Instantly, the sound of wooden crossbows clattering to the ground resounded, and the crossbowmen in front of the dais also dropped their crossbows.

"That includes you and your friends who have swords, drop them now!" Razim pressed the dagger threateningly into the soft flesh of Raheena's throat. Vitaeus, Yolif, Hilam, Yousel, and others nearby who had a sword buckled at their waist complied quickly.

"Good, now everyone back up; everyone past that pillar! Vitaeus you stay." Razim growled. As he led Raheena after the retreating crowd, he stooped down and yanked Raheena's hair down violently, and she went with him to the floor. Razim picked up a crossbow and released Raheena's hair. "You whore, go stand next to your forbidden lover." With the crossbow, he shoved her towards Vitaeus.

Vitaeus looked around helplessly to see if anyone was perhaps hiding with a weapon, but there was no one. Everyone else in the room was as helpless as he was, watching the events unfold with the same horror. Razim, though old, walked with hardly a limp visible, and his knees that only earlier were hardly able to support him, seemed fine now. Razim's hatred carried him; despite any physical ailments that tried to hold him back. A dark scowl clouded his face, and he was hardly recognizable. He looked like a monster coming to have his vengeance, like a viper slithering to its helpless prey. Vitaeus felt Raheena pressing herself against him at his side, but he dared not take his eyes off Razim, even for a second. His Vulcan dagger was gone. Razim had it, and his Vulcan sword lay on the ground far out of reach. Vitaeus watched intently; all the while praying that Razim would trip and fall as he climbed the steps to the dais. Razim struggled with the last step, but he didn't fall.

"Sit!" Razim commanded Vitaeus and motioned with the crossbow. Vitaeus complied and sat down slowly, afraid that any sudden movement might make Razim react by firing the crossbow, and it was clear that Razim had the crossbow aimed at Raheena, standing to his right. "Your grandfather died from poisoned wine; so it's only fitting that it's wine that should end his line. Princess, serve your man that bottle of champagne." Raheena walked slowly, trying to stall time as she walked around to retrieve the bottle that stood on the center of the table. Razim continued to give his instructions. "You will drink the wine from that bottle, and the moment you stop drinking, the princess dies."

Vitaeus's mind raced on how he could delay the inevitable. He watched as Raheena picked up the wine bottle.

"The glass on that bottle has been blown way out of proportion, and the size is too big for any man to drink by himself. I will fall over way before I finish it. Can't I get a smaller one from a table below?" Vitaeus asked, though he knew that Razim would never fall for the ploy.

"No, you will drink from that bottle, and when you finish it, the princess will have another one ready for you. You keep drinking until you're pissing wine and then continue on drinking until the wine is pouring out your ears and nose. Even then, you better keep on drinking because the moment you stop drinking is the moment the princess dies." Razim's voice had lightened up some, and it sounded like he was beginning to enjoy himself.

Raheena was holding out the bottle for Vitaeus; not seeing a way out, he took it from her. He squeezed the bottle between his legs as he struggled to pry the waxed top of the bottle.

"Quit stalling, or I will simply shoot her." Razim shouted impatiently.

Vitaeus looked up to see that Nepides was still stationed on the fourth floor balcony where he had been the whole time, and his crossbow was still trained on him.

"Princess, come stand over here and away from the table," Razim commanded.

Out of the corner of his eye, Vitaeus could see Raheena start moving, *she will be right behind you,* he thought. He pretended to drop the bottle, catching the wide bottom, but smashing the narrow neck against the floor. He instantly lunged at Razim. Two bolts struck him in the chest, but the momentum of his thrust carried him forward. He stuck the narrow neck of the bottle with its sharp, ragged teeth of glass underneath Razim's chin. As he released the bottle, blood squirted from the gaping hole under Razim's chin, and Razim snatched the bottle, allowing the crossbow to fall from his hands to the ground. Like a mad man, he frantically tried to plug the hole under his chin with the bottle. Vitaeus hearing a commotion and looked up to see Nepides being thrown off the balcony, head first. His head hit the rock floor and seemed to sink inside his body. On the floor before him, Razim was opening his mouth as if to say something, but no sound came out. His eyes were dancing around wildly as he lay down and tried to tilt his head upwards, in a futile attempt to stop the flow of blood. In shock, the King lay on the floor holding fast to the bottle, as the wine continued to pour inside, drowning him. Slowly, his hands released the bottle, and it rolled away, spilling its contents on the floor. Razim's eyes rolled up into his head, while the yellow wine trickled from his nose and ears, and yellow tears were frozen on his eyes.

Vitaeus's eyes finally left the now still corpse of Razim, and his gaze settled on the silent hall full of people before him. Raheena was suddenly at his side inspecting where the crossbow bolts had struck him.

"That's amazing." She whispered, as her fingers probed the tiny holes in his shirt. "Aside from ripping a bit of fabric, the bolts didn't leave a mark on your armor."

Vitaeus was overjoyed. Raheena was safe. Only moments ago he had feared that he wouldn't be able to save her, and now she was here beside him. With his hands, he pulled her in against his armored chest and held her tightly. He felt Raheena's pulse at the back of her neck, and tears of relief sprang from his eyes as he gently began to kiss the top of her head. She looked up at him; her big, teal eyes gazing into his. Even as the hall broke out into applause and shouts of joy could be heard all around, Vitaeus's lips embraced the soft flesh of Raheena's lips, and he felt the warmth and moisture of her mouth against his.

"I love you Raheena."

"I love you too." She replied; her voice small and choked up.

Vitaeus faced the joyous crowd with his right hand still holding Raheena's hand. The men hooted and yelled their well wishes to the couple; as the women stood with smiles displayed on their faces looking on.

"Thank you all." Vitaeus yelled in order to be heard above the noise of excited chatter. The large hall quickly died into silence as everyone strained to hear the new King speak. "I thank you all for your support of me as your new king, and I am as overjoyed as you are that the usurper has finally been defeated and that my family name, Arkonis, has once more been restored to its rightful place as the royal name of Rosmir. To see the murderer of my family brought to justice, certainly brings some closure to me. However, this also signals the beginning of a long and hard journey for all of us. As King, I will not sit idly by in the safety of Caminia; while the rest of our kingdom in Rosmir is brutalized by Rakirian armies. Our nation will once more be united, and starting tomorrow morning, our armies will begin preparing for war."

All the men of war shouted hurrah, and the rest of the crowd joined in shouting and chanting Vitaeus's name.

EPILOGUE

A month later.

Achledis urged his horse to go faster, but Desiani's horse still managed to stay slightly ahead. They were racing for the grove of trees near the northwestern corner of Seredine, right next to the Seredine River. He glanced in her direction, and she looked back at him with laughter in her green eyes.

"I told you," she shouted. "A lion can't outrun a gazelle." When she glanced back, however, Achledis had gained on her, and once more she focused her attention to the grove of trees.

No, Achledis realized, I suppose it can't. Achledis couldn't help but notice the beauty of Desiani's white-blonde hair flowing like a streamer in the wind and marveled how gracefully her body moved in rhythm to the gallop of her horse. The prairie grass seemed to flow past at a blurring speed, and the trees were drawing near. They both sped past the first row of trees at full speed, slowing down only after they had crossed the finish line.

Desiani dismounted and hugged her white horse. It was the same one she rode during her escape from Rakirian captivity. She named him Leto. Achledis dismounted off his destrier, whom he had named Ronen, and gave him a firm pat. Then he leaned in and whispered in the horse's ear. "I know, it was my fault we lost."

The horse whinnied and looked at him accusingly, then tossed his head in Desiani's direction. "I know, I know, I watched her too you know, and she is a much better rider than me."

Desiani jabbed him in the ribs from behind. "Well, I could train you, I suppose. Summer may be over, but we still have a little bit of fall left." As she spoke, Achledis watched as a golden yellow leaf floated from a tree above and landed on her hair. She reached to brush it off, but Achledis stopped her.

"You know as presider, you should have some kind of a crown made up, and this golden leaf just gave me an idea."

"No, wearing a white gown to symbolize my position is enough, and I will wear that only when I must." With that, she brushed off the leaf.

Achledis snatched it before it hit the ground and put it in his pocket. A breeze picked up just then, and more leaves started to rain down. Achledis could see that Desiani was cold; so he took the blanket that he had used as a saddle and wrapped it around her. She accepted it gratefully, and the two sat on some rocks overlooking the river, with a broad oak tree serving as their backrest. Neither one spoke as they were both lost in their thoughts, dreading to speak of it yet knowing full well that tomorrow Achledis would be leaving for the Gateway Fortress on the Rakirian Isthmus.

A month had passed since the victory over Viserate and the Rakirian army. And Desiani had done a terrific job governing the city since then. Already the army had tripled in size as young men hearing of the successful revolt flocked to the city. The only problem with that, however, was that it meant a lot more mouths to feed, and not enough food in the city's supply to last the winter. The Rakirian plunder of Southern Rosmir and part of the country around Seredine itself had left very little crops for the city's reserves. Desiani had sent letters to Caminia asking the King for assistance. There had been no response thus far; and some messengers had come back and reported that Rakirian troops garrisoned at the fort near Caminia had sealed off the isthmus.

Achledis would take a force of 5,000 men with him to seize the Gateway Fortress. The plan was to take it before the cold winter set in. If they didn't succeed in conquering the fortress by then, many of them would die from hunger, and even more from the cold. However, it was agreed by all in the council that the time to strike the fortress would be now; as it would be heavily reinforced through the winter months and by spring, Rakiria could mount an even greater invasion. The other benefit, though no one wanted to be the one to voice it, was that 5,000 men leaving the city would also alleviate the burden of feeding so many mouths. A remaining force of 1,000 men would remain to guard Seredine in case neighboring occupied Rosmirian provinces, headed by Rakirian viceroys, attempted to move against the city. This scenario was highly unlikely; however, no one wanted to be trapped in a siege during the winter months.

The march would take Achledis past Pavanti, and Achledis closed his eyes as he thought of the village he grew up in. It would give him a chance to bury the bones of his parents, and yet he was afraid of what else he might find in Pavanti. A part of him still strongly believed that his friend Vitaeus and his family had somehow escaped the Rakirian attack. But he believed that less and less lately. He had searched for Vitaeus among the Rakirian prisoners that were freed during and after the battle, but he hadn't come across anyone that knew or even heard the name. That brought his thoughts to the cave that he and Vitaeus had found. They had sworn a pact to keep the cave and its treasures a secret. At times, he had wanted to share the secret with Desiani, but the oath he swore to his friend remained firm.

Desiani took his hand and held it in both of hers. "Find out about my grandfather, would you? Let him know of my whereabouts."

Achledis knew that Perat had been on Desiani's mind a lot, and more visibly so since the victory over Viserate. He gave her hands a squeeze reassuringly. "Absolutely."

The breeze from the river was wet and chilling as it picked up force, and Achledis felt Desiani shiver through the blanket around her.

"It's getting cold. We should head back to the city." Achledis said, and Desiani readily agreed.

As they got up and got ready to go, Desiani stopped and pointed at a speck nearing the city. "Look over there." She said.

Achledis took out his looking-glass and looked. It appeared to be a procession of knights with olive green standards.

"Take a look." Achledis said, as he offered the looking-glass to Desiani.

After observing through the looking-glass, she handed it back to him. "Let's go." She said, as she hurried towards Leto and swung on the horse's back with ease. "We need to find out who that is."

Achledis swung onto Ronen's back, and together they rode along the wall towards the northern gate. They heard the sound of a bugle blaring a warning, and on the battlements above, a handful of archers appeared. A host of Seredinian horsemen rode out of the northern gate and joined Achledis and Desiani, followed by a procession of armed guards that stood protecting their flanks. The olive green standards were visible now, and the sigil of a silver wolf was emblazoned on them. The procession stopped, and a lone horseman rode out. The man wore no armor, unlike the knights around him who were fully encased in metal from their shoulders to their toes, leaving only their heads exposed. The man was young, early twenties at the latest, with sandy colored hair and grayish blue eyes; which seemed to be studying the defenses of Seredine. As Achledis and Desiani rode out to meet him, he acknowledged them with a slight bow.

"Sir," he addressed Achledis, then acknowledged Desiani. "My Lady, who is in charge of this city's governing?"

"I am." Desiani replied. "And as for you Sir? Where do you come from?"

"I am Yolif, the head of His Majesty's embassy. We come from Caminia, and we bring tidings of exciting news for all of Rosmir. The old usurper who sat on the Caminian throne is now dead, and the Grand-Prince, the grandson of King Krepedes now reigns. The Arkonis line has been restored once more."

Achledis was filled with joy at the news; perhaps the new King would even come to their aid against Rakiria; which was bound to attack once more, he thought.

"Please send our congratulations. I have indeed heard good things of King Krepedes." Desiani replied politely, yet her voice was neutral and didn't sound excited. "I have received word that the isthmus to Caminia had been sealed off by Rakirian troops. How did you get past?"

"His Majesty's forces swept the Rakirian forces aside and laid siege to their fortress on the Caminian border. The Grand-Prince is confident that the fortress will capitulate before winter sets in."

"I have sent messengers to your King, err Grand-Prince, do you know if any of them made it?" Desiani asked.

"Yes, we received your message, and the Grand-Prince is preparing a massive shipment of food and warm clothing."

Desiani smiled at the news; perhaps they would survive this winter after all. "Why don't we head this party inside; you and your men must be famished."

"Yes, My Lady, that would be much appreciated." Yolif replied, his face keeping its stoic appearance.

Seredinian guards parted for Desiani, Achledis, and their guest Yolif, as the three rode at the front of the procession. Seredinian horsemen flanked the trio, followed by Caminian knights, and the city guards followed at the rear as the procession made its way inside the city.

Yurosi met them inside the gates, and he bowed politely as he rode up. "Lady Presider, my apologies for intervening in this procession, but I just received urgent news that you must hear right away."

Desiani apologized to Yolif and excused herself from the group as she and Yurosi rode out of earshot.

"What is it?" Desiani inquired.

"I just received a pigeon with a message from one of my scouts. The Rakirians have sealed the gate off from the Gatehouse Fortress to Rosmir, and Rakirian forces are massing on the Rakirian border. The other bit of news is this." He held out a note; which Desiani accepted. "We shot down the pigeon that was carrying that message."

Desiani read the note, then looked at Yolif apprehensively. "Make sure the city guard is on the highest alert and don't allow any of our guests out of your sights. Even now, they are studying the defense of the city. She wished Achledis could stay here to help protect the city but knew deep down that Achledis would have to leave by tomorrow morning. He had to take the Gatehouse Fortress before Rakiria managed to reinforce it completely and before the snow started to fall.

Vitaeus and Raheena were standing against the cliff in the back courtyard of the New Palace, overlooking into the stormy waves below. Vitaeus knew that Raheena was worried; her family should have arrived yesterday. Yet there was still no sign of any Rok ships, and the waves below weren't exactly encouraging. He took her hand reassuringly and thought of something he could say to put her mind at ease, but nothing came to him.

In the past month since he began to rule Caminia, he had sent out envoys to Celesta and Seredine to inform them of the change in leadership that had taken place. He had also sent out messengers, through all the provinces of Rosmir, to inform them of the change, as well. It was his first step in unifying Rosmir with Caminia and of driving Rakirian forces out of Rosmir's lands for good. At this point, his armies were still too small to face a direct confrontation with the large and powerful armies of Rakiria; so he had to recruit more men to his cause. He had received the news of Seredinian's successful defense against the Rakirian army, and he had hoped to relocate the capital there once more. At the very least, his coronation had to take place there, he decided. It would be powerful and symbolic for the morale of all his people.

Raheena nudged Vitaeus, "Look over there." Her finger pointed to the east, not at all the direction that the Rok ships should be arriving from. A flock of birds were coming their way. Their size seemed to grow larger and larger as they drew nearer. "Oh my, what is that?" Her voice was high with excitement, and she clenched Vitaeus's hand nervously.

"Eagles," Vitaeus replied; his voice carried the awesome feeling he felt. "With passengers on top."

A total of ten eagles circled around the courtyard where they stood before diving down towards them. Their wings were massive as they unfurled before landing on the ground. The birds were larger than the men they carried. Their passengers slid off their backs and formed a group before approaching Vitaeus and Raheena. These were the tallest people that Vitaeus had ever seen, each at least ten feet tall, dressed in all white, their hair was a white-gold color, and their blue eyes stood out like jewels.

Vitaeus only noticed his own heart beating in nervous anticipation as he felt Raheena's hand clenched tightly around his. Protectively, he stepped in front of her, and his hand dropped to his Vulcan blade at his side.

The man at the very front of the group stopped, and everyone behind stopped on the dime. "That would be most unwise." The man said, and though he spoke calmly, his voice was loud like that of a trumpet, and yet eerily peaceful. "Not only is it rude to greet your guests that way, but also dangerous to threaten emissaries from the upper tiers of Celesta. We have not come to threaten you, only to make contact, and to give warning. The cloud of darkness is growing. It will be you and another who will have to rise to confront it. You will defeat it, by the knowledge of the book, the Book of Mysteries. Find it. It will be your greatest weapon."

Vitaeus was shocked and speechless at the phantoms in front of him. He tried to say something, but no words came out.

"You, Vitaeus, will be a good king and the Princess will be a great queen, congratulations to both of you. Your emissaries who came to Celesta were indeed sincere; you are both regal and of good courage. May the Creator's Spirit be ever with you in guidance."

"Who are you?" Vitaeus asked, finally able to break the awe that had gripped him speechless, thus far.

"We are from a world that is not of your world, my friend. A world where mere mortals do not live, nor can they. We are from the upper tiers of Celesta."

Vitaeus was more confused than ever. He knew that Celesta was a mountain in Northern Rosmir. The Celesta Straight cut through the mountain; the side north of the straight had no inhabitants, as far as he knew. It was a rock wall, the boundary of their world to the north. The tops of the mountain went far beyond the clouds into the heavens above. Growing up, the place had always seemed more legend, but his parents had told him that such a place actually did exist. Its inhabitants lived longer than normal people, this he heard.

"Mortals?" Raheena asked in a mesmerized voice.

"Yes, our cousins at the lowest tiers of Celesta are the ones that you have contact with, but we are from a world beyond them. We mostly stay out of the world of men, but the rising tempest in the South has brought us down into your world so that we may warn you of its coming. Prepare yourselves with the time at hand; for the time is short."

"From the South? Celesta is north. How would you know of the whereabouts in the South?" Vitaeus asked.

The Celestian being smiled warmly. "You saw us fly in on eagle wings, and yet you ask? These eagles fly higher than any other creature in your world. They fly above the heavens, and we hover over all the world. We know more of the lands and what's happening, than any mortal. We see all, and we hear all. You Vitaeus are a remarkable being, with a good heart, and a caring soul, selected by the Creator himself for a precarious time in men's history. Your answers lie at the location where that armor of yours was taken from. Farewell, and may you succeed; for failure would doom your world."

The Celestian turned and headed back for his eagle, and the other Celestians mounted theirs. With a swoop of giant wings, the eagles floated off and soon disappeared into the cloudless sky above, with only a few green and yellow feathers floating down as a testament of them ever being here.

Long after the eagles were gone, Vitaeus and Raheena stared into the skies above.

"Did this really happen?" Vitaeus asked. Raheena simply held up the eagle feather in her hand.

Suddenly Vitaeus noticed Daenis approaching with a host of his palace guards headed by Captain Yousel. "My Prince." Daenis said, as he bowed in reverence before him, "it appears that a group of ships are approaching. Perhaps you and the princess should prepare yourselves to personally greet the Rok King and his family."

Sure enough, a fleet could be seen coming in from the west.

"We are ready; prepare the lift." Vitaeus commanded as he took Raheena by the hand, and they headed in the direction of a small building that housed the oxen which operated the lift.

"Do you think anyone else saw those men and the eagles?" Raheena asked Vitaeus as they walked away from the others.

"You would think they would have said something, or at least their facial expressions would have told us if they would have, but no, they didn't see them." Vitaeus replied.

The cold ocean water smashed against the floating wooden dock beneath Vitaeus's feet, sending the dock into a wild swaying motion, and covering him with its icy, salty mist. The dock was anchored by heavy iron chains to the ocean floor, as well as by chains that kept it anchored to the cliff below the new palace. The bay of Caminia City lacked a proper beach for landing; so Razim had ordered a dock at the foot of the cliff to be built. After the dock had been built, the problem of getting to it arose. The narrow stairway that was chipped out at the side of the cliff proved to be impractical and very dangerous, as numerous incidents occurred that resulted in deaths. That was when a young engineer came and proposed a plan to build a lift.

The oxen powered the lift by turning a giant winder which would then either hoist or lower a rope through a series of pulley systems. This soon became the main means to get to the dock. It had only been engineered and installed a few years ago, but the technology had left Vitaeus impressed.

Vitaeus's thoughts snapped back to the present as he watched a lone Rok ship separate itself from the fleet of fifteen ships that had accompanied it here on this voyage from the Rok Isles. To his right stood Princess Raheena, and an escort of knights stood behind them. They all had warm fur cloaks wrapped around their shoulders to keep the cold autumn wind from the Rok Sea from chilling their bones. Fall had come quickly, and winter was coming even faster to this Northern peninsula. Yet there was still so much to do.

"Father will like you, and he will be so happy for me as well." Raheena said as she looped her arm around his.

Only a month had passed since Vitaeus had become the ruler of Caminia, but it seemed almost a lifetime ago. So much had happened; so much had changed. Along with pigeons being sent to notify the Rok King of the changes that had occurred in the Caminian Kingdom, the two Rok Princes had gone back to the Rok Isles to make the formal announcement of the engagement of Grand-Prince Vitaeus to Princess Raheena. Vitaeus had sent the crew of the White Swan, along with a small embassy headed by Daenis, to retrieve his mother and Perat. Perat had left the Rok Isles a couple of weeks prior to the White Swan's arrival. He had set out to find his granddaughter Desiani. But the message that the pigeon had brought Vitaues assured him that his mother was on her way.

"Your Majesty." Shouted a knight behind him. Vitaeus turned around to see a messenger coming to him from the stairway. "Should we allow him to pass?" The knight asked.

"Let him pass." Vitaeus commanded. His intrigue mounted at what could be so important in the message to have the messenger take the risk of descending the dangerous stairway in these windy conditions down to the docks. The messenger stooped to one knee and bowed before Vitaeus; as he offered two separately sealed messages. The first one was from the commander announcing that the Rakirian fortress across the border in Rosmir had surrendered. The second one was from Yolif. Vitaeus opened it excitedly and read the short message. His expression quickly turned to dismay, and Raheena noticed.

"What is it My Prince?" Raheena asked.

"A matter too trivial to ruin the event of the arrival of the entire Rok royal family." Vitaeus responded as he smiled at Raheena. "Excuse me a moment Princess." Vitaeus pulled the messenger aside and commanded him to write a message for him. "Write, suspend all aide to Seredine immediately and deliver this message to my aide Daenis," Vitaeus commanded. "The second message is for the general in command of the army at the Rakirian Fortress; write and tell him to prepare his army to march."

The messenger finished writing the messages down and placed them inside a leather binder; which he then tucked away inside a satchel at his side. The messenger bowed and headed for the stairs. Vitaeus turned around in time to see the broadside of the Rok ship nudge itself against the dock. Dock hands hurriedly tyed the ship down to the dock. The Rok King had arrived.

The story continues in book two, Legends of Rosmir; A Clash of Duty and Brotherhood

www.ingramcontent.com/pod-product-compliance
Lightning Source LLC
Chambersburg PA
CBHW050907250626
47155CB00001B/140